TASH SKILTON
HOLLYWOOD ENDING

KENSINGTON
PUBLISHING CORP.

www.kensingtonbooks.com

ISBN-13: 978-1-4967-3068-8 (ebook)
ISBN-10: 1-4967-3068-2 (ebook)

ISBN-13: 978-1-4967-3067-1
ISBN-10: 1-4967-3067-4
First Kensington Trade Paperback Printing: September 2021

10 9 8 7 6 5 4 3 2 1

Printed in the United States of America

HOLLYWOOD ENDING

Also by Tash Skilton

Ghosting: A Love Story

For E and J. There is no universe where I didn't choose you.
—S.S.

For my parents, Haleh and Hossein, for always letting me come home again.
—S.T.

When you kiss a friend, the friendship dies.

—J. J. Westingland, *Castles of Rust and Bone*

HOLLYWOOD ENDING

CHAPTER 1

CoRaB Viewing Party

Where: TV Lounge, Emerson Hall, Ithaca College, Upstate New York, Finger Lakes Realm, KINGDOM OF SIX

What: The Best Night of Our Lives???

When: Sunday, 7:30 p.m. until the End of Time

Why: If you have to ask . . . Okay, fine: This Sunday is the 5th Season Finale for *Castles of Rust and Bone* and we are doing ALL the things. Potluck Feast (sign-ups below)! Refreshments of a Boozy Sort! Trivia Games! Rap Battles! *Watching the Episode!*

COSTUMES ARE MANDATORY. (Really. Don't show up if you're not decked out.)

$5 gets you across the drawbridge plus one (1) tankard of fermented mead and a trencher of bread upon which to sup

~ HOWEVER ~

Gold is not enough. You must prove your worth in one of the following ways:

- Unicorn Horn (whether the unicorn is still attached is up to you)
- Bouncy Castle
- Cauldron of Doom
- Farm-Fresh Goat's Milk
- Defeat one of us in a duel
- Perform a monologue from Seasons 1, 2, 3, or 4
- Mummer, Minstrel, Jester, or Juggling Act
- Hammer Throwing
- Fire-Eating
- Gaze into the Abyss (but Stop Before it Gazes Back into You)

Ready to complete a quest? Show us the fruits of your labor on Saturday afternoon, and you'll receive a ticket for Sunday. OR YOU WON'T. Mwa-hahahaaaa.

Questions? Contact Nina Shams & Sebastian Worthington, party hosts extraordinaire.

And it was ever thus . . .

SEBASTIAN

I know every inch of this couch.

I know which stains are from coffee (trying to stay awake during midnight study sessions), which are from Sharpies left uncapped (falling asleep during midnight study sessions anyway), and which are from wine (celebrating the end of midnight study sessions). I know where the furniture is slightly faded from the sun hitting it through breaks in the blinds.

Every Sunday night for the past four years I've parked my ass on this saggy, threadbare, marmalade-brown couch to watch *Castles of Rust and Bone* with Nina. Run-down, lived-in, and shockingly comfortable, it's a couch made for watching and analyzing the show we love more than anything.

It's never been used in judgment of real live people before, but the lounge only fits, like, thirty, so this is the best way of figuring out who gets into our party tomorrow night.

Also, it's fun to lord it over people because, really, this is *our* place.

Nina holds a clipboard, which would make her look all business if not for the bright orange paper crown on her head. My crown's pickle green and keeps slipping over my eyes.

Some company in England made *CoRaB*-themed Christmas crackers last year filled with wind-up toys of the characters along with the usual lame jokes ("Where does Santa work out? Down the gymney!"). Naturally, my little sister gave me a box of them when I was in Sherborne for the holidays last December, her caveat being that Nina and I must not open them until our finale party in May. (Yes, we've been planning this party for months.)

So here we are, king and queen of the dorm lounge with the paper crowns to prove it, deciding the fates of the masses regarding the party-to-end-all-parties.

"Why is 'Castle on a Cloud' from *Les Miz* the first song in your suggested Spotify playlist?" Nina asks Contestant #1. "I'm concerned it might affect the mood of the party."

"Do you think anyone will dance to 'Castle on a Cloud'?" I add.

"It's an EDM remix," Contestant #1 retorts testily. "So yes, I think people can and will."

Nina peers at her clipboard, then looks at me. "Sidebar," she announces.

We convene behind the couch.

"She put any song with the word 'castle' in it on the list," Nina whispers. "Sixteen of them are covers of 'Castles Made of Sand.'"

I feign indignation. "Why not songs with 'bones'? Justice for bones! Why can't we get down to 'B-B-B-B-Bad to the Bone'?" I do my best sneer and rock out for a second.

Making Nina laugh is a daily goal of mine.

We pop our heads over the top of the couch. My paper crown dips over my left eye. I rearrange it and tuck my longish, needs-a-cut hair behind my ear to keep the crown in place.

"Thank you for your time," I tell Contestant #1.

"Am I in or out?" she asks.

"As much as we love Jimi Hendrix, and we do love Jimi Hendrix, we're going to put you on provisional status until we've seen the rest of the contenders," Nina says.

"And it was ever thus," I intone.

Contestant #1 reluctantly curtsies and takes her leave.

Contestant #2 rolls in, pushing an inflatable bouncy castle on a dolly.

"Is this happening?" Nina mutters from the side of her mouth. "Is this real?"

It's probably a good time to point out that every item on our quest list was tongue-in-cheek, designed to terrify or annoy our former RA, Stanley, aka "We Have No Choice But to STAN . . . ley."

Stanley is a six-year senior who no longer holds any recognizable authority over us, yet constantly threatens to "shut us down" whenever we make dubious plans in the TV lounge. Back when he was our actual resident advisor freshman year, he would hold us hostage during endless monthly dorm meetings ("Snuggles dryer sheets and a towel shoved under your door do not mask the smell of pot, you guys, come on"), to lecture us on the alleged downward trajectory of *Castles of Rust and Bones* episodes.

"Still watching CRAB?" he'd snicker faux-casually, as though it didn't matter to him either way, when the truth was its continued existence—despite his disapproval!—was eating him alive. "I stopped watching after they killed off—well, I won't spoil it in case some of you haven't seen it yet, but when they killed off REDACTED . . ." (he actually shouted the word "redacted") ". . . I realized they had no fucking clue what they were doing and it was time to bail. Saved myself a LOT of time and energy that way."

So you can imagine our surprise that Contestant #2 *is Stanley.*

"Shams." He bows. "Worthington."

We stare back, temporarily unable to speak.

"My niece's birthday party was this morning so I snagged the rental for an extra day. You guys want it?" Stanley says, not meeting our eyes. "Doesn't take long to blow up."

"Won't you have to 'shut us down'?" I ask. "It'll take up half the room when it's inflated."

"I'll let it slide this once. It being your last hurrah and all that."

Nina and I glance at each other.

"You guys, come on," Stanley blurts out. "Can I come to the party?"

We have no choice but to Stan.

"Let's take a moment to appreciate what just happened," I tell Nina once he's left, a spring in his step.

"What *did* just happen?"

"I'm glad you asked. In short, Nina, you've achieved power beyond your wildest dreams. You summoned a bouncy castle. Nay, you summoned a bouncy castle from the show's fiercest critic."

She falls apart laughing and gives me a gentle shove.

"Ow," I joke.

"That's for saying, 'Nay.'"

Fifteen minutes and two impassioned—albeit inaccurate—monologues later, Nina turns my words around on me: "You win. You summoned a goat."

And by goat she doesn't mean Greatest of All Time. She means an actual goat, straining joyfully against a leash held by Contestant #5.

"For your . . . royal . . . consideration . . ." Contestant #5 grunts and pulls the energetic goat toward us. "May I present: farm-fresh goat milk. Ta-da!"

"It's a baby goat," Nina points out. "Baby goats don't produce milk."

I tilt my head. "It's also male."

Nina's giggle is unhinged. It reminds me of the time she made me braid her hair *CoRaB*-style using a YouTube tutorial and then laughed till she cried at how awful it turned out.

"This one's on you," Nina warns me. "Good luck explaining it to Stanley."

"Maybe we can hide it behind his bouncy castle."

"Where did you get him?" Nina asks our resident Doctor Dolittle.

"Rent-a-Goat in the Adirondacks. We drove all day, didn't we, li'l goatie? Who's a good goat? His job is to eat weeds, but I thought I'd give him the weekend off and let him join the revelry."

"You need to take him back," I insist.

"I don't have time to make the return trip again—I'll miss the party," Contestant #5 pouts.

"Leave him in your room and lock up everything you value. You can't attend if you bring him."

"Why did none of our jokes land?" I groan after Contestant #5 scowls and backs out of the lounge, tugging the feisty creature along. I'm pretty sure li'l goatie has already left us a gift in the hallway. "*You* knew I was joking, didn't you?"

She grins. "Your indicator light was definitely on."

I can be pretty deadpan—Nina says it's because I'm British—but Nina also says I get a glint in my eye that reveals the humor, if people know to look for it.

To speed things up over the next hour, we see contestants separately.

NINA	SEBASTIAN
"So you brought us a battle-ax signed by the main cast? . . . Just by the extras, I see . . . you found it on eBay for a steal . . . Right. While we appreciate the candor of straight-up bribes, only verbal weapons are allowed tomorrow night. You saw the part about the rap battle, I assume?"	"Here's the thing—it was fine to do a speech by him, but, you know, he doesn't exist in the books. It's like I always say about A. A. Milne and the *Winnie-the-Pooh* adaptations: That whistling gopher DOES NOT and SHOULD NOT exist on our screens, right? So I'm afraid I'm going to have to ask—"

"I already forbade the battle-ax," I remark to Nina. At the same moment, she turns to chastise me: "Literally no one has time for your A. A. Milne thesis."

"Can you imagine if that was really a thesis I wrote?"

"Like you went to all that trouble of applying to grad school and spending all those years learning and studying and paying all that money—"

". . . and it culminates in writing a nine-hundred-page screed about that fucking gopher and the way he fucking whistles every time he talks?"

My roommate calls this our "Fugue-GetAboutIt state": a fugue state in which we forget about anything and everything that isn't us; in which we can follow the conversation the other person's having while conducting our own, and pipe in without missing a beat because the rest of the world has fallen away.

I separate from our personal time flow and watch her for a second.

Moments like this, I think we'd make an awesome couple.

Things We Have Going for Us:
1. The Vivarin Incident
2. We're best friends
3. She loves my cooking
4. I love everything about her

My gaze drops to her lips, which are so kissable it hurts to sit this close to her lately and *not* kiss her. The late afternoon sun through the window reveals cognac highlights in her long dark hair. (Never said I was a poet, though in my defense, "cognac" is a prettier description than "Guinness foam," is it not? Point being: I'm drunk on her; her warm brown eyes, her heart-shaped face, her wit and humor.)

She's equally intoxicating to me in a plaid red shirt and shredded blue jeans as she is in a dress and heels, like the one she wore last year when she won an undergraduate award in critical studies. Nina's Persian but was born and raised on Long Island. Sometimes it blows my mind that a boy from muddy, mossy Dorset ended up at the same college with someone as luminous as Nina, her cheeks flushed, her eyes mischievous, her rose-scented shampoo wafting in the air between us.

Did I mention her kissable lips?

However.

Things We Have Against Us:
1. The Vivarin Incident
2. We're best friends
3. When you kiss a friend, the friendship dies.

It's a line from the books, so Nina doesn't know about it (she's a show purist, which I respect; the books are two thousand pages long and spend half that time describing people's clothing).

If I didn't have Nina in my life, I don't know what I'd do, which is why in the four years I've known her, I've never kissed her.

NINA	SEBASTIAN
"The party is going to be so amazing!"	"The party is going to be so amazing!"

Spoiler alert: It wasn't.

By the end of the next night, we're no longer speaking.

By the end of the next week, the show's been canceled and so has our friendship, and neither of them is ever coming back.

CHAPTER 2

NINA

Five Years Later

Bzzzz. *Bzzzzzz.*

I roll over in bed, and confusedly slap at my phone, thinking I've accidentally programmed in some new age ringtone as my alarm. But, no, that doesn't stop the buzzing.

I blearily stand up and open the door to my bedroom, only to be greeted with the sight of my roommate, Celeste, adoringly staring at a glass hexagon that she's placed up against the wall. She's holding it in one hand while she precariously traces the top of it with a pencil. The hexagon is where the buzzing is coming from because it's filled with bees.

Actual. Goddamn. *Bees.*

Celeste turns at the sound of my footsteps and stares at my gaping expression. "Oh, good. You're up," she says. She places the glass hexagon on the table and then proceeds to hammer a nail on top of the mark she's made on the wall.

Everything inside me is screaming to shut the door, try and get another hour of sleep, and forget this episode ever happened. But I'm too curious for my own good. "Celeste. What in the fuck?"

"I know. Aren't they *adorable*?" she says, touching the glass. "I'm starting with one, but we can expand so that we can make this whole wall into a hive. *And* we can eventually collect our own honey."

"Honey," I repeat dumbly, staring at Celeste's preternaturally smooth face and her wild, springy hair. She could be anywhere between twenty-five and sixty-five years old; the walk-in Botox-and-boba center around the corner makes me think she's closer to the latter but that's mostly conjecture.

"I'm thinking if they produce enough honey, we can set up a stand at the farmers' market and get a huge tax break on our rent. Maybe we'll call it . . ." She stares off into the distance as she makes imaginary rectangles with her hands, like she can see the name on a marquee. "'Micro-collected honey,'" she intones dramatically.

"Mmm-hmmm," I say. "I'm just going to . . ." I can't think of what to finish that sentence with, so I shut the door, crawl back into bed, and burrow underneath two pillows.

My body's self-defense against the actual swarm on the other side of the door is to go back to sleep. But then I glance at my phone again. 7:23 a.m. My real alarm is set to go off in exactly seven minutes anyway. Might as well take the extra time to get a head start on what I'm about to walk into at work.

I go to my laptop, open up Hootsuite, and, through a fog, check the socials to make sure nothing dire has happened in the eight hours since I dared to go to sleep and take my eyes off them.

The *CoRaB* Twitter still only has the one tweet from three weeks ago that turned out to be Clarence's farewell message:

@CastlesofRandB ✓: Halt, Rustiers and tell us . . . ARE YOU READY TO REBOOT?!

Ah, Clarence. I hardly knew ye. Seven hours into training on my first day on the job at WatchGoNowPlus—the streaming service that acquired the *CoRaB* reboot—Clarence quit in a flurry of shouting (from our boss, Sean Delaney, not Clarence), stomping (also Sean), a smashed centaur mug (yup, still Sean), and an HR huddle/human litigation barricade gathered around—guess who?

On my second day on the job, I got a temporary promotion to "interim social media coordinator." This promotion comes with no monetary gain or title change on my email signatures. But I am now responsible for taking over Clarence's duties while they interview for a permanent hire. Because, as Sean put it through gritted teeth and while squeezing the life out of a WatchGoNowPlus stress ball that came at the suggestion of his mandatory anger management courses, "I know strategy. Not the minutiae of sending out tweets to the masses. Which I'm sure you're . . . you're . . . great. At." He spit that last part like it physically hurt him to dole out positive reinforcement. *Ah, little Seany*, the part of me that once studied child psychology whispered in my head, *who hurt you?*

Despite that, I still haven't gotten the password to the Twitter account. Clarence has been holding it hostage while he negotiates his severance/here's-what-I-need-you-to-give-me-so-that-I-don't-sue-your-asses package. Our interactions may have been brief, but I'm still rooting for him.

As of now, all is quiet on the *CoRaB* social front. So I get dressed, swipe on some makeup, wait until it's exactly 8:03 a.m., and then open up my phone to summon the LA version of my knight in shining armor: my Uber driver.

It's a classic story.

Girl moves to Los Angeles in the hopes of becoming a screenwriter.

Girl is terrified of driving.

Girl meets a nice and handsome (because it's LA and handsome is a requisite for anyone who's hopped on their flight with a dream and a cardigan) boy/Uber driver on her first day in the city.

Boy asks girl out at the end of her ride.

Girl thinks, eh, why not? At least she can get chauffeured around for another week. Besides, Craigslist has paired her up with a roommate straight out of a "wacky neighbor" casting call and she could use some face time with someone with a semblance of normalcy.

And before she knows it, two months have passed and boy is nice enough, and—let's face it—girl needs a ride to work (not as a screenwriter, natch), so she doesn't see any reason not to keep the mutually beneficial relationship going.

Tale as old as time, really.

At this point, Ennis and I have figured out the system pretty well. At a predetermined time, he drives close enough so that when I summon a car, he's the one who gets pinged. He picks me up; I get a discount, since 75 percent of the fare money goes straight to Ennis and he kicks half of that back to me; and he gets a little something for picking up his girlfriend (thus slightly mitigating my guilt that he's become my chauffeur). Everybody wins.

He gives me a dimpled grin as he pulls up in front of the WatchGoNowPlus offices, his blond hair blowing just slightly in the SoCal breeze. If there was ever going to be a "California Boys" song to counter all the many Girls/Gurls versions, there's probably a program that could just scan him in and use its algorithm to make one. (He shockingly doesn't surf, but that's about all I can think of that doesn't fit the stereotype.)

"Pick you up at five thirty?" he asks.

"Yup. I'll text you if I'm going to be late."

"Righty-o, babe." I mean, come on. He even has his own catchphrase. Ennis leans over to give me a sloppy peck before I get out of the car.

I look up at the glass building, take one deep, centering breath, and enter.

It's noon and I'm eating my desk salad at—where else—my desk, when a piece of paper floats onto my keyboard to join the soggy piece of lettuce that has inevitably landed in between my B and N keys.

"The password," Sean says when I look up. I guess Clarence finally got what he wanted, which might explain why Sean has two stress balls today—one in his left hand and one, inexplicably, tucked in under his armpit. The original one he had was a prototype, but an enormous box of them got delivered yesterday—his idea to brand them and therefore expense them as a marketing tool. Because when you think of WatchGoNow-Plus, you want to be thinking about stress?

Sean is breathing out puffs of air in between every third word he says.

"Lucky us because—*puff*—I have something—*puff*—for you to—*puff*—do Monday to—*puff*—actually earn your—*puff*—paycheck."

I wonder if HR/Sean think the words are less biting when they're said slowly and with extra enunciation.

"Sure thing," I respond with the enthusiasm that five years in the workforce have ingrained in me. "*Could you drop an atom bomb?*" a supervisor might say and I'd probably retaliate with an exuberant, "*You got it, boss!*"

Sean closes his eyes, collects himself, and opens them before he says in what I'm sure he thinks is a zen voice, but sounds more like a spam callbot failing to sound human. "Get yourself over to Vasquez Studios by nine a.m. This Twitter Q&A was announced two months ago and now someone has to go transcribe Roberto's words of fuck . . . I mean *f-r-e-a-k-i-n-g* . . . wisdom into a hundred eighty characters."

I don't bother explaining to him that Twitter expanded its character count years ago. And it was never 180 characters anyway, it was 140.

Because the thing is, he said Roberto . . .

"Roberto . . . Ricci?" I squeak out. The lead actor in *CoRaB*? Sean stares hard at me and loses his robot voice for just a second when he says, "Are you going to fangirl all over his shoes and embarrass the company?"

"Of course not," I reply, in as professional a voice as I can muster, while my inner self is squealing: *OMGGGGGG, in three days I am going to meet Prince Duncan of Briqlian. THE SILVER PRINCE . . .*

"Super." Sean goes back to the voice that sounds as dead as his soul. "Don't forget to validate your parking with security before you leave."

"Right. Of course," I say calmly, in lieu of pointing out that it might be difficult to validate an invisible car.

Instead, as soon as he's out of earshot, I scroll through my phone and dial Ennis.

"Hey! Monday morning, do you think you could drop me off at Vasquez Studios instead of the office?" I feel compelled to give him a heads-up before the weekend because it's a much longer commute, even though if I had to guess his answer, it'd be . . .

"Righty-o, babe."

CHAPTER 3

SEBASTIAN

"Don't do this to me. My death-row dessert? Right now?" My best friend, Matty O'Brien, rolls his suitcase across the bubbled-up linoleum floor—does anyone still believe it looks like wood?—and into the apartment hallway. "I'm supposed to be carbo-loading."

"Your game's not until Thursday. Eat up."

I hand Matty a fork and a slice of seraphim food cake so large it makes the paper plate sag. I've been putting together a *Castles of Rust and Bone*–themed cookbook in my spare time, testing ideas out and modifying them for fun on the weekends. The dessert in question—one of two in the fridge—is a modified angel food cake that includes white-chocolate feathers everywhere, over blood-red icing.

Matty grins and leans against the wall to shovel it in. He's claimed for a few years now that he'd request this for his final meal, should it, er, come to that.

Speaking of final moments . . . "Your last photo as a single man," I announce.

His smile is cake filled, and right before I snap the pic, he straightens his tie and shakes his shaggy brown hair out. He used to mock my ponytail, but now he steals my hairbands.

When we moved here together after graduation, Matty swapped his archetype from squeaky clean baseball captain to rakish advertising executive, complete with suit-and-tie aesthetic, which is rarer than rare in LA, land of zero dress code, and thus catnip to some of the girls out here; no wonder his girlfriend, Maritza, wants to lock that down. One mitigating factor: The tie he's wearing is a Boston Red Sox tie because *those are the only ties he owns.* This one's eye-wateringly awful, siren-red with diagonal stripes and random Bs everywhere.

Our other best friend, Sam Jeong, barrels through the door. Sam lives down the hall, just like he did in college. We managed to re-create our dorm here in the Park La Brea apartments, stretching out senior year like taffy these last five years.

Sam groans and flicks Matty's tie as he walks by. "Uggh, O'Brien, we talked about this. I'll take you shopping."

Matty sets his cake plate down and slings his final piece of luggage, a duffel bag, over his shoulder. Despair grips me at the sight.

"What's the rush?" I ask. "Food's on."

Every Sunday I cook dinner for the three of us—two of us now, I guess—and throw on a movie. Dessert's first because I have my priorities. Now that the cakes are done, I'm about to braise ribs in the oven.

Sam cringes. "Shoot, I forgot to tell you, I'm interviewing a new band at Molly Malone's tonight for my podcast."

"Oh."

"And I'm meeting Maritza at Ray's before we head to her place to start unpacking," Matty says. "You should come, too, save the ribs for another time."

Ray's is the outdoor bar a block away near the Urban Lights, the restored streetlamp installation on Wilshire that shows up in everyone's 'grams.

Apparently I made dinner for one tonight.

Matty waves a hand in front of my face. "You there?"

"I have to get up early tomorrow, but thanks."

"Oh, right! It's your big day."

He sets his duffel bag on the floor again and my shoulders relax. I've bought us a few more minutes of roommate time.

"Did you ever tell your news to 'Mi-chelle, ma Belle'?" he sings, butchering the Beatles.

Belle was our codename for Nina back in college, so we could talk about her without her knowing. (Matty's favorite band at the time was Belle & Sebastian. Also, Nina was beautiful and smart like Belle from *Beauty and the Beast*.) Every guy in the dorm used to bust on me about her. They couldn't understand why she and I never dated.

The last time we saw each other was . . . bad. "Torture scenes from season three" bad.

We haven't spoken in five years, but I've had her on my mind all month. How could I not? As the newest production assistant at Alex & Company Productions, I'll be working behind the scenes at the *actual fucking reboot of CoRaB*. Way behind the scenes, because I'm not an on-set assistant. I'm producer Janine Alex's personal assistant, which mostly means running errands for her all over town in my 2007 Toyota Corolla. But still! I'm part of it! I'm within the sphere of its existence!

When I got the job six months ago, I *attempted* to friend Nina and *attempted* to follow her, but increasingly frantic searches for her yielded nothing but 404 Not Found / No Longer Exists screens. Her phone number's still in my phone, but it's a 607 area code from Ithaca, New York, and I doubt it's still good. Besides, I can't text her out of nowhere after all this time. What if she didn't text back?

I also worried it would come across like I was only getting in touch to shove my good fortune in her face. Did I imagine, or even hope, that she might be impressed? Definitely. But the main thing was that I wanted to share it with her, like old times.

Tomorrow's too important to risk oversleeping. It's my first visit to Vasquez Studios, out past rugged and dusty Canyon Country, where the show is shooting.

With the prevalence of hackers and techno-savvy fans, no one can email important files anymore; the show's so paranoid that multiple times a week yours truly will be making the pickup and drop-off of sensitive materials between offices. I feel as though I'm part of a long Hollywood tradition, a once-thriving brotherhood long since dwindled down: that of the messenger.

"No, I haven't heard from her since graduation," I say quietly. "What about you?" I ask Sam, in what I hope is a nonchalant voice. "You and Nina ever connect?"

Sam grins and runs a hand through his slicked-back, pomaded hair. "Ahh, my favorite ex. I wish."

Matty frowns. "Dude, show some respect. You know Sebastian was cuckoo for Nina's Cocoa Puffs."

"I've given it a lot of thought," I remark, "and I've concluded there was no worse way you could have said that."

"No, I never hear from her, but I could check with our mutuals," Sam offers. His eyes are kind, and I know he and Nina only dated for a few weeks, but it still grates on me that he can refer to her as a former girlfriend.

"That's okay," I say quickly. "Don't bother."

"Are you sure?"

"Yeah, forget I asked."

"All right, guys, you know I hate drawn-out goodbyes." Matty lifts his duffel bag once more, and this time he means it. "I'll probably see you tomorrow at Baja Fresh anyway."

"Nah, you're closer to Poquito Mas now." The words stick in my throat.

Maritza's place is in Studio City, practically a different time zone from the Miracle Mile.

We hug and that's that; he's gone.

Sam opens my fridge, as though he lives here now that Matty's gone. "Why did you make two cakes?"

"One's for us, and the other's a gift for the show. I'm bringing it to craft services tomorrow." When I started the cookbook, it was a lark for me and my friends. I never would have guessed I might serve one of my recipes to the actual cast and crew.

"Save me some of tonight's leftovers?" Sam asks, angling to leave.

"Yeah, definitely. Come by whenever."

"Sorry I can't stay tonight."

"You're fine—have a good interview."

"I sorta overdosed on pork already today too."

Sam is Korean American, and his family lives about four miles east, in Koreatown. I occasionally join him and his parents for services at the Methodist church on Sunday mornings, but only because they go to a restaurant called CHD for kimchi fried rice and grilled pork dumplings afterward. They spend half the meal berating Sam for wasting money renting an apartment when he could be occupying his childhood bedroom. It's hilarious, obviously.

"Don't suppose you want to take over Matty's room?" I ask, only half joking.

"Nah, I like the studio life too much."

He chose the studio floorplan when we all moved in, and transformed it into an actual studio for his indie music podcast. We slap hands and he's out the door too.

"Knock 'em dead tomorrow," he calls before letting the door shut behind him.

My apartment's abruptly silent. I finish cooking and then, for the first time since it aired, I pull up the season five finale of *Castles of Rust and Bone*. Every episode is available on Watch-GoNowPlus, to drum up renewed enthusiasm for the reboot. I already own the first four seasons on Blu-ray, but I couldn't stomach paying for season five; too many bittersweet memories.

Part of me thinks I've been numb ever since the show ended.

It doesn't take a psychologist (or a little sister who used to ship me and Nina) to know the two events are linked in my mind: our friendship breakup and *CoRaB*'s cancelation.

I can't help thinking that if the show gets it right this time around, it could heal more than just my broken fandom heart.

Monday morning, I wake at 5:45 and hit the apartment gym. My energy needs an outlet, and I go a bit overboard with bench presses and chin-ups. I'm sure I'll pay for it later, but right now adrenaline shields me from pain.

I'm showered, shaved, dressed, and eating breakfast (cake and ribs) by seven, which should give me plenty of time to make it to Vasquez Studios by nine with the other cake, pristine and carefully packed in its bakery box. I'll be heading north to the middle of nowhere, yet within the thirty-mile zone of LA County so production can take advantage of the tax incentives.

In the garage I check my Sigalert app for a live traffic report, and holy shit, there is apparently a "pig in lanes" on the 101, aka Satan's Freeway. Scratch that, *several* pigs. A big-rig truck carrying livestock overturned fifteen minutes ago. No animals have been injured but they're running amok, and the on-ramp at Highland Avenue has been closed.

My on-ramp.

No. No. No. This can't be happening. Not *today*.

I'll have to go a half hour out of my way on surface streets to reach the 5 instead, which is what everyone else will be doing too.

My boss, Janine, needs the briefcase in time for a ten-thirty meeting at the production office in West Hollywood. As it is, I'll need to turn around almost immediately upon arrival at Vasquez.

I slam my hands on the steering wheel, let loose some creative expletives, fly out of my car, then run back up the stairwell and into my apartment.

"Your day has come. Don't let me down," I command the

life-size cardboard cutout of *CoRaB*'s Queen Lucinda standing in the corner of my living room.

I squeeze one of Matty's left-behind Boston Red Sox caps on Lucinda's head and carry her sideways out the door, ignoring the looks I get in the elevator.

Aware of the garage cameras judging me, I click Lucinda's seat belt into place and continue a steady stream of pep talks to myself. The only way I'll arrive on time at this point is if I sneak into the carpool lane, which requires two people. Fingers crossed we'll be going so fast no cop will see that she's not flesh and blood.

Stop-and-go traffic consumes me for a nightmarish hour before I reach the 5. As I'm scanning my rearview windows for CHP officers and mentally preparing to slip into the forbidden lane, WhatsApp bleats with incoming video calls: first my sister, then both my parents, each chiming in from a different location in their house in Sherborne, Dorset. I silence my phone and toss it to the floor of the passenger seat.

For ten glorious, eighty-five-mile-per-hour minutes, my plan works flawlessly. I bounce and glide past endless rows of unmoving, law-abiding suckers, wondering why I've never done this before.

I merge onto the 14, out into unexpected farmland, and zip past Newhall, Santa Clarita, Shadow Pines, Sand Canyon, and Soledad Canyon. LA is a distant memory now. I take a moment to appreciate the perfect, cloudless sky above and the majestic mountains and hiking trails off to both sides. Green fuzz coats the beige peaks like a wrinkled blanket. I bet the view is peaceful from up there.

My wandering thoughts are blasted away when some asshole in a Mitsubishi Mirage merges in front of me, going the speed limit. What the actual fuuuuuuck?

Whoever he is, we're headed in the same direction. Every time I attempt to pass him, he steps on the gas enough to thwart me, then retreats and slows down again. At least my exit's coming up. But then the Mirage takes the off-ramp at Agua Dulce Canyon too.

Now I'm ultra fucked because we're on a winding, two-lane road with CAUTION: ROCK SLIDE AREA signs everywhere and I can't pass him. I grit my teeth as we amble in slow motion past Sweet Water Ranch and a series of horse farms.

At long last, the gormless slowpoke and I arrive at our shared destination: Vasquez Studios. Enormous, diagonal planes of rock jut out behind the soundstages and offices, making the world feel tilted. The image is otherworldly, stunning in its strangeness, and reveals the brilliance of Vasquez Studios: Production can film indoors *and* outdoors, using the natural beauty of Vasquez Rocks for location shoots.

The security guard checks my name off a list. His eyes flick to my cardboard passenger.

"Phone," he commands. I retrieve it from the car floor and hand it over. The security guard places a bright-orange sticker over my phone's camera lens and hands it back, expressionless. The implication hits me like a sugar rush: I'm about to see things no other fan will see! Top-secret, incredible things!

I thank the security guard and push on, heart pounding. My glee is short-lived.

In front of me, the Danger to Us All pulls over to the loading zone and slams on his brakes, which forces me to do the same, which sends my beautiful cake careening into the dashboard.

"Dammit," I yell, as buttercream and white chocolate feathers explode, dripping goo and splatter everywhere.

Heedless of the destruction he's caused, my nemesis turns to his passenger, a woman with long dark hair, and kisses her goodbye. I roll my eyes and look away to give them privacy. Once I hear the car door slam, indicating the woman's exit, I yank my steering wheel to the left so my car rolls up alongside the cake destroyer.

"Learn how to drive!" I shout out the window.

The other driver exits his car. "You almost rear-ended us," he says lazily. "Many times."

I exit, too, slamming my door shut. "What's the point of using the carpool lane if you're not going faster than all the other lanes? It's an abuse of the carpool lane!"

"'Abuse of the carpool lane'?" he laughs. "You're using a doll!" He peers through the passenger window. "Who *is* that? What's-her-name . . . Wanda? Miranda?"

"Lucinda," the female voice and I correct him simultaneously. A premonition casts its shadow over me like the wings of a passing angel, and I swear to God time slows down as I turn to look at her.

The woman he dropped off, the one he kissed, who's standing on the curb . . .

. . . is Nina Shams.

CHAPTER 4

NINA

Time stops. Almost like in episode 207 when Jeff the warlock is temporarily able to harness Mount Signon's power to manipulate the passing of hours.

I'm immediately thrown back to the endless debates Sebastian and I had—not about the many plot holes that time manipulation immediately caused. But about the sort of world in which an evil warlock is named . . . Jeff.

And then, just like old times, we talk right over each other again.

NINA	SEBASTIAN
"What are you doing here?"	"What are you doing here?"

A pause.

"You two know each other?" Ennis asks in his drawl, and I find myself deeply envious of how relaxed he is. Then again, I guess he's not the one who's just been confronted with his biggest regret, dressed in bright salmon shorts and checkered

Vans. My heart seems to give one extra beat at the sight because if I were to Los Angelify the Upstate New York version of the Sebastian that I knew, this is exactly what he would look like, extra muscles and all.

"Yeah," I say.

"We were friends," Sebastian adds.

I blink at the use of the past tense, not expecting it to give me a little buzzing over my skin since I know it's unequivocally true. We haven't even spoken in five years. I try to mask my discomfort by giving Ennis more details. "In college."

"So," Sebastian says. "I can't imagine it's a coincidence that *CoRaB* is getting rebooted. And you're here."

"'You've sussed me out, Queen Lucinda,'" I quote with a small smile. "I'm working for WatchGoNowPlus. On the digital media team."

Sebastian's eyes widen as his face breaks out into a huge grin, giving me another little buzz. "Nina! Oh my God. That's *incredible!* Congratulations!" I can tell he wants to go in for a hug but then he holds himself back.

I can't help smiling. Sebastian knows the significance of this for me, no matter how long it's been since we've spoken. He was there for all of it, including the *CoRaB* fanfic I wrote and made him read, and he knows how thrilling it is to be here, *on the set* of the very show we debated and dissected and adored within an inch of its life. "But wait, there's more! I'm about to go in to interview"—dramatic pause—"Roberto Ricci." I roll my Rs to add some extra oomph.

Sebastian's jaw drops. "Please, please, please tell me you'll ask about his beard-care routine." It was a source of much debate between Sebastian and Stanley back in the day.

"Well, I have to ask him fan-submitted Twitter questions," I clarify. "So . . . if you want to go ahead and at the official *CoRaB* account sometime in the next hour, beard care will be within your grasp."

He takes out his phone. "Already on it," he says as he starts furiously typing away.

I watch him for a second, taking in the miracle of having the best friend I've ever had and lost in front of me again. "You never answered my question, though. What are you doing here?"

He looks up at me with a smile. "I'm a PA for Alex & Company, on an important briefcase mission."

"Get out!" I say. "Congratulations to you!" Because of course I know the significance of this for him, too.

We grin at each other until Ennis's phone dings.

"I've got to go pick up another rider," he says. "Good luck, babe." He kisses me again on the lips and then turns to Sebastian. "Nice to meet you, uh . . . sorry, I didn't catch your name."

NINA	SEBASTIAN
"Sebastian."	"Sebastian."

"Got it. Ennis," he introduces himself as he shakes Sebastian's hand. "*Lucinda*." He makes a mock bow to the cardboard cutout lying on Sebastian's passenger seat as he gets into his own car.

"Lucinda," I point out as Ennis is driving off, "would never be a passenger. Elevor, maybe. But Lucinda, never."

"True," Sebastian says. "I was hoping I wouldn't run into any superfan traffic cops who would accuse me of ruining the canon."

"Is that an extra fine?"

"In LA, yes."

I smile at him. "It's good to see you."

"You too," he says.

But then we are plunged into something unfamiliar: an awkward silence. Because barring jokes about our shared fandom, when it's been five years, there's no more small talk, only big talk: the broad strokes of what each of us has been up to that the other one would know nothing about. I wouldn't even know where to begin.

"I don't want to be late," I finally say.

"Right. Let's go in."

We walk together in silence. He opens the studio door for me, and suddenly tenses. "Oh, wait, I still have to park my car. Don't let me keep you." We look at each other. He dips his head. "Bye, Nina."

Hearing him say my name in that low, soft way takes me back to late-night conversations in the dorm again. I shake my head in wonderment as I enter the studio.

There's a perfect banana at the top of the fruit bowl in Roberto Ricci's dressing room. I'm about to compose a poem in iambic pentameter dedicated to this banana's ripeness—I'm already thinking of words that might rhyme with "chartreuse." Clearly I should've had breakfast this morning. But fixating on the banana is also distracting me from my jumble of nerves. I can't believe, somewhere in this building, is Roberto Ricci and Francis Jean Taylor (Lucinda) and David Sherman (Jeff). I equally can't believe that somewhere in this building is Sebastian.

"Okay, right. What asinine task do you have for me now?" I hear the unmistakable voice before I see him. Roberto Ricci walks in, dressed in slouchy jeans, a white T-shirt, and a white trucker hat. He's followed by a redheaded woman wearing a bright yellow dress and leopard print cat-eye glasses.

Roberto sees me sitting on his couch and yells, "Dry skim cap. Extra shot."

The redheaded woman rolls her eyes and walks over to me. "Hi. Are you here from the network?"

"Um, yes," I say, standing up to shake her hand. "I'm Nina. Here to facilitate the Twitter Q&A."

"Great. I'm Sabrina. The publicist for the show. We'll probably be working together quite a bit." She smiles at me and I smile back.

I turn to Roberto then. "It's such a pleasure to meet you," I say.

"I'm sure it is," he replies before adding, "Does this mean I'm not getting my coffee?"

"Yeah, sure, I can get that for you," I reply, trying to remember what he just ordered.

"Never mind that," Sabrina says, coming to the rescue. "I'll get the coffee. Roberto, please just answer the questions Nina puts to you and she'll take care of putting them up online. Right, Nina?"

"Definitely," I say. Sabrina nods and leaves the room.

Roberto gives a deep, dramatic sigh. "How long is this going to take?"

"Well, your Twitter takeover is set to run for an hour," I say.

"You have twenty minutes," Roberto replies.

"Um, okay. No problem." I'll just get his answers down and dole out the replies over the hour.

I open up my laptop, scroll over to Twitter and the Word doc where I'd cut and pasted some of the best questions we'd gotten over the week, and search for a nice, softball one to get things started.

I clear my throat. "This one's from at-stevienicks4eva . . ."

"Rule number one," Roberto interrupts. "I one hundred percent don't care about anyone's screenname or obsessions with hair bands."

"Uh, right, of course," I say, and then feel compelled to add, "Of course, Fleetwood Mac isn't a hair band. . . ."

"Rule number one," Roberto replies in a singsong. "Next."

Sabrina comes back into the room with a paper cup that she hands off to Roberto. "How's it going?"

"Splendid," Roberto says sarcastically.

Sabrina raises her eyebrow suspiciously and then throws a questioning look over at me.

"Yup. It's great," I reply. It's perfectly normal that Roberto would be guarded with a new person. He'll warm up after he's had his coffee, no doubt.

"Oookay," Sabrina says, sounding unconvinced. "I have to go check on Francis Jean, but I'll be back in a few." She smiles at me encouragingly before leaving the room and shutting the door behind her.

"You have until I finish this coffee," Roberto says as he takes an inhumanly large swig of the scalding cup.

What happened to twenty minutes? I want to ask. But, of course, I don't. Instead I say, "Got it. So, easy one. How does it feel to be back?"

Roberto's eyes widen in surprise. "Wow. That *is* easy," he says slowly. "So easy you could, I don't know, probably write the answer yourself instead of wasting my time."

"Um . . . okay," I say, typing out the word "splendid" in the Word doc. It isn't technically a misquote. He did just use it a minute ago. I'll just . . . finesse it.

"Is there anything you can tell us about what happened in the intervening five years between season five and the up-coming new season?" The show announced just last week that the reboot is going to have a five-year time jump to match the real-life time jump between seasons five and six. Very meta.

"I sure can. I auditioned for about three hundred roles and the only ones I ever got callbacks for were the ones that required wearing armor, being in a makeup chair for twenty hours a day to play the latest Spiderpool villain, and/or utilizing the fake

British accent that I honed in the depths of Central Jersey. Usually all three."

"Mmm-hmmm," I say, jotting down "something about armor" for myself. "How do you feel about some of the discrepancies between the books and the show?"

Roberto laughs. "No one really thinks I read that shit, do they? It's thousands of pages about fucking corsets and chainmail."

Honestly, this I agree with. In the past few years, I missed the show so much that I finally, finally hunkered down and read the five-book series. A lot of it was somewhat torturous, and not in the way that poor little Pathoro gets methodically skinned in book two/season three.

"They are a little wordy," I say to Roberto with a conspiratorial smile, hoping this will be the shared opinion that will finally win him over. But he doesn't even see it since his coffee cup is currently covering his face. (Is his tongue made of the same heat-repellant metal as Duncan's sword?!) At this rate, I'll have a two-minute Twitter takeover.

I look at my next question. I'm probably going to regret this but I don't have time to hunt for a different one. "Are you Team Duncinda or Team Lucivor?"

"I'm team getting off your couch and taking a shower so that maybe a real, live person will actually want to fuck you."

Cool. Cool.

"Is there any juicy, behind-the-scenes info you can give us about the infamous wedding scene between Duncan and Lucinda?" The question gives me a little jolt. Because how could I have known, when I curated it, that I'd have seen Sebastian just minutes before? He and I had our own behind-the-scenes drama related to that very scene.

I'm snapped out of my thoughts by Roberto's short bark of a laugh. "Well, everyone knows that Lou Trewoski and Francis Jean were sleeping together for the duration of the show.

Whenever things were going well, she got a power grab scene and whenever things were going poorly . . . Queen Lucinda got betrayed."

My jaw drops. "Is that . . . is that actually true?" I can't believe it. All the little nonsensical plot twists that Sebastian and I would endlessly debate. Was this the real reason for all of them? The head writer and lead actress were sleeping together?

He smirks at me. "Yup. Print that." He takes one last swig of his coffee. "And we're done here."

He's about to leave when I realize I only have answers to five questions. "Wait," I say in desperation. "Can I ask just one more?" What I really want to ask is how he manages to play the soulful hero when he's clearly a certified asshole in real life. Instead, my eyes fall to one line of text and before I can second-guess myself, I ask, "Can you give us any beardscaping tips?"

He stops at the door and turns to me, a gleam in his eyes I haven't seen before. "An infusion of lemon verbena, coconut oil, lavender, and witch hazel. One drop in the morning, one drop at night. A close shave with a safety razor at a trusted barber every ten days." He stares off into space and then intones, almost wistfully, with a hint of Central Jersey–crafted British accent: "Most important rule: Never, ever trim your beard when wet. EVER."

He exits with a flourish, as if he's delivered a Shakespearean soliloquy, leaving me alone to schedule out the tweets over the next hour.

@stevienicks4eva: @CastlesofRandB How does it feel to be back? #AskRobertoRicci

@CastlesofRandB ✓: Roberto Ricci: Splendid! Truly splendid. I feel like every audition I've been on over the past five years has led me back to this.

@CoRaBCoBrA: @CastlesofRandB Is there anything you can tell us about what happened in the intervening five years between season five and the upcoming one? #AskRobertoRicci

@CastlesofRandB ✓: RR: Hmmmm . . . there will be . . . armor, corsets, and chainmail. 😏

@ejs5785: @CastlesofRandB How do you feel about some of the discrepancies between the books and the show? #AskRobertoRicci

@CastlesofRandB ✓: RR: I respect both author J. J. Westingland and showrunner Lou Trewoski so much. One of the most interesting things about the craft of writing is how the same base material can inspire so many different paths.

@sebworthington: @CastlesofRandB Can you give us any beardscaping tips? #AskRobertoRicci

@CastlesofRandB ✓: RR: An infusion of lemon verbena, coconut oil, lavender, and witch hazel. One drop in the morning, one drop at night. A close shave with a safety razor at a trusted barber every 10 days. Most important rule: Never, ever trim a wet beard. 💀 👍

@thefandomlife32: @CastlesofRandB Are you Team Duncinda or Team Lucivor? #AskRobertoRicci

@CastlesofRandB ✓: RR: Team Jeffcan.

I decide not to use the gossip he gave me about Lou and Francis Jean since a) I have no idea if it's true and b) even if it were, I'm pretty positive the execs at WatchGoNowPlus would *not* want me sharing that.

But the Team Jeffcan answer I feel good about. Let's set the Rustiers' tongues wagging by getting the warlock and the Silver Prince together. After all, that's really my job here, right? Drum up some hype?

And besides, the Duncan/Jeff fanfic was some of my best work.

CHAPTER 5

SEBASTIAN

I wish I could inhale this moment, save it inside me, and exhale it later to examine from every conceivable angle. I'm here at Vasquez Studios, and *so is Nina. Nina!* It took everything I had not to celebrate via dance moves in the parking lot. I'm not even mad about the cake anymore. I'll have plenty of chances to try again. *And plenty of chances to run into Nina.* I hope I didn't make her late for her Q&A with Roberto.

The light above the soundstage doors is on. It's green, meaning . . . what? That I'm allowed to enter and find the person with the briefcase? Or does green mean they're filming and I shouldn't, under any circumstances, enter? It would make more sense for red to indicate that, but maybe not.

I have no idea how much time I waste staring at the pulsing round light above the doors, willing someone to exit or enter so I'll know what to do.

No harm in looking for the bathroom first, after that long drive from Park La Brea. Maybe by the time I get back the soundstage light will be off.

A posh female voice interrupts my thoughts. "You seem lost, love. Are you looking for wardrobe?"

"No, I'm—" *Holy crud.*

I didn't think it was possible, but Francis Jean (aka Queen Lucinda, Our Lady of the Cardboard Cutout) is even more stunning in person. Her dark skin glows and her pulled-back hair isn't gray but actual, real-life silver, which I didn't think existed outside of fantasy novels or wigs from the prop department. The molecules in the air seem to pulse with her presence. She's shorter than me by a lot. She's tiny, in fact, but emits a larger-than-life energy, a radiance that renders me speechless. She hasn't been to hair and makeup yet, she wears a plain cotton T-shirt, wide-legged, black-and-blue-striped trousers, and worn-in ballet flats, but it takes everything in me not to bend the knee and whisper, "Your Grace."

"You're . . . ?" she prompts.

I take a deep, anchoring breath, and look her in the eyes. "I'm supposed to pick up something to take back to production, but I'm not sure where to go."

"Probably Dani and Dom's office. I'm headed in the same direction. Follow me." She glides down the hall toward an elevator, waits for me to join her inside, and presses the button for floor two.

I nod at the script she's holding, which reads *Lucy's Donuts* on the front cover. "It's a cute code name, huh?"

Lucy's Donuts is the secret title for the *CoRaB* reboot (Lucinda and Duncan being the stars of the show; Dunkin' Donuts, get it?). Production uses it whenever they need to hide something in plain sight, like a casting notice or the CAST AND CREW signs at location shoots.

"I lobbied hard for Lucy's Donut *Shop*," Francis says. "Make her a proprietor, give her some agency, you know?"

I laugh and mentally add donuts to my show-themed recipe book. "I'm a Krispy Kreme lad myself, but . . ." I smile like a dope and trail off. "Do you have a favorite donut flavor?"

Do you have a favorite donut flavor? I scream inside my head. *What kind of question is that?*

"Cream-filled. Scratch that: jam-filled."

"Brilliant."

"Are you English as well, or one of those people who pick up contact-accents?" she says, not unkindly.

"Um, both. My family are from Sherborne, but I've lived in the States most of my life." (Wait, my family *are* or my family *is*? Which is American and which is British, and do I sound like a poser either way?)

The elevator doors open, and we walk into the hallway. "Down the hall to the left." She points. "You're good? Are we good?"

"Yes, thanks very much."

She swans off in the opposite direction. A cartoon heart might as well appear above my head.

Daniela and Dominic are siblings in their thirties who inherited the studio from their grandfather and run the day-to-day aspects of it from their command center in a corner office. They're both on calls via AirPods when I knock on their open door.

Daniela waves me in. Every square inch of the walls is decorated with framed posters of the film and TV shows that have called the studio home over the years, from Westerns to sci-fi. I perch on the edge of a chair facing her desk until she double taps her earpiece to end her call.

I stand, eager to prove myself. "I'm here for the briefcase, if it's ready."

That's when I notice Dominic has already retrieved it and is moving toward me at a rapid clip. "Yeah, I know," he says to whoever's on the other end of *his* call. "We're sending it now."

I'm dying to know what's inside the briefcase but I've been warned lawsuits await anyone foolish enough to attempt to open it. The NDA I signed already threatened my firstborn child.

I reach out to accept the briefcase from Dom's hand, but he ignores me, shifting the handle to his other hand instead and reaching into his pocket, from which he pulls a pair of hand-cuffs.

Click!

He's attached one cuff to the handle.

Click!

He's attached the other cuff to my right wrist. He lets go of the briefcase and it slams into my thigh. I gasp. The pain is blinding.

"What—why—?" I croak out.

"At Vasquez Studios we take security *very* seriously," Daniela says. "Sign here, I'll be the witness, and Dom will stamp the notary mark."

She holds out a sheet on a clipboard. I automatically raise my hand to sign the outtake form and feel another white-hot smear of pain because of course the briefcase is attached, and once again it has swung into my thigh. I'll be black-and-blue before long. *A souvenir!* I think stupidly.

Dom nudges me out of the way and stamps the sheet twice.

I clutch the briefcase to my chest, where hopefully it will do less damage to my joints.

The siblings seem annoyed at my continued presence in their lives.

"Anything else?" Daniela taps her earpiece, getting ready to make a new call.

"Just go straight to production," Dominic adds by way of instruction. "Janine has the key."

Daniela shoots him an irritated look, no doubt perfected during their childhood. "No, do not go 'straight' there. Our security consultant recommends you drive in a zigzag fashion, double back a few times, exit the freeway and get back on at random, to throw off anyone who might be following you."

Who would be following me?

"What I meant was, don't make any *stops* on the way," Dominic clarifies with a roll of his eyes.

"Do you have Waze?" Daniela asks me. "Use that."

"It's—heavy," I gruff out, rattling the cuff. "Going to be difficult to drive with this. . . ."

"Others have managed. See you next week."

Am I in a Tarantino movie? *What is inside this briefcase?* Gold bars? Body parts? It can't be scripts; it weighs like twenty pounds.

More to the point: Is my life in danger? Why do I need to be handcuffed to the briefcase? What do they think is going to happen to me on the 405?

I peer out the window, looking for snipers on the roof, before warily taking my leave.

It's unsanitary to bring the briefcase inside the men's room with me, but what choice do I have? I definitely need to use the head before getting back in my car.

When I emerge from my stall, the briefcase thumping rhythmically against my legs, I notice a familiar dark head of hair hunched over the sink. Roberto Ricci! He's putting in a contact lens. Or, actually, doing a line of coke.

I mean, I have no *proof* it's coke. It could be Ritalin he's snorting, or some new-age vitamin, but—nah. It's coke.

Surely the Twitter Q&A isn't already over? It only started twenty minutes ago. It must be on pause to accommodate his "re-up." I send good vibes to Nina that it's going smoothly.

"I guess that means Duncan survives, huh? Congratulations," I say after washing my hands.

Roberto sniffs and stands up. Even at full height, he's shorter than me. Apparently, I'm a giant among actors.

"I'm not playing Duncan anymore. Nope. He's deader-than-dead. This is a new character, Dun*can't*, Duncan's identical cousin. Like *The Patty Duke Show*. It's a whole thing. Don't tell anyone. . . ." His inflated pupils focus on my ID lanyard. "Sebastian. Or I'll know it was you."

A beat. Then, "Ha ha, look at your face," he crows. "That was sarcasm. Idiot."

"Oh. Okay."

He looks me up and down. "Did you jizz yourself?"

If I could spontaneously combust, now would be the perfect time. "It's. Icing," I grit out. I brush at the white streaks on my shirt.

He peers at himself in the mirror; futzes with his million-dollar hair, sniffs. "What are you, a gofer?"

"I work for Janine, in production."

"Stay here a sec. I have a job for you."

"I've actually got to go." I hoist the briefcase up to my chest and the movement sends a tight circle of pain to my wrist as the handcuff digs in.

He points at me, pinning me in place. "I said stay here."

I'm torn. My direct supervisor is Janine, but she'd want me to accommodate requests from others, right? Especially the star of the show.

The Silver Prince heads into a stall, locks it behind him, and proceeds to make noises that belong in a gross-out comedy. Noises I'll never unhear, no matter how long I live.

I'm paralyzed, and I can't help thinking, *I've seen his butt on TV. Or at least his butt-double's butt. And now I've heard what it can do.*

Then I picture him as Duncan, in a slow-mo hero shot, astride a horse and swinging a mace, bravely defending a group of helpless villagers. The juxtaposition splits my brain in half.

Roberto emerges, and I can't help but notice that he didn't flush.

He turns on the faucet and washes his hands. "What are you waiting for?" He jerks his chin toward his vacated stall.

I laugh. It's got to be a hazing ritual. He's not really asking me to . . . "Good one, you had me going there."

His face is blank, his eyes like a coked-up shark's. "Do your job, Sebastian. Unless you think you're above it?"

"Oh. Um." Isn't *everyone?*

"You might want to wrap a paper towel around your hand.

Awful germs on the handle. From other people, all day long. That's why I never touch it." He flicks his wet hands impatiently. "I come from a long line of germaphobes."

"Don't you—have your own bathroom in your dressing room?" I blurt out, after completing the task God has seen fit to test me with. (I used the toe of my sneaker.)

"Are you crazy?" Roberto says. "I never take a dump in there. With that ventilation?"

Ninety minutes later, after a harrowing commute that found me searching my rearview mirror for assassins every twenty seconds, I knock on Janine's door at Alex & Co. in West Hollywood, at the corner of Sunset and Doheny. We're across from Soho House, a fact my little sister discovered when she Google Mapped my location.

The important meeting has already started. Janine quickly emerges from her office, her curly hair bouncing, and closes the door behind her so I can't even see who's in there with her.

"Here you go—"

Janine yanks on the briefcase, realizes I'm still attached, and yelps as we collide.

"I'm so sorry!" I cry out.

"No, *I'm* sorry," she says. "I should've remembered. Let me get the key. Stay here."

Stay here. A shiver rolls through me. I can never use the men's room at Vasquez again, lest Roberto be lying in wait like a spider.

Janine locates the key in an empty tin of mints and unlocks the cuffs. I rub at the tender spot on my wrist.

"Are you okay?" she asks. "You look like you've seen Duncan's Ghost. Did he say something obnoxious?"

"Sarcastic. And then categorized it as such, to make sure I was clear. Unless that part was sarcasm too. Maybe it's like the turtles holding up the world, sarcasm all the way down."

"Sarcasm is the lowest form of wit. I should've warned you. I hope the others were more professional?"

"Francis Jean was lovely."

"Unless she's had dairy, yes," Janine murmurs cryptically. "Anyway, you've earned a reprieve. Take the rest of the day off. Maybe ice that wrist."

Since I'm home so early, and it's only seven p.m. in England, I FaceTime my sister Millie. She's nineteen and sounds like an air raid siren when she's excited (which would be now). Seeing a familiar, friendly face after the bizarre day I've had makes my heart lurch. We have similar coloring—sandy hair, hazel eyes— but she takes after Dad and I take after Mom in terms of looks.

My parents moved from Upstate New York back to England right after I graduated high school, and obviously Millie, who was ten at the time, went with them. As a result, we had completely different childhoods, yet with the same parents.

I squint behind her. "Where are you?"

"Callo's!"

Callo is her best mate, though they muddled through an awkward phase for a while after Millie came out to her as bi last year. Not because of the information, but the fact that Millie hadn't told Callo sooner (which Millie understandably took issue with). For their gap year, they're working together as docents. I'm relieved their friendship remains strong, but disappointed Millie's not at home; she probably can't chat for long.

"How'd it go, how'd it go? Tell me everything," she demands.

"It was amazing in some respects and a bit naff in others."

I get a flash memory of Nina teasing me about my wandering accent back in college. She once told me, "Whenever you're on the phone with Millie, you go from All-American Joe to Dick Van Dyke in *Mary Poppins* in under five seconds."

Speaking of Nina . . . "You'll never guess who was there."

"Way to bury the lede, Seb!" Millie groans once I've filled her in. She plans to study journalism at university next year.

"The whole day was ledes," I protest.

When I said that Millie ships me and Nina, I mean she actually ships us. She has a notebook filled with things I've told her over the years, a timeline of cute moments that have occurred. Stuff I never even told Matty about.

"It's fate!" Millie shouts. "It's prophecy! Did you get her number?"

"No, but—"

"WHAT? Why not? Call WatchGoNowPlus and ask for some personnel numbers, say it's for Janine."

"Being in contact isn't the issue. The issue is, do I have a right to."

She taps her chin, deep in thought. "Okay, I see what you mean."

"Yeah. It's not that simple, right?"

"It's so weird that you've been in the same city for who knows how long, and not run into each other before."

"It's not like London, Mill. It's a sprawl out here. But yeah, I know."

"I still think you should call her."

"She has a boyfriend."

"Really?" Millie's face falls, and it's nice to be validated. It's as though she's allowed to express everything I'm feeling but can't show.

"I think she lives with him too; he dropped her off today."

She bites her lip. "Are you okay?"

"Yeah." I shrug it off. After all, Nina with a boyfriend is the Nina I know best. It was only when she *didn't* have a boyfriend that things got strange between us.

In other words, this is good. This I can do.

Since Nina has a boyfriend, we can slip right back into our original roles.

Call it a reboot. A chance to fix the past and move forward. And if we *are* getting a second chance at friendship, all the pain of missing her these last several years will have been worth it.

An incoming call interrupts us, audio only.

It's an LA number I don't recognize, but instinct tells me to pick up. (It wouldn't be out of character for Janine to send me home early and then summon me back.)

"Gotta run, talk soon?" I ask Millie and she flashes a thumbs-up in return. I miss my dorky kid sister.

I switch over to the new call. "Hello?"

"Sebastian? Hi . . . it's Nina."

Chapter 6

NINA

Sebastian hesitates for the briefest of moments before bursting forth with a loud, "Hi."

"I hope it's okay that I got your number," I say quickly. "I called the production company. . . ." I trail off. My intention was for it *not* to sound stalkerish but now that I hear my confession out loud, it's decidedly not turning out that way.

"Of course not! I'm so glad you did," he says. "I didn't know how else I'd find you, to be honest. I mean, no 'gram, even?" I can hear the teasing note in his voice.

A few days after college graduation, I deleted all of my social media accounts. The move was initially spurred by a photo of the newly minted couple, Sebastian and Heather, who got together the night of the season finale party. But it was finalized by this feeling I'd had for a while, that instead of living my life, I was scrolling through a fictionalized version of one. It felt like everyone I knew was starring in their own highly edited reality show and I suddenly needed to opt out.

"Don't worry," I reply. "The irony of someone without any social media accounts being a temporary social media manager for a major streaming service isn't lost on me."

"I was going to say," Sebastian snarks. "Wait, temporary?"

"The manager left my second day on the job and I'm just a stop-gap until they find a real replacement. I think my boss put it as, 'You're twenty-seven. You know how to viral a meme or whatever.'"

Sebastian laughs on the other end. Making him laugh feels good. More than that, it feels right.

"That sounds uncannily like 'doing a violence,'" he replies.

Now it's my turn to laugh. In season three, during a pause in one of Jeff's tense speeches, the closed captioning read *[off-screen: someone does a violence]*. The phrasing and vagueness of it cracked us up for weeks afterward. "Maybe my boss was in charge of the closed captioning before clawing his way up the corporate ladder," I reply. "Anyway, I was wondering if you want to grab some food sometime? Catch up?" I'm about to reach the office, which means I don't have a lot of time to get to the point of my conversation—and if there's one thing I know about Sebastian and me, it's that we can get lost for hours just riffing off each other. Or, at least, we used to be able to.

Ennis's client after me had turned out to need a ride to Ojai, which is, apparently, a million hours away from Los Angeles, so he hadn't been available to pick me up from Vasquez. That means I'm currently in a real, honest-to-God, non-Ennis-driven Uber . . . which is why I feel comfortable having this conversation at all.

Not that Ennis has anything to worry about with Sebastian and me romantically. Nope. I learned that lesson the hard way and I'm not going back down that road; my friendship with Sebastian is way too important to risk ruining again. When I finally did read the *CoRaB* books, somewhere in between the tributes to leathermaking and insanely minute descriptions of the types of herbs that grow in the fictitious Kingdom of Six, there was a line that jumped out at me and has haunted me for the past two years: *When you kiss a friend, the friendship dies.*

It was true for Lucinda and Elevor. It was true for Sebastian and me—even though, irony of ironies, we never even kissed. Not once.

"Absolutely," Sebastian says. "What days are good for you?"

"Let me double-check with Ennis," I reply, wanting to make it triple-clear I know this is just a friendship thing. "But I think Thursday or Friday night would work."

"Either of those would be great," Sebastian says.

"Awesome. I'll confirm which one ASAP. And I'll leave it to you to pick the place? I still don't feel like I have my feet under me in LA."

"How long have you been here?" Sebastian asks.

"A little over two months," I say as the car pulls up to the WatchGoNowPlus offices. "Listen, I have to run. But I'll text you the day and you text me back with the spot?"

"You got it," Sebastian says.

"See you soon."

"See you."

I hang up with a smile on my face. The simplest words but ones I never thought I'd hear in that faint accent again. I hug my phone to my chest for a second before I step out of the car and back into the real world.

REDDIT
r/fandom_wank
Posted by u/bleeeeet 10 min. ago
1, 2, 3, 4: I declare a ship war!
Did you guys see this?? According to the Associated Press, the offices of WatchGoNowPlus were bombarded with hundreds of CANS of Chef Boyardee (with the word "Chef" crossed out in silver Sharpie and replaced with "Jeff") from a bunch of hyper-organized, LA-local Jeffcan shippers this morning after some Twitter Q&A Roberto Ricci did! Ha ha ha ha!
Literally no one:

Jeffcan Shippers: WE WON! Roberto confirmed it! WE
ARE ENDGAME!!

Sane CoRaB Fan: Unless an actor is also an executive
producer, they have no say in the scripts, nor do they
know what will happen in future episodes (even ones they
appear in), nor would they be allowed to say what little
they DO know, for fear of breach of contract.

Jeffcan Shippers: lalallala we can't hear you *singing*
"We are the champions . . ."

Duncinda/Lucivor Shippers: STFU! *sobbing*

Correction: this is not the real world. This is a world of lunacy.
I can't see my desk from the hallway that leads to my cubicle.
Instead, all I see is a wall of red boxes surrounded by a moat
of tin cans. At first I think I may have taken a wrong turn, but
then I see the wall is being guarded. By Sean.

He's sitting on an exercise ball and breathing like he's in a
nineties sitcom episode taking place in a Lamaze class.

"Um, hello, Sean."

"So," he says in between cartoonish exhales. "How did it go?"

"Well . . ." I begin, but then get a closer look at the red boxes.
Originally, they were labeled:

DUNCAN HINES DEVIL'S FOOD CAKE MIX WITH
WHITE FROSTING

Only someone has carefully replaced most of the letters so it
now reads:

JEFFCAN HINES WARLOCK FOOD CAKE MIX WITH
SILVER FROSTING

The DELICIOUSLY MOIST CAKE MIX tagline has been left almost untouched, except CAKE MIX has been replaced with FAN
REMIX.

I'm impressed by the mad graphic design skills and the quick mobilization of the fanbase, because it's barely been an hour since I sent out Rob's tweet. Of course, I also quickly realize that Sean's question about how everything went was sarcasm. "I guess the fans were really impressed with Rob's answers," I say calmly.

"Idiots," Sean breathes out, abruptly getting off his exercise ball and inadvertently knocking the wall of boxes down. "Get rid of these," he seethes.

"Will do," I say, as I start re-piling the boxes. Sean is walking away by the time I get a good look at the cans. Chef Boyardee Beef Ravioli. The "Chef Boyardee" has been crossed out in black Sharpie and scrawled over in serial killer handwriting with *JEFF.*

Jeffcans. I get it. Though I can't help comparing it to the intricate, seamless work of the cake mix boxes. Oh, well. Guess we can't all be artists, even if our fandom runs just as deep.

I rearrange the boxes and cans again in an aesthetically pleasing way and snap a photo. I'm sure I can use this in one of the socials. Then, after only the briefest hesitation, I text it to Sebastian, too. **The Jeffcan shippers are not here to play.**

Getting to casually text Sebastian is not something I ever thought would happen again. The unexpected feeling it gives me makes the rest of my workday go by much more pleasantly, even if half of it is spent trying to find someplace that'll accept an enormous donation of boxed and canned food.

After work, Ennis takes me to two different shelters where we off-load about three-quarters of the boxes and cans. The problem was that more kept coming as the day progressed— eventually joined by three cans of tomato paste halfheartedly declaring JEFF in faint blue pen—and there's only so much a shelter can do with cake mix and canned ravioli. So now I have about three dozen containers to stow in my apartment before I figure out what to do with them.

Ennis is helping me bring them in but gets a ping to go pick someone up.

"I got the rest," I assure him. "Thanks for your help."

"Righty-o, babe." A quick peck and he's gone.

By the time I'm bringing the last load in, Celeste has appeared like a genie in a cloud of Gap Dream perfume. (Which, I'm pretty sure, hasn't been manufactured in at least two decades, but Celeste has a large supply stockpiled under her bed.) The bees, I am disturbed to realize, have mysteriously vanished from the walls.

She's holding a can, her protuberant blue eyes even wider than usual. She points to the scrawled *JEFF* and whispers, "Does this *mean* something?"

"Uh. I guess it means the fanbase is still going strong."

"Is he listening in?" She raises her eyebrows significantly toward the door. I mean, I assume it's significant for her because I have no idea what she's talking about.

"Who?" I whisper back.

She looks at the can and then back at me. "Jeff," she mouths.

Jeff is a fictional warlock, potentially in control of Mount Signon and all of its powers (I don't have the clearance to read the pilot script so I don't know for sure). But I still doubt he's listening in. "No?" I mouth back.

"Blink twice if you need me to call 911," she whispers.

Okay, I give up. "Celeste. What are you talking about?" I say in my normal voice.

"*Jeff,*" she emphasizes, looking at the door again. "You're in an abusive relationship and this is a cry for help." She says this not as a question, but a statement, holding the can in her hand defiantly as if it's irrefutable evidence.

"First of all, my boyfriend's name is Ennis. Jeff is a fictional character on a show I'm working on. And this isn't a cry for help. . . ." I flick at the can. "Except maybe for some Photoshop lessons."

She looks back and forth between me and the can. I step around her to start putting some of the food away in the kitchen, which I do in silence for about a minute. Until . . .

"He *is* listening in, isn't he?" she whispers.

It takes me another hour to convince Celeste that all is right in my world. I finally get her off my back by telling her it would help me out if she could find a worthy cause to donate the extra food to. I have an email from Sean that just says DON'T THESE PEOPLE HAVE JOBS?! in the subject line with a photo attachment of a rebuilt wall of boxes in my cubicle, so I know I'll have more to deal with tomorrow.

I close out of my email and switch over to texting, sending Sebastian the latest photo.

This is dedication, he replies back. Also, how did it get there so fast? Drone delivery is eerie.

Supernatural, I reply. Maybe they should work a medieval version of it into an episode.

It would turn into drone carnage.

Naturally, I write. Anyway, how's Thursday? For dinner? The reason being: It's one day closer than Friday and the sooner I feel like I have a real friend out here, the better.

He responds right away. Great. How's this place?

He sends me a link to a Mexican place located . . . somewhere in Burbank. Honestly, I'm still overwhelmed by the massive sprawl of this city. When I first moved here, my one touchstone for LA geography was a line from Cher's dad in *Clueless*: "Everywhere in LA takes twenty minutes." It's a line that nearly cost me my job because I was over forty minutes late for my first interview. (Luckily, it turns out saying "traffic" with a disbelieving head shake is a pretty standard LA greeting so I was immediately accepted as one of their own.)

Looks great. I haven't had Mexican here yet, so . . . I write.

NINA.
NINA.
A long text bubble appears. I smile in anticipation of whatever he's going to write. Talking to Sebastian again is like stepping back into your childhood bedroom years after you left it and realizing you still remember the pencil marks in the closet and which parts of the floor squeak.

I know whatever he says is going to make me laugh and spur me to try to make him laugh in return.

I settle into my bed feeling, for the first time in the two months since I moved here, that I may finally be home.

CHAPTER 7

SEBASTIAN

The night Nina and I met is burned into my brain like a tattoo.

Even the date left an imprint: Sunday, October thirteenth, the premiere of season two of the original *CoRaB*. Fresh snow coated the ground. It had started falling that afternoon, and cast an ethereal glow over every tree and building. My little sister used to call it fairy dust. To me, the first snow of the year looked like icing, glossy and untouched, but that night I would've agreed with Millie. Fairy-tale magic infused the air.

I'd brought my dinner to the TV lounge of my dorm. I pretty much always grabbed a to-go bag in line and either ate outside by the weird orb sculpture (allegedly a fish) or on a bench near the chapel with a book.

Matty had a built-in group of friends from baseball, and I didn't want to impose on him. By leaving the cafeteria, maybe I could get him to infer I had my own group of friends. For weeks I'd operated under the principle that the less he and I interacted, the more highly he would think of me. Even if it hadn't snowed, I'd be inside because it was *CoRaB* night.

The show wouldn't air for another fifteen minutes, but I wanted to stake my claim to the channel before anyone else arrived and challenged me to a clicker duel.

T minus five minutes to showtime, food cleared away, and book set aside, I simmered with anticipation. One minute to showtime, a girl burst through the doors.

"Did it start? Is it on?" she demanded, her long dark hair swishing.

Startled, I moved out of the way and made room on the couch.

Her foot tapped. *"Castles of Rust and Bone,"* she clarified. "Did I miss anything?"

"Not even the Previouslys," I assured her.

"Oh God, I don't watch those," she said. "The Previouslys spoil everything."

"How do they . . . ?"

"Because they pick and choose what to remind us about and it's always a foreshadowing. I mean, you can totally watch it but I'm going to turn my back away and cover my ears. Tap my shoulder when it's done?"

Before I could reply, she pivoted from the screen, squeezed her eyelids shut, and clamped her hands over her ears.

I tapped her on the shoulder. "I'll mute it."

I took one for the team and watched the Previouslys in silence, unmuting at precisely the right time to hear the theme song pour out. I swayed to the music the way I always did, letting it transport me.

Nina still hadn't sat down. She stood sentinel, rapt, in front of me but to the side so the screen wouldn't be blocked.

She swayed in time to the beat too.

Throughout the episode, I was aware of each breath as it left my body, conscious of how I sat, my posture, where my arms fell. We shared the couch by the first ad break, and as we chatted about the show during commercials, a thrilling thought swam below the surface of my mind like a shark: This lovely girl with the heart-shaped face thinks I'm a regular guy, just some normal dude, someone worth talking to. She has no idea who

I used to be. No idea that in high school and middle school, I never fit in.

As far as Nina was concerned, I could be anyone. Anyone at all.

I didn't cheat or steal to get this job.

I did, however, lie like a rug.

Janine believes I've seen a handful of *CoRaB* episodes but not all of them. She certainly doesn't know I have a quilt depicting the show's family trees, purchased on a dare while drunkenly surfing Etsy with Nina junior year. (In return, Nina had to wear medieval tippets on her sleeves during her fullest course load day, but not respond to questions or acknowledge them in any way, even if she stumbled over the floor-length fabric.)

The Kingdom of Six family tree quilt is in storage because Matty banished it from our apartment. He called it Sex Kryptonite. Anyway, Janine has no clue I'm the definition of a Rust & Boner (derogatory name for superfans) because I didn't want her to worry I'd be a security risk.

When I first arrived in LA, finding a job in film or TV was about as easy as climbing a rampart outside a castle while javelins flew at you from everyone who'd gotten there first. Internships were the tunnel inside the fortress. I worked at La Brea Bakery mornings and weekends so I could afford to accept unpaid industry gigs. (Matty popped for groceries since I cooked for us so often, which helped, too.) For my internships, I reviewed reels for a talent agency and wrote script coverage for a lit agency, only to see both agencies bought by outside conglomerates and my role deemed "redundant" before I could be promoted. After two more years of sporadic employment—in a mailroom, as a grip for low-budget films, and for three soul-confusing months, a fit model for a French cowboy-themed denim company in the garment district downtown, during which I tried on thousands of pairs of jeans and stood in awk-

ward positions while designers measured my thighs, waist, in-
seam, and ass—I'd had enough. I got serious about networking
and hosted alumni nights multiple times a month to connect
with other graduates and get the inside scoop on legitimate production jobs. My home-cooked buffets were the main draw of
these events, and eventually my efforts paid off: I got word that
a boutique production office, Alex & Co., sought an assistant
for a hush-hush new contract they'd landed. The "Co." part of
the name is purely decorative. There's no one else; it's Janine
Alex and me. Luckily, she's down-to-earth and easygoing, and
she rarely interrupts my weekends. When I'm off the clock, I'm
off the clock.

If you ask ten people what a producer is, you'll get ten different answers, but the gist of it is that Janine's in charge of
overseeing the physical creation of the show from start to finish. Budgets, contracts, above-the-line talent (directors, writers,
actors), and below-the-line talent (crew members). In short, her
job is to find the right people to do all the *other* jobs.

Since there's nowhere to advance in the position, Janine
switches out assistants every two years. The job is intended
to be an overview, a launching pad in any direction I choose,
which means I get to experience every aspect of television production. When my two years are up, I should have a clearer idea
of where my interests—and future in the industry—lie.

Today, Wednesday, I'm driving to Manhattan Beach with
one-third of a script page in hand so J. J. Westingland's research assistant can approve the song lyrics used by the noble
children's choir during a serenade to Queen Lucinda. I've been
instructed to eat the script page if anyone stops me en route.

After that I'm meeting Matty for dinner at Don Cuco's in
Burbank, the very restaurant I chose for Nina and myself tomorrow. My plan to not screw anything up with her includes a
practice run so I can determine the best place to sit, and advise
her if she asks for suggestions from the menu.

I arrive first at Don Cuco's and scan the restaurant's layout. A booth in the middle would be ideal for tomorrow—low-key private, not too close to the entrance or the kitchen. We can sprawl out and I won't fall into the "Should I or Should I Not Pull Out a Chair for Nina?" dilemma. I don't want her to feel awkward or uncomfortable at any point of our meet-up. It needs to go perfectly.

The last words Nina said to me senior year are easy to recall, despite my wishing numerous times over the years that I could forget them.

It was the first week of June. The finale party we'd spent so long planning felt like a distant memory, and the news of *CoRaB*'s cancelation had just hit, so I'd sought her out in a daze to discuss it. I had assumed she'd be as devastated as I was.

Instead, she seemed . . . blank. Above it all. Her voice coiled around me like a snake, slowly squeezing the air from my lungs.

"It's fitting, don't you think? Because that's what we had in common and now it's done, just like college is about to be done. We don't want the same things, Sebastian, so let's just . . . chill and get through graduation so we can go our separate ways and start our real *lives, okay?"*

It didn't make sense then, and it doesn't make sense now. Each clipped, angry word had sliced at me, confusing and cryptic and painful, but I respected her wishes and backed off. We sleepwalked through graduation and "went our separate ways." She dropped off the face of the earth, leaving me to navigate life alone.

I've ordered three dishes to test out by the time Matty wanders through the door. The advertising firm where he works is around the corner, which is the other reason I chose this restaurant; I couldn't ask him to drive out of his way for my weird little exercise. Not that he's unaccustomed to my bizarre requests; he was my roommate for eight consecutive years, which is longer than I lived with a comprehensible Millie (I don't count ages zero to three, aka the Incessant Pattycake Years).

Eight years of listening to me natter on every few months

about my feelings for Nina, equivocating and obsessing, must have taken its toll.

And yet. Here we are.

Matty waves and saunters toward me, leather briefcase strapped around his shoulder. I'm so Stockholm syndrome'd from my own briefcase experience, I can't figure out why his isn't handcuffed to his wrist.

We slap hands, and after ordering a taco salad and a margarita to match mine, he doesn't waste a second. "How'd she look? Are you still into her?"

The instant I'd gotten off the phone with Nina the other night, I'd texted Millie about our plans, then texted Matty and filled him in too. My cheering section didn't disappoint (if by cheering section I mean a GIF Matty sent me of a jubilant Xander Bogaerts celebrating with his Red Sox teammates in a piggyback jump).

"Technically I never *stopped* being into her."

He points at me. "Tell. Her. That."

"She has a boyfriend!"

"If you wait for her to be single, you'll never do it."

The urge to defend her clicks into place, like notching an arrow. "What's that supposed to mean? She's allowed to date whoever she wants."

He groans. "I know that, but has it occurred to you the only reason you never dated is because she didn't know it was an option? If you tell her how you feel, she can decide what to do with that information. I'm not asking you to lure her out of a committed relationship. I'm telling you to come clean for both your sakes. Clear the air already."

My pulse speeds up. "Tomorrow? Right away?"

"What's the worst that could happen?"

"Um, the worst that could happen is we go our separate ways for *another* five years."

He leans back in the booth and grins at me. "Negative, my friend. You work together now."

I laugh, but it's not a happy sound. "All the more reason to shut my fucking gob. I don't want to make things weird for her whenever we cross paths."

"What's the plan, then? You'll take this to your grave, never give her a chance to say 'Yes, my long-legged British darling, let's bang it out'?"

I snort and take a large swig of my drink. If he busts out another falsetto impression of Nina, I need to be at least halfway sozzled. "You know what, yes. If I have to 'take it to my grave,' to have her in my life again, that's what I'll do." I cross my arms for good measure but not even my arms believe me.

"Look. The worst thing that could happen already happened," Matty points out. "And it wasn't because of an honest conversation."

"That's the problem, though. I don't *know* what caused our rift. And until I do, I'm not going to freak her out by telling her how I feel."

"Fine. Get to the bottom of it, and *then* tell her. If she's not into it, at least you'll finally know, and you can move on."

His subtext rings out loud and clear. "And you won't have to hear about it anymore."

He chuckles and shakes his head. "I can hear about it all you want. All I ask is that *Nina* hears about it too. It's not like she's going to be completely shocked, right? I mean, you did almost kiss that one time."

Early on in my friendship with Nina, there was an incident involving the caffeine pills that came with our freshman welcome packs. During the course of that evening we spent together, kissing seemed 100 percent plausible. The problem was, I had zero experience. I hadn't even held hands with a girl at that point.

When I confessed my secret to Matty, he finagled an invite to a frat party that weekend at Cornell University, our collegiate neighbor. Ironically, a school called Ithaca doesn't have a Greek system, and Matty thought I should make out with a few girls to boost my confidence. He marched me into the living room of the house party and shouted, "Who wants to teach my friend how to kiss?" Unbelievably, we got three takers from amongst the sorority girls, as well as a dude whom we politely declined but set up with a classmate of ours. Last I heard, they're still together. Lucky bastards.

Anyway, we kept this up for several weekends in a row, everyone had fun, no one got hurt, and I upped my game significantly. By the time I felt as though I could show Nina a good time in the kissing department, she was dating someone else. Which, again, she had every right to do.

Still, Matty's right. I need to come clean. I just have no idea how I'm going to do it.

"I got this," I insist, when the check arrives.

"What?" Matty lunges for the bill. "No, we're splitting it."

I've already signed the slip and crammed it back in the holder. "Your money's no good here. Consider it a thanks for the pep talk."

Matty squints at me and pulls out his wallet. "Let me handle the tip or drinks, at least. Those margaritas weren't cheap."

"It's all good," I assure him. "Hit me up next time. By the way, I have your monkey bread for tomorrow's game. It's in the car."

He grins. "Seriously? Thanks! But you know you don't have to make it every week, right?"

"And break the streak? Please." The La Brea Lemurs have won their last eight baseball games and I like to think Matty's pregame snack is the reason.

I take another bite of my tamale. It's slightly better than the burrito and has thus earned a slot on my recommendation list for Nina tomorrow night.

CHAPTER 8

NINA

One hour. I can make it one more hour.

Here's the thing: The bees *are* gone. But they've been replaced by something far, far worse.

"Medicinal leech therapy dates all the way back to the beginning of civilization," Celeste is telling me as she's covering a large tank with a navy bath sheet. "They like the dark," she explains.

The tank is almost the size of our love seat and is currently sitting across from it, like it's come for tea. Or, more accurately, blood.

"Uh-huh," I say.

"But my new holistic therapy practice is going to bring the practice to the twenty-first century. You see, when you're menstruating . . ."

Oh, dear Lord. "Please say no more," I beg.

Celeste raises an eyebrow. "Nina. It's not natural to be squeamish about your own cycle."

"That's really not what I'm squeamish about," I assure her as I catch a glimpse of a swishing black tail at the bottom of the tank. The bath sheet is not big enough to cover the whole thing. "Also, do you have any sort of experience with holistic therapy? Or, like, a license."

"I've got something better!" Celeste squeals, her eyes shining. "My ex is dating someone whose ex works PR for Goop. If I can just get Gwyneth to put this in her newsletter . . . I mean, this could be THE next yoni egg, Nina." She smiles at me. "Do you want to be one of the very first to experience the magic? I'll give you a discount."

"So generous. Too generous," I say as I slowly back away to my room. "Unfortunately, I have dinner plans, so . . ." I can feel my room's doorframe with my foot, so I scurry in, still smiling at Celeste as I close the door and then lock it for good measure. Not only do I not trust Celeste to refrain from barging in but, with my luck, she's managed to "get a good deal" on some incense-based sedative and will drug me and perform the procedure without my consent.

Fifty-four minutes. Sebastian is coming in fifty-four minutes.

I look at my phone. I guess I should do it. It's been a while since I checked in. I pick it up, scroll to "Mom" and hit the FaceTime button.

"Yo." A familiar heart-shaped face, perfectly contoured and framed by lavender locks, answers. Not my mom, obviously. Sayeh, my twenty-year-old sister.

"Hi," I say. "How are you?"

"Good," she says. "Just about to use Mom's phone to make my latest video. She got the latest iPhone for herself but not, you know, for the person who actually makes her living from using her camera." She rolls her eyes.

I refrain from mentioning that if she's making such a great living from her videos (she is), then she could just buy herself the latest iPhone. Last I checked, Sayeh's YouTube subscriber count had just passed 1.5 million. "What's the topic today?" I ask.

"Eyebrows. I have a duty to save the overpluckers from themselves. Before it's too late," she adds ominously.

It still boggles my mind that my little sister has created a makeup empire over the fact that her name means "shadow" in Farsi—in fact, EyeSayeh is the name of her channel. She started out as a precocious eight-year-old showing other kids how to paint their faces to look like their favorite Pokémon and has moved on to beauty store endorsements and a contract in the works for her own line of eye shadow: Sayeh Sayeh, I believe is the working brand name.

"What's up with you?" she asks, as she brings her face closer to the phone, looking at herself instead of me in order to swipe some mascara on. "Still keeper of all the nerd gossip that's fit to tweet?"

That's the weird thing about my sister. When she started out with the Pokémon, I was sure she was set to join me in my geeky, pop culture junkie ways. But then, somehow, she switched tracks, becoming trendy and fashion-obsessed instead.

"Yup," I say. "I interviewed Roberto Ricci this week."

She racks her brain for a sec. "Oh, yeah. He used to be cute. Is he even in anything anymore?"

"Um, yeah. He's in the reboot of *Castles of Rust and Bone.* The thing I'm working on?"

"Right. Right." She brings her other eye closer and evens out her mascara.

I suddenly realize something. "Wait, aren't you supposed to be in school?"

"Oh. I'm taking a sabbatical," she says casually as she picks up a tube of lip gloss.

"Now?" I ask. "Three weeks before the semester ends?"

"I actually left last week," she explains. "It was getting to be too much dealing with all this—" She indicates the spread of products before her. "Like, who has time to write a paper and be a mogul, you know? Besides, I think the school of life is teaching me more business sense than my stupid statistics class."

"How is Maman taking that?" I ask. If there's one thing my

mom is a stickler for, it's school attendance. A very angry nurse once sent me home with chicken pox when my mom had decided I wasn't contagious anymore (read: There was a "highly important" elementary school standardized test I apparently needed to take instead).

"Oh, she doesn't care. Now that she's got a new man in her life."

My heart is suddenly soaring, lodging itself somewhere in my throat. Can it possibly be true? "What?! Who?" I squeak out.

Sayeh starts laughing and gives me a withering look. "Really, Nina? You're way too gullible. How have they not eaten you alive in LA?"

"Ugh," I say in disgust, even though she's sort of right. Our mother hasn't so much as looked at another man since our dad left when I was ten. While I was at college, Sayeh sneakily created a bunch of dating profiles on her behalf and all she got in return was a week of muffled crying from Maman's room when she found out about them. Even the concept of looking for love is too painful for her.

"Well, this has been fun, but I gotta start my livestream in exactly one minute, so, later," Sayeh says as she takes one final look at her own image and then ends the call without waiting for me to say goodbye.

"Khodahafez, you narcissist," I say to my own face long after she's gone. And then sigh. Might as well put my own makeup on. Sebastian will be here in forty-five minutes. I can try to drag out the process.

I slip out of my apartment barefooted, waiting to put on my shoes when I'm already outside. I've had enough Celesteisms for the evening and think I could do without having to say goodbye.

Sebastian has texted me that he's outside my place but I don't see him. I take out my phone to message him when I hear something that sounds like a horn section. I don't mean a car horn, I mean a literal horn section in the philharmonic.

I look up to see a sleek silver spaceship in front of my building, with a profile so low it practically stops at my knee. That's why I didn't notice it; it looks like set decoration from *Fast and Furious 27*, not a real live mode of transportation. Somehow, Sebastian has folded himself into it. He grins at me from the driver's window.

I know enough to realize that this car costs more than my college education, but I have to glance at the back to find out what kind of car it actually is (a Jaguar), because otherwise I'd have no clue. My eyes glaze over whenever anyone mentions automobiles of any kind—a fact that holds true with medieval modes of transportation as well. There was an unfortunate fifteen-minute interlude in *CoRaB* episode 303 involving a certain combination of horse and chariot during which, I swear to God, I blacked out. When I came to, Jeff was inexplicably petting a centaur tail. Sebastian had to give me a recap on what happened.

Speaking of whom, he's getting out of the car now to open the passenger door for me. Grinning, he asks, "Are you okay? You didn't black out again, did you?"

I can't help smiling. Five years later, and we're on the exact same page, thinking of the same moment, the same episode, and we're not even watching it. I feel my body instantly relax. Being Sebastian's friend is my destiny. And if I continue to think of him like the brother I never had, then everything will work out the way it was always meant to.

"I got worried for a sec you forgot everything there is to know about me and rented this to impress me," I tease as I get into the (surprisingly) roomy interior. Is the car so expensive because it has actual TARDIS abilities? That might make it slightly more interesting.

"Believe me, I couldn't even *rent* this thing on my salary,"

Sebastian assures me. "My boss is letting me borrow it while I housesit for her. I only found out this morning, so the timing's pretty great for our dinner, huh? I thought it'd be a fun way to explore Los Angeles. Check this out."

He presses a button on his steering wheel. My door swings open.

"Uh. By foot?" I joke.

"Crap. That's not what I meant to do." He presses the same button again, but nothing happens. "How do I get the door to close?" he mutters.

"I have an idea," I deadpan, and lean out, grab the handle, and manually shut my door.

"Wow. Analog. Who would've thought? Okay, let's try this again."

He presses the button next to the original one. The Sirius XM station changes to the Radio Margaritaville channel.

"Did you mean explore Los Angeles or explore South Florida through the musical tastes of a seventy-year-old man?"

"Shit, no. That's not what I meant either." Sebastian starts haphazardly pressing buttons. The windshield wipers go, the brights get turned on, an alarming mist starts filling the car . . .

"Does this car also give you a facial?" I ask. "Because that truly might be the most Los Angeles thing I've heard of."

"Damn it!" Sebastian says.

"Seb. What exactly are you trying to do?" I ask.

"Open the top so that it's a convertible!"

"Oh." I take one glance at the unfathomable panel. There's no way I have any idea how to do that either. "Okay, next best thing . . ."

I take my phone and find the app that simulates the night sky at our exact location. Then I raise my hand so that it's touching the ceiling of the car. "See? And no light pollution to worry about. The perfect LA night. Artificial and everything."

Sebastian glares at me playfully. "Okay, fine. Obviously the way to your hardened heart is through your stomach. I'd like to see you make fun of the restaurant, missy."

He pulls into the street and starts driving. A silence settles over us but Sebastian doesn't let it go too long. "So . . ." he says.

"So . . ."

"Your top three highlights of the last five years. Go," he says, as the GPS butts in to tell us to continue on Los Feliz Boulevard until we reach the freeway in one and a half miles.

"Top three?" I ask.

"I know, I know. It's hard to whittle down," he says.

I don't tell him what's giving me pause is the opposite. So much seemed to happen in my four years of college: There were so many different classes, so many ideas flying around, so much growth between freshman year Nina and senior year Nina (both figuratively and literally: I actually was a super-late bloomer who grew my last two inches in college) . . . most of all, so much *fun.* How can it be an even longer time out of college than in it when it seems like nothing of significance has happened since? Just a sort of . . . melancholy I seem to be doing my best to grope my way through. The last five years haven't really been about living; they've been about surviving.

"I'll give you a freebie," Sebastian cheerfully interjects, having no idea of the dark turn my thoughts just took. "You now work on your favorite show ever."

I give a wan smile. "I work for the new streaming service that my favorite show ever is on."

"But you got to interview Roberto Ricci! You got to be on set!" he exclaims.

"That's true." It could be a good time to tell him how that interview really went, how Prince Duncan is forever ruined for me but . . . I don't want to ruin it for him, too.

"Rain check on a high five on that?" he asks.

"As soon as we park," I promise. "Okay. I got one. I moved out of my mom's house."

"And over to the best coast!"

"Mmmm . . . that's still TBD," I say as I look at the bumper-to-bumper traffic ahead of us. We now have a mere 1.1 miles to go, which will take us at least twenty minutes.

"Come on," Sebastian says, drum soloing on the steering wheel. "Sunshine. Every freaking day? How is that not an improvement?"

"Would you like me to list weather as one of my top three highlights?" I ask mock sweetly.

"No. Next."

Oh! I know exactly what to tell him! "I found all the Koroks!"

I'd like to think that, had we been moving, Sebastian would have hit the brakes in a cartoonish manner. Instead, his eyes nearly bug out of his head. "WHAT?! You. Did. Not."

"Did so," I say proudly. "All nine hundred." *The Legend of Zelda: Breath of the Wild* came out our senior year of college. For two months, Sebastian and I played it obsessively together. It's a one-player game but we'd take turns, raptly watching the other one solve puzzles and fight Lynels, freely doling out advice though neither of us minded the other one's back-seat gaming. We tried to hit every side quest and collect every one of the Korok seeds in the massive game.

"When did you find them?"

"Oh, sometime . . . after," I say awkwardly. And I know we both know exactly after what.

The finale party. Where I had put way too much thought into my costume. Like, would anyone notice that I had a tiny fake dagger sewn into my corset just the way Lucinda did in a pivotal scene from season three? Of course not.

That's not entirely true. Sebastian would've noticed. And, honestly, that was the whole point.

For days afterward, I told myself that I hadn't been planning what I was actually planning. That I was drunk (I'd had half a glass of homemade mead which—quite frankly—I'm pretty sure was just a sickly sweet shot of rotting honey because what college kid knows how to properly ferment honey?). That it was a good thing I hadn't ruined four years of friendship and fandom by doing something so cliché as admitting that I wanted us to be more.

But the thing was, I ruined everything anyway.

Sebastian knew I was going to be Lucinda and I knew that he was going as Duncan, but we'd kept which version of the characters we were planning a secret from each other.

So when I saw him from across the room, dressed in the bloody wedding suit, my hand had gone to squeeze the fake dagger of its own accord. Of course we'd dressed as the characters from the same scene, the moment when the star-crossed lovers turned to mortal enemies. (After all, it's sort of hard to forgive your newly wedded wife when she attempts to murder you as soon as you've completed your recessional.)

Also hard to forgive? Watching your crush stick his tongue down the throat of someone else dressed as Wedding Dress Lucinda, $29.99 Halloween Store Version.

It was like I was watching it in slow motion. It was like one of the fanfics I'd started (and abandoned) about Lucinda really having an evil twin that would explain her constant teetering on the edge of heroine or villain. (Sebastian and I would discuss it as brilliant, subversive writing. It's only now, and thanks to Roberto Ricci, that I know the real reason was the behind-the-scenes drama between Francis Jean and the head writer.)

I saw Sebastian spot me. I saw his eyes widen as he broke away from his make-out partner.

I didn't know how else to react so I did what most women do when their heart suddenly seems to be in a million pieces but they don't want anyone to know it.

I smiled.

I grabbed another shot of the atrocious mead off a tray, held it up in the air in a salute to him, and downed it.

Then I left the party and went to a place he wouldn't think to look for me.

But it all fell apart anyway. I couldn't stand seeing him and Heather together. I tried, I really did. If it was any other guy, I think I could have swallowed my feelings.

But I wasn't used to doing that with Sebastian. So when he found me to talk about—of all things—the cancellation of *Castles of Rust and Bone*, I snapped. I said all those things about us being over, about college ending and it being time to move on. I said it with such force that I ended up believing it myself. And then I went out of my way to make sure we never saw each other again. I had my mom come pick me up early from school. I deleted all my social media accounts (though that, quite frankly, turned out to be a blessing). And I told my mom that I wanted a new phone number, making up a stupid story about some guy stalking me.

I canceled us, just like that.

But things are different now. Five years later, maybe the most significant highlight is that I *know* I want our friendship to work. I need it to.

Sebastian makes a harrowing maneuver to merge onto the 5, and I think back to his question. I guess, for highlight number three, I'm going to go with . . . "And then there's Ennis."

"Your boyfriend," Sebastian says, nodding. "He seems nice."

"He is." Definitely not a lie.

"Do you live together?"

"No." I should've said *not yet* but I can't bring myself to deceive him that deeply.

"How did you meet?" Sebastian asks. "Nightclub? Tinder? Settlers of Catan tournament?"

"You know only one of those is even remotely likely."

He grins and shrugs. "I'm glad some things never change."

I sneak a glance at him. No, some things never do.

"Okay, ready for the most LA story ever?" I ask and he nods. "Ennis . . . was the Uber driver who picked me up from LAX."

CHAPTER 9

SEBASTIAN

Traffic speeds up so I'm saved from responding right away. I exit at Olive Avenue and make my way through Burbank, all the while trying to decide what to say.

If I'm interpreting Nina's previous statement correctly, it means if she'd gotten a different driver that day at LAX, she *might not have a boyfriend right now*. That's the thin line we're talking about, folks, and one I'm painfully familiar with.

Boyfriend 1, pre-freshman year: The campus tour guide, aka the first person she could possibly have met upon arrival at orientation.

Boyfriend 2, freshman year: SAM JEONG. Yep. After I'd concluded my Making Out 101 coursework, with a concentration in bra clasp efficiency, the guy Nina started dating was Sam. Witnessing it was agonizing, a monthlong torment that firmly put her off-limits.

By the time they broke up after a few weeks, the words, "Did I mention I'm a good kisser now . . . want to test me out?" did not seem appropriate.

We spent most of our free time together anyway, so if you ask me, I was the lucky one. If she'd dated me instead of him, we never would have become best friends. Freshman year in particular, friends were a luxury I didn't take for granted.

For whatever reason, Nina's boyfriends came and went with no lingering after-effects; at least, none that I knew about. Sam, et al. never lasted long. In my biased opinion, they were temporary distractions. Nina and I were an institution. Nina and I were forever.

So I thought.

Boyfriend 3, sophomore year: the brother of her roommate's boyfriend who was, quote, "always around."

Boyfriend 3.5, sophomore year: the cashier at the 24/7 convenience store located between East and West Tower where she hung out to eat sandwiches while studying. You could say he was the most convenient aspect of the store, and you would not be wrong.

Boyfriends 4 through 6, junior year: one or two dates each, as I recall, with guys who sat next to her in class.

God, stop.

"Is that how you keep track of him?" I joke. "Through his Uber?" At least, I *intended* it as a joke, but the look I get in return tells me it didn't land.

"I don't 'keep track' of him—"

"It's great you can carpool together to work," I add hastily, and sincerely, because who wouldn't want to shave minutes off their commute?

"It has been nice," she answers vaguely.

We arrive at Don Cuco's and park in the free lot up the street. The moment we enter the restaurant, the host proceeds to blow my cover.

"Back so soon?" he booms happily. To Nina: "He was here last night, too."

It's still light outside, but as the heavy wooden doors close behind us, the restaurant turns dim and velvety.

Unfortunately, a loud birthday party is happening right beside the booth I had picked out so carefully last night. My hope for a quiet evening is murdered in its sleep.

"Do you mind if we find a different spot?" Nina asks.

"Definitely. I mean, no, I don't mind. Sorry about that."

She looks confused. "It's not your fault."

"I know, but . . ." I shrug, feeling helpless. I wanted tonight to be flawless.

Once we're seated at a smaller table, away from the celebration, Nina smiles and says, "You ate here last night, too? This place must be killer."

My cheeks burn. "Matty says 'hey,' by the way."

"Matty? Your college roommate."

"Yeah, we still live together. Or, we did. He moved in with his girlfriend, Maritza, on Sunday. But we came out to LA together a few months after graduation. Sam was already here, living with his family again and being slowly driven insane until we rescued him and convinced him to move in down the hall."

I steal a glance at her, wondering if Sam's name will provoke a response, but her expression remains the same.

"Wow," she says. "Emerson Hall, second floor, transferred over to the West Coast, huh?"

I smile. "Something like that."

Matty's directive to tell Nina the truth about my feelings had seemed obvious and simple last night, but now it feels impossibly far away, as though I agreed to it in a dream. Even his text message this afternoon—a GIF of Woody Harrelson in *Zombieland* saying, "It's time to nut up or shut up"—seems like a relic best left unheeded.

I give her a rundown of the menu, we order, and Nina leans forward, excitement shining in her eyes.

"Tell me all about the PA job."

"Yes! The office is peak LA. It's on Sunset Boulevard, and I never know which celebrity will hop on the elevator with me. Oh and my boss, Janine, lives across the street in a luxury apartment, on the tenth floor."

Nina's in awe. "No commute? That's power."

"She has floor-to-ceiling windows and the sickest view, too: you can see all the way to Dodger Stadium *and* the ocean."

"That's right, you're house-sitting."

"And car-sitting."

"Very cool." She snaps her fingers. "You're still coming up with recipes, I hope?"

"Of course. Remember Jeff's eyeball necklace from season three?"

"Do I 'remember Jeff's eyeball necklace'?" she scoffs, tapping her finger to her chin. "No, hmm, can't seem to recall. Did Jeff have an eyeball necklace?"

"The show's fake production name—"

"*Lucy's Donuts*, how perfect is that?"

"—inspired me. I was thinking of stringing a bunch of donut holes together with licorice laces, and then using icing and Skittles to make them look like eyes. And people can be like . . ." I make a *nom-nom* sound as I pretend to eat the eyeball necklace conveniently located under my mouth. "Like those candy necklaces for kids. Millie used to crack out on those."

"I love it. Great idea."

"Can you believe no one's done a cookbook yet? Not a licensed one, at least."

"You should pitch it to them," she says. "Why not, right?"

Speaking of all things *Why not?,* I'm on the verge of bringing up our estrangement when our food arrives. Nina seems to enjoy everything I recommended, so at least the cuisine aspect of the night is going well.

My phone dings. I apologize and check the message in case it's from Janine with a house-sitting instruction. Nope, it's Matty, who's sent another GIF, this time Schwarzenegger in *Predator* ordering me to "Do it! Do it now!!!" I quickly silence my phone and shove it in my back pocket.

"Did you meet any actors when you were at the studio?" Nina asks between bites of food.

I can't say *Roberto in the men's room and I'm still traumatized,* so I blurt out, "Only the queen regnant herself."

"Whoa. How did that go?"

Her eyes are so curious and welcoming I want to fall into them. I feel dizzy with the wonderfulness of it all, the effervescent rightness of sitting here with her and telling her about my run-in with Francis Jean.

"She couldn't have been cooler. She even showed me where to pick up that briefcase that's going to get me killed."

"Any idea what's in it?"

"I was hoping *you* might know."

"No clue, but I'll keep my ear to the ground."

"And what about you? Roberto was—nice? He was nice to you?" It's one thing for Rob to dick *me* around, but if he hurt or harassed *Nina* . . .

She takes a sip of her Mexican Coca-Cola, seeming to relish the infusion of real sugar instead of corn syrup. "Mm-hmm. He was fine."

Huh. Okay. Maybe he plays up his heartthrob status with women but doesn't bother to be polite—or even human—to men. An alpha thing? I'm relieved for her and double down on my decision never to reveal what happened with Roberto. Her *CoRaB* experiences appear to have been positive so far, and I refuse to burst that bubble.

Instead, I clear my throat. "There's a pretty big elephant sitting next to us and I don't think I can ignore it much longer, so I'm going to ask . . . what happened with us?"

She looks like a deer in headlights, and my pulse is so jacked up the room vibrates. If I lose her again, after just getting her back, I'll regret it forever, so I fill the air with a possible explanation to see how she reacts.

"I thought you might have been upset about Heather—like you were worried I'd spend all my time with her or something, but I never would have done that. I still wanted to hang out with you, take that catering job over the summer, do all the things we planned. I was surprised when you said all we had in common was . . ."

"The show. Right. I think," she says slowly, "that I figured that was how *you* saw us, and it didn't seem right to drag things out."

My face wants to make the scream emoji because that's such a batshit interpretation of how I viewed us. "I *never* thought all we had in common was the show."

"So then why didn't you confide in me about the rest of your life?" she asks, her voice wavering. "I thought we were close enough to share important things, like our crushes."

I'm running alongside her train of thought, desperate to jump on. "So it *was* about Heather?"

"No! But . . . you could've *told* me about her. You know? That you liked her and everything." Nina's nostrils flare, and fuck me a million times, even that small movement of hers is adorable.

"I didn't, though! I mean, I did, but it wasn't some long drawn-out situation the way you're making it sound."

She nods. "I know it's mostly my fault. I felt foolish—God knows I bent your ear about my boyfriends—and I lashed out. If I could take it back—go back to our friendship the way it used to be—I'd do it in a heartbeat."

"We can do that," I say quickly. "Let's do that." My heart feels both clawed open and restored. I'm devastated *and* grateful, a pendulum swinging between two extremes. I suppose eventually the pendulum will come to a stop in the middle, peaceful. Because it's dead.

She wants friendship? I'll friendship her till effing dawn.

"For what it's worth, I know what you're saying," I continue. My voice sounds far away. "I feel that way about Matty sometimes. I would tell him about, you know, girls, and I sometimes worried he was only putting up with me because he had to. But

Heather was my first. There were no girlfriends to talk about before her."

Just people I kissed so I'd be worthy of kissing you.

"I'm not saying it makes sense," Nina says quietly. "But I want you to know I'd listen. If we end up hanging out, I'd listen. I'm sorry I didn't stick around to do exactly that, and prove that I could."

"Me too. I'm sorry I didn't try harder to find out why you were upset." A weight's been lifted off my chest, but I *miss* the weight. It represented the possibility that we could've been more than friends, and now it's gone.

She offers me her hand across the table. "To friendship?"

We shake. I try to ignore the smooth feel of her palm. "Want to go cruisin', friend?" I ask, and the radiant smile she gifts me in response makes my throat hurt.

The first place we drive is CarMax Burbank, a used-car dealership, because it's making me crazy that I can't put the top down in Janine's Jaguar.

Shoving aside all pride, I lay it out for the salesman, who isn't thrilled to be helping non-customers with their rich-people shit.

"Little does he know we can barely make rent," Nina whispers, and I almost crack up in front of the dude.

Nevertheless, the salesman explains which buttons to push, and his irritation is more than worth it when the roof folds back on itself, revealing the night sky above our heads.

"Yes!" I pump my fist, and we're on our way again, wind tickling our hair, as we soar along Barham Boulevard to the overpass at the 101. I coast over to the right lane and exit on Mulholland, so we can climb the twisting, slender path of the mountains for a spectacular view.

"Sebastian Worthington in a Jaguar convertible," Nina muses. "Quite a long way from the Klepto-car."

Back in New York we christened my piece-of-junk Nissan the

"Klepto-car" because I hoped someone would steal it. Whenever we went to the movies at Pyramid Mall or over to Cornell to rollerblade around their campus, I deliberately left the car unlocked with the windows down. The insurance payout from its theft would have been about $300, i.e., the cost of treating all our friends to a night out at La Café Cent-Dix on Aurora Street, our goal at the time.

Heather hated that car.

"Oh, this is amazing," Nina says quietly when we reach our destination, a secluded overlook bathed in the day's last streaks of sunlight. The sky is a saturated, incandescent mix of purple and pink, but not for long; soon it's going, going, gone. The irony, of course, is that the most spectacular sunsets are caused by smog.

Within minutes all is dark, save for the intricate pattern of lights shimmering below us, backdropped by the dark silhouette of the mountains. From this high up, traffic becomes a harmless stream of colors and sounds that can't touch you. The stretched-out vista embodies promise and possibility, a great wide-open city that urges you to ask, over and over, "Is this real? How can this be real?"

I'm not sure how much time passes, the two of us side by side as the night air turns chilly, before Nina breaks the silence. "Are you seeing anyone now?"

"Not at the moment. I dated a few actress-slash-models the last few years, and—"

"Not to brag," she teases.

"They're the only people out here! But I'm not interested in doing that again."

"Can I ask what happened with Heather? Is she still doing theater?" Nina asks. "In Chicago, wasn't it?"

"Yeah, she moved home to Evanston the same time I moved out here. She was thinking about joining me at some point, but it never happened. Last I heard she booked a commercial for probiotic yogurt."

"Nice! Lifetime supply!" Nina says in a high voice. "I'm guessing?"

I'm perplexed. "Maybe?"

"You don't keep in touch, then?"

"Not really."

Unlike the abrupt excommunication by Nina, Heather and I never had a blowout. We floated off in our own directions with no hard feelings.

I have photos of her filed away somewhere, and I liked her a hell of a lot, but for the life of me, I can't recall a single evening we spent together in detail. The entire summer is one soft blur, undefined, no edges.

In contrast, the days and nights I spent with Nina on that ratty old dorm couch shift like splinters beneath my skin, specific and sharp, poking out when I least expect them. And here we are, five years later, sitting not on a couch but in the front seat of a luxury car, gazing out at a view that belongs in the movies.

"What?" Nina asks, tilting her head.

The lump in my throat dissolves enough to let me speak. "I'm glad you're here."

My tone is lighthearted, but I try to strengthen the impact of the words by looking her directly in the eyes.

I can get used to this again, being with her but not *with* her. I did it for four years and then I lived without it for five years and I know which one I prefer, even if they both kill me in different ways and to different degrees.

"Don't get too sappy on me," she says.

"I won't. But I do have a request: Let's take the long way home."

CHAPTER 10

NINA

We're pulling onto my street, having talked the whole way home. Non sequiturs that jumped track from the first time we met to an observation about smog being LA's original ultra-chromatic filter to a snippet of season one dialogue from a baby-faced Duncan, and back again. What we don't discuss is the little lie I just told.

I *was* upset that Sebastian hadn't mentioned Heather to me before, of course, but that mostly had to do with my own humiliation—with me leading myself on that I had a chance. It's too much too soon to fully reveal that to him now . . . and maybe it always will be. Maybe the way to hold on to this friend-ship now is to extricate it from the messy entanglements of the past. And I really do want that. I forgot what it's like to bounce around so smoothly in conversation with someone that it's like the dialogue was written for us. To have it be so fun and easy that time flies by. Sometimes, I would wonder how college and high school had both taken four years, when one felt as if it was over in the blink of an eye and the other felt as if it lasted an eon. Now I think the answer is in front of me. Maybe it turns out we can all manipulate time without Mount Signon, if only we're allowed the luxury of having a true friend at our side.

"This was really lovely," I say.

"It was," he says, smiling at me.

NINA	SEBASTIAN
"Let's do it again sometime?"	"We should do it again sometime."

I smile back. "Definitely." I look at the latch for the car door. Once I open it, I'll be well on my way back to Crazytown, aka Celeste's house. I take in a deep breath.

"You okay?" Sebastian asks. "Do you want me to find the button that opens the door again?" He looks over at the panel and I can tell he doesn't have a clue which button that is.

"No, I could use the exercise." I waggle my fingers. "I just kinda don't want to leave. My roommate is sort of . . . bonkers, actually."

Sebastian looks toward the house. "Where did you meet her? Him?"

"Her. Celeste. And I met her on Craigslist."

"That might have been your first mistake."

"Don't I know it."

He stops smiling. "Wait, do you feel unsafe?"

Images of bees and leeches flash before my eyes, but I know what Sebastian really means. "No, not like that," I say firmly. "She's harmless." Even if her pet projects—emphasis on pet—aren't. "But I think I definitely need to move out soon. It's just finding someplace solo on my salary seems impossible. And as far as roommates go . . . I mean, better the devil you know? Maybe?" A black tail swish floats in front of my eyes again.

"Huh. Well, actually . . ." Sebastian runs his hands through his shaggy blond hair. "You know, Matty just moved out. So I have an extra room, and I'm looking for a roommate . . ."

"Oh." How wonderful would it be to live with a roommate who's also my friend? To have that friend be *Sebastian*. On the other hand, would it be too much too soon to be that close to each other—literally—when we're still figuring out *how* to be friends again?

"It could be temporary," Sebastian says quickly. "And I'm not going to be there for the next two weeks while Janine is away. So you could use it as a quiet base to find a more permanent living situation. Feel free to think it over. No pressure."

"Okay, I will," I say. "But for now"—I place my hand on the door—"I shall take my leave, with my sincerest wishes for a successful joust . . . with LA drivers."

"And it was ever thus," he responds without missing a beat.

"I'm sorry, but that fuzzy handcuff teaser image is completely the wrong shade of lavender. Stu Stu would never." The voice that speaks the absurd words is calm, professional, wrapped in a pleasant Australian accent, and currently coming out of the black flying saucer in the middle of the conference table. Sean glares at me over it.

"Oh, is it?" I say. "I just posted it as is. It's the image I got from . . ." I scroll through my phone to find the email. "Jake D'Addario."

The woman sighs on the other end. "Figures. I'll get the right image over to you. Please take that one down."

I go over to the multiple tabs and delete the offending posts from Twitter, Tumblr, Facebook, Instagram, and Snapchat. The images were meant to tease our huge upcoming announcement but apparently they're the wrong shade of purple to do so.

"So, Jeri, are we all set with everything else? The commenting?"

"Stu Stu texted me a thumbs-up emoji but, er, I will try to get a firm confirmation on that. But, yes, I believe we are all set."

"Helena?" Sean asks.

"Everything is good on our end," Helena confirms.

"Dana?"

"I don't see an issue from us."

"And Bill?"

"Um . . . well, Stu Stu has decided that he's going to be in charge of his own social media from now on. Or . . . at least this week," Bill chimes in.

"What does that mean?" Sean growls.

"It means, well, I'll be with him, of course. But he's going to be doing the actual typing and posting."

Sean groans.

Stu Stu, aka Stuart Stutter, is former front man for the Hot Flashes, now brooding, Australian solo artist. Jeri is his personal publicist. The absent Jake (he of the wrong-colored fuzzy handcuffs) works PR for Stu Stu's label and has apparently sent me the incorrect ten-pixel image from his first album art. Helena runs the wildly popular Comments by Stars account on Instagram. Dana works at Instagram, though I have yet to figure out what her wordy title actually means. And Bill is Stu Stu's manager. We are all currently finalizing the most strategic way to make our big announcement: Stu Stu, longtime *CoRaB* fan—his first hit single "Queen of My Heart" is allegedly an ode to Lucinda, not his girlfriend at the time, popular Australian soap star Alma Rogers—will be making a guest appearance on the pilot episode of the reboot.

And not a single person is content with announcing this the old-fashioned way: via, say, a press release, or as an exclusive to a popular website.

"The fans need to *discover* this," Sean ordered me. "Figure out a way for them to feel like they're fucking Sherlock Holmes. Go."

It took me a few hours of soul-searching and browsing around on the socials to hit upon an idea. What if we posted something as a benign ode to "Queen of My Heart," then Stu Stu commented on that post, asking if he could come on the show, and then the Comments by Stars account "caught it" as a screenshot. And we let it take off from there, not confirming or denying anything for a few days. It should create a frenzy. I know because it's the type of thing Seb and I lived for in college.

Sean had not gone so far as to say my idea was brilliant or even good. But he'd immediately had me set up this conference call so I had to infer that it was.

So here we all are, making this "spontaneously viral social media moment" happen. Via a two-hour conference call. And endless coordination.

"Okay, great. So, since Stu Stu is in London at the moment, it'll be eleven thirteen a.m. UK time on Saturday. That's tomorrow morning. That's what'll work for Stu Stu, correct?"

"Affirmative," says Bill.

"Yes," says Jeri.

"Works on our end," says Helena.

"Us too," says Dana.

There's silence until I realize Sean is glaring at me, expecting me to chime in.

"Of course, I'll be there," I say.

"Okay. Great. Let's make this happen, people."

11:13 a.m. UK time is 3:13 a.m. LA time. Because of the ungodly hour, on a Friday night no less, Sean is letting me work from home. But I know if I fuck this up, I'm in severe trouble. So I think it's best to power through and stay awake rather than go to bed and risk being so deeply asleep at three a.m. that I miss my alarm clock.

I turn on the old TV I have in my room. It's a tube TV, a tiny fifteen-inch one that I found on a corner a couple of weeks after I moved here. It's not connected to cable or anything. But I did splurge on the latest Nintendo console a couple of months ago. And that's what I turn on now to relax, instantly navigating to *Breath of the Wild*.

The funny thing was—is—I've always thought Sebastian looks like Link, the main character of the game. Long, shaggy blond hair, wide clear eyes with a sweet mix of curiosity and virtue, a propensity to get overexcited and willingly dive into a cave of trolls (aka 4chan). The only thing he's missing is the elf ears. I never told Sebastian this. I don't know why. Maybe it's because I once mentioned, early on, that I had a crush on Link and thought he was—for a video-game character—sorta hot. Even before I realized I might feel the same way about Sebastian, something in my subconscious had protected me and stopped me from revealing too much.

For the next couple of hours, I explore shrines with an avatar version of Sebastian. My two cups of coffee have long run out. I could make more, I guess. Then I remember something that once made me alert and awake (and certifiable) for a solid twelve hours.

I take out my phone and text Sebastian. **Remember the Vivarin Incident?**

His reply is immediate. **Who could forget that? The vision of you sprawled out at the 40-yard-line at Butterfield is seared into my brain.**

I can't help but smile. It was the third week of college and Sebastian and I hardly even knew each other. Our freshman orientation packets had come with a selection of small Ithaca swag, coupons for local businesses, and some sample-size products. A lip balm, I think. A trial size of Tums. But the one I remember most acutely was a small bottle of something called Vivarin, which was touted in bold yellow writing as A STUDY AID.

The tinier writing told me they were caffeine pills. My first college exam was the next morning and I wanted to study. So why not get "aided"? There were six pills in the bottle. Knowing my body was pretty tolerant of caffeine thanks to the coffee addiction I'd had since I was ten, I took three.

Big mistake.

It was Sunday night, *CoRaB* night, so Sebastian was there for my extra-jittery, extra-opinionated viewing of the episode. He was also there when I had to get up and pee approximately twenty-five times during a fifty-two-minute episode. It took us almost three hours to watch the show because he kept having to pause it. And, finally, he was there when I decided sneaking into the football stadium would be a great idea, the kind of prank that would be a lasting college memory. "Come on, Worthington, have some balls!" I believe were my exact words to the kid I had known two whole weeks.

He stayed with me throughout the entire thing. I know he thought it was funny (my loud giggle fits made it clear that I certainly did), but I also knew he was concerned. And the thing I knew most of all was that, despite his being practically a stranger, I felt safe with him. I felt safe being goofy and a little high. I knew nothing would happen to me except that lasting college memory I was looking for.

I sorta wish I had some now, I text to Sebastian.

What?! That stuff made you crazy. Do you remember the CRASH the next day?

I snort, remembering weeping into the thin fabric of Sebastian's pale aqua button-down, convinced that I would fail my first exam and be forced to drop out of college entirely.

I know. I know. I just have to stay up until 3 AM for something important and I don't want to miss it. But I pinkie swear I'm not actually taking it, I write.

Okay . . . but if you do manage to get your hands on any, please call me. I'll be right over.

Now that's one way I know I could stay up for a long time: having Sebastian to talk to. For a second, I think about asking him to come anyway. But without the buffer of hallucinatory caffeine pills to make me brazen, I can't. No matter how close we were five years ago, that gap of time is a wedge that has made us into near strangers again. I can't just ask him to drop whatever he's doing on a Friday night to come entertain me.

I promise. Good night, I write.

I do manage to stay awake on my own, without caffeine pills or my tall, nerdy Brit as a stimulant. A little more Zelda, the last hundred pages of the Lisbeth Salander/Queen Lucinda fanfic I was reading on my phone, some surfing around on the internet and—bingo—it's three a.m. Just have to make it another thirteen minutes and I'm golden.

I open up a new tab on my laptop's browser, about to navigate over to one of the biggest *CoRaB* fansites, along with the biggest Stu Stu fansites, so I can make note of when the buzz starts happening for my weekly meeting with Sean. I'm greeted with a pixelated dinosaur, letting me know my computer is offline. What?

Then I notice that my laptop screen has gotten a little darker, indicating it's no longer connected to a power source. I glance at the power strip underneath my desk. The red light is off. I'd been working without the lights on so I go to switch them on now. Nothing.

I emerge from my room to a dark apartment—not surprising since Celeste must be asleep at this point. Only she's not. She's on a ladder in the kitchen with a flashlight, futzing around with the fuse box on the wall.

"What's going on?" I ask, so afraid of the answer.

"Oh. You're up. Sorry. I was testing out my new microdermabrasion machine and I guess it shorted something out."

My first thought, inexplicably, is that Celeste is really serious about this holistic spa business. My second, of course, is that no electricity means no internet. I look at the clock. 3:07 a.m.

Okay. It's fine. My phone and its cellular data should still work.

I go back to my room and pick it up.

It's dead. I was so absorbed in the Lisbeth/Lucinda fanfic that I didn't realize how low the charge had been running. Fuck. Me.

I grab the laptop and run outside. Celeste is humming "If I Had a Hammer" to herself softly when I leave.

I open up the network connections tab on the computer as I'm jogging with it, hoping to find any unsecure network I can log onto for just two minutes while I respond to Stu Stu's comment. Little padlocks mock me from my screen.

Shitshitshit.

What are the chances an Australian rock star is on time though? I think, as I see the clock going to 3:11 a.m. Then 3:12.

I'm running now, past an ocean of stucco houses with apparently no Good Samaritans who feel like gifting their neighbors with a passwordless connection. It takes me three blocks before my brain finally thinks of another destination to try.

I sprint over to my closest Coffee Bean, carrying an open laptop in my arms like I'm an ER doctor rushing around with an unresponsive baby. I'm a sweaty mess by the time I reach the café's parking lot, but I also see those miraculous curved bars that indicate I'm now connected to its internet. Thank God I brought my computer here to work last week, otherwise I'd never have the saved password on it.

I sit my ass down right in the handicap spot in the parking lot and go over to Instagram. Right on time, a whole six minutes ago, Stu Stu has commented on the image. **What's a guy got to do for the honor of becoming a fallen soldier in the Kingdom of Six, eh?**

I type quickly, double-checking once for any typos, and then hit send so that the official *CoRaB* Instagram account has responded: **You have an open invitation for a beheading anytime, sir.**

I slump back in relief against the wall of the Coffee Bean, my savior.

I can't believe I almost messed this up. Or rather, *Celeste did.*

It's the last straw. I need to leave her house ASAP. I'm going to let Sebastian know first thing in the morning that I'm taking him up on his offer of a place to crash while I figure something else out.

CHAPTER 11

This confidential information is the property of Casting Services, Ltd. — DO NOT COPY!!!

LUCY'S DONUTS (RUSH—Auditions Today)

1-hour Drama

Episodic

Alex & Company/Vasquez Studios

Draft: 4/28

Network: WatchGoNowPlus

ELECTRONIC SUBMISSIONS ONLY—SUBMIT ASAP!!!

AGENTS AND MANAGERS: DO NOT DOUBLE-SUBMIT

<u>**We do not break top of show.**</u>

SEEKING:

[BROTHEL OWNER] 50s, male, portly, balding, all
ethnicities, acts like he owns the place, because he does . . .
NO NUDITY. 2 lines, 1 scene. MUST SPEAK WITH A
BRITISH ACCENT. **Auditions today, shoots Monday!!**
SAG Scale.

[SEX WORKER] 18 to 28, female, pretty, all ethnicities,
NOT jaded (yet), first day on the job, would rather not
participate in an orgy . . . NO NUDITY. 2 lines, 1 scene.
MUST SPEAK WITH A BRITISH ACCENT. **Auditions**
today, shoots Monday!! SAG Scale.

[ADDITIONAL SEX WORKERS] 18 to 28, female, fit/
attractive, all ethnicities, happy to be part of an orgy—at
first . . . 3 grunts, 2 moans. NON-SPEAKING EXTRAS.
NUDITY REQUIRED. SAG + 10%. Casting off photos.
Shoots Monday!!

[ORGY PARTICIPANTS] 28 to 75, male, all ethnicities
and body types, presumably wealthy, happy to be part of an
orgy, until it turns into a bloodbath . . . NON-SPEAKING
EXTRAS. **NUDITY REQUIRED. SAG + 10% Casting**
off photos. Shoots Monday!!

SEBASTIAN

Makes you wonder what sort of donut shop this Lucy is
running, eh? I text Janine, who's in Minnesota scouting loca-
tions and securing film permits. It's still snowing there, and is
projected to do so throughout the summer. Janine's hoping to
take advantage of the world's extinction to save a few bucks on
the ice-field battle scenes.

She responds a minute later with an eye-roll emoji. Is that really your question?

No, sorry. My question is, do the "Additional Sex Workers" have to grunt/moan with a British accent?

She doesn't respond, so I dial back the jokes. It's my first time seeing a *CoRaB* casting notice, and excitement got the better of me.

Sorry, I type. 1). What's "top of show"? 2). What's the "+10%"? Hazard pay?

She's a slow texter and opts to call me instead.

"Hi," Janine says when I pick up. "Top of show means each episode has a casting budget—created by yours truly—that cannot be exceeded. So once the series regulars and recurring roles are accounted for, if there's a guest star like Stupid Stupid . . ."

"Congrats on that, by the way."

"Who sucks up all the guest-star money, the costars, underfives, and background actors have to make do with scale."

"Ah."

I already know that "under-five" means the role has fewer than five lines.

It *boggles the bean*, as my dad would say, to realize that while Duncan, Lucinda, and Jeff hang out fully frocked for half a million dollars each, the naked people will be paid nothing more than SAG daily rate (plus 10 percent) for eight hours of bare-assed work, their uncloaked visages living on for eternity, to be paused, scrutinized, and meme'd for years to come, pun intended.

Even before today, I pitied actors. Not the A-, B-, or C-listers; everyone else. The 98 percent striving to prove themselves for scraps, with scraps being a best-case scenario.

Screenwriters might be lower on the totem pole in terms of visibility and outside respect, but at least they're not rejected for a job they're otherwise qualified for because someone didn't like their *face*.

Their height. Their weight.

Or their teeth.

For example.

A year ago, long before Janine hired me, I was briefly one of the 98 percent. Having borrowed money from Matty to keep the lights on, and desperate to pay him back, I swan dived into the murky waters of T4P jobs on Craigslist, the same platform Nina used for roommate hunting. T4P (Time for Prints) means photographers, makeup artists, hair stylists, or anyone else trying to build a portfolio will pay you in photos if you model for them.

I got free headshots that way, with my stats printed below like a prize fighter (or, less ruggedly, a prize poodle): 6'0" height, 32-inch waist, 40-inch chest. Ridiculously, those stats meant I fell within the parameters for a male model. When I went out on go-sees, most companies liked what I had to offer.

Until I smiled.

At which point the model wrangler would approach, way too close for comfort, and tell me to show my bottom teeth. Then he or she would tell me to come back after having my canines "dealt with." I'm ashamed to admit I considered it before Matty shook some sense back into me.

"Repeat after me: Hollywood is not reality. If your teeth were any straighter, it'd be creepy as hell. Don't do that to me."

"Oh, so it's all about you, huh?"

I guess he was right, because I managed to secure a job as a fit model for Vachère, a start-up clothing brand in the garment district compiling a lookbook for investors.

The vast majority of the time I was a human mannequin, my body the quality control that ensured the "fit" remained consistent. If I gained 1/16th of an inch anywhere on my body, they'd know. My diet was strict, my gym regimen nonnegotiable. I was hungry *all the time*. Not only for food but mental nourishment. Laughter. Human connection.

I was frequently told how lucky I was to pose in the catalog;

it's rare for the fit model to double as the print model. *They* were the lucky ones, actually; my fees were a pittance compared to a print model's rate, but I didn't know that at the time.

Vachère means "cowboy" in French, and their signature outfit was a pair of dark-wash jeans with a bandana sewn into the back pocket. I was shirtless for every image—they didn't even *make* a line of shirts—and the denim was so tight around my crotch it left little to the imagination. ("How you say, 'Packing heat, yes?'" according to the designer.) I didn't recognize myself in the photos. Who was this oiled-up sex machine, Stetson cocked, muscles glistening, thumbs tucked into his waistband, fingers grazing his thigh, as though about to peel off his clothes any second?

"Smolder. Smollllllder," the photographer ordered me while Kid Rock's "Cowboy" played relentlessly in the background for inspiration. Heady days.

My female counterpart and I decided to hook up.

Picture two paper dolls joylessly inserting tab A into slot B. Or don't, actually. The whole time I'd be thinking to myself, "You are sleeping with a model."

It didn't occur to me to think, *So is she.*

We lasted three Instagrams and two side-by-side waxing sessions before she moved to Japan to pursue modeling there instead. Prior to her red-eye flight, I tried to wholesome-ize our narcissistic coupling by cooking for her. London broil, English peas, crisp fingerling potatoes, and bread pudding with caramel sea-salt sauce.

She looked at the food. She looked at me. "I can't eat any of that," she said.

". . . Right."

We abandoned the bulbous feast and chain-smoked on the balcony until it was time to leave for the airport. I'd banked enough money for two years' worth of rent, but I'd never felt more empty.

The next week, I called Vachère and told them I'd be moseying on to greener pastures. My agent tore me a new one but stopped short of terminating our contract, advising me to reach out once I came to my senses. He may as well be waiting for the earth's rotation to reverse.

Quitting modeling *was* me coming to my senses. Reviving my senses. Honoring my senses. Luxuriating in them. Good food is the JOY OF LIFE. When a perfect combination of flavors opens your taste buds and melts your eyes shut with pleasure, all is right in the world. And if you can share that experience with friends or family? Bliss.

After a few days of lazing around, I returned to the apartment gym voluntarily but less obsessively. The mood-boosting morning regimen was the only element worth retaining from that time in my life.

For today's crash course in TV production, I'll be participating in a casting call from the other side of the power structure. While the casting assistant sets up the video camera and doles out water bottles in a nondescript, white-walled room off Maple Drive, I reread Nina's text from last night: **If the offer still stands to crash at your place for the next two weeks, I'd like to take you up on it.**

After responding **ABSOLUTELY!**, I restrained myself from hitting send and stabbed the delete button over and over. Then I typed **sure**. Aura of ambivalence in place, I called down to the garage for Janine's Jaguar and raced over to my own apartment to vacuum and scrub the place down, spending extra time sprucing up the sole bathroom. I also instructed Sam to roll out the red carpet for Nina whenever she arrived.

"I don't know exactly when she'll get here, probably after work, but could you buzz her in and give her my key and the garage clicker?"

"Anything for my favorite ex," Sam said, and arched an eyebrow.

I may have imagined shaving that eyebrow clean off.

This morning, five minutes before the first audition starts, my head's still buzzing with the knowledge that Nina will be moving into my place.

It's good I won't be there with her, I tell myself for the millionth time. *She deserves peace and quiet after her looney-tunes roommate.*

A text from Sam arrives: **Should I tell her you're single and ready to mingle?** He's attached a photo of himself in my kitchen standing next to a spread of food on the island, looking like a perfect host.

My spine straightens. **Is she there already?** I text back. **And what's with the buffet?**

No, I'm meeting that rep from Audio-kinetic, remember?

Sam's small, messy apartment contains wall-to-wall sound equipment, monitors and microphones, so he uses my place to conduct business. Audio-kinetic is a big podcast network he's hoping will add his show to their slate. At the thought of his podcast, a burst of stress detonates behind my eye; I'm eleven episodes behind, with little hope of catching up because new, ninety-minute episodes drop every single day. I tried listening at 1.5 speed once and it gave me a headache. When I refreshed the page, he'd already uploaded a bonus episode!

After that I'll be rolling out the red carpet for Nina, per your request . . . mwahahaha

I can't explore that ominous statement any further, because the first actress has entered the casting room. I silence my phone and focus on work.

Janine's on my laptop screen, chiming in from the Minnesotan arctic, and the casting director, casting associate, and casting assistant are all female, so I'm commissioned to portray Brothel Owner and feed lines to the actresses.

My line: "Go on and join them, then."

Sex Worker: "This wasn't part of the deal."

My line: "You need to do as you're told."

Sex Worker: "Triple my fee or I walk next door." (I know from previous seasons' sexposition that there are competing brothels on this particular street.)

After thirty read-throughs with thirty different women, a lunch break, and a bathroom break, I pass through the waiting room in a daze. As far as I can tell, there are no front-runners for the role, just an endless stream of pretty faces and dubious British accents. My trance is broken by the appearance of a specific pretty face.

Her bobbed, honey blond hair looks different—frothier—and she's wearing a skirt with heels, which I rarely saw during our relationship, but it's definitely her. I let her finish mouthing her lines before I approach with a wave.

"Hey, Heather, it's me, Sebastian."

"Oh my God! What are you doing here?" She hugs me and as my hands press lightly into her back, I fall into memories of summer nights in Upstate New York: crickets chirping outside, our calves sore from hiking Buttermilk Falls or kayaking in Cayuga Lake, her head on my shoulder as she dozed off in front of a movie.

Heather always intended to move west at some point, but the fact that she and Nina have reappeared in my life at almost the same time is jarring.

"Are you auditioning too?" Heather's eyes are bright and curious. "I thought you quit that scene."

After my liberation from Vachère, I'd posted a video of Matty and me singing "La Marseillaise" on a private Ithaca College alumni group, and she must have seen it.

"No, I'm a PA for the show and my boss wants me to experience every part of production. I swear I'm not trying to casting couch you," I joke.

"You hate couches. I remember," she jokes back.

I don't "hate" any pieces of furniture, it's just that we had an opportunity to do it on the couch in the Emerson Hall TV lounge once and even though Nina had made it clear how she felt about me by then, there was no way I could have had sex in such a sacred place. I made up a story about my back hurting, with the unintended, karmic consequence of Heather insisting on giving me a massage. This meant she hammered my spine and pinched me at random while I suppressed groans of pain.

Heather may not be good at backrubs, but she's terrific at playing a defiant lady of the night, complete with authentic-sounding accent. The powers that be agree with me, because following our read-through, the casting director asks Heather if she's available all day Monday. We both know what that means!

I give Heather a thumbs-up before she leaves, her back straight, her head held high, her blond hair like golden wheat swaying in the sun. I'm glad we exchanged numbers in the waiting room so I can send her a congratulatory text later.

Twelve Brothel Owner readings later and time is running out. "I didn't care for any of those guys." The casting director yawns and stretches. "And it's almost five o'clock."

"Why don't we have Sebastian do it?" Janine suggests from my laptop screen. "He's got the lines down."

I gasp. "Really?"

"Do you have a SAG card?"

"No." My stomach drops.

"We'll Taft-Hartley you. That's a waiver so you can take the job. We'll say nobody but you had an authentic accent, given our limited time to fill the role."

"Okay! Great!" I don't entirely understand the words she just said, but I figure it's best to nod vigorously.

"It shoots Monday at Vasquez, so it's perfect," Janine replies. "You'll be there anyway for the briefcase."

I should accept this amazing turn of events and shut my gob, but I can't help remembering the description of the brothel owner. "'Fifties, portly, balding,'" I quote from the casting sheet. "Is it okay to disregard all that?"

Janine waves me off. "Eh. It's fine."

No one contradicts her, so it appears to be settled, but the disdainful words from my previous life as a model return to haunt me.

"Are my teeth okay?" I ask.

"They're fine, what are you talking about?" God bless Janine.

"He has no idea, does he?" the casting director says with a shake of her head. "How good-looking he is."

"None," Janine replies. "And let's keep it that way so he doesn't ditch me for the runway."

"I don't—I'm not—" I begin.

"And here comes his 'Hugh Grant oopsy-daisy' right on cue," Janine interrupts, but she's smiling at me. "Break a leg next week. And don't forget the briefcase."

I smile back.

In three days, I'll be making my acting debut on *CoRaB*, and I won't even have to be naked!

CHAPTER 12

TUMBLR

rustierorbust

Taking bets now on who we think Stu Stu is going to play in the pilot of *CoRaB*. My guess is traveling minstrel.

Chis45

A ghost.

imaTRex

A merman.

TheWestinglandGame

Book 5, chapter 3, paragraph 2, line 4, there is mention of "a redheaded wretch begging for gruel." The clues made it OBVIOUS this is the role that Stu will be undertaking. If any of you morons were real fans who'd read the books, you'd already know this and wouldn't be wasting valuable print space asking.

junJI26

hi. this is the internet. there's no such thing as valuable print space. moron.

StuuuStuuuuStuuuuudio

Ohmygodddddddd. Do you think he's going to perform anything off of his new album?!

NINA

"Nina, Nina, bo bina," a familiar voice says as soon as I buzz apartment 2G.

I'm instantly transported back to the second floor hallway of Emerson Hall. Me, Sebastian, Sam, Matty, and our other friend Asher could often be found there, our backs to the walls, shooting the shit about classes or the latest Netflix documentary or occasionally even the weather which, with that crew, still managed to be fun. There was a rotating cast of significant others, too, for me and all the boys except for Sebastian. Well, until the bitter end, but there was no final hallway summit to try to mitigate that explosion. Heather may have ultimately tainted the common room for me, but she never set foot in that hallway.

"Sam-I-Am," I reply with a smile. "How the heck are you?"

"I'm great now. Come on up," Sam says as he buzzes me in.

The building is sleek and modern, a condo that looks like it was built in the last decade. A lot of buildings in Los Angeles feel that way. It's a town that likes everything young, fresh, and looking like it came into existence only yesterday, even if that illusion is cosmetic. In some ways, it's the opposite of New York City, with its longstanding skyscrapers that promise to remain unchanged long after you're gone. I only spent two years living in New York, but sometimes I feel like that might ultimately be more my speed than LA, despite the abundant sunshine.

The elevator opens to a full head of dark hair and a warm smile. Sam, too, seems to have bulked up since our Ithaca days but I think a gym membership is just a foregone conclusion in SoCal.

"My favorite ex! Come here, you," he says as he opens his arms wide.

I walk right into them. "It's good to see you." I inhale his subtle cologne. It's only now that I realize that, although I missed Sebastian the most, he wasn't the only person who was suddenly gone from my life once I unceremoniously left Ithaca.

Friends of all shapes and sorts have been scarce since. "What have you been up to?"

"I'm working my way up the sound department ladder. Just got off a booming gig for Maalox. Real A-list stuff, ya know?" He gives a sheepish grin.

"Still hoping to do something with music?" I ask. Sam was notorious for dragging us around to see every band who ever came through the Finger Lakes. He'd spend every set break geeking out about the band's "tone" while Sebastian and I pretended we had any idea what he was talking about.

"I actually do! Well, not professionally in that I don't get paid for it yet, but I've been hosting a podcast about the indie music scene, and I might be added to a network today. Mostly it just means that I'd get comp tickets if the band's small enough. Want to catch a show sometime? With Sebastian, too, of course," he adds quickly.

"Sure! That sounds fun." I'm unprepared for the soul-lightening wave of nostalgia that breezes through me.

"So where's your stuff?" Sam asks, glancing at my purse. "Do you need help bringing anything up?"

"Nah. My roommate let me leave my furniture at my old place for now, since this is just temporary. And my boyfriend will be here soon with my suitcase. He had to go park the car."

"Ah," he replies.

"So . . . can I see the place?" I ask.

"Right this way." He guides me to the door of 2G.

As soon as I walk in, my first thought is that Sebastian's apartment smells like him, an inviting mix of olive oil, sugar, and his cedar-scented deodorant. It feels like him, too, with its giant pot rack neatly stacked with an assortment of matching pots and pans, its tasteful mauve curtains and shag rug, and its classy framed map of the Kingdom of Six that I recognize from one of the exclusive print editions of *CoRaB* that came out before the TV series was a thing. And then I realize that Sebastian's apartment . . . looks like him.

Neatly taped up to every other kitchen cabinet and wall are professionally shot pictures of Sebastian, torn from a catalog of some sort. In each of them he is wearing a cowboy hat, a very, *very* tight pair of jeans . . . and nothing else. They must have caught him after a particularly good round of bicep days if his arms, which are often posed with their thumbs in his belt loop or casually leaning against a crate aggressively stamped **APPLES**, are any indication. Some of the images are strictly from behind but, despite not being able to see his face, I realize I'd recognize Sebastian's long, lean physique anywhere. It's . . . disconcerting. It's . . . hot.

I can't help taking a closer look at the glossy image that's closest to me, the one that's taped to the back of the couch. It has a scrawled speech bubble coming from Sebastian's mouth. "Need to rest your legs after a long day of wranglin' steers? Saddle up here, cowboy."

I look up to see Sam barely stifling laughter.

"Sebastian's been keeping this part of his life from me," I say, trying to sound casual and hoping Sam doesn't notice the flush crawling up my cheeks. "I'm hurt."

"He probably didn't think you were ready," Sam says. "Sometimes a cowboy's gotta be a lone coyote out in the desert." He indicates an image of Sebastian inexplicably sitting on the arm of a cactus. "This is your room by the way." He opens the door the image is taped to. "Well, Sebastian's room. But he said you wouldn't have furniture and Matty's room is empty."

I peek into a neat room with a tall mahogany dresser, a four-poster king-sized bed, and a black-and-white rug. A novelty Jeff the Warlock clock holds a place of honor on one of the walls. The cedar scent is stronger in here. I'm about to walk in when there's a knock on the apartment's front door. "Babe?"

And just like that the spell is broken. Suddenly, I'm not an eighteen-year-old college freshman hanging out with her friend, talking about what band we're going to see that weekend, and thinking she has all the time in the world to figure out what she wants to do with her life. It's probably a good thing Sebastian's only here via his, er, modeling photos. I don't want to get too suckered into nostalgia and lose all sense of what I'm doing here in the first place: trying to find a permanent living situation so that I can focus on building my career out here in La La Land.

"Hi, I'm Ennis." My boyfriend is introducing himself to Sam.

"Ennis," I say. "This is my old friend Sam." And I smile. Because it feels good to say it.

Over the weekend, Ennis offers to help me explore my new neighborhood. "There's a museum I think you'll like," he tells me over the phone.

"A *museum* in Los Angeles?" I retort. "Let's do it."

Forty minutes later, I get a text that he's outside. I put on some lip gloss and get in his car.

"You look beautiful," he says as he gives me a kiss.

"Thanks," I reply, smiling. This is nice. Ennis is nice. It's nice to have someone to do stuff like this with. "Want to tell me where we're going?"

"I could . . . but wouldn't you rather have it be a surprise?"

"You know what? Yes!" I say. Why not? Ennis puts one hand on my knee while he drives and that feels nice too.

Eventually we park, get out, and start walking toward one of the coolest buildings I've ever seen. It's made of undulating silver metal, almost like zebra stripes, and peeking through the empty space is a bright red color.

"Modern art!" I say, pleased. I've always liked modern art, how it leaves so much open to interpretation, how you're allowed to feel whatever you like when staring at globs of paint, or a banana peel, or a shark preserved in formaldehyde.

"Well, yeah!" Ennis says. "At least *I* think so."

I'm a little confused until we enter the building and I see the sign.

The Petersen Automotive Museum.

"Wow . . . cars." I don't know what else to say. Whereas just a few days ago Sebastian knew my every feeling about cars, down to the moment in a particular episode when I basically went into a coma, Ennis doesn't seem to understand the most blaring facts about me. Doesn't the fact that I don't even own a car in *Los Angeles* give me away?

But then Ennis smiles and says, "I know cars aren't really your thing but I thought . . . well, they might surprise you. For example . . ."

He pays for our admission, takes me by the hand, and leads me down a set of metal-railed stairs to . . .

"Wait. Is that *the* DeLorean. From *Back to the Future*?" I exclaim.

"Sure is!" Ennis says, and grins at me as I marvel at the interior of the famed car, with its controls set to 1985.

"Take my photo!" I command, and Ennis gladly obliges. Then gets in for a selfie. I grin like a lunatic and then we make our best "Great Scott!" face for the second take.

Ennis guides me around, showing me an original Batmobile from the 1960s television show; a groovy, psychedelic VW van; and a mirrored, black, flattened pyramid that looks more like a UFO than a car. We see boxy cars from the seventies, perfectly preserved Model Ts from the twenties, and bright, teal convertibles that surely spent some time in a 1950s drive-through. We take photos with Bumblebee from *Transformers*, and Lightning McQueen from *Cars*, but also with some vehicles that look so strange and cool, they probably *are* more modern art than functioning automobile.

When we're getting ready to leave, Ennis looks at me and asks eagerly, "Did you have fun?"

"I really did," I reply.

"Good," he says as he kisses my hand, and I can't help looking at him a little in wonder. Because the cars weren't the only thing that surprised me today.

* * *

When we get back to the apartment, Ennis starts kissing me in earnest and I respond. We're standing up and he's slowly walking me back toward the bedroom as his hands push down the strap of my tank top and he moves his lips to the dip between my collarbone and shoulder. I sneak my hands under the hem of his T-shirt, feeling his smooth, toned abs.

He pushes me down on the neatly made bed and my nose is suddenly infiltrated by the scent of cedar.

"Wait," I say, putting a hand on Ennis's shoulder to push his lips away from my neck.

"What's wrong?"

"It's just . . ." I look around the room. "This isn't my bed. I feel weird about doing stuff on it."

"Oh," Ennis says. "We can wash the sheets?" he adds hopefully.

"Um . . ." I catch sight of one of the shots of Sebastian that Sam put up next to his dresser. "Yeah, no. I don't think so."

Ennis follows my line of sight and sees the picture, too. "Okay," he says as he moves an inch away from me. He points at the catalog image: shirtless Sebastian on what I'm positive is an adult-sized rocking horse. "Remind me again how you know that guy? Your ex in college?"

"No, no," I say immediately. "Just a close friend. But . . . it feels weird. On a friend's bed. When I get my own place and have my own bed back, though . . ." I waggle my eyebrows at him.

He laughs. "Okay. Fine."

"Want to find a show to watch?" I ask. "It can be an episode of *Top Gear* if you want?"

"Really?" he asks me, surprised.

"Sure," I say, knowing I owe him one for both the fun date and the abrupt halt to his other plans for the night.

He happily settles on the couch then, pulling me to him, as he finds some more cars to stare at on the TV.

CHAPTER 13

SEBASTIAN

Monday arrives in a rain-soaked blur. Despite the traffic problems this will cause, nothing on earth could dampen my elation today, the day Brothel Owner as Interpreted by Sebastian becomes part of *CoRaB* canon.

I lay awake in Janine's apartment for hours last night in jittery euphoria, counting the minutes till morning. Outside, wind shook the traffic lights and rain crashed against the windows of Janine's tenth-floor apartment like cymbals. Janine's cat even ventured from her hiding spot to pace and fidget, as though she knew something big was on the horizon.

Vasquez Studios is equidistant from Janine's building and my own place, so I don't get any sort of commuting perk by leaving from West Hollywood instead of the Miracle Mile. Every time I take the 405 I wonder if the last thing I'll see before I die will be an upside-down vanity plate, but today's worse than usual; no one uses their headlights in the rain, so the freeway turns into *Mad Max: Torrential Downpour*. The Getty has disappeared within the ghostly fog, as though it's been airlifted out, or never existed at all.

Miraculously, I arrive on time, shake off the cramps in my hands from gripping the steering wheel extra tight, sign in, and head to the wardrobe department for my costume. It's a belted tunic that's alarmingly close to my skin tone and risks making me look naked if viewed through squinting eyes. Better that than a body stocking, bikini, and robe, of course—which is what the nude orgy members squeeze into.

As strangers in various stages of undress swarm in my peripheral vision, it's difficult to know where to look.

The aggressively silent wardrobe mistress, complete with pins in her mouth and a cloth measuring tape around her neck, changes her mind about my outfit and holds out a black/blue tunic, shaking it at me until I get the hint and swap it for my previous one, which is promptly tossed in a bin marked Laundry.

The darker tunic doesn't fit. At all. It's three sizes too large, and my face poking out the top looks consumptive, floating pale and wan above my body, but that must be what she's going for, because she waves me away with a grunt and turns to the next person in line.

My fingers barely peek out of the sleeves, and I don't think of myself as having particularly short arms. I roll up the sleeves, but the material is so slippery the cuff doesn't hold.

"Is this the right . . . ?" I trail off.

The wardrobe mistress's eyes slam toward me. She has problems of her own, helping an elderly gentleman step into his gherkin holder. He may very well be capable of playing King Lear, but alas, the world will never know.

"The right what?" she snaps.

"The right fit? The right size?"

"WARDROBE DOESN'T MAKE MISTAKES," she roars and I decide this is not an argument I'm equipped to have.

I tug my sleeves up as best I can and leave the room. Was this how Nina felt wearing the tippet sleeves outfit in class that one time? Despite everything, the memory of those ludicrous sleeves spiraling and flapping around her brings a grin to my face.

Okay, so my costume is absurd. Who cares? I'm living the dream. Life is good!

I make my way to craft services: a mountain of pastries, each box of which is stacked behind signs indicating "gluten-free," "dairy-free," or "sugar-free." Jesus, they are practically crying out for my seraphim food cake. I wasn't comfortable cooking in Janine's kitchen (where every available surface is covered in gift baskets celebrating her *CoRaB* contract), or rebuying the necessary ingredients for the cake, but next week I'll bring a fresh one. I'll resurrect everyone's dead taste buds and remind them food is an expression of love, not a chemical experiment.

I can't bear to taste any of the "-free" items so I opt for a third refill of coffee to fill my empty, gurgling stomach. Shit. That's what Sebastian the Hungry used to do, Sebastian of Last Year, who drank his coffee black and smoked cigarettes in lieu of eating snacks. Must be some kind of survival instinct from the last time I was on a set. I shake off Vachère's demented influence and slide the first pastry I see into my mouth.

A short man sporting a Vandyke goatee flits over. He looks like the devil's pesky little brother. "Do you need a bib?" he says with a smirk.

"Beg your pardon?"

"Careful with those crumbs. The tunics stain easily."

I wipe my hands on a *CoRaB* logo'd napkin, wishing my tunic had pockets so I could take a fistful home with me.

Devil Jr. consults his stack of index cards. "Sebastian, right? Janine's pet? I'm the assistant director, aka Background Herder."

"Good Moon Day to you," I say with a courtly bow, a standard greeting of the Kingdom of Six.

He doesn't blink. "Yeah, that never gets old."

I straighten up. "Actually, I'm not background. I have a couple of lines."

"Good, great, whatever, I'm in charge of under-fives, too. When you're done eating, head to hair and makeup." He glances down again at the index card. "Says here we're supposed to give you a haircut."

"Really?"

I bounce lightly on the balls of my feet. How exciting! Who else gets to say their latest haircut was performed on the set of their favorite TV show? I could use a trim, and if that means they'll use Roberto's products on me, I'm game as hell.

The AD flips the index card over so I can see. My character name and real name are printed at the top, with the brothel owner's original description below: "50s, portly, balding."

A premonition slithers through me.

I grab the premonition with both hands and strangle it. Janine assured me I didn't need to match the age or description. Everything's fine.

The AD calls out to a woman scurrying past: "Donna. Donna! He's the guy." Donna slows down and waves at me. She looks my age, with a mohawk and green eyeshadow, ripped jeans and a white T-shirt that appears to double as a rag; smears of foundation, eyeliner, and other spackling decorate her shirt from the bottom hem to the V-neck collar.

"Follow her to makeup," the AD tells me. "When she's done with your hair and prosthetics, we'll block the scene—show you where to stand—and rehearse with the girl, okay?"

"Prosthetics?" is what I should be thinking. Instead, I wonder how Heather's faring this morning. You can bet her costume isn't oversized; they'll want to accentuate her body. I'm curious what wardrobe plucked for her to wear. Rumor has it wardrobe doesn't make mistakes.

I've settled into my swivel chair in front of the bulb-framed mirror in the hair and makeup room with Donna, when a pair of scissors rises up behind me. Reflexively, I duck and weave away.

"Careful," Donna says. "Hold still."

Snip.

My ponytail is on the floor.

MY PONYTAIL IS ON THE FLOOR.

"What! Why?" I bellow.

"*They* wanted to shave your head. *I* said there isn't time. Put this on," Donna replies calmly, and hands me a flat, shriveled-up, circular contraption from her drawer of horrors. It's a pinkish, Sebastian's-flesh-tone-colored bathing suit cap.

I'm so stunned I comply, tucking and shoving my shorn locks inside, stretching and pulling at my scalp. My eyebrows have relocated upward in a perpetual state of surprise, which seems an accurate summation of my morning thus far.

Donna's only getting started. The prosthetics turn out to be a fake belly strapped under my XXL tunic, and remarkably realistic boils on my cheeks and forehead, attached like barnacles to my makeup-thickened skin with some type of glue gun.

Presenting: Brothel Owner as Interpreted by What's Left of Sebastian.

Donna scrutinizes me in the mirror and nods to herself, pleased.

I *really* don't feel like saying "thank you," but I can't risk a reputation as a surly under-five, especially since I'll be coming back several times per week for the production briefcase.

The words "I appreciate your help," fall quietly from my lips. The boils pinch each time I move my mouth.

"Happy Moon Day," she chirps as I wobble out the door like a swaying egg.

I'm so relieved to see Heather on set for our scene that I open my arms for a hug.

She screams and backs up.

"Oh God. Sorry. It's me, Sebastian," I say, arms falling dejectedly to my sides.

"Holy shit," she says tentatively.

"You look pretty and . . . painful." The pretty: She wears blond hair extensions that have been curled into thick, tumbling locks, and her makeup accents her lovely cheekbones. The painful: a cinched-tight corset. I remember wearing tight blue jeans for Vachère and release an empathetic shudder.

"Do you want me to free you?" I mutter out the side of my mouth. "Blink once for yes, twice for no."

She laughs, then winces. I wince too. Corsets are the most vindictive outfit ever devised. She wore something similar but less punishing the night of the costume party in Emerson Hall.

And look at us now.

"What did they do to your face?" she asks, her hands traveling up toward my "naked scalp" before she thinks better of it and halts, midair.

"They gave me boils. And this belly, obviously." I pat my stomach. "I think they used it for Lucinda's pregnancy in season four."

Our scene takes place outside the doorway of the brothel bedroom, where the orgy is being staged. We huddle together, two clothed ships in a storm of nakedness.

"You'd think nudity would provide a pay bump on par with, say, horseback riding, wouldn't you?" I ask, motioning to the poor saps entangled with one another in what looks like an obscene sculpture.

"Nudity's not a skill, though," Heather points out.

"Depends if you're doing it right," I say with a shrug. "It's never *happy* sex on this show, is it?" I sigh, watching as the orgy rehearsal segues into a choreography of death. Hooded, sword-wielding bandits pour in to lop off heads and limbs left and right. Donna and the rest of the makeup team stand by, ready with buckets of blood for the actual take.

She grins. "I forgot how funny you are."

The AD walks among the bodies, frowning. "Dead people don't twitch. You're dead, be dead."

Someone referred to as an intimacy coordinator trails him, leaning down to consult with the naked actors and offer them support. Hiring said intimacy coordinator was Janine's doing; she told me it never would have occurred to a male producer.

An hour passes before the assistant director gets to us, and once he's satisfied with our blocking, he digs into our dialogue.

Brothel Owner/Me orders Heather/Reluctant Sex Worker to join the orgy with the straightforward command, "Go on and join them, then."

"No American accents," the AD interjects. "Try the line again."

"Go on and join them, then," I repeat with a sneer. My boils pull against the skin of my forehead and cheeks each time I talk.

The AD frowns and speaks to someone via his headset. "I thought you said he had an accent. That's why we Taft-Hartley'd him."

I tap his shoulder. "I do have an accent."

"Barely," he says, into the headset, but also at me.

"What do you think British people sound like?" I mumble. "That we go around saying 'What ho, Jeeves' all day?"

"Or cockney rhyming slang?" Heather adds. We indulge in a discreet low-five.

"Just give me . . . *more*," the AD demands vaguely.

"I am actually British, though," I say. "This is how British people talk."

"Please, *I'm* more British than you. Look, we're wasting time. Repeat after me, exactly like this: 'Go-wan 'n joy-ner, den!', and give her a smack."

My vision goes blurry. "What?"

"Give her a smack. A spank. *On her butt*," he clarifies.

Good God. "I'm *so* sorry, Heather," I whisper.

"It's okay. I can't feel anything from the neck down," she replies, hands pressing on the thick lines of the corset frame.

We somehow record the scene, assisted by the intimacy coordinator (who was activated the moment the AD yelled the word "butt"). I'm glad Heather and I could laugh about it at least.

On my blessedly sunnier drive back to Alex & Co. Productions three hours later, briefcase handcuffed to my wrist, I replay the rest of the morning in my head.

Heather and I finished our day by helping each other scrub our makeup off and grabbing a quick bite together in the cafeteria. We lamented my ponytail-ectomy and wondered if we could find it on the makeup room floor and graft it back on somehow. I apologized again for the unnecessary spanking.

"I had *no idea* he would make us do that."

"I know you didn't." She waves me off. "Though if you want to make it up to me . . ."

"Anything."

Her voice takes on a suggestive timbre. "Cook me dinner some night."

"Done."

Should I invite her to Janine's, where she can bask in the best view of LA, or wait until I'm back at Park La Brea? I'd have to hit six different grocery stores to stock Janine's pantry, and I'm more comfortable in my own kitchen, but when else would I have the opportunity to show off Janine's luxe apartment to a pretty girl?

Also: Does Heather consider our dinner plans a date, or a platonically friendly catch-up between exes? I wonder, as I exit the 405. Then it hits me. This is the perfect opportunity to prove to Nina that I took her words to heart. I can call her tonight from Janine's, tell her about my conversation with Heather, and ask for her insight. She'll see how much I trust her and value the idea of opening up to her about my dating life.

She'll want to hear every detail about my day on set too. We'll need hours for that.

I'm so caught up in the idea of chatting with Nina all night that I don't notice at first that Janine's car is parked in the reserved spot in the underground parking area.

She's back from Minnesota early.

CHAPTER 14

NINA

After another workday in the books (spent mostly on a twenty-five-page "postmortem" doc on Stu Stu's social media reveal), I take an actual honest-to-God *subway* and then a bus back to Sebastian's apartment. Public transportation in LA? A freakin' miracle.

I immediately recognize several things as I enter the apartment: my lower heart rate, a sense of independence at not having to rely on Ennis to get me home (cue some Beyoncé please), and the novel feeling of not bracing myself for whatever lunacy awaits me courtesy of my roommate. This is the first time in my life I don't *have* a roommate. I enter an empty apartment with no one to answer to but myself.

It is *delicious.* I change into my tank top and shorts and realize I don't have to wear a bra. I find a karaoke version of the *CoRaB* theme song on YouTube and tunelessly belt it out to my heart's content:

'Twas a castle, of rust and bone
And all who lived there, died alone.
An inheritance of fools, thieves, and tricks.
For all who reigned o'er the Kingdom of Six.

I'm just about to get to the meat of the song (a soaring chorus all about the merits of Queen Lucinda), when I hear a tinny instrumental version of the same melody coming from the couch.

It's my phone, a FaceTime call from an unknown number with a foreign area code. The UK?

With a strange premonition, I answer it.

Suddenly my screen is filled with a familiar face, though much more grown-up than I've ever seen her. She has the same sandy blond hair and adorably crooked teeth as her brother, on full display as she grins at me.

"Nina!" she squeals.

"Millie!" I squeal back.

"You look amazing!" she says.

"*You* look amazing!" I respond, and it's true. Nineteen, as it does on most people, looks good on her. She doesn't have a stitch of makeup on that I can tell, but her fresh face is beaming, smooth and unmarred by the worry lines that seem to come standard with your college diploma (or whenever you are forced to enter the real world). "What's going on with you? Tell me everything."

"Gap year before uni. Still living at home with Mum and Dad for the time being, though might get a dorm next year. Blah, blah, blah. Now *you* tell me everything. I heard that you met Roberto Ricci." She waggles her eyebrows.

"Sure did."

"Is he just as handsome in person?" she asks and I can hear a hint of the twelve-year-old girl I knew best.

"Yes," I answer truthfully. But before I have to go into any further detail about how the inside does not match the outside, I change the subject. "How are Jane and Harold?" Sebastian's whole family came to Ithaca for spring break of sophomore year and I stayed behind too. They were kind enough to invite me out to practically every meal they had, so I got a delightful dose of the Worthingtons. By the end of the week, I felt like an honorary daughter/sister.

"They're great. They were just as excited as I was to find out that you and Sebastian had reconnected," she says as I see her grab a cat from out of frame and bring it into her lap.

"Me too. I'm so glad we met up." I squint to see whether the cat is still Tigger. He'd be well over twelve by now so . . . maybe not?

"*CoRaB* brought you together!" Millie gushes. "Just like it did in the beginning."

"You're right," I reply, catching sight of the telltale orange triangle at the tip of Tigger's tail as he jumps out of Millie's arms. I smile, relieved. "I owe *CoRaB* for one hell of a friendship."

Millie blinks at me and looks as if she's lost her train of thought. "Right. Yes. So . . . are you seeing anyone?"

"I am," I say, settling into Sebastian's couch. "A very nice guy named Ennis."

"Ah. I see." She nods and crosses her legs to settle into her own couch. "How long have you been together?"

"About two months."

She inexplicably brightens up. "Oh. Okay!"

"What about you? Are you seeing anyone?" I ask.

"I'm attempting to woo a girl I met last month at a pantomime show," she says. "But I doubt anything will happen before my TrekUSA trip. I might have to settle for an American this summer."

She wrinkles her nose and I laugh, but am impressed at her unaffected confidence in what a catch she is.

"I hope it's okay that I called you," she says, suddenly sounding unsure for the first time. "I asked Sebastian for your number. . . ."

"Of course it's okay!" I exclaim. "I'm so glad to hear from you, Millie. You have no idea."

I really don't know if she has any idea that I've always considered her to be the little sister I never had. I mean, I have my own little sister, of course, but this is one who actually seems to look up to me and find my thoughts and advice worthwhile.

Case in point, Millie starts asking me about what classes I think she should pick for her first semester.

"There's this really cool class on the *Arabian Nights*. Has nothing to do with journalism of course but . . ."

"Take the really cool class," I say firmly. "Trust me, you don't have much of an opportunity in real life to explore a subject just for its own sake. Take advantage."

She grins. "I was hoping you'd say that."

Just then, I get a text on my phone. "Hold on, Millie. It's Sebastian."

"Of course."

Bad news, he writes. **My boss's trip got cut short so I'm no longer housesitting. Would it be okay if I came back tonight?**

Okay? It's your apartment! I write him back.

I know. But I realize you need more time to find a place. And I can always crash at Sam's.

Come back. The kettle corn's on, I write, referencing our favorite TV-watching snack. **That is . . . if you have some.**

I'll come back with something better.

I smile as I switch back to Millie. "Sorry about that. But looks like your brother is heading back here tonight if you want to call later."

"Nooooo problem," she replies. "I'll give him a call soon. Maybe I can catch you both together sometime."

"Definitely," I say. "Well, until I can find my own place, which will hopefully be soon. I don't want to impose too much on Sebastian's hospitality."

"I'm pretty sure you can impose as long as you like. See you later, Nina!"

Why is it so hard to find a place to live in a city that, according to Google, has 110,000 empty apartments?

The answer is: because the half-empty apartments, aka the roomshares which are the only ones I can currently afford, are apparently filled with lunatics. I *cannot* deal with a Celeste of a different color.

Maybe it's time I asked Sean for a raise. I reluctantly open up my work calendar and add a note to myself to maybe put a meeting in his calendar. I need to summon up the courage first.

I've gone back to the depressing job of scouring whatever the latest roomshare site endorsed by Jeff Goldblum is when I hear the door open.

"Honey, I'm home!"

I look up from my laptop to see Sebastian walking in with two paper bags of groceries: one from Trader Joe's, and one from Sprouts. Did he hit two separate stores on his way over? I go to help him.

"What's all this?" I ask.

"Our snack!" he says.

And then I notice his hair. It's lopsided with a particularly floofy tuft sticking up in the back. It's *short*. "What's all *this*?" I exclaim again, taking my hand to the poufy section.

He grimaces. "Right, so . . . being on the show might have come with some sacrifices."

"Oh, man. And your Link cosplay was going to be so good this Halloween."

"I know!" he says. "Now I need a thoroughly unconvincing wig."

"Do you have scissors? I think I can try to at least even it out."

"Um . . . yeah. Let me put this stuff away."

He takes out a jar of fancy-looking mayo, a couple of pomegranates, a package of thick bacon, and a tub of ice cream that I immediately notice is Talenti Pacific Coast Pistachio—my absolute favorite. I doubt that's a coincidence and I smile at his back as he stacks the items away in the fridge. The rest of the bags he leaves on the kitchen counter.

Then he rummages around in one of the drawers until he emerges with a pair of kitchen shears.

I look at them skeptically. "Is that all you have?"

"Yeah. Why? You don't think they'll work?"

I immediately think of Sayeh and her three-part series on cutting your own bangs. "Rule number 1," she said. "For God's sake, get a pair of hair scissors and *only use hair scissors.*"

I take the kitchen shears and test them out. To Sebastian's credit they at least seem pretty sharp and clean.

"Listen, it can't really look worse," Sebastian says in response to my thoughtful expression. "I trust you. Just go for it."

He gets one of the barstools from behind his kitchen counter, brings it to the middle of the floor, and plops down on it.

I lightly touch his thick blond hair. I'm close enough to notice the way the light catches the fine hair at the very nape of his neck, turning it golden for just a second before it disappears into his pale skin again.

"Do you have a water spray bottle?" I ask, mentally replaying Sayeh's tutorial.

"Sure," he says. He gets up and brings me a small green one from next to the plants on his windowsill before sitting down again.

I spray down his hair, darkening it a few shades. I run my hand through it, bringing the uneven edge to the end of my fingertips.

"You sure about this?" I ask.

"Yup. Do your worst."

"My worst would definitely involve a beheading. Battle of Signon–style," I muse. "Actually, in between apartment hunting, that's what I was working on," I say, indicating my laptop on the couch.

"Beheading memes?" he asks.

"No but . . . that's an idea. I'll bring it up to Sean. I was on my old Neener96 account."

"Ack! You're writing new fanfic?" he asks, practically jumping out of his stool and almost getting stabbed in the head in the process.

"Easy there, cowboy," I say. "Speaking of which, we are going to have to have a deep discussion about the whens and hows of those pictures."

Sebastian looks around at the catalog images, which I still haven't taken down, and groans. "I'm going to kill Sam . . . but, hold up, don't change the subject. What were you writing?"

"Oh, you know . . . my specialty."

"Jeffcan?"

I grin. "Yup. Let's just say the enthusiasm of the fandom has fanned the flame." I don't tell him that I even opened up Final Draft and wrote one of the scenes in screenplay format. Not that I'm ever getting anywhere near the real *CoRaB* writers' room but it still felt a little thrilling to see *my* Jeff and Duncan dialogue written out in Courier New font.

"I will need to read this."

"Obviously. Now, hold still." I gently move his head down so that he's looking at the floor, and using the scissors, start trimming the ends of his hair in a vertical line toward my fingers. We're silent for a moment, giving me time to realize that touching someone's hair—someone I've known for so long and so well—is somehow very . . . intimate. As many times as I've sat next to him, or hugged him, or playfully touched his arm, I've never done this before.

I clear my throat and grasp for another topic of conversation. "By the way, I *am* apartment hunting. I hope to be out of your hair within the week," I say, as I move over to a different section of his head and trim. "Literally."

"Oh." I can't see his face, but I feel his body shift. "Or you could stay."

"What?"

"I mean, I need a new roommate anyway. You need a new

roommate. You already know my bad habits. You already even know the neighbor. It seems like a no-brainer." He turns his neck now to grin at me.

I smile back haltingly. In some ways, he's right of course. But we've also just gotten back into each other's lives and this seems like it might cross a line somehow. Too much, too soon.

Sebastian must sense my reluctance, because he turns back around and casually says, "No pressure, of course. Just a suggestion. Hey . . . you'll never guess who my scene partner was today."

"Uh . . ." I give his hair one last brush with my hands. It's evened out at least. "Milo Ricci?"

Sebastian snorts. "If only. I have so many questions." Milo is Roberto's little brother and for about five minutes, seven years ago, he tried to launch an unsuccessful teeny-bopper career (which included an ill-advised cameo on his big brother's hit show). Duncan's urchin little cousin, Lance, made one appearance in one episode, was immediately called out for being a strong indication the show was about to jump the shark (the Medieval Cousin Oliver effect, it was dubbed), and then promptly disappeared, never to be spoken of again. This somehow also stalled poor Milo's career, and he's been relegated to starring in VH1 "celebrity" dating shows ever since.

"You're done by the way," I say, flicking a strand of Sebastian's hair.

He places his hand behind his head, brushing my fingertips for the quickest of moments. "Thanks," he says, and then turns around to face me. "It wasn't Milo. But it was . . . Heather."

"Heather . . ." I say. "*Heather* Heather?"

"Yup. Like salmon swimming upstream, all actors end up in Hollywood eventually." He smiles at me. "We had fun. I think we might go out on a date soon." He gives a pregnant pause and suddenly I realize what he's doing: confiding in me about a girl—*the* girl, in fact—the very thing I said I wanted him to do.

If I don't recognize this for the reboot that it is, then I deserve to have my imaginary Writers Guild membership revoked.

I slap on a big smile. This is my second chance, right? This is one step closer to us becoming real friends. And if he has a girlfriend soon—and I have a boyfriend—maybe I can even take him up on his offer to become his new roommate.

"Tell me more!" I exclaim. "What was her part? How is she doing?"

He hops off the stool. "I will. Over dinner?" He goes over to the bags and starts unloading more groceries. "How do you feel about avocado and bacon sandwiches with garlic aioli and pomegranate seeds?"

My stomach groans in response. I laugh. "Is that enough of an answer for you?"

He smiles and indicates the stool. "Go ahead. Take a load off."

"Oh, I plan to pull my own weight." I head to the corner of the living room where I dropped off a small bag after work today. With a flourish, I bring out a bottle of Kingdom of Six cabernet.

Sebastian gasps. "A tie-in wine?"

"It's a prototype," I say happily.

"Avocado, aioli, and merchandised cabernet. This might be the most LA meal there ever was."

I rummage around in the kitchen until I find a corkscrew, pop open the wine, and find us two glasses.

"Did you know it's illegal in the state of California to go an entire day without eating an avocado?" he says as he's slicing one up. "I'm just saving you from a life behind bars."

I grin as I hold a glass out to him. "To freedom, then."

"To freedom," he bellows in a terrible *Braveheart* accent.

He takes his glass and clinks it with mine. I take a sip. And nearly choke before swallowing it.

"That is . . ." I hack away. "Absolutely disgusting."

Sebastian's face is lined with repulsion. "Yup," he says. "Is this meant to be poisoned or something? Is this specifically a season three prototype?" He picks up the bottle and starts perusing the label.

I look over his shoulder with concern. "How seriously does Hollywood take its tie-ins?"

"Very," he says as he puts down the bottle. "I think it'd be best to . . ." He takes both of our glasses and dumps their contents down the drain and then does the same with the whole bottle. Then he reaches into his bag and takes out another bottle of wine. "Two-Buck Chuck to the rescue."

I hold out my glass as he pours.

"What shall we drink to this time?" he asks as he positions his glass an inch away from mine.

"To reboots," I say firmly before we clink them.

CHAPTER 15

SEBASTIAN

I wake up on the couch with a crick in my neck and a smile on my face. Nina and I negotiated for half an hour last night about who should take the bed and who should take the couch. I insisted she sleep in the bed and she eventually agreed, with the caveat that we'd alternate nights.

I have no intention of honoring that agreement.

The point of her staying in my apartment was so she'd be more comfortable than her other situation; I'm not booting her from the bed just because my boss returned early.

Logistical problem of sleeping on the couch: morning wood in the living room. *Please don't let her walk in*, I pray, flinging the sheet off and making a ponderous yet mad dash in my boxer shorts to our shared bathroom. I splash water on my face and through my shortened locks, my hand jerking outward in memory of where my hair used to be. I pivot between mirrors, admiring Nina's handiwork. I'd walked in wearing a tragedy on my head, and while her fix isn't *perfect*, it has the distinction of at least looking *deliberate*. The memory of her fingers moving through my hair, soft and fragrant, pulls at me and for a moment I close my eyes and revel in it.

When my eyes snap open, I'm a man with a plan: move the

bulk purchase that arrived last night (my monthly subscription of cleaning supplies) into the entryway, and busy myself in the kitchen. I can't retrieve my clothes from the bedroom until she wakes up, but I don't want to wake her if she's tired, so I gather ingredients as silently as possible, ticking items off my mental list. Eggs, butter, parmesan and cheddar cheese, tomatoes, salt, pepper. I undressed so rapidly last night in an effort to claim the couch before she changed her mind that I didn't think to "pack" today's clothes, so I'm shirtless when I put the burner on and a toss a thick slab of butter into the pan for omelets.

I'm so focused on cooking that I don't hear her glide up behind me until there's an audible thump, followed by a wail. "Ahh! Oh, no!"

She's tripped over the enormous box and crashed into me. Instinctively, my arm goes around her back. With my other hand, I turn off the burner and then steady her, gripping her upper arm until she finds her balance. She wears a "Yasss Kween Lucinda" tank top and plaid boxer shorts, she's sleepy-warm, and her hair smells like milk-and-honey shampoo.

We're practically hugging, and I move my pelvis backward so our hips don't touch.

She avoids my gaze, and her words come out in a rush of embarrassment. "Sorry! Apparently, I can't walk until I've had coffee. That box was *not* here last night. Was it?"

My hands move from her arms to her face, which is about a centimeter from my naked chest. I love the way her warm, shallow breaths hit my skin. I gently cup her cheeks and wait until her gaze slides up to meet mine. "Are you okay?"

She clears her throat and backs up. My hands fall to my sides.

"That was definitely not there last night, and neither was—this." She motions in wide circles in a vague encapsulation of my upper body.

I grin. "My chest wasn't here last night? Where did I put it?"

"No, I mean your chest wasn't this . . . *chesty* in college."

"Chesty?" I shouldn't tease her, but it's flattering, the way her eyes sweep over my pecs and abs.

"Chest-like."

"If my chest wasn't chest-like, what *was* it like? A bowl of fruit?"

She puffs out a laugh and waves in the direction of Sam's apartment down the hall. "Same with him. When you crossed the state line into California, did your T-shirts automatically cease to fit?"

"They tore right off."

She snaps her fingers. "I knew it."

"Actually . . ." I lean closer and cup my hand to the side of my mouth, as if imparting a secret. "It takes a *little* more effort than that."

"Right, I can see you've—worked hard to achieve . . . that." She shakes her hair out and rolls her eyes at herself. "Apparently, I can't walk *or* talk before I've had my coffee."

"Let's rectify that. Beans are in the cabinet above the grinder. I'll get dressed."

"Sounds good." She moves to the side, giving me a wide berth.

I duck my head and walk quickly to my room.

Pushing, sweating, and straining my way through hundreds of early-morning workouts over the last year was worth it for five minutes of Nina's ogling.

Even if it doesn't mean anything.

I shave, brush my teeth, and pull on a collared shirt, khaki shorts, and Vans. By the time I emerge from my room, Nina's made coffee for both of us. Sunlight coats her in a hazy, angelic hue as she lifts my mug toward me.

"Do you still take it with cream, no sugar?" she asks.

"Good memory."

She pours the exact right amount of cream in my mug and swirls her spoon through it before setting it on the island for me. I unpack the box that sent Nina careening into my arms and finish making our omelets.

Her eyes go round when I set the plate before her. "This looks fantastic, but you know you don't have to cook for me."

"I was making it for myself anyway, no big deal."

"In that case, I accept." She points her fork at me. "But don't make a habit of it."

She slides one of the omelets onto the plate I'd set out for her, and we tuck in, our forks clinking against the plates.

"So, Worthington, is there something you want to tell me?"

For a horrible second, I think she means about my feelings for her. The confusion/horror must be evident on my face, because she swings her leg and points with her cute bare toes at the box, stacked high with 480-count packages of baby wipes. "About your secret baby?"

"Ah. Right. Let me explain how we keep Chateau Worthington clean. Dare I say dazzling clean."

"Now that you mention it, I *am* dazzled. Please enlighten me."

"Do we use spray bottles? Harsh chemicals? Scrub brushes? A bucket and mop? No, we use wipes. Wipes are safe for every surface. Wipes bring joy to every heart. Wipes are life. They arrive in bulk the first of the month, and we use them for mirrors, floors, countertops, bathrooms, tables, dressers, windows, and, for my new roommate, should she desire it: makeup remover."

"I didn't know you performed infomercials in your free time."

"Look, Matty was disgusting and wipes were the only solution. Did you know he had two piles of clothes on the floor of his room at all times? God forbid he use his dresser. One pile was fresh from the laundry, and the other pile was dirty. Every day he'd pick his outfit from the clean pile, iron it, wear it all day, and then place it in the dirty pile before bed. *Sometimes he'd forget which pile was which.*"

Nina shudders theatrically. "I'm a significant improvement, then."

"You have no idea."

"Are those the only house rules? No clothing piles of dubious origin, and when in doubt, use wipes?"

"That's about it. Oh, and I allow myself one emergency cigarette per week on the balcony, but if that bothers you, I can take it farther away."

"I can live with that, but since when do you smoke, Worthington?"

"Since I became a 'Cowboy, Baby,'" I sing, complete with hip swivel and whip crack. She laughs and my heart soars. "I've cut down almost completely since then. One pack lasts me six months."

I gather our plates and utensils for the sink, but before I can grab the sponge, Nina's beside me. I yank the water on, as though that will dispel the fact that my apartment suddenly feels warmer, smaller, and more cramped.

"I can wash up," Nina tells me, nudging me sideways. "The cook should never be on dish duty."

"Tell that to Sam and Matty." I shift to the left to give her space but continue washing. She picks up the sponge and gets to work as well.

Our elbows touch amid the suds. I never considered my elbow an erogenous zone before, but apparently, I've been missing out for twenty-seven years. Nina's proximity is torturous. Her sleep-tousled hair, her soft-looking skin, the way we've fallen into step with each other so effortlessly . . . it's cruel and unusual and I want to keep it going as long as possible.

"I meant to ask, did you sleep okay on the couch?" Nina says.

I ignore the pinched nerve in my neck. "Definitely."

She grabs a dish towel and efficiently dries both our plates. "Don't fight me tonight, okay? I'm taking the couch, end of discussion."

I open my mouth to refute her statement when a voice calls to us from the hallway.

"Is Nina decent?" Sam shouts. "Can I come in?"

"I'm never decent," Nina yells back.

I open the door and Sam walks in, surveying the kitchen.

"I knew it," he grouses. "Nina snaked my breakfast."

"First come, first served," I reply.

"Are you at least on for dinner this Sunday?" For Nina's benefit he adds, "We're supposed to binge *Crash Landing on You*. I've seen it twice but I'm trying to enlighten this heathen. You in?"

"Sure. What's on the menu?" Nina asks me.

"Bangers and mash, in'it?" I say with a terrible Cockney accent. If the assistant director could hear me now, he'd probably say, "Was that so hard?"

"Bangers and mash?" Nina's face lights up. "Will we be dining at midnight? Will there be shortbread?"

Sausages and mashed potatoes were our comfort food junior and senior year, prepared in the shared kitchen of Emerson Hall at ungodly hours, and scarfed down in the lounge while cramming for exams.

"Here's my list, by the way." Sam places a torn-out notebook page on the kitchen island. "I'm off to record my new 'cast, live from the Wiltern. Hey, Seb, did you catch yesterday's? What'd you think?"

I'm now fourteen episodes behind. I will never catch up.

"Mm," I say vaguely. "Did you hear back from the podcast network yet?"

He slumps. "Yeah, they want me to gain an extra five k listeners before they'll add me. As though it's that easy."

"Sorry, man."

"Anyway, gotta go." He shoots a friendly smile at Nina, all K-Pop charm and (agggggh!) the dreaded words, "See ya, favorite ex."

"See ya," Nina replies, and while I'd give a month's paycheck for Sam to never call her that again, my heart twitches happily when she doesn't repeat the honorific.

As quickly as he arrived, Sam exits into the hallway, the heavy door slamming shut behind him.

"I checked out his podcast," Nina says. "He updates *every day*?"

"He does."

"And you listen to all of them?"

"That's what friends are for, right?"

"What's this?" She picks up the piece of paper Sam left on the island.

"Supermarket Shuffle." I pull additional grocery lists from my back pocket and lay them down in a row. "Sprouts, Trader Joe's, Ralphs, Whole Foods, and on special occasions, Gelson's."

"Aren't they basically the same?"

I clutch my heart. "You—what—how—NO?"

She looks at me like I've grown two heads. "You aren't really going to all these stores."

"Of course I am. And you're coming with, because a statement like 'aren't they basically the same' is so shameful it proves you need guidance to live here. First lesson: Sprouts is like if Whole Foods had Trader Joe's prices."

She continues to stare at me. "Just go to Sprouts, then! Problem solved."

"Sweet child. So naive. Every grocery store in LA has certain items and brands the others don't have. You don't want me cooking with subpar ingredients, do you?"

She regards the list-covered table with skepticism. "Why can't you, Sam, and Matty split up, and everyone takes a different store?"

"We used to, when Matty lived here, but this is easier, because I'm selective about Sunday night dinner. I'm going to all these places, anyway, so . . ."

She drifts closer. My skin prickles and my heart races. Will it always be like this, for me? Will I never become inured to her presence?

Her eyes are soft. "That's what you said to me about break-fast. You don't need to treat me like a guest. I'm perfectly happy with cereal from now on, and I'm paying for half our groceries. Got it?"

"Got it. In my defense, though, Sam and Matty would live off Jack in the Box, egg noodles, and Cheez-Its if I didn't take charge."

I gather the lists but Nina's quicker. "Speaking of egg noodles, that's on Sam's list and he wrote 'H Mart' next to it. Tell me that's not another grocery store."

"Er. It's in Koreatown. Because they have the best egg noodles. I like them too! I make a garlic sauce that's—"

Fast as a hawk swooping down, Nina lunges for her phone, her eyebrows pinched together in concentration.

I peer over her shoulder. "What are you doing?"

"Putting an end to this nonsense. I bet he goes there twice a week when he visits his family."

Get your own egg noodles at H Mart, she texts. **And buy a second set for us.**

Sam's response is swift: **Yes, ma'am.**

Nina smirks and puts her phone away. "See? Easy."

After work, I make good on my threat to drag Nina around every grocery store in LA. Once we've crossed the items off our list, we drive to a storage facility on Highland Avenue. My unit's the smallest available, a five-by-five one where I've stacked sweaters, a winter coat, a pair of skis, and heavy blankets. (In case it drops below sixty.) Today, one particular blanket shall be freed from its prison.

"Why are we here?" Nina asks, shielding her eyes from the sun as I lead her to the unit and unlock it.

"You were right this morning. I do have a secret baby, and this is where I stash her when I'm at work. She's got a Nintendo Switch, a water tube, and an exercise ball. Should be fine, right?"

"You just described a hamster."

"Eh, pretty much the same."

Her eyes fall on the real surprise, which provokes laughter and applause. "You still have it! The Kingdom of Sex quilt!"

Nina's nickname for it stems from the fact that it's a family tree of the show's main characters and lays out exactly which incest produced which characters. I shake off the dust and hold it out for Nina to view in all its glory.

"Matty called it Sex Kryptonite and forbade me to hang it." I address the quilt directly. "Guess what, you gorgeous thing you, there's a new queen on the throne and your banishment ends today."

Playing along, Nina mimes holding a sword with which to knight the quilt. "Sir Quilt, your trial is at an end, and you are hereby restored to your rightful place of honor behind the couch." A sidelong glance at me. "Unless you want it in your room?"

"Are you kidding? Behind the couch for sure."

Back at my apartment, we unpack the groceries and hang the quilt.

If the quilt *is* sex kryptonite, that's a bonus, as far as I'm concerned. I really don't need to hear Nina and Ennis the Menace through the walls. Maybe we should instigate some type of sock-on-doorknob code to keep the other one away should either of us intend to make the mattress squeak.

"Will Ennis find this weird?" I ask, but only after it's too late to unhang it. That thing is *earthquake-proof* now, clamped between a wooden frame that's secured deep through the wall. Heh.

She shrugs. "Doubtful. Does Ennis find anything weird?"

I swallow and force the next words out, because talking about our dating lives is what we do now, or at least, it's what she *wants* us to do.

"Let's figure out a way for you to alert me whenever you and Ennis need privacy. If you give me a day's notice, I can make myself scarce."

Nina seems surprised. "Oh. Okay. Same goes for you and Heather."

"I don't know if that'll ever be the case, but okay. What should our code be?"

Nina's gaze travels the length of the room until it lands on the cardboard cutout of Lucinda in the corner, a Burger King crown dangling from one of her hands. "If the crown's been moved from her hand to her head, the other person will know to steer clear for a little while."

I resist the urge to ask, "So Ennis only takes a little while?" and instead head to the gym for an extra-punishing workout.

Night falls and the crown remains on Lucinda's hand. Thank God.

Sam stops by to extract his groceries, and I settle in on the couch to email Millie about her upcoming visit. The final item on her gap-year check list is a six-week camping trip with TrekUSA, a small-group tour company for young travelers. She'll be staying with me at the beginning and end of the tour.

Millie emails back right away, so we switch to instant messenger.

Sebastian: how r u awake??

Mills: HOW'S UR ROOMMATE

Sebastian: fine.

Mills: nice try. When are you telling her you 🐥, 💀 her?

Sebastian: Never.

Mills: whyyyyyy dammit!

Sebastian: Remember how upset Callo got when you didn't tell her you were bi?

Mills: yes, which was completely unfair, because I wasn't ready to share and she doesn't get to dictate my timeline

Sebastian: I agree, but my point is, Nina thinks I didn't open up to her the way a friend should, and it hurt her so badly she wanted nothing to do with me for YEARS. So I have my marching orders: open up to her as a friend, AKA tell her about my love life.

Mills: This is a terrible plan. It's not "opening up to her," it's hiding the truth more than ever. You realize the irony, at least?

Sebastian: We're in good form right now. I'm happy to have her in the next room, happy to have her in my life again. It's enough!!

Mills: You're useless.

Sebastian: How's your cellist? How was the fancy dress party? What'd you wear?

She met a cute musician at a pantomime show in Yeovil, and they've gone out a few times since, most recently to a friend's costume party (called fancy dress there).

Mills: The theme was 90s pop music and we both went as All Saints. I thought it was brill, but ever since, she's been impossible to read.

Sebastian: Mixed signals?

Mills: Exactly. She "wants to stay in touch" while i'm camping, but "doesn't want to tie me down."

Sebastian: meanwhile you're gagging to be tied down

Mills: gross!

Sebastian: LOL but you are, you're in love with love. You always have been

Mills: guilty 💀

After we say good night, I print out my weekly meal plan, which I affix to the fridge with a *CoRaB* magnet. I prepared dinner for two at least twice a week when Matty lived here, so folding Nina into that schedule is easily accomplished, assuming she's interested.

I've no clue what my inimitable roommate has been up to the last several hours, but around ten p.m. she enters the living room with a pillow and sheet.

"Move it," she instructs me, plopping elegantly down on the

couch. Yes, she plops elegantly. "You get the bed tonight, re-member?"

"Au contraire," I say, stretching my arms wide and resting them on the back of the couch. "I claim this couch in the name of England. You'll have to take the bed again, I'm afraid."

She groans. "Come on, we had an agreement."

"I prefer the couch, actually. The bed's awful. Way too roomy."

"Very funny. Move your ass."

"Nope."

She folds her arms. "Well, I'm not leaving either."

"*Breath of the Wild* till one of us concedes? You can show me where the Koroks are."

Four hours later, bleary-eyed and punch drunk, we've moved on to Mario Kart, having decided that speed champion of Hyrule Circuit gets the couch. I beat her latest time by half a second and shake my ass obnoxiously, nestling farther into the couch cushions and challenging her to respond.

Except Nina can't respond. Nina's asleep, her head lolling forward, her breaths soft and steady. I clear my throat. "Nina, your turn."

She doesn't stir.

I'm a complete git. The neon clock on the microwave reads 2:45 a.m. Adrenaline and stubborn idiocy kept me awake when we should have called it quits by midnight at the latest. We both have to get up in four hours; she deserves the bed more than ever at this point, but how to relocate her?

"Nina, can you walk to the bedroom?"

Nothing. No murmur, no movement. She remains upright at a painful-looking angle, her neck a loose pivot point that spasms forward and back in an involuntary jerk. I release a long breath and move to the outside of her armrest, torn between leaving her where she is and carrying her to the bed. It's only a fifteen-foot distance, and lifting her will probably require less effort than my typical workout at the gym.

"Hey, Nina." I nudge her shoulder. "Want me to take you to bed?" Aaah, no! My heart slams inside my chest as I quickly correct myself. "I mean, take you to *your* bed. For sleep."

On the plus side, my verbal madness seems to have roused her somewhat.

Her eyelids lift partway. Her voice is soft, slurred. "Time for sleep."

"Yes, it's time for sleep."

Her arms encircle my waist. She pulls me toward her, snuggles closer, and rests her head against my hip. How is it possible that earlier today I thought standing next to her at the *sink* was torture? I had no clue what torture was.

"Right. I'm going to lift you, okay?"

"Okay, honey," she mumbles, chin lifting.

I freeze. I know it was only a sleep-induced reflex and she has no idea what she's saying, but it kills me all the same. Is there a world out there where she calls me "honey" and means it? And if there is, does the Sebastian of that world know how lucky he is?

I scoop her into my arms and try to ignore the fact that her nose is nuzzling my neck.

I make the trip in five strides and settle her gently atop my mattress. She curls into a ball, eyes closed. The sweetest yawn overtakes her face before she murmurs, "Thanks, Seb."

I back out of the room, turning the light off as I go.

"Good night, Nina," I whisper, and shut the door.

CHAPTER 16

NINA

I wake up enveloped in the scent of cedar.

"Sebastian?" I croak in a haze. Though as my brain unfogs, it quickly realizes that he wouldn't be asleep next to me. I had a couple of drinks last night, but I would remember that.

I open one eye. I am, however, in Sebastian's room. And I distinctly remember making him promise that we'd switch off every other night. But then I get a vague memory of my head against his chest. Did he carry me into his room last night?

I open the door to the living room, starting off by saying, "You're in big trouble . . ." But then my words fail. I'm unprepared this early in the morning for the sight of a sleeping, shirtless, boxer-clad Sebastian on the couch. A longer lock of his hair has fallen across his mouth and is gently rising and falling with his breath. He looks younger like this, with the muscles in his face completely relaxed. He looks so much, in fact, like the Sebastian I watched dozing on the common room couch that I have to quickly shut the door. It feels like it echoes the slamming of a door in my own heart. *No, we will not go down this road again.*

I go about the business of quietly getting dressed for work

and putting on makeup. I take a fortifying breath before I open the door to the living room again. Turns out I didn't need to. The couch is vacated, and the sound of a flushing toilet lets me know exactly where its former occupant is.

Though when the bathroom door opens I realize: still no shirt. I remember our run-in from yesterday morning too and wonder if this is just how he walks around. I will the answer to be no. But also yes. But no.

"Hey," he says through a sleepy, lopsided grin.

"Hi," I manage, before flurrying past him to the bathroom. It's only when we have the safety of a closed door between us again that I feel comfortable chastising him in my normal tone of voice. "You broke our pact, Worthington. *I* was supposed to take the couch last night." I feel a little weird talking to him while I pee but, then again, if we're going to be normal run-of-the-mill roommates, I have to get over that. So I sit down on the toilet and do my business.

"A humble squire never lets his queen suffer," he quotes.

I raise an eyebrow in the mirror as I turn on the faucet to wash my hands. "I don't recall a centaur raid preceding my bout of unconsciousness last night."

"Centaurs. Lynels. Different side of the same coin."

"And anyway," I say, right before I stick my toothbrush in my mouth. "You can't die at the end of this episode. I definitely don't have enough saved up to make rent on my own."

I hear Sebastian's snort laugh through the door and I can picture exactly what he looks like when he does it. It brings a toothpaste-smeared grin to my face.

Something is sizzling on the stove by the time I open the bathroom door and I'm hit with the impossibly tempting smell of bacon. Sebastian has also, thankfully, thrown a shirt on.

"Breakfast?" Sebastian asks.

"Don't change the subject," I reply. "You're getting the bed tonight and that's final."

He shrugs. "I'm comfortable on the couch. Honest. I swear on the long, lustrous, and stain-free life of the Kingdom of Sex quilt."

My jaw drops. "Not the quilt!"

He raises his hand in a Scout's honor. "May an entire bottle of prototype poisoned wine spill on it if I'm lying. Besides, I know your neck's messed up."

He's not wrong. I've been getting pinched nerves in my neck on and off since I was a preteen. "It's fine now," I say unconvincingly.

"*For* now," he replies. "One bad night of sleep and it'll be weeks of agony."

I have no response to that because he's right. Though I'm floored that he remembers.

"I'm fine on the couch," he says again firmly. "I swear. If I'm ever not, I promise to tell you."

"You swear?" I ask. "On the quilt?"

"On the quilt," he responds solemnly. "Now, breakfast?"

"I can't," I say, feeling as sorry as I sound. "I'm already late for work."

"No problem. Hold, please." He takes out a container and makes quick work of adding a couple of slices of bacon and then, from a different pan that I hadn't even noticed before, a thick slice of French toast.

"How did you . . ." I start.

But he just hands me the container with a wink. "A squire never spills his secrets."

I don't know how popular I'm going to be on the bus eating a whole plateful of Sebastian's breakfast without any to share . . . but just this once, I decide not to care.

"My life is abject torture," Sean says as he comes up to my desk in his designer suit, designer wingtips, and Hermès messenger bag. "Let's get this over with."

"Get what over with, Sean?" I ask, my voice still chipper from the last half-hour's bus breakfast.

"Ughhhhh. Can't any of my assistants be bothered to check their calendars?" He's pulling at his temples so tightly that he's like a before and after for a miracle face-lift cream.

I bring up my calendar right in front of him and show him my docket for today. Empty.

"How is that possible?" He takes out his phone and starts irritatingly scrolling through it. "I sent it to you last night at 2:07 a.m. See . . . oh. Stuck in my outbox." He presses a button and my computer whooshes with the sound of incoming mail. "Well, there you go. Now let's get a move on."

I take a look at the words that just popped up on my calendar and my eyes nearly fall right out of my head: *Castles of Rust and Bone* Official Cosplay Contest Sponsored by Duncan Hines.

It's happening in one hour at a convention center downtown. I grab my bag and start following Sean to the elevator.

"Oh wow," I say. "So Duncan Hines is officially in?"

"They're in," Sean grumbles. "And to celebrate, I now get to spend three hours of my life staring at spray-painted dragon turds or whatever the fuck."

"Centaur turds," I correct. Sean shoots me a look of death. "Sorry, it's just there are no dragons in . . ."

"Nina. Does. It. Look. Like. I. Care?!" He's gritting his teeth so hard that I'm afraid he's going to snap one off and then, undoubtedly, my day will be spent finding an emergency oral surgeon instead of judging (or at the very least observing) a *CoRaB* costume contest.

"Sorry," I say.

Sean is doing his Lamaze breathing again and he's rummaging around so hard in his fancy briefcase that I'm convinced the lining won't survive it. "Where the fuck are my stress balls?"

I give a quick glance down the hallway where the entire HR department sits. "Er, Sean. Do you have to be the one to judge this contest? Isn't there someone else at the company who could go in your stead? Someone who might even be a fan?"

He shoots me a withering look. "I don't think 'interim social media coordinator' is going to impress our sponsors much."

"I didn't mean me," I say.

"Oh no. You are definitely co-judging with me because I know absolutely nothing about the Kingdom of Six . . ."

"But that's right!" I say beaming. "It *is* the Kingdom of Six."

He shoots me another look. "Yes, that's what the boxes of wine staring me down from the corner of my office tell me. As I was saying. *You're* the real judge. I'm just the suit and the title and the person who is probably going to have to call out sick because of a fabric glue–induced migraine for the rest of the week." He gets a buzz on his phone and looks at it. His face falls. "Oh my dear God. There's a line around the block. That *is a lot* of pale skin and chest hair for ten a.m. on a Monday morning."

He shows me the photo. Apparently, the Caveman Tal contingent—a minor character who appeared on a three-story arc involving a whole lot of spelunking—has come out in full force. When I glance up at Sean, he looks as if he's about to burst into tears.

"This is probably a stupid question," I start.

"Probably," Sean agrees.

"But . . . do any of the sponsors know what you look like? Because I know a guy, an actor . . ." Not technically a lie. He just came off an acting gig, after all. "Who's a huge fan. He's got a suit. And he can totally pretend to be Sean Delaney, SVP of Digital, for a couple of hours."

Sean stares at me for a second and I think I may have totally stepped over the line. But then he lets out a huge sigh of relief, and gently puts a hand on my shoulder to keep himself from falling over. "If that's true, Nina, you'd be my hero."

I grin. "Really? I can call him?"

"Book him. Offer him a case of wine if you have to."

"I don't think that'll be necessary," I say, but Sean has already turned away, an extra jaunt in his step as he heads toward his office.

"Good," he replies as the elevator opens. "Because I was kidding. We don't have that in the budget."

He steps into his office as I step onto the elevator, then take out my phone, press some buttons, and wait for that British-tinged "hullo?"

"What are you doing today? Actually it doesn't matter what you're doing today. Drop it," I say through a huge smile. "I just booked us the gig of a lifetime."

"Your tippets were better," Sebastian whispers to me as we sit behind a black desk a few feet away from a small stage. We look like we're the stern headmasters of a performing arts school about to crush some dreams, except that we have an assortment of corsets, chainmail, and centaur tails in front of us. "*Fame* but make it medieval" might be a good TV show pitch, I think vaguely.

I look at the brothel denizen twirling before us. "Yeah, but the knife wound on the back is the real star of the show. That is some exquisite scar work."

"You're right." Sebastian jots something down on the score sheet in front of him.

"Thank you," I say into the microphone. "Next."

A veiled girl steps forward. I'd tried to mentally prepare for this; after all, Queen Lucinda's wedding dress is a popular enough costume to be mass-produced. Not that this girl's costume is. The lace looks too fine and too accurate to the detailed design of the original, down to the tiny seed pearls that I'd seen up close at the traveling *CoRaB* museum exhibit a few years ago; Sebastian and I had blown class to go down to New York City to catch it. Even I hadn't reproduced all those details when

I'd worn the dress. Which, in retrospect, was a good thing since I tore the thing trying to get it off as quickly as possible on the night of the costume party.

Atypically, Sebastian doesn't turn to me to make any comments about the dress, just quietly jots down some notes on his scorecard. I stop myself from making some biting remark about how this version is better than Heather's.

"Thank you, next," I tell the girl, after we've had enough time to take in her costume.

But before the eager twin centaurs behind her can move ahead in line, I hear someone yell out, "No live animals!" It's the poor, frazzled freelancer hired to help run the contest. "Honestly, doesn't anyone read the rules?"

And then we hear a bleat.

Sebastian and I stare at each other, me nearly choking on a bite of devil's food cake I'd just stuffed in my mouth courtesy of our sponsor. We crane our necks and can see, far down the line, the telltale horns of a goat.

Sebastian stares back at me and we both burst out laughing.

Our *CoRaB* finale party is being re-created right in front of our eyes. It's another sign that the universe is giving us a second chance. And this time, I will not screw it up.

"Hey, so, did you make official plans with Heather?" I ask Sebastian casually while a contestant is setting up her papier-mâché Mount Signon backdrop. "When are you guys going out?"

"We haven't set a date yet," Sebastian replies.

"Well, you'd better get on that," I say, as I take out a fresh scorecard. "Beautiful girls won't wait around forever, you know."

"Yeah, I know," Sebastian responds, as he clears his throat and squints up at the stage. "Oh my God." He points at our contestant, who has just whipped out two enormous containers of baking soda and vinegar. "Do you think she's about to make that mountain erupt?"

CHAPTER 17

SEBASTIAN

That. Fucking. Wedding. Dress.

Maybe it's pathetic to blame a cosplay outfit for what happened the night of the finale party, but in my defense, I wasn't thinking straight and hadn't eaten much that day. More to the point, my heart was a battering ram, lurching frantically inside my chest as I surveyed the lounge for Nina, desperate to know if we'd come as corresponding scene partners. Desperate to know if our shared brain had worked its magic again.

When I saw a masked girl in a wig and a veil wearing Lucinda's wedding gown, I felt dizzy with relief.

If I'd been paying closer attention, I would have noticed the lack of detail on the gown. Christ, the family crest wasn't even the correct house colors, the blood splatter looked more like pink lemonade, and a biodegradable spork from the cafeteria was duct-taped to the outside of the dress, as a pathetic representation of Lucinda's dagger. Which—I mean—it's unforgivable. (Of *me*, obviously, for not noticing those details.)

Also unforgivable: trying to slot Nina into a role that wasn't meant for her.

The *CoRaB* books and Westingland were clear on the issue. "When you kiss a friend, the friendship dies."

Nina wasn't any old friend. She was my *best* friend.

If I'm being completely honest . . . my first friend.

Back up. So. My family's originally from Sherborne, in northwest Dorset. There's an abbey in the middle of town, two castles—"New Castle" and "Old Castle," the latter of which is in ruins, and was my favorite—a high street, pubs and shops. It's also home to the boys' school where John le Carré spent an infamously miserable couple of years, but my childhood memories were an idyllic blend of treehouses, netball, and second-hand bookshops.

When I was seven, halfway through the school year, we moved to Upstate New York. Elmira. My accent was one most of the kids hadn't heard live-and-in-person before. That first day at recess, classmates circled me, calling out words and demanding I repeat them back ("Say this! Say that!"), and laughing at the result. After several days of this, the school librarian invited me to spend recess in the library whenever I wanted to, which turned out to be most days. I was a dreamy kid, lost in fantasy worlds, with little interest in team sports, though I loved running and hiking.

My parents were proud that we lived in the same town for a decade, taking me from seven to seventeen. They thought it gave me stability and security. What it really meant was spending grades two through twelve with the same group of people, ostracized as "that weird Brit." By middle school, some of them felt bad about the way they'd teased me, and by high school, some of them tried to befriend me, but I preferred the company of stories, films, telly, and like-minded people I'd met online.

I taught myself how to cook. Turns out you can spend half of every Saturday at a farmers' market, and the other half preparing a meal from scratch. No time to feel lonely if you're always busy. My parents provided a meal budget and I repaid them with three-course dinners on the weekends. Starting at age four, Millie drew the week's menu in crayons and served as the perilous water refiller.

I experienced all the "American school system milestones" of Senior Ditch Day, the SATs, prom (in a group of eight), and a slightly inebriated graduation. My yearbook was signed with bland aphorisms. One anonymous person wrote, "Sorry we gave you so much shit." Realizing that the message could have come from literally anyone in my graduating class was a gut punch.

The August after high school ended, my parents moved back to England with Millie. I stayed in Upstate New York to attend Ithaca College for a degree in film/TV. A merit scholarship provided more than half my tuition and it seemed easier, somehow, to stay put. I may never have belonged in Elmira but that didn't mean I belonged in England. Not anymore.

I knew how to survive, socially: head down, do the work, don't smile too hard at anyone, don't draw attention, don't let anyone look too far down into the gaping maw of your personality. Don't take up too much of anyone's time or expect anything from anyone.

Form only the most superficial of friendships.

And then I met Nina.

The night of the *CoRaB* costume party, I never intended to blurt out what I blurted out. I'm not a writer; that was always Nina's forté. I can appreciate good writing and I can tell when something works for me, and sometimes even why, but I can't create like that.

When I saw her in the bloody wedding outfit, though, a speech formed in my head, so rapid-fire and vital it overrode my circuitry. I'm not saying it was award-worthy or anything, but it happened to be true, and when you're twenty-two years old, and a self-conscious late bloomer, sometimes true is the most you can hope for.

Throat tight, I tugged on her hand and drew her through clusters of people to a quieter section of the lounge. Seeing what'd we built together—a community, a room full of friends—gave me strength.

What I thought: *Hey. You look great.*

What I wanted to say: *I've never fit in anywhere, but I fit with you, and this proves it for the millionth time. The best part is I didn't have to change who I was, I didn't have to pretend to be anyone other than who I am. Except for one thing. I've hidden a part of myself, the part that's* crazy *about you. I'm so crazy about you. That is . . . I think you already know I think the world of you but what I'm asking is . . .*

What I actually said: "Do you want to spend the summer together?" Nina and I were already planning to stick around and get catering jobs after graduation, so I quickly clarified: "Like, *really* together. Together as a couple."

As I said, it wasn't award-worthy. Just pure and unfiltered.

"Yeah, okay," Nina said, before shifting her opaque veil a little to the side, stretching upward, and kissing me. If I hadn't been horrified/proud of myself for laying everything on the line, I might have noticed she didn't smell quite like Nina. But all I could think was, I am kissing Nina. Nina is kissing me. This is actually happening. She's kissing me and—

What I saw: Nina was also, somehow, at the entrance to the lounge, in the same Lucinda wedding dress, only a thousand times more accurate and detailed and thought out. A veil covered her face, too, but I'd know her anywhere.

So who the hell was I kissing?

I ripped my mouth away from the mystery kisser to gape at Nina. Was that a *guy* with her? Did she bring a *date*?

In that instant, everything became clear to me, in a way it never really had before.

She will never show up to a party with you.

"I'll meet you there," she'd said earlier in the day.

She will never be your girlfriend.
She will always be someone else's girlfriend.

"Sebastian, are you okay?" The mystery kisser removed her veil. Heather. An attractive theater major who hung out with us in a group sometimes for Sunday-night *CoRaB* viewings. She'd gotten into the party because she'd provided a bugle horn. The idea was that someone posted at the door would blow on it and announce each guest as they arrived, but it was such an eardrum splitter and conversation destroyer that after the first four people, the instrument was abandoned in the corner.

In retrospect it would've been goddamn helpful!

"I didn't think you remembered about me being a few credits short," Heather marveled, eyes sparkling. "It's so funny we'll both be here this summer."

"Yeah! Ha ha! Right!" My teeth hurt from smiling. They were tiny daggers trying to stab my own mouth.

"I like you, too, by the way. If it weren't already obvious."

"Cool, that's—yeah, very cool."

I wasn't in the room anymore. I was up on the ceiling, looking down at myself in the bloody wedding suit, wondering how I'd gotten there. To anchor myself, I leaned down and gave her another kiss. Heather pulled me closer and deepened the kiss, and the feel of her body against mine was irresistible. She might not smell like Nina, but she smelled nice all the same, like a ripe summer peach. I was tired of being alone, of watching Nina date other people. It was *my* turn, dammit.

When you offer a dehydrated man a bottle of water, he doesn't often check the label. It was exhilarating to be desired.

It didn't matter that the guy I'd seen walk in with Nina had planted himself beside someone else shortly afterward, or that Nina disappeared for most of the night; my epiphany remained. What a relief I hadn't made our friendship awkward! What had I been thinking? This way I got to keep Nina as a friend *and* date someone.

My nervous stomach settled, and I focused on the girl who was to become my first girlfriend.

"Have you been to Cornell Dairy Bar yet?" I asked Heather, already concocting a list of summer fun activities for us.

I couldn't take them back, the things I'd said to her. There was no point in taking them back. Besides, I didn't want to.

Wasn't it time I stopped pining for someone who didn't want me and gave it a shot with someone who, apparently, did?

Or who was happy to give it a try, at least, for the summer?

CHAPTER 18

NINA

On Saturday, I make a point to set my alarm so that I'm up before Sebastian. After three days in a row of him making me breakfast before work, the man deserves an omelet at least.

I work as quietly as I can in the kitchen, chopping up some green peppers, tomatoes, and onions. Sebastian definitely has some fancier ingredients available in his refrigerator (one looks like . . . a cactus?), but I decide to stick with simple and therefore (likely) edible rather than try to out-gourmet-chef him.

By the time the eggs are sizzling, he's up. He walks over to me, groggily mussing up his hair. "What's going on?" He's so confused at the sight of his electric stovetop that he looks like a time traveler frantically wondering how the devil created fire without flames.

"You . . . made me breakfast?" he asks with such wonder in his voice that I have to laugh.

"You do it for me all the time!"

"I know, it's just . . ." He stares at the omelet again. "I don't think anyone's ever made me breakfast before."

"That can't be true. I'm sure your mom's made you breakfast." I take a spatula and carefully flip over the omelet.

"I think she poured some milk into a cereal bowl for me

once," he says as he stares off into the distance. "Froot Loops, if I remember correctly. We had just moved to the States and were trying to assimilate the local cuisine."

"Well, this isn't much fancier," I admit as I slide the omelet onto a plate. "But . . ."

He places a hand on my shoulder. "Thanks, Nina. I love it."

"You haven't tasted it yet!"

He grabs a fork from his silverware drawer, quickly puts a bite into his mouth, and then closes his eyes in pleasure. "Thanks, Nina. I *love* it," he says slower and more emphatically.

"Okay, okay," I say, putting my hands up. "Don't get all actory on me."

"Not acting," he says as he takes a much larger forkful. "This is the nicest thing anyone's done for me in months."

I frown. "And why would that be? Don't the guys ever do anything for you?"

"Oh, of course they do." He waves his hands dismissively. "I'm just the only one who really knows how to cook. You know that. And I like doing it," he adds quickly.

"Sure, but it doesn't mean someone can't order a pizza once in a while. Or . . . make eggs." I gesture to the counter, trying to indicate the whole ten minutes it took to do so.

"It's no big deal. Anyway," he says, changing the subject, "one guess as to what I woke up thinking about."

"Caveman Tal winning the cosplay contest."

He nods at me vigorously. "I mean, I know it's been *three* days, but . . ."

"It's all anyone's been talking about on the socials, too," I say. "But you know we had to give it to him. Anyone who brings in his own stone enclave . . ."

". . . and does live cave painting . . ."

". . . photorealistic live cave painting . . ." I amend.

"Deserves to win. I know," Sebastian concludes.

My phone buzzes. My face falls as I read the message. "Oh noooooo."

"What?" Sebastian says. "What's wrong?"

"It's from Celeste." I show him the text message, her response to my text the night before, asking when would be a good time to pick up my furniture. **You wanted them back? I'm so sorry. I thought you left them for the Salvation Army. They came to pick everything up yesterday.**

"Just . . . why would I do that?" I sputter at Sebastian. "And without telling her?"

I have your bed still though, she writes.

And I only have one second to feel a small sense of relief before an image comes through that is so horrible, I actually drop my phone. Sebastian heroically catches it before it smashes all over the tiled kitchen floor. He looks at it and does a double take.

"Is that . . ."

"Leeches," I squeak out. "All over my bed."

"Um . . . she wrote you another message." He holds the phone up for me to read.

I thought "relaxed leeches, relaxed client." But I can take them off and have the bed ready for you by tonight. (Off-topic: do you think I can trademark the "relaxed leeches" line?)

I just stare at Sebastian from in between my fingers, shaking my head in horror.

He claps his hands together. "Right. So who's ready to go to a mattress store?"

"Firm. But is it too firm?" Sebastian asks, his voice a little flattened from his prone position.

"There's no such thing as too firm," I say, staring at the ceiling from the mattress next to him.

"That's what she said!" Sebastian says.

I flip over to my side to arch an eyebrow at him. "Really?"

"Sorry," he says with a shrug. "I forgot you weren't Matty for a second."

"Story of my life," I say as I get up from my mattress. "This one's definitely a sinkhole." I walk over and press my hand down on the one Sebastian's lying on. "Hmmmm."

"Well, hop on in and give it a test drive." He pats the spot next to him but makes no move to get up.

Right. *It's just like I'm Matty,* I think, and lie down next to him. My first thought is that queen beds are smaller than you think, especially when a long-limbed person you're determined to keep friend zoned is giving off body heat mere inches away from you. My second thought: "This is pretty perfect."

Sebastian glances down at the tag under his elbow. "And it's on sale."

"So it just upgraded to perfect." I press one more hand down on the mattress. "Unless you really think it's too firm?"

"Well, it's *your* mattress. You're the one who'll be sleeping in it. Well, you and . . . Ennis."

And right on cue, my phone buzzes. I look down. "Speak of the devil," I mutter.

Sebastian clears his throat and sits up, swinging his legs off the bed. "Do you want him to come try it out too?"

"That won't be necessary." I don't add, *Because I'll be shocked if my relationship with a new mattress doesn't outlast this romantic one.*

I get the salesman's attention. "We'll take this one."

"Oh, great," he says as he checks his tablet. "Our soonest delivery date is Wednesday. Is that okay?"

"Guess it has to be," I say with a smile. "Thanks."

"I'll start ringing you up," he says as he scans the tag.

I turn to Sebastian. "So, Ennis wants to hang out tonight and I was thinking, maybe he could come over and hang out with the two of us."

"Uh, like a third wheel thing?" Sebastian asks, looking confused.

"No! Of course not. Just a meeting my friends thing. He actually hasn't. Met any of my friends, I mean. Except Celeste, but you know, 'friend' might be too strong a word there."

"Oh, okay then. Sure."

But he definitely doesn't look too sure about it so I add, "Maybe you can invite Heather, too? Sort of like a double date?"

His face lights up. "That could be fun. I could make dinner!"

"Or we could order in," I offer.

"We could, but there's a garlic noodle dish with ginger soy glazed chicken that I've been dying for you to try. Works great with the egg noodles Sam got us too." He adds, almost as an afterthought, "And I promised Heather I'd cook for her."

"All right. Let's do it then."

We smile at each other.

"And how will you guys be paying?" the salesman asks.

"Uh. Me. I'll be paying," I say as I dig through my purse for a credit card. "We're just roommates," I tell him unnecessarily.

"Sure, great," the salesman says as he swipes my card, completely unbothered by whatever our relationship is or isn't.

"Okay, how can I help?" I ask as soon as I've washed my hands at the kitchen sink.

"Help?" Sebastian says. "No, see, I'm supposed to be cooking for you."

"You're supposed to be cooking for *Heather*," I correct. "And *my* boyfriend. So, yes, I'd like to help."

Sebastian eyes me skeptically.

"What?" I ask, mock-offended. "You think I can't cook?"

"No, of course I don't . . ." he says quickly.

"Well, you'd be right. Honestly, the omelet was the extent of my skills. But I can learn. I'm a quick study."

He gives me a grin. "Well, the vegetables were very well chopped. So if you'd like to mince the garlic and slice the green onions, that'd be great."

"Sure," I say, taking the vegetables out of the bag and placing them on the cutting board Sebastian has already gotten out for me. But as I pick up his übersharp chef's knife, I realize there's already a problem. "Uh . . . there's a difference between mincing and slicing?"

"A little. Let me show you." He takes the knife, puts the flat surface on the garlic, and then uses the heel of his hand to whack the knife down. When he removes the knife, the peel slides right off, like a magic trick. Then he rocks the knife back and forth across the clove, somehow making tiny, perfectly square pieces in the process.

I have no idea why but his precision is . . . sexy?

What is wrong with you, Nina? It's literally tiny garlic. Tiny garlic is not sexy.

"And then with the slicing, just curl your fingers under to make sure they're out of the way. About this size is good." He demonstrates with a few strokes on the green onion, making small, bright green cylinders, then turns the knife handle toward me.

"Got it," I say, as I take the knife from him, careful for our fingers not to brush. It's obviously been too long since Ennis and I had sex if mincing is making me all hot and bothered.

But then he slides behind me to get to the stovetop and his shirt brushes against my back anyway and somehow, the sliding of soft fabric between us is even more electric than if we actually touched.

We're just roommates. I echo in my head what I said to the salesman. And ex-best friends trying to return to that.

"If you could do six cloves of garlic and four green onions, that would be perfect," he says. "I need some for my chicken marinade, too."

"You got it," I say as I slowly start to chop. There's no way I have Sebastian's speed, but I can try to have his accuracy.

In the ten minutes it takes me to get the vegetables ready, he's already mixed up two different sauces and has them bubbling on the stove. When I ask him for another task, he asks if I'm up for making the noodles.

"Pasta! That I can do!" I say with slightly more enthusiasm than required. He laughs at me. "I just don't want you to think I'm totally inept in the kitchen."

"I think you're perfect at everything," Sebastian says while checking on his marinade and therefore not looking at me.

He takes a spoonful of his sauce, blows on it, and holds it out to me. I taste it. It's sticky, sweet, and completely delicious, of course.

"Ohmygod. Wow," I say as he grins at me. "Heather is going to flip."

He nods and gets back to work.

Once the pasta is drained, Sebastian puts the marinade in a Ziploc in the fridge. "Got to give that half an hour." He looks at the Jeff the Warlock clock that we moved from his bedroom to the kitchen wall last week. "They'll be here in about an hour, right?"

I nod. "Plenty of time to get ready."

We're facing each other, and he leans over to reach behind me. It takes me a second to realize he's just wiping some sauce off the counter.

"Right. So I'll get to it then," I say as I head to my room. "I already took a shower this morning, so the hot water's all yours," I call out behind me.

"I know. Thanks."

I close the door to my room, and rummage around in my suitcase and closet for something to wear. (Note to self: Go to the Salvation Army to see if I can salvage my own dresser and desk, or at least find some cheap replacements.)

It's a date. But a casual at-home date, I think. My hand goes to a flowy top with little embroidered flowers at the collar and a pair of black ankle-cut jeans. *But my boyfriend is going to be there. And, judging by my abject horniness, I probably do need to get laid at some point soon.* I move my hands away from the jeans to a short denim skirt, eyeing a pair of black espadrilles at the bottom of my closet that I know make my legs look at least two inches longer than they are.

Heather will be there too.

And it's this thought which, inexplicably, leads my hand over to the coral dress I bought on a whim from ModCloth's sale section. It has a sweetheart neckline that dips just low enough to reveal a hint of cleavage, a slightly flared skirt that's perfect for a confidence-boosting mirror twirl if not actual dancing (which I doubt is happening tonight), and a thin gold belt that cinches in at the perfect place on my body. Its color complements my olive-toned skin (I once went on three dates with an artist who explained why, chromatically, the green undertones of my skin pair well with anything in the red family). The hem of the skirt comes up about an inch above my knee which means that, with the espadrilles, yup, mile-high legs. Or, at the very least, kilometer-high, if we're thinking in Sebastian terms.

He's already out of his room by the time I emerge from mine. I hear his breath hitch when he sees me, and I pretend not to notice, focusing on clasping a statement necklace filled with chunky emerald-colored stones.

I look up when I'm done. He's dressed in jeans and a soft hunter-green T-shirt that were clearly picked to bring out his hazel eyes.

"That's a great dress," he says as he opens his George Foreman Grill to check on the chicken. "You look great."

"Thanks," I say, just as the door buzzes. "I'll get it."

I press the intercom, hear Ennis's voice, and buzz him in. Then I wait for him by the door while Sebastian continues to futz around in the kitchen.

"Hi!" I say enthusiastically when I see Ennis.

"Wow," he says, looking me over. "You look great!"

"Thanks!" I say as I fling myself into his arms, trying not to overanalyze why those same exact words coming out of Sebastian's mouth gave me more of a zing than they did when my boyfriend said them.

I kiss Ennis and then walk him over to Sebastian. "A more formal, non-parking lot introduction is probably in order. Sebastian, Ennis. Ennis, Sebastian."

Ennis grins and shakes Sebastian's hand; then he nods his head toward the cutout Lucinda in the corner of the living room. "Aren't you going to more formally introduce me to your girlfriend too?"

Sebastian gives a tight smile. "Good one, man. Hey, Nina, would you mind getting the salad out of the fridge?"

"You made a salad?" I ask, perplexed. "When?"

"I threw it together while you were getting ready. It's a really simple one," he says.

It looks anything but when I take it out. Feta cheese, a perfectly sliced egg, and walnuts all artfully arranged over a bed of romaine in a teal ceramic bowl.

The doorbell rings just as I've grabbed the bowl and Sebastian is heating up the noodles in his garlic sauce.

"I'll get it," Ennis volunteers.

I take the salad to the table, then go to the cabinets to get plates and silverware. I'm not looking when the door opens but I hear Heather's voice.

"Oh, hello," she says to Ennis. "Are you Sebastian's roommate?"

"Not me," he says. "That would be her." I turn around in time to see him pointing at me.

Heather follows the trail until she's looking me full in the face, and I can tell she recognizes me, even though we only saw each other a few times before I made my dramatic exit from Ithaca.

"Oh. Huh," she says. "Hello. Nina, right?"

CHAPTER 19

SEBASTIAN

"Tell us more about the scene you were both in." Nina twirls her fork around the last noodle in her bowl and lifts it to her mouth, her eyes darting between mine and Heather's.

"Viewer discretion is advised," I warn. "This may not be appropriate dinner talk."

"Sex or violence?"

"Both!" Heather announces cheerfully. I grin at her.

"Wait, oh, no," Nina says. "Does someone get beheaded during a BJ?"

"No, but you're in the right ballpark," I reply. "Shit, I sounded like Matty again."

"How *is* Matty?" Heather asks, leaning forward. She's wearing a Henley shirt tucked into wide-legged jeans with fringe at the bottom, as though she drove down from Laurel Canyon, circa 1971, to join us for dinner. I like it.

"He's good," I tell her. "He moved in with his lady love recently, hence my rooming with . . ." I indicate Nina and also turn back to Nina to finish answering her question: "Let me put it this way: *CoRaB*'s tradition of depressing nudity is alive and well."

"So you're saying there will be a lot of confused boners when it airs."

"*Every CoRaB* boner is a confused boner. Your boss should use that in the promos: 'If you miss being disturbed by your own reactions, the wait is over.'"

Nina laughs and my heartrate skyrockets. Will her laugh ever stop feeling like a prize? I tear my eyes from Nina and pivot toward my date.

"Food all right?" I ask Heather, in what I hope is a curious tone of voice rather than a concerned one. I can't help noticing that half of her meal remains, in stark contrast to everyone else's cleaned-out bowls.

"Could've used more garlic," she says.

"Oh. Really?"

"I'm kidding. It's good, thank you. I just had a big lunch. Hey, remember Moosewood?"

"From *Rocky and Bullwinkle*?" Ennis cuts in. It's the most energized I've ever seen him.

"This great vegetarian place in Ithaca, where we went to school," Heather explains.

"Seb swore to never go," Nina says.

"Did he?" says Heather, before glancing back at me. "We went there, what, twice a week?"

"I saw the error of my ways," I admit. "Although keep in mind the only vegetarian meal I'd had before that was . . ."

"The veggie sub at Subway." Nina again. Our eyes meet and I wonder if she's remembering the look on my face when I bit into that limp lettuce.

"So Nina, did you move out here the same time as Sebastian and the guys?" Heather asks.

"No, I only got here about two months ago. I'm still in denial about the lack of public transportation."

"Oh my gosh, same. I miss the 'L' so badly. That's what we call the subway in Chicago."

"What made you decide to head west?" Nina asks. I'm grateful that she's chatting so warmly with Heather. I should probably return the favor with Ennis, but I have zero interest in anything he has to say, and I'm not a good enough actor to pretend otherwise.

"I'm not sure how long I'll stay . . ." Heather begins.

"Famous last words," says Ennis.

". . . but it seemed important that I give it a try before I turn thirty, and see if I can make in it in film or TV. If not, I'll head home and keep up my theater work."

I glance at Heather's half-eaten bowl of food again, wondering if she's avoiding carbs and wishing I'd known beforehand. "Shoot, I should've asked if you have any dietary restrictions. Is your team . . . ?"

"Starving me?"

An actress's team, I've learned over my years in LA, consists of, but is not limited to: agent, manager, publicist, stylist, Reiki healer, hypnotist, "exhaustion expert" (dealer . . . of . . . let's call them vitamin B12 shots), and masseuse. The first four typically put pressure on talent to lose weight, and the last four enable it. Either way, it's not a topic that women in showbiz can avoid.

"No, though an agent I met with on Friday casually dropped the info that, contrary to popular belief, people don't need *all* their ribs."

"Jesus!" I shout and Nina and Ennis, who've been talking to each other, look over.

Heather laughs and points at me. "Gotcha. Again. I've never had the 'ribs are overrated' chat because I decided early on to niche myself in best friend roles instead of leading lady. That way, I'm allowed a quirk, and my quirk is 'Looks like an adult woman.'"

"Excellent. I'm glad they're not pressuring you. You look amazing by the way." I reach for her hand across the table and squeeze it. Her manicure's impeccable and her skin is smooth and cool to the touch. "But then you always did."

She seems pleased. "Thanks, Sebastian. You too. Wait—

unless your team's trying to starve *you*, and the reason you asked me was a veiled cry for help?"

"I am no longer in possession of a team, thank God. Or at least, they no longer send me out for anything."

"Was your agent good to you in general, though? My manager in Chicago's been setting me up with meetings, and I'm always curious to hear about who to trust and who to avoid."

"I basically parted ways with them, but I'd be happy to refer you."

"Thanks. I'd appreciate that."

Heather and I continue to hold hands across the table. It felt natural when I reached for her, but now it feels forced, as though we're back at the costume party and I've been paired up with her for reasons that don't entirely make sense.

"You guys are both, like, obsessed fans, right?" Ennis asks. "What's the best part of working on the show? I don't watch much TV myself, but I remember what it was like to be into something."

"Like the *Rocky and Bullwinkle* show?" I mutter under my breath.

Ennis either doesn't hear me or doesn't care.

Then the weirdest thing happens. I can't answer his question about the best part of working on the show. I rack my brain for pleasant anecdotes, but all I can see is Rob in the men's bathroom during my first visit to the studio, my ponytail being chopped off by the hair and makeup department, that obnoxious AD telling me he was more British than I am, and the endless hours driving back and forth on the 405 and never seeming to get anywhere. I drop Heather's hand and rub at my wrist, which is perpetually bruised and sore from being handcuffed to the heavy briefcase three times a week.

"Was it something I said?" Ennis jokes.

"There are so many great things, who can even begin," I reply in a bright voice.

Nina tilts her head at me. Something about her expression prompts a genuinely good memory from my job.

"I met Westingland's Wiki when I had to drop off a script page at her house. That was cool," I say.

Ennis looks to Nina for a translation.

"J. J. Westingland is the author of the books the show is based on, and she created such a rich and detailed world she had to outsource her research to this woman named Olive," Nina clarifies. "We call her Westingland's Wiki."

Nina clears her throat, and anticipatory joy sparks up my spine, because that's the noise she makes when she's about to launch into an impression: "'As you know,'" Nina says, in a pitch-perfect parody of Olive from a behind-the-scenes clip we saw once, "'J. J. only came up with five words for the Ageless language: 'ancestor,' 'honor,' 'duty,' 'love,' and 'slop.'"

I laugh so hard I start coughing.

Nina doubles down: "'Using my advanced degree in linguistics, I extrapolated outward from those sounds and meanings to construct a guidebook of terms and phrases using a combination of Old English, Latin, and the sound my cat makes when she would prefer not to go on a walk.'"

I slap the table, startling Heather. "I saw the cat! Or at least, *a* cat, staring at me from on top of her bookshelf, with a leash and collar dangling from its neck."

"And you didn't liberate the poor creature?" Nina says.

"That's a question that will haunt me the rest of my days, Nina."

"Anyone up for dessert?" Nina stands to clear the dishes.

"Does the Yiga Clan like bananas?" I reply and Nina guffaws.

Ennis and Heather look at each other. Heather shrugs.

"Is this more TV stuff?" Ennis asks.

"Sorry, it's from *Breath of the Wild*," Nina replies. "*Legend of Zelda?*"

Heather's smile is strained. "I've actually got to be up early tomorrow, so I'm going to head out, but thanks for the offer."

Ennis meanders to the couch—aka *my bed*—and stretches out on it. As predicted, he didn't bat an eye at the Kingdom of Six quilt, but when I steal a look at Heather, she's squinting at it, perplexed.

I suddenly feel self-conscious, and move to block her gaze. "Sorry you have to go. Can I walk you to your car?"

"Sure. Nice seeing you again, Nina, and nice meeting you, Ennis."

We ride the elevator in silence and emerge from the building onto Third Street.

"Have you been to the Farmers Market at the Grove yet? I love having it within walking distance," I remark.

"Mmm, I bet."

"Also, Molly Malone's is a block away and has decent live music, according to Sam, anyway. I'm all, 'They sure sang and played those instruments, didn't they?'"

She nods but doesn't take the conversational ball and run with it. The air feels heavy with something and I don't have to guess what it is. Nina and my Fugue-GetAboutIt state is alive and well, despite going missing for five years. A familiar apology, honed from past conversations with Matty, rises up my throat.

"Sorry that Nina and I got a bit hyper back there. The show tends to bring that out in us, but it was rude and I should've been more aware of it."

"It's not that. You guys are friends and of course you're going to be laughing together about your favorite show when you both work on it. But when I asked you to cook dinner for me, I thought it would be the two of us. We didn't get to catch up as much as I was hoping."

"Then we'll make it you and me next time. If you'd like a next time, that is."

Her shoulders relax. "That sounds great."

"Okay, I'll plan something. Does next weekend work? Oh, wait—my sister's going to be here, but I'd love to see you after she heads out."

"Of course. Mindy, right? In England?"

"Close. She's called Millie, but yeah."

"Enjoy your time with Millie. She's quite a bit younger than you, if I remember correctly?"

"Yes. My parents like to birth a child in one country, raise it till the age of seven, and then bugger off with it to the opposite side of the Atlantic. We were both raised as only children, in a way."

"Like some type of social experiment."

"So *that's* why a documentary crew was always following us around."

Heather smiles and this time it looks genuine. Crisis averted.

"Do you really have to get up early tomorrow, or were you trying to escape?" I ask gently.

"No, that was true. I'm hiking Kenter Canyon."

"Oh, cool! Have fun. I still haven't made it out there, but it's supposed to be really scenic."

Heather and I hiked a lot during our summer together, and I know it's important to her that she have that outlet.

She climbs in her car and I do that thing where I smack the top of the vehicle before she drives off, which I've never understood but have seen in countless movies. I should ask Nina where it comes from.

No, actually, I should not ask Nina anything. She's trying to spend time with her boyfriend right now and I need to make myself scarce. My phone's in the apartment so I don't have any way of knowing when she and Ennis will be—ugh—"done" with each other, so I walk around the Tar Pits for a while, empathizing with the woolly mammoths and dire wolves who got sucked into a deadly morass from which they'd never climb out.

Eventually I find myself back in my building, knocking on

Sam's door. He greets me with a pizza slice in hand and an action flick on TV.

"Hey, how'd the noodles turn out? Did you bring me any?"

"Shit, I should've made extra. I'm sorry."

"I'm joking, I didn't expect you to. How'd it go with Heather?"

"Iffy. I wasn't a good host."

"I find that difficult to believe."

"Anyway, Nina and Ennis need space." I spread my hands open in a helpless gesture.

"Mi couch-bed is su couch-bed if it comes to that." He makes room for me on the couch and we watch the movie to the end, and then through every credit, which is something I never did until I moved to LA. It's the respectful thing to do when you work in a one-industry town.

"Is it possible to have the Sunday blues on a Saturday?" I ask.

Sam frowns. "The name suggests no."

"Right."

Sunday blues stemmed from my childhood. After I moved to New York and started second grade, every Sunday afternoon brought with it an insidious feeling that struck around four p.m., asking me if I'd *truly* finished my homework, and casually dismantling whatever pleasant feelings I'd managed to accrue from not being at school the past day and a half.

I haven't felt this sensation in ages, and I can't pinpoint why it's hitting so hard now. Killer job? Check. Awesome roommate? Check.

Maybe if I focus on the next movie Sam chooses, I can pull up the drawbridge before the blues slip past my castle walls and take the throne.

My "Sunday" blues lingered for days. By Tuesday, the sensation had grown rather than abated. It didn't help that I woke up Tuesday morning to the sight of the Burger King crown on

Cardboard Lucinda's head, indicating that Nina and Ennis wanted privacy tonight. Nina was long gone already, and now Ennis would learn about her day before I did. He was *completely* unworthy of that honor. I craved a cigarette, and I could've channeled my misery into a gym workout, but instead I channeled it into baking a masterpiece seraphim food cake. The briefcase wouldn't be ready at Vasquez until eleven a.m. today, so I had extra time before I had to leave.

When I drove past the security gate of the studio, cake in tow, there was nowhere to park; the lot was overrun with Star Waggons (trailers for the actors), as well as a brigade of aluminum buses I'd never seen before. The air rippled with tension and an unpleasant smell as I trudged a quarter-mile to the studio entrance from the alternate lot.

Arms shaking, legs sore, sweat gathering along my temple and spine, I couldn't shake the sensation of dread that increased with every step closer to my destination.

So that's *what this is. Not Sunday blues; dread.*

I dreaded my sojourns at the studio.

If I hadn't been so perplexed and disturbed by this revelation, I might have been aware of certain noises surrounding me.

What noises? Oh, just hoofbeats and a scream of "Loose horse!" before a galloping destrier in blinders and medieval armor thundered past within a foot of me, causing me to holler, jump backward, and drop my cake.

Heart bashing against my rib cage, I windmilled pointlessly with my arms before landing squarely on my shoulder on the asphalt next to the smashed cake, all of which was witnessed by six horse trainers and David Sherman, the show's resident three-time Emmy winner for his portrayal of Jeff the Warlock.

"So *then*, when I'm convalescing with an ice pack in Dominic and Daniela's office—have you met the siblings yet? They run the place—Janine calls and goes, 'Before you leave, I have a quick, easy task for you. A charity auction needs a hundred and fifty signed scripts by the weekend, so try to get as many cast members as possible to sign them—the more signatures, the more they'll be worth.'"

"No," Nina groans sympathetically, as I recount the incident to her that evening at home.

"Oh, yes."

"In what universe is that task 'quick' or 'easy'?"

"Agreed. I hobble outside to the set, with the briefcase attached, of course—I swear it gets heavier each week, and I still don't know what's inside it. I'm also carrying a pile of scripts and trying to figure out how I'm going to fulfill Janine's command, when David Sherman comes to my rescue again."

Nina grins ear to ear and claps her hands. "Yessss! Tell me!"

"He goes, 'You took quite a fall earlier—are you okay?' in the nicest voice, and I was struck mute."

"The most evil character on the show. . . ."

"Was the *only* person to inquire about my well-being. Yep."

I sink back into the memory. David stands four feet eight inches, but I'd never realized until meeting him how he always hunched himself even further to play Jeff. Also, he looked completely transformed with a smile on his face and his signature goatee shaved off. I'll remember our interaction the rest of my life.

"You're my favorite character!" I'd blurted out. "I mean, your *character* is my favorite character. You're my favorite *actor*."

"That's very kind. Are you with craft services?"

"No, I'm a PA. I made the cake on my own time, because I wanted . . . anyway, it doesn't matter. I'm still feeling my way around."

"Young blood," David said in his creepy, croaky Jeff voice before giving a hearty laugh. "The show is lucky to have you, making cakes for everyone like that. Better luck next time; what was it, three layers?"

"Yeah."

"Mr. Sherman, that's a wrap for you, see you tomorrow," the AD called out.

David nodded at me and walked away.

I came to my senses before he got too far.

"Wait! Would it be—could you mind . . . I mean, *would* you mind signing a few of these?"

I set the enormous stack of script title pages on a table.

David stared at me, deadpan. "A few?"

Between my embarrassing fall, my throbbing shoulder, my ruined cake, and my fanboy flailing, I felt reduced. Utterly, crushingly reduced.

"Any amount would help. It's for a charity auction."

He considered this, then pulled over a chair and sat down. "I'll do fifty. How about that?"

"Brilliant, thank you."

"Then what happened?" Nina asks, pulling me out of the memory. I stare into space, barely cognizant of her question.

"Let me get you some water." She returns with a glass filled to the top. She places it carefully in my hand, but even so, it nearly slips from my grasp.

"Thanks. Yeah. It was a long day."

"You drifted off there for a sec. Take a moment."

I scratch the hair at the nape of my neck, stalling, uncertain how I can possibly finesse the next part to spare her the truth about Roberto. "Right. What happened next was, I noticed Rob squinting at us. He seemed curious about what David and I were up to, so I waved him over, trying to be friendly, hoping that if he saw his castmate signing scripts, he might feel inclined to join us, or even slighted if I didn't ask him, too."

"Oh, God. What did he say?"

"Um, I'm not sure I remember."

Our eyes lock. "Yes, you do," Nina says. "It was something awful, wasn't it?"

I swallow. "He came over, got up in my face, and whispered: 'NEVER make me walk to you.'"

Nina's jaw slowly drops.

"He was probably joking," I say weakly.

She looks down and shakes her head. Her jaw is tight. "No. He wasn't. Because he's awful."

We stare at each other for another long beat.

I break first. "So awful!"

"He's the worst!"

"I didn't want to say anything because I wanted everything to be wonderful for you."

"I wanted everything to be wonderful for *you*!"

Hoping to entertain her, I slide onto the floor and curl into a fetal position, rocking to and fro. "I hate him so much! Why is he allowed to exist!"

She joins me on the ground, two traumatized, low-level pawns, rocking for their lives.

"They don't reimburse for gas," I tell her. "So every time I drive to the studio I *lose* money. It's like I'm paying *them* to work there."

She makes a sound between a laugh and a howl. "They made me stay up until three a.m. on a Saturday to announce Stu Stu's cameo!"

"I need workers' comp and physical therapy from the briefcase! And now my shoulder!"

"I had to look at Pathoro's torture scene frame by frame to find the exact right one to meme!"

"Roberto made me flush his toilet!"

Nina stops rocking. "You win."

"That's not winning!"

Frenetic laughter overtakes us. The absurdity of our surroundings—*CoRaB* quilt on the wall, Lucinda cardboard cutout in the corner, Jeff clock glowering from the kitchen—launches us into another fit of laughter.

I rub my eyes and sit up with a groan, unable to determine which part of my body is in the most pain. "What I'm about to tell you can never leave this room."

"I swear on the quilt."

"Picture me standing there on set, with Roberto's rancid, entitled breath still warm on my face. Are you picturing it?"

"In high-def, with smell-o-vision."

"It was in that moment I made a decision. I gathered up all the Sharpies and script title pages and I decided I would go home and forge everyone's signatures one hundred and fifty times. This is an act for which I will no doubt be fired, should it be discovered. Worse, I'll be sent to fandom hell after I die. So if you want plausible deniability, I suggest you leave while you still can."

"Sebastian," she jokes, her hand on my good shoulder. "We're already *in* fandom hell."

Chapter 20

NINA

"How's this?" Sebastian asks as he shows me his facsimile of Francis Jean Taylor's signature. It was easy enough to find examples of all of the main cast members' autographs online (we stuck with the three main actors and Lou Trewoski since we have to do everything times 150). Less easy is getting those signatures to match.

Case in point: Sebastian's attempt looks like it was definitely done by an under-five . . . as in under five years old.

"Er . . ." I say as I look at the shaky capital F. "Maybe I should try to handle her. That's some pretty impressive cursive. And I do have calligraphy experience."

He grins. "I almost forgot about your Etsy enterprise." For a few summers in high school and college, I did some wedding calligraphy for extra cash. I had to put an end to it when tendonitis and my shoulder pain merged into one giant mess of pinched nerves and strained muscles and my physical therapist basically banned me from the surprisingly lucrative world of place cards.

Speaking of which, I look over with a worried expression at Sebastian's wrist. It looks bruised and angry.

"Is that from the fall?" I ask.

He looks down. "No. Not this. This is from the briefcase. *This* is from the fall." He rolls up the sleeve of his shirt, where the upper part of his bicep is starting to turn a deep shade of purple. Even he looks surprised at its appearance. "Oh. It didn't look like that a few hours ago."

"That must really hurt," I commiserate.

"Eh. It's all relative. The abject humiliation was worse, honestly."

"Okay, new plan," I say, as I go into the kitchen and fill a Ziploc with ice, wrapping it in paper towels before I bring it back to him.

"Is your other arm okay?" I ask. "Can you use it to hold this on your shoulder?" I give him the ice.

"Sure. But, like I said, I'm fine." He doesn't move to take the ice from me.

I press it into his hand. "Rest up. I'll take care of the signatures. You . . . watch this." I turn on the TV and navigate over to a random season of *Top Chef Masters*.

He visibly relaxes as soon as he hears the first sound effect of a sharpening knife and Curtis Stone announcing that this season will be their "toughest competition yet."

In the meantime, I text Ennis to cancel our plans and apologize for the late notice. There's no way I can abandon Seb right now. Then I pick up a Sharpie and practice Francis Jean's signature a couple of times on scrap paper before I give it a go for real on one of the scripts. Not bad.

"Wow, that looks really good," Sebastian says as he looks over my shoulder and then compares it to the one he attempted. "I'm an embarrassment."

"You're right," I say solemnly. "You'll never get into forgery school."

He smiles and then leans back. For a while, there's just the sounds of Sharpie on paper and the chefs on TV running around. I've reached the end of the stack and moved on to practicing Roberto Ricci's signature by the time Sebastian speaks again.

"Seriously though. Why is he such a dick?" He points to Roberto's name.

I shrug. "Isn't that the modus operandi for most actors?"

"Not really," Sebastian says. "Or at least a lot of the struggling ones I know are nice. And normal. Just trying to make it in a cutthroat business. I guess I don't understand why, if you've managed to do it, managed to make an impossible dream come true, you wouldn't be . . . I don't know, nice? Or, at the very least, grateful."

I think for a second as I move on to signing Roberto's name on the real script pages, too. "I think if you have something long enough, it becomes the norm. Fame, money, power. It's human nature to crave more than what you have and if you already have a lot . . . well, that doesn't stop the craving."

"That makes sense," Sebastian says after a moment. "You know, you were always good at figuring out character motivation."

I smile. "Thank you."

"Did you ever consider trying to write?" he asks. "As a career?"

I shrug as I dot a "Ricci" and move on to the next page in the pile. "I sort of moved out here for that," I admit. "To try and get one of the writing internships on the networks."

Sebastian sits up. "You did? Why didn't you tell me?"

"Because I didn't get into any of them. And then I got this gig. And . . . I don't know. It hasn't been the best, seeing how the sausage is made so to speak. I just wondered if it was going to be worth it to spend so much time and energy pursuing this thing—this impossible thing as you just so astutely pointed out. Only to be disappointed by it if I ever did manage to 'make it.'"

"By that logic, no one would ever try anything," Sebastian says gently, forcing me to look up at him.

"I know . . ." I say softly. "I guess . . . I don't know. I've been here less than three months and all I see is a land of crushed dreams. The Uber drivers with a screenplay . . ."

"Does Ennis have a screenplay?" he asks.

"A voice-over demo actually. Even though I keep telling him he's the opposite of that saying, 'You have a face for radio.'"

Sebastian laughs. "In LA, even the radio faces are beautiful."

"Yup," I say as I continue to write. I'm getting into the groove now and am almost through with Roberto's signatures, too. "What about you and pursuing your dreams?"

"Ah," Sebastian says. "That's where I've figured out the secret. If you don't have a dream, no one can crush it, Nina."

"What about cooking?"

"What about it?"

I raise an eyebrow at him. "You love it. You're great at it. Why not do something with that?"

"Because I love it," he replies. "And I don't want to stop loving it."

"See?" I say smugly. "That's exactly what I said."

"Touché," he replies.

I switch over to the tab with David Sherman's signature and start practicing that. "What about that cookbook you mentioned the other day? The *Castles of Rust and Bone* one. Don't you already have a few recipes for it?"

"Eight or nine," he says. "The Seraphim Cake. The Baby Backstab Ribs. The Mount Signon Flambé . . ."

"So put together a proposal. I know the marketing guy who's heading up the show's merchandising. Put in some Duncan Hines ingredients and, honestly, I think it'll be an easy sell." I don't hear anything so I look up again to see Sebastian staring at me in wonder.

"Really?" he asks.

"Of course, really. What's the point of having these degrading jobs if we can't use them to get our foot in the door for something we actually want to do?" I point at him with my uncapped Sharpie.

"Well, yeah but . . . how exactly are you following that philosophy for yourself?"

"What do you mean?"

"Don't you have the cast and crew's contact info at your fingertips? Couldn't you, say, email Lou Trewoski and see if you could get into the writers' room, just to observe it?"

I laugh. "Sure. I could also get myself fired. Pretty sure that's a huge breach of my responsibilities."

Sebastian shrugs. "Maybe if we've learned anything from this conversation, it's that getting fired wouldn't be such a bad thing."

"Right. Except for that whole rent and groceries thing," I say as I finish off another signature.

"I think you'd be surprised how much of getting ahead in LA is just getting up the nerve to talk to people. Especially people you genuinely admire and who, more likely than not, are dying for an ego boost." He leans back and does his best Jack Nicholson impression. "This is Tinseltown, Jake."

I shake my head. "I do not think Lou Trewoski is sitting around waiting for a twenty-seven-year-old interim social media coordinator to cold call him and tell him how much she admires his work."

"Wow. You know nothing about Hollywood," Sebastian says.

"Ew," I say as I hit him softly with a pillow.

"Hey! I'm injured," he replies.

"I know. So why don't you go brainstorm some more punny recipes and let me finish this in peace, will you?" I pick up the pillow and gently place it behind him.

He stares up at the ceiling and I can practically see a cartoon circle of ingredients dancing around his head. "If I can only figure out how to make Warlock Fingers into a thing."

I grin as I get back to work.

* * *

An hour later, I've finally gotten through all the scripts. Sebastian is in his room, dictating recipe ideas to his phone.

My hand is cramped up. I wiggle it before I go knock on his door.

He opens it, his eyes slightly manic with inspiration. I smile. I know that look. I would get it myself sometimes when I was on a particular roll with a scene I was writing or a story arc idea I had. "How's it going?"

"Great," he says. "I have at least twenty-five ideas going."

"Awesome," I reply. "I'm done with the scripts." I show him the neat pile stacked on the coffee table.

He walks over and picks up the top sheet. When he turns to me, he almost looks like he's going to cry. "You're an angel," he whispers.

I shrug. "I'm sure you'd do the same for me. You know, should I ever need you to forge six hundred celebrity autographs at a moment's notice."

"I can't ever thank you enough." He starts to lift his arms, maybe to envelop me in a hug, but a wave of pain ripples across his face. He clamps his hand down on his injured shoulder.

"Can I take a look at your arm again?" I ask.

He nods, sits down, and rolls his sleeve up.

I touch it gently. It feels hot. "I think you should maybe see a doctor," I say.

"The on-set medic said it was fine. Just a bruised bone maybe." He winces as I gently press on his shoulder.

"I think it would help if I wrapped it up. So that you don't move it in your sleep," I say.

"Okay," he replies.

"Do you have bandages?"

"Medicine cabinet."

I nod and go to find them. Then I sit down on the couch and stare at his shoulder for a few seconds before I realize I have no idea what I'm doing. I grab my phone and find a video that guides me on how to wrap up a shoulder injury. I try to work as gently as I can as I follow the instructions.

"I feel like the millennial version of Belle," I joke, thinking of the scene where she's tending to the Beast's wounds. "YouTube instead of a magic mirror."

I look up, smiling at Sebastian, expecting him to crack a joke back. Instead his face looks oddly stricken.

And then I remember. He had a crush on a girl named Belle at Ithaca. I once overheard him and Maddie talking about her, and I'd been hurt that he'd never brought her up to me. I once even casually broached the subject of crushes, specifically trying to cajole him to spill the beans. I'd been unsuccessful.

And judging by the look on his face, it's probably not worth bringing up now either.

"All done," I say in a chipper voice, using the clip to secure the bandage around his arm.

"Thanks," he says, clearing his throat. "If you don't mind, I think I'm going to call it a night." He reaches into a storage trunk by the couch and takes out his pillow, placing it on the head of the couch.

"Yeah, of course," I say. "Except you know there's no way in hell I'm going to let you sleep on the couch tonight, right?" I point to his arm. "You're going to murder that. Off to bed with you." I get up and open the door to his bedroom wider.

"Nina," he says seriously. "You must have *murdered* your own neck and wrist doing all those signatures."

My arm is tingly and sore and a little numb, which is what happens when my pinched nerves get inflamed. "I just need to do some stretches," I assure him. "I'll be fine here for *one* night. My bed's getting delivered tomorrow, remember?"

Sebastian goes over to his door, looks into his room, and then back at me. "I mean, it is a king-sized bed."

"What are you suggesting?"

"I'm suggesting we both take our prematurely creaky old bodies and sleep on either side of an enormous bed," Sebastian replies calmly. "I think we can trust each other to stay on our own sides."

"Of course we can," I say with what I hope is a casual laugh, trying to belie my sped-up pulse. *I can stay on my own side.* And then to prove it, I follow him to the door of his bedroom and check out the bed. It does look big.

"I'll probably be asleep in five minutes anyway," he adds.

"Okay. Let me just get into my pajamas." I go to the door and then realize something. "Do you need help getting changed?"

He shakes his head. "I'm all good."

Relief floods through me as I nod and head to my own room.

Sebastian is already in bed by the time I get back, his eyes closed. I notice he's kept his T-shirt on and I can't see anything else underneath the sheet he has over himself.

I've kept my bra on, intending to take it off once I'm safely under the comforter.

I try to memorize the dimensions of the room and the placement of the bed before I switch off the light. Sebastian's taken the side closest to the door, so I have to make it to the other side of the bed. I fumble around a little, reaching out for the mattress once and accidentally brushing my hand against his foot. He doesn't stir.

Finally I make it. I sit down, unclasp my bra and expertly pull it out of a sleeve.

Then I lie down, staring at the ceiling, eyes wide open. This was a mistake. I'm never going to sleep.

"Don't worry, Lucinda," Sebastian says softly from his side, startling me. I look over, just barely able to make out his face. His eyes are still closed. "A knight always keeps his word."

I grin. "You're only a knight in the streets," I quote back the next line. Sebastian's eyes open and he turns his head.

We're staring at each other when we say, at the exact same time, "But a freak in the sheets."

We're both grinning. Not a real line from the show, of course, but exactly what we turned and said to each other simultaneously seven years ago, watching that scene from the common room couch. I was just as physically close to him then as I am now, I realize. Maybe even closer.

But that was before I ever developed feelings for him. Or, at least, before the feelings had gotten so strong that even I, the queen of avoiding any real emotional attachments, could deny them.

For just a moment, I let myself think about what could have been if I had confessed my feelings for him at the costume party before I saw him kissing Heather. Would he have chosen me instead?

Would he choose me now, if I leaned over and kissed him? In the darkness I can just make out the contours of his face. His lips are slightly parted, soft and open, and I can't help picturing it. In a world where he wanted me back, what kind of kisser would he be? He's always been handsome, and he gave the best hugs, back when we used to hug each other like it was nothing. He'd smile and duck his head, enveloping me—as if I was precious and valuable. Would his kisses make me feel the same way, but with the added sensation of desire, possession? Would they start out soft and slow and teasing before turning deep and passionate and fierce, until we're both breathless, eyes shining at each other, hearts pounding?

But then I shut that down. Because that possession part is something I've never had and never wanted. That all-consuming feeling is exactly what consumed my mom, swallowed her whole, and I had a front-row seat to the devastation it brought. *This* love, though—this powerful feeling I have for Sebastian— is way more important than any fleeting kiss could ever be.

Sebastian had Heather then. He has Heather again now. And I have a chance to get my best friend back.

"Good night, Sebastian," I say as I turn to lie on my back and close my eyes.

"Good night, Nina."

I fall asleep content, knowing for a fact—by trial, even—that having Sebastian as a friend is better than not having him at all. I won't do anything to lose him again.

CHAPTER 21

SEBASTIAN

Nina's gone when I wake up.

I can't speak for her, but I slept better than I have in months. I could pretend the stress of the day overtook me, but the truth is, having my favorite person next to me while I drifted off after a tough day was a balm to my soul, a draft of warm ale, a time-out from reality.

I forgot about the pain in my shoulder and wrist. I forgot how much I dread my trips to the studio. My last thought before I drifted into dreamland was *Everything will be okay. You can rest, now.*

Dreamland . . .

Oh crap. I may have had a sex dream about her. I definitely did; it returns to me in a rush: tangled sheets, soft moans, heated confessions.

Right, no more of that. Time for an ice-cold shower.

I don't get out of bed, though. Not yet. If I get out of bed, the evening's officially over and I'm not ready for it to end, to condemn it to the history book of my mind. Her new bed arrives today, and this will never happen again.

The sheets on her side of the bed are neatly tucked and folded, and her pillow's propped up against the headboard, which makes me imagine something much more chaste than my dream, but no less endearing: her lying in bed and reading a book or magazine late into the night, muttering to herself when she thinks no one can hear her, the cutest bookworm ever. Speaking of bookworms, I nearly lost the plot when she mentioned Belle the night before.

I force myself to leave the bed and walk into the living room. Lucinda's crown is back in hand and I realize Nina must've canceled on Ennis last night. I feel drunk on that knowledge, that she picked me, her injured knight.

In the shower, my mind splits into angel and devil factions.

Angel: It's a good thing Nina's bed gets delivered today.

Devil: You'll never sleep that well again. Sabotage the bed!

Angel: Millie's visit will take your mind off Nina and provide a buffer between you and her before you do or say anything foolish. And by the time Millie leaves, you'll have put this foolishness behind you.

Devil: What are you talking about? Millie *ships* you and Nina.

Angel: Time to lay down some ground rules.

I finish showering, towel off, get dressed, and compose an email to my sister.

Under no circumstances will you light candles in the apartment, ask Nina about her love life, queue up nonstop romances on Netflix, or propose a Truth or Dare drinking game.

Her response is immediate: **Unsubscribe.**

On Thursday, my PA adventure finds me mediating a turf war between the Super Loopers and the Walla-Wallas. It seems the good folks in postproduction accidentally double-booked rival vocal groups for an ADR (additional dialogue recording) session. Yesterday's scene at the market in Bastardstown got messed up audiowise, and requires sweetening.

From what I've been able to gather, the Super Loopers were formed first, in the 1990s. "Looping" is an archaic term from the days when rerecorded dialogue was cut into physical loops of film to replace the previous recording. Hollywood loves its lingo.

The Walla-Wallas came together a decade later and were apparently founded by a disgruntled Super Looper. The phrase "walla, walla, walla" refers to the sound of background murmurs and originated in the world of radio, but apparently its use right now is controversial. I know this because the voice-over artists are currently screaming about it.

The Super Loopers insist that everyone say "peas and carrots" for the recording. The Walla-Wallas insist that "peas and carrots" is used by background players who are *seen on camera*, "because it makes their mouth flaps look real," whereas "walla-walla is for voice-overs, you assholes."

"What does Janine want?" the sound tech asks me, while fiddling with the controls. We're watching the battle play out from above, safe in our sound booth. "Does she give a single fuck?"

"Who knows?" A part of me died about five seconds ago when the term "mouth flaps" entered the lexicon. And since I'm not about to text Janine and ask her where she falls in the great peas-and-carrots/walla-walla war, I suggest, "Let's do one of each and let the editors decide."

The sound tech shrugs and unmutes his mic so I can be heard on the miniature soundstage below.

I address the actors in my sweetest, bullshittiest tone: "I hate to see you all hurting your voices right now when we need you in top form. Super Loopers, you march clockwise, Wallas, you march counterclockwise." According to Janine, if a group of people tramp about in a circle saying their respective gibberish, it more authentically duplicates the sounds of a crowd.

I wonder if Ennis the Menace has an opinion. Mr. Voice-Over. I try to picture him doing voice-over work in that sleepy drawl of his, and the only thing I think he'd be suited for would be audiobooks where the listener is trying to fall asleep.

The reason we're all here at a sound booth in Van Nuys is because at yesterday's outdoor shoot, a car alarm went off, blaring out over the actors' dialogue, and once the alarm stopped, the local birds mimicked the same noise. It was during a Roberto monologue, so I'm firmly Team Birds. In the outtakes you can see Roberto scowling and Francis Jean laughing. Anyway, the footage *looked* amazing—they shot during magic hour, that moment when the sky glows orange-pink as the sun goes down—but now the sound techs need to remove the car and bird noises and replace the ruined dialogue, as well as add believable background murmurs of the market-goers beneath it.

As I watch the scene on the monitor, I realize I haven't been paid yet for my under-five role. It's not a ton of money, but I don't wear pregnancy bellies and bald caps for free.

Roberto and Francis Jean will fix their own lines at a later date. I'm relieved I don't have to be there when it happens.

"You ever work with Her Royal Cheesiness?" the sound tech asks.

I frown. "Francis Jean? She was nice when I met her," I assert, ready to throw down if the sound tech besmirches her good name.

"Yeah, no, don't get me wrong—she's a sweetheart. But one time there was a plate of cheese out and she kept going back and forth with herself. 'Dare I? Dare I not?' I figured it was a vocal cords exercise thing, she didn't want to clog the pipes or whatever, but then her hand darted out and I'm telling you, eating that cheese *changed* her . . ."

I tune him out because a voicemail from Millie has arrived, with a text immediately following it: **whoops i messed up the time difference ha ha just landed**

It's only four o'clock. I wasn't expecting her for another two and a half hours.

Shit, really? I text back. **I can't leave yet, you're going to have to sit tight.**

While I'm waiting for her response, other messages swoop in from a group text. Matty checking in, wondering if Millie and I want to come to one of his baseball games while she's in town.

I ignore him for now and wait tensely to hear from my sister. She finally chimes in: **don't worry, a free van service will drop me closer to you, halfway thru H-wood. it's called Mad Men**

"Janine has an emergency. Excuse me, please," I tell the sound tech before ducking out into the hallway to call my sister.

"Mildred Digby Worthington!" I shout when she picks up. "Do not get in the Med Men van!"

"'Med Men'? No, *Mad* Men, it's a TV tour. Oh, wait, it does say Med Men."

"It's going to take you to a marijuana dispensary. STAY PUT."

"Ha ha, even better!"

"Do not get in the van. Hold on, hold on." I can't leave in the middle of work. I'm on thin ice as it is; Janine noticed that one of the autograph forgeries looked wobbly and asked if I'd gotten the actors drunk first. (Which in retrospect couldn't have hurt. I made a mental note to include a cocktail section in my cookbook.)

I thumb out a flurry of texts, receive a response, and then say to Millie, "Good news, Nina's coming to get you."

Millie gasps. "Is she there with you? Has she been listening? Does she know my full name is Mildred Digby? Oh God."

"Yes, and she's writing it in huge letters on a sign. Soon, everyone in Los Angeles will know."

"Shut up."

"No, she doesn't know your full name and she doesn't need

to, *if* you listen to me and do what I say. And honestly your priorities right now are alarming."

"Don't be condescending."

I know Millie's almost twenty, but she'll always be my baby sister and if I didn't at least *try* to stop her from taking a free van to a weed store, what kind of brother would I be?

Was it wrong to enlist Nina in this task? Should I have called someone else to pick up Millie, like Heather? No, the very idea is ludicrous; Millie's never met her, and Heather doesn't owe me any favors, especially not that level of favor. Neither does Nina—it's just what friends do for each other.

You're the best, I text Nina before heading back inside the sound booth.

CHAPTER 22

NINA

"What does she look like again, babe?" Ennis asks.

"Like a girl version of Sebastian, but shorter," I reply. "At least . . . I think."

It took me a few minutes of looking into thirteen- and fourteen-year-old faces to realize that I haven't seen Millie in person in five years. She's an actual adult now and she probably won't be shorter than me.

I get a text. I still can't find you. Are you at the Tom Bradley Terminal?

"Er. What's a Tom Bradley Terminal?" I ask Ennis as I look up to try to find the name of the terminal we're in, but all I see is a number five.

"Oh, hold on," Ennis says. "I think that's the international terminal." He looks up at the number too. "Righty-o, babe. We gotta get back in the car."

Sorry! We went to the wrong spot. Hopefully be there in a few minutes, I text Millie back.

By the time we drive around to the right terminal, I don't have to worry about Ennis parking the car again. Millie's standing at the curb, a few inches taller, sure, but with the same blond hair, fair skin, and freckles I was expecting.

She sees me through the windshield and her whole face lights up. By the time I've undone my seat belt and stepped out, she's already beside me, arms outstretched. "Hi!" she says.

I reach out and embrace her. Finally a Worthington I can hug without question, without constantly having to set boundaries for myself.

"Hi yourself!" I respond, and then step back to take her in. "You look great!" She really does. The braces she sported the last time we saw each other in person clearly worked out for her.

"So do you!" she says. Her accent is more pronounced than Sebastian's, presumably owing to her having spent the past twelve years of her life in England. Though she also has something of a hybrid British/American lilt. "I'm so happy to see you!" She hugs me again and I laugh.

"Hi there," Ennis says, reminding us of his presence.

"Sorry. Millie, this is Ennis. Ennis, Millie."

"The boyfriend. Right," Millie says as she sticks out her hand.

"That would be me." He shakes her hand and then grabs the handle of her silver suitcase. "Let me put that in the trunk for you." He wheels it to the back of the car.

"He's nice," Millie says, looking at me.

"He is," I agree.

"Ready to go?" Ennis asks as he closes the trunk.

"Yup," I say. "Hey, is it okay with you if I sit in the back? Millie and I have a lot of catching up to do."

"Sure. Would be like my usual fare," Ennis says as he gets into the driver's seat.

Millie looks a little confused so I explain, "Ennis is an Uber driver by day."

"And Nina's driver by night," Ennis chimes in affably. There's no malice in his words, but they still feel a little strange, hearing them said out loud since I have undoubtedly thought much the same thing for the last few months.

"Uh . . . yeah. I suppose that's true."

"Still not driving then?" Millie asks. "Even in Los Angeles?"

"Negative," I say. "I'm just waiting for self-driving cars to finally go mainstream and then I'll . . ."

"Dump Ennis?" Millie asks.

My jaw drops, but Millie immediately laughs and so does Ennis. In fact, he winks at her through the rearview mirror. "Exactly what I'm afraid of!" he says.

"Don't worry," Millie replies as she gets into the back seat. "I wouldn't really trust Elon Musk's word on how soon that's going to happen. I mean the man said space tourism would be a thing, like, two years ago."

Ennis nods. "Good point."

I climb into the back seat after her. She leans forward to check Ennis's Waze app where his phone is mounted on the windshield. "Okay, it says it'll take us thirty-two minutes to get home . . ."

"First rule of LA," I say. "Always tack on an additional thirty minutes for traffic."

"Forty-five if it's between eight and ten a.m. in the morning and four and six p.m. at night," Ennis chimes in.

"Excellent!" Millie says. "That gives us well over an hour for you to fill me in on your life over the past five years."

I blush a little. "Ha! Well . . . I'm embarrassed to say it probably won't take that long."

"What happened right after college? Where did you go?"

I think I know what she's asking, but I'm going to pretend I don't so I answer her literally. "New York City. Well, first home, to Long Island. And then to New York City. I got an internship with a clinic that worked with high-needs children."

"Wow," she says, her eyes bright. "New York! My parents only took me once when we lived upstate, to see *The Nutcracker*. Did you like living there?"

"I liked it," I admit. "It was frenzied but in a good, energetic way and, best of all, I didn't have to drive."

"So why did you leave?"

"I was there two years," I explain. "And the internship turned into an administrative job. And though I really liked working with the kids, I realized . . . I don't know. I think I didn't have the passion that was necessary to really be good at that job. And I wanted to be really good at my job, you know?"

Millie nods. "Yeah. I think about that a lot. It's what my gap year is meant to be for, to figure out what I want to do for real. I always thought it'd be journalism, but lately I'm wavering."

I laugh. "Well, if you still haven't figured it out at twenty-seven, don't be so hard on yourself, okay?"

"That's a relief," she says. "I was starting to get worried since I only have three months before uni begins."

"Don't let her fool you," Ennis pipes up from the front. "Nina knows she wants to be a screenwriter."

I look at the back of Ennis's head in surprise. I mean, I'm sure I told him once in the beginning that's why I initially moved out here, but I didn't think he remembered. Lord knows I don't really remember what he wants to do in voice-overs. Animation? McDonald's commercials? Is that even his end goal?

"Oh my gosh, that'd be so perfect for you!" Millie gushes. "Do you still keep up with the fanfic? I . . . okay, I admit I subscribed to your Wattpad account. But I haven't seen anything posted in years."

"That's sweet of you, Millie. I haven't posted there in a long time. Though I . . . well, I actually started another secret account a few months ago."

"OMG! Please tell me what it is. Please, please, pleaaaase! I would love to read more of your work. I think I read that Jeffcan-trapped-in-the-dungeon story at least ten times."

I laugh. "Thanks! But I don't know if it's any good. I'm a little rusty."

"Pleeeeeease?!" She grins and bats her eyelashes at me. I have a hard time saying no to those hazel eyes or either of the faces they occupy.

"Okay. Fine. Hold, please." I take my phone, navigate over to the URL and text it to Millie.

She grabs her phone and hits the link, looking as if she's settling into the seat to read. I laugh as I gently push the phone down from her face. "You can look at that later. Now it's your turn to tell me what you've been up to for the past five years."

"Oh, you know. Sixth form. A-levels. Gap year. Giant crush on someone I've left behind for America because I have *great* timing. That pretty much sums it up."

"Uh-huh," I say, glancing at Ennis again. "We'll have to dissect some more of that later. Girl talk," I whisper.

"Sure." She smirks at me. "So how long have you guys been together again?" She points to Ennis. "Three months?"

"Um, let me think . . ."

"Yeah, that's exactly right!" Ennis replies cheerfully. "Our three-month anniversary was last week."

It was? I blink. But then I just turn and shrug at Millie, who's smiling in an odd little way, like she's in on some sort of secret.

"Cool, cool," she says. "By the way, you guys have Netflix, right?"

"Obviously. We're not savages, Millie. Why?"

"Oh, there's just this new rom-com that came out yesterday that I've been dying to see. Maybe we can even have a rom-com marathon? You know, for our girl time?"

"Sure. Why not?"

She grins at me as she leans back in her seat. "I really missed you. You were the only person who ever felt like the sister I never had."

I smile back at her. "Me too. Well, the missing part I mean. I guess I, uh, have a sister. Though, frankly, I think you and I have a lot more in common."

Millie beams at me.

"Hello, sister!"

I'm at the door of the apartment, blocking either Ennis or

Millie from entering, but it's probably going to take a minute to unstick my jaw from the floor.

Is Sayeh like Beetlejuice? Or more accurately, Mary Jane? Does the mere mention of her make her appear?

I take in the unfathomable sight of Sayeh and Sebastian sitting on the couch together, chatting. Sayeh has toe separators and a fresh coat of polish on each foot. So she's clearly been here awhile and, naturally, made herself at home.

"What are you doing here?" I ask.

"Good news! I'm moving to LA," she says.

Sebastian gets up and looks over my shoulder to see his own sister. "Millie!" he yells with much more warmth than I just greeted mine. I finally realize I should stop blocking the door and get out of the way so that Millie can run into her brother's arms.

Sayeh and I look at this display of sibling affection, her from the couch and me from the door, and make no move to create one of our own.

"How was your flight?" Sebastian asks Millie just I walk closer to the couch so that I can start my own interrogation.

"What do you mean, you're moving to LA?" I ask.

"I had a lot of meetings set up for possible sponsorship deals. Plus the distributor of the makeup line is based here. It just seemed like a no-brainer." She waves her hands over her wet toenails.

"So that means you're never going back to school?" I ask.

She shrugs. "Like I told you. I don't actually need a business degree when I'm already on my way to becoming a mogul."

"And what does Maman say about this?" I ask. I have a vague notion that Sebastian is taking Millie into the kitchen to offer her some food and probably give us some space for our bickering.

Sayeh reaches into her bag. "She sent this for you." She holds out a plastic container and I lean over to see that it's filled with noon-nokhodchi, crumbly, clover-shaped cookies made out of chickpea flour.

But I won't be distracted, not even by my very favorite dessert. "Right, but what does she say about *your* plan?"

"She's fine with it as long as I'm with you," Sayeh says with a smile. "That's what you get for being the 'responsible one.'" She puts the container down long enough to make air quotes and then picks it back up, about to return it to her bag. "Sounds like you don't want these?"

"Give me that," I say as I grab for the container. There's a part of LA that's known as Tehrangeles because there are so many Persian people—and therefore Persian restaurants, grocery stores, and bakeries—there. I've kept meaning to go, and pick up things like noon-nokhodchi for myself, but it's hard without a car. Though, I suppose, I could always make a date at a kabob place with Ennis. If I ever get around to asking him if he'd want to eat at one.

"Hello," Sayeh says over my shoulder and I realize Ennis is, obviously, still standing right there. "You must be . . ." She drags the sentence out long enough that Ennis is forced to give her his name, without his learning that I've never once spoken to her about him. Infuriatingly clever as always.

"Ennis, right," Sayeh says as she shakes his hand. "I'm Sayeh. Nina's little sister."

"So who wants a snack?" Sebastian says from the kitchen. "How about some homemade spinach dip and pretzels?"

"Yum," Sayeh says. "After you, Ennis." She lets him walk ahead of her to the kitchen, then stops in front of me to say, "Don't worry. I'm not staying here permanently. Just crashing until I find a place."

I snort. "Um, great. But even if you were staying here *temporarily*, you should've told me. *Asked* me, even . . ."

"Where's the surprise in that?" she asks.

"I don't like surprises," I say through gritted teeth.

"I know. That's what makes this so fun."

"For *you*."

She shrugs, but doesn't deny it. "This"—she points back and

forth between Ennis and Sebastian, who are having a heated debate about the merits of pretzel twists versus pretzel rods—"is interesting."

"I have no idea what you're talking about," I reply.

Sayeh smirks. "If you say so." She hoists herself up on the kitchen counter, watching the two of them for a minute before she chimes in. "You know, I've always been a fan of braided honey wheat pretzels myself."

"With a savory dip?" Sebastian asks her.

"Yup," Sayeh responds.

"Like a spinach artichoke dip?" Ennis asks.

"Uh-huh," Sayeh says.

ENNIS	SEBASTIAN
"Are you crazy?"	"Are you a sociopath?"

Millie laughs, Ennis and Sebastian look at each other, and Sayeh turns around and gives me a wink.

Crap. No matter the pretzel type, this clearly is a recipe for disaster.

CHAPTER 23

SEBASTIAN

Invasion of the Sisters has me pulling an Ennis and carting both Millie and Sayeh around today. Per the girls' request I'll be dropping them at Rodeo Drive on my way to work.

Janine earned a potential World's Best Boss mug when she told me I could leave by noon today and start the weekend early since I have family in town. (Nina's boss either didn't offer the same option, or Nina didn't ask; both are equally likely.)

"Works in Beverly Hills," Millie murmurs from the back seat of the car, her pencil scratching rapidly in her journal. The miniature notebook hasn't left her side since her arrival yesterday. "Glam-o-rous," she adds loudly.

We have a tally going about my life in California. She's convinced every aspect of it is glamorous; I'm convinced otherwise.

"I don't work in Beverly Hills, I work in West Hollywood." I check the side mirror to see if I can slide to the curb without cutting someone off or getting us all killed.

"*Eats lunch* in Beverly Hills whenever he likes," Millie amends.

"Hmm, and yet I *don't*, because A) it's too expensive and B) my lunch hour is more like fifteen minutes because I have to get Janine's lunch sorted first. Unglamorous."

Scritch, scratch. "*Drives past* Beverly Hills every day en route to work," Millie says through clenched teeth, determined. "Whilst complaining like an utter—"

"I never take this route; this is solely for your benefit. I take Melrose or Third Street."

"Oh my God, give it a rest," Sayeh interjects in a bored voice. "You can drop us here. This is where Julia Roberts gets shit on by the boutique staff."

Sayeh is on a mission to re-create various pop culture moments today for her followers. She calls it "hashtag Ironic Iconic."

"Speaking of Melrose, can you take us to the Pink Wall later?" Sayeh adds. "I need some shots there, for obvious reasons."

"The pink wall?"

"Paul Smith's store. He like, denounced it as a landmark or whatever, but that's where the irony comes in."

"Sure, I can take you both there later." I see my opening in the left lane and jerk the steering wheel. The girls unlock the door and tumble out, eager to start their day.

Millie wears a skirt, tank top, and ballet flats, and Sayeh rocks a crop top, high-waisted pants, and immaculate gold sneakers. In comparison I feel shlubby in my LA production uniform of T-shirt, jeans, and Vans.

"See you in three hours. Have fun," I call out the window. Furious honks behind me drown out my words.

When I arrive at the office, coffees in tow, Janine is bemoaning her Friday evening fate. "I have an engagement party to go to tonight, I don't have a gift, and I feel a migraine coming on," she reveals before I've even set the beverages down.

"What's your price range?" I ask, poised to retrace my steps to the parking garage.

UNGLAMOROUS, I text Millie from the gas station twenty

minutes later, alongside a photo of me filling up my car. **AND UNREIMBURSED**, I type for the caption.

My shoulder's killing me, so I take two ibuprofen and send Millie a picture of that, too.

By the time I've purchased a present for Janine, had it professionally wrapped, dropped off Janine's dry-cleaning, and retrieved Janine's lunch, it's already time to pick up Millie and Sayeh. Janine says it's fine to bring them with me back to the office.

Alarmingly, Sayeh and Millie have shopping bags with them when they slide into the back seat of my car. We zip along Wilshire and hang right, heading northeast along Santa Monica Boulevard.

"Are Mom and Dad homeless now so you could buy trinkets in Beverly Hills?" I ask Millie.

"Relax, all I got was a package of postcards and a pen from a stationery store."

"I hit Saks," Sayeh says casually.

I'm too frightened to ask what Sayeh purchased, although apparently she can afford it, based on what Nina's told me about her sister's job; not to mention those high-tops she's wearing, which I now remember being the subject of a headline, announcing that the only thing more outrageous than their price tag was how fast they sold out.

Millie sniffs the air. "What's for lunch?"

"It's Janine's, from Cluck It All Chicken. I'm bringing it to her now, so you can both meet her if you want. TV producer," I add, in case that matters to Sayeh.

Sayeh shrugs, immersed in scrolling through her phone, though in my rearview mirror I see Millie vigorously nod her head.

"The office is across from Soho House," I add. Sure enough, Sayeh perks up at this tidbit of info, offering a "Cool."

"Across from Soho House," Millie repeats, uncapping her new, expensive pen and putting it to paper. "Glamorous."

"I'm not a member and therefore not allowed on the premises. Unglamorous."

"Could become a member if applied himself," she grits out. "Glamorous."

"Millie, just now I had to scoop a ladle of baby tomatoes up to my nose in public at Cluck It All Chicken to see if they smelled, Janine's term, 'fishy' before including them in Janine's lunch. She never clarified whether she meant 'fishy' from the sea, or merely suspicious. Luckily, we were in the clear today, or I'd have had to dump everything out."

Sayeh leans toward me. "Sorry, my dude, it definitely smells fishy. I have a superb sense of smell."

I groan. "Seriously?"

We swing down Doheny and over to Beverly Boulevard, *back* to Cluck It All, fill up a fresh chicken salad *sans* tomatoes for my boss, and two #7 plates for the sisters. In all the chaos of the day, and taking care of everyone else's needs, I forget to order food for myself.

Up at my desk, where countless emails and voicemails await me, Millie gifts me a chicken leg and Sayeh tosses me one of her rolls. I introduce the two sisters to Janine, who has an eye mask pulled up to her forehead and has evidently spent the morning asleep on her couch.

"How's your migraine?" I ask.

"Terrible. I have to cancel on the party and return the gift."

Translation: *I* have to return the gift. I struggle to keep my expression neutral, like a vassal who's pledged fealty to the wrong lord but will be killed if his thoughts on the matter become known.

"Ms. Janine, do you know any movie stars?" Millie's eyes are saucers. They're also rimmed with green eyeliner; Sayeh's handiwork, no doubt.

"I *only* know movie stars," Janine replies. "Why are you still here? Scram, have fun."

We gather our trash from lunch and set about leaving. Janine watches me, as though weighing something. *Please don't send us on another errand,* I beg silently. My shoulder throbs, sending tension through the rest of my body.

"Why don't you take my Jaguar?" Janine hands me her key fob. "In fact, keep it all weekend."

"Bagsy," Millie whispers, the Brit version of "shotgun."

"You'll take turns sitting in front," I correct her. Great, I sound like Dad.

We thank Janine profusely and head out with the excitement of lowborn serfs about to hit the town on the finest steed in the realm.

"Oh my God," Millie squeaks, trembling, when she sees the car. "I'm so chuffed."

Thanks to the evening Nina and I spent in the car, I can fool the sisters into thinking I'm an expert at unlocking its secrets. Sunglasses on, top down, radio blasting, we take about fifty selfies before exiting onto Doheny.

Sayeh graciously offers Millie front-seat privileges in exchange for curating our itinerary.

Besides the pink wall on Melrose Avenue, Sayeh's checklist of Ironic Iconic landmarks includes Santa Monica Pier, Abbot Kinney Boulevard in Venice, the Getty Villa, Chateau Marmont, and the Infinity Mirrors at the Broad, which requires advance ticketing and is therefore not possible today. Still, we accomplish all but the last one, and the weather remains in the low eighties with clear skies the whole day.

"It's really chockablock, isn't it?" Millie remarks from the back seat as we linger in another traffic jam, sunburned and cheerfully knackered after a long day. "Still glamorous," she adds quickly.

We left the Alex and Co. production offices seven hours ago, and I'll need to vacuum Janine's car to get the beach sand out, but I'm proud to have delivered an ideal Cali experience.

Millie and I drop off Sayeh at the Urban Light installation outside LACMA so she can vlog there as night falls. She'll walk back to the apartment afterward, while Millie and I enjoy our final destination: Hollywood Boulevard.

I wonder how Nina's doing today. Will the four of us spend Saturday and Sunday together or split into factions?

"They're polar opposites, aren't they?" I ask Millie once we're alone in the car, meandering north. "Nina and Sayeh."

"You think so?"

"Yeah, one lives for social media, and the other . . ."

"Works in it?" Millie finishes.

"I was going to say hates it. Although you're right, technically they both work in social media." An observation I won't be sharing anytime soon with the elder Shams daughter.

"Speaking of Sayeh, she said something brilliant while we were in Saks, that I've been dying to tell you."

"Okay . . ."

"She said, and I quote . . ." Millie flips backward through the pages of her journal until she finds what she's looking for. "'My sister and your brother should have boned ages ago. They clearly belong together. Or should at least fuck and get it out of their systems.' End quote. She basically confirmed Nina's up for it!"

My heart races, but the neutral expression I've perfected for Janine locks into place like a mask. "She only said that to see how you'd react. She and Nina aren't close; she doesn't know what she's talking about."

My hands clench around the steering wheel. I tell myself it doesn't matter; even if they did discuss me, which I doubt, it means a decision was reached to NOT bone.

Unrelated qualm: it was weird hearing my little sister say "fuck." To prevent any further discussion, I fire up Sam's podcast.

Millie groans. "Not again. Can we please listen to the radio?"

"I'm so many episodes behind it's not even funny." I conked

out last night listening to them, dreamt I caught up, woke to harsh reality, and felt more stressed than ever about it.

"Your friendship does not hinge on whether you listen to his podcast. Or if it does, he's not a good friend."

I ignore her. Millie has no clue what it was like for me, growing up without friends. I can't assume they'll stick around if I don't give them a good reason to. Next time Sam asks if I caught his latest episode, I need to be prepared.

We park Janine's Jaguar in valet at Hollywood & Highland, and wander around at Millie's leisure.

Janine told me celebrities wouldn't have been caught dead in Hollywood twenty years ago, unless it was to fly up in a limo, lean out, press their hands in cement outside Mann's Chinese Theatre, pose for a photo, and whip back to Bel Air.

The only establishments for ten blocks each way were dodgy tattoo parlors, pizza joints with C-ratings from the health department, Ripley's "Believe It or Not!" Odditorium, Trashy Lingerie (actual name), and tourist shops selling cheap plastic Oscars with your name misspelled on them. Tourists called home frightened and confused. Where was Hollywood *really*?

Today, of course, there's a Gap, Lucky Strikes bowling alley, the Academy Awards in the Dolby Theatre, *Jimmy Kimmel Live!*, and a huge, three-story shopping complex to make the place safe for visitors.

"I need more postcards," Millie announces.

It's an easy request, but she already has thirty or forty. "Why do you need so many?"

"I'm trying to woo the cellist from Yeovil! I'll be sending her postcards at strategic intervals over the next six weeks to retain her interest. Obviously."

We grab take-away from In-N-Out Burger and Millie yammers excitedly all the way home, before getting ready for sleep and shifting the sheets and pillows around her on the couch. I make sure she has a glass of water on the coffee table and bid her good night, but she refuses to stop talking.

"Guess what, I read the first *CoRaB* book on the plane. Well, half of it, anyway."

I sit on the armrest of the couch. We only have a few days together before she joins up with TrekUSA, so I should savor her presence while I can. "Prove it."

"'When you kiss a friend, the friendship dies.' Please tell me that hasn't been your guiding principle with Nina. Because if it has been, you are *completely* mad."

I motion for her to lower her voice. Nina and Sayeh are tucked away in Nina's newly furnished room and sharing her new bed while Sayeh's here, and I can't risk them hearing.

"We love the show, Millie. We don't use it to plan our lives. Did I want more than friendship with her in college? Yes, of course," I hiss as quietly as possible, with a nervous glance toward Nina's room. "But I know better now."

If my relationships—platonic, romantic, whatever—are doomed to be unbalanced, I think I'll always be the one who loves more.

And I'm okay with that.

I have to be.

"Are you really saying you stopped wanting it?" Millie presses me.

I think about Nina cutting me out of her life five years ago. Unfriended, right to my face. Would she do it again, if I behaved in a way she didn't like, or that she perceived as unforgivable, somehow? Even if I didn't understand what I'd done wrong? I have no reason to suspect she would—we've been getting along fantastically in our friendship reboot—but then, we'd been getting along fantastically in college, too. So I'd thought.

"Before I leave, I'm going to find out once and for all how Nina feels. Stay tuned," Millie vows, yawning her biggest yawn yet.

I stand and rub my eyes. "Go to sleep, Millie, and no scheming this weekend. I mean it."

"Ugh. You're useless."

"No," I remind her with a kiss to her forehead. "I'm glamorous."

CHAPTER 24

NINA

I wake up Monday morning relegated to a corner of my own bed, again. It's been like this all weekend, with Sayeh sprawled belly-down on most of the mattress, her long lavender curls fanned across her back, popping against her golden skin and black tank top. How does she look like a ready-made Instagram post even in her sleep?

I tiptoe out of the room, more for a sleeping Millie's benefit than my own sister's. Millie's curled into a ball on the couch, heroically having convinced Sebastian that his still-injured shoulder needed his bed more than her perfectly healthy nineteen-year-old body did.

I tiptoe back after I use the bathroom, only to render the whole procedure moot when I give a loud yelp upon opening my bedroom door. Sayeh is sitting on the edge of my bed, already dressed in a thigh-length, sixties-inspired crocheted dress and burgundy combat boots. She's applying the final touches on her mascara.

"Good news," she tells me as she puts down her mirror.

I look over in alarm at the couch in the living room where, thankfully, Millie hasn't stirred. She's still technically a teen-ager, I remember, so maybe she sleeps like one.

I quietly close the door before I turn to Sayeh. "How did you get ready so fast?" I ask.

She shrugs. "You do a few 'Look Like a Ten in Under Five Minutes' tutorials, you get the hang of it." She looks over my mussed hair, bare face, and pajama-clad body. "I can cue one up for you if you need."

"I'm good," I grumble as I go over to my closet.

"I'm going to hitch a ride with you to work today," she says matter-of-factly. "I have a few meetings starting at noon that are close by."

"Is that your good news?" I ask.

She thinks for a moment. "No. Though I guess it could be. *More* time with your little sister, amirite?" She smirks.

I roll my eyes as I remove a navy dress from my closet.

"Ugh. No, not that one," Sayeh says as she comes over. She looks disapprovingly at the rest of what's hanging up. "Why is your wardrobe so depressing?"

"It's called professional, Sayeh. Some of us have regular jobs in regular offices?"

She touches one of the black dresses in my closet, then one of the beige ones and looks over at the navy one in my hand. "Are these the same dress in different colors?"

"As a matter of fact, they are," I say. "I found this great website for professional women who don't have the time or desire to shop."

Sayeh looks back at my closet, disgusted. "You didn't."

"Saves me a lot of time and aggravation," I say as I turn around and make quick work of taking off my pajamas and putting on a bra.

"Just. How? You live in Los Angeles. And before that you lived in New York. These are fashion capitals. You can walk out of your door, into any store, and buy practically *anything* and it would be on point."

"Actually, I can't *walk* anywhere here," I say as I feel around with my hand for the dress I just put down on the bed behind me. "And not everyone cares about how they look."

"Well, they should," she says. "Because everyone judges you by it anyway. And it's to your advantage to present yourself as best as you can. And this dress . . ." I now turn around to see that she's holding up the navy dress. "Is so not you."

"Great. Thanks for the personality and wardrobe analysis. Now can I please have that so I can get dressed and go to work? You're going to make me late."

She doesn't make any move to hand the dress over as I continue to stand in front of her in my underwear. "So now I have two pieces of good news: First, I found a roomshare. I'm leaving this afternoon."

"That *is* good news," I say as I go to snatch the dress from her. She pulls it behind her.

"My second piece of good news is that I'm your stylist for the day."

Honestly, it was going to cost me much more time and effort to argue with Sayeh rather than just give in to her, which is how I find myself sitting in the front of Ennis's car in a bright blue blouse with an intricately cut-out neckline, an armful of noisy enameled bangles, and a pair of ankle-cut heather gray slacks.

Sayeh is in the back seat, inexplicably feigning an interest in Ennis's life story.

"What's your middle name?" she asks.

"Steven," he responds. "After my dad."

"Are your parents still together?" she asks him.

"Nope," he says.

"Ours neither," she replies. "Do you find that keeps you at an emotional distance in your own relationships?"

"Sayeh!" I interject, annoyed. "That's a real personal question for nine a.m. on a Monday morning, don't you think?"

Ennis laughs. "I don't mind." He glances quickly at Sayeh in the rearview mirror. "Maybe. Depends on the relationship. They're both happily remarried though. What about yours?"

"Oh, hasn't Nina told you about them?"

"Not really," Ennis says lightly, not looking over at me.

"Hmm," Sayeh says. "Well, no one is happily remarried. Our mom is unhappily single and our dad is about to be unhappily divorced for the third time."

"Wait . . . he is?" I ask.

"Yup," Sayeh says. "And you'd know that too if you gave him a call once in a while." She addresses Ennis. "Nina really took my mom at her word that our dad was a cartoon villain."

"I did not!" I say, indignant. "But maybe you haven't realized that one parent *stayed*, and one parent *left*, Sayeh."

"Yeah. Baba moved to California. A whole one hour south of here. Have you ever even considered visiting him?"

"You know what? I'd rather have this conversation in private, thanks," I say through gritted teeth.

"Why?" Sayeh says as she relaxes back into her seat. "You don't have any secrets from your boyfriend, do you?"

I place my hand behind my back and give her the middle finger. In the rearview mirror, I see her smirking.

Since Sayeh's first meeting doesn't start for two hours, she comes up to my office with me. By which I mean, she just follows me out of the car and to the lobby without asking me if it's okay or not. Typical.

"Look, if my boss isn't okay with this, then you're going to have to leave. Got it?" I say as we make our way up the elevator.

"Why wouldn't he be okay with it?" she asks, her nose buried in her phone as she posts one of the fifty selfies she managed to take in the back of Ennis's car.

"Uh, how about because there's no such thing as Take Your Little Sister to Work Day?" I say. "Besides, he's not okay with most things. He's halfway between giving himself an ulcer or getting himself a toxic work environment write-up. . . ."

The elevator door flies open and the words die in my mouth because Sean is standing right there.

"Oh, great, write-up," he says to me. "I assume you're talking about the social media PowerPoint for episode 601. Do you have it ready? The presentation's tomorrow but I need to give you my notes by one so you can revise it before EOD today."

"Uh . . ." Shit. This was something he actually told me about. At five thirty p.m. on Friday, but still, he mentioned it. And normally I would've spent the weekend on it, except that as soon as I came home to a full house of Worthingtons and Sayeh, I completely forgot.

"Who's this?" Sean says, looking over at Sayeh.

"Sayeh Shams," Sayeh says, sticking out her hand. "I'm Nina's sister. But, more importantly, I'm an influencer and social media consultant. Here." She reaches into her tiny clutch and hands Sean a gorgeous robin's-egg blue business card with gold foil-embossed writing. It does, in fact, read:

SAYEH SHAMS

SOCIAL MEDIA CONSULTANT

"Nina wanted me to take a look at the PowerPoint before it got to you." She gives Sean her brightest, camera-ready smile.

"How much do you cost?" Sean asks her suspiciously.

"It's free! I mean, just this one time. As a sisterly favor, obviously."

Sean breaks out into an equally award-winning grin that I've never seen before. It shows more teeth than his usual grimace. "Great!" He presses the elevator button and the door pops right open. "Can't wait to see the presentation."

"You got it," Sayeh says. "We'll have it to you before noon."

Sean nods and steps on the elevator. The door closes after him.

"Before noon?" I ask Sayeh.

She shrugs. "I'll have it done in an hour, honestly."

I sigh. "I don't want you doing my work. . . ."

"It's called helping you out, Nina. You could say thank you. Now, which one is your desk?" She walks into the rows of cramped cubicles. I point mine out and she sits down. "You want to log in?"

I do and then, true to her word, she does take over, expertly putting together a PowerPoint presentation with a shocking amount of speed and finesse.

"Wow," I say after a few minutes of watching her. "You . . . really know what you're doing there, don't you?"

"Don't act so surprised," she replies. "Do you think getting to the top of your social media game is all selfies and preloaded filters? Besides, I'm only fifteen credits short of a BA."

"You're right. I'm sorry," I say as I watch her work some more.

"Do you have a write-up of what you're already doing on the socials?" she asks.

"Yeah, it's right here." I click over to the document.

"This isn't half bad," she says, which is probably the closest she's come to paying me a compliment in years.

"Thank you," I say.

"You're welcome," she replies while typing away. "Though your Instagram strategy is a little thin. Maybe you can pitch a Stories takeover with one of the cast. Or behind-the-scenes with the crew?"

"Actually, I had this silly idea to try to see if I can get into the writers' room. Well, it was Sebastian's idea really."

"Why is that silly?" Sayeh asks.

I shrug. "Would anyone care to see a TV show writers' room?"

Sayeh stops typing to stare at me. "Would you, as a superfan of the show, care?"

"Of course."

"Then there's your answer." Her fingers go back to flying

over the keyboard. "Social media strategy is nothing more than tapping into what people want to see. And the best way to do that is to tap into what you—as a fan—would want to see."

"But would I really be doing it as a fan?" I wonder. "Or as a writer trying to get into the room myself?"

"Why can't it be both?" Sayeh says. "At the end of the day, you'd be doing your job. If you get something else out of it, then good on you."

"Yeah, but they're also super secretive about the writers' room." Now I'm voicing every concern I've ever had about bringing this idea up to Sean. "I doubt they'd let me in at all. And with a camera to boot?"

"You never know if you don't ask," she replies simply.

I look at Sayeh, confidently typing away and I realize something: As obnoxious as I sometimes find her, she's gotten where she is because she's never been afraid to ask for things. She's never been afraid of getting a no.

"And ask it the right way," she adds. "Look." She types a bullet point into the presentation:

AN EXCLUSIVE, NEVER-BEFORE-SEEN PEEK INTO THE WRITERS' ROOM VIA AN INSTAGRAM STORIES TAKEOVER (CONTENT WILL BE PRERECORDED AND VETTED SO THAT IT REMAINS SPOILER-FREE)

I blink. "Wow, that's . . . good."

She smirks. "Naturally. Just pitch it to Sean when you hand this in to him. It should make for good content and—as I'm sure the SVP of Digital Media is well aware—content is king."

"Okay. Thanks." I watch her finish up converting the rest of the document into slides. "By the way, where did you get an apartment?"

"Oh, it's in . . ." She checks her phone. "Los Feliz. There's a roommate. Someone named Celeste Holybrook. I interviewed with her over FaceTime. She seemed chill enough."

I stifle a laugh. Oh, man, if only I could be a bee on that wall because I'm actually not sure who's going to drive who crazy first.

Sayeh's already gone by the time I get back from work, having picked up her stuff after her meetings. I was planning on telling her in person that Sean loved the Instagram writers' room idea and said he'd run it by Lou Trewoski that week. I'm excited to tell Sebastian at least, but when I get in, it's only Millie.

"Where's Sebastian?" I ask.

"He's . . ." She pauses. "On a date with Heather."

"Okay. Cool," I say, and then go into my room to get changed. On second thought, maybe I'll tell him only if Lou Trewoski actually okays the idea. When I come back out in my lounge pants and a T-shirt, I ask Millie what kind of takeout she wants for dinner. "And didn't you want to watch a movie on Netflix?" We haven't gotten around to it yet and Millie's only here one more night before her camping trip begins.

"Whatever food you want is fine with me." She seems extra subdued tonight. Maybe I can get her to open up about what's on her mind once we've settled in.

I've ordered the burritos, and the opening credits of the movie have just revealed the names of the two romantic leads when Millie's dam bursts open without my even trying to pry out a word.

"Is it really 'cool,' Nina? That Sebastian's out with Heather?" she blurts, staring at me with wide eyes.

"Uh . . . I thought so," I reply. "Why? You don't like her?"

"It's not that I don't like *her*. It's that I like someone else more. For my brother."

"Um, okay. Who's that?"

She stares at me. "You really don't know?"

"I mean, to be fair, I haven't met many other girls that Sebastian knows."

She blows out a puff of air and picks up the notebook she's

always carrying around. She opens up to a page and starts reading from it. "'One: He definitely thinks she's beautiful because she is objectively beautiful. Two: He lights up around her. She lights up around him. Three: They can make each other laugh without saying a word. They can have whole conversations without saying a word.'"

I'm starting to get an inkling of what she might be talking about. "Millie . . ." I start, but she keeps talking over me.

"'Four: They share the same interests, especially the same fandom. Five: He's been in love with her for *nine years*.'"

She looks up at me. We stare at each other, the words hanging in the air. My heart is suddenly a techno beat in my ears.

I laugh to try and drown it out. "I didn't know you were writing your own fanfic," I say, attempting to sound as casual as I can.

"*Why* aren't you two together?" Millie asks. "Everyone around you can see it. Me. Sam and Matty. Sayeh."

"Sayeh?" I ask.

"Yup. She told me so herself."

I shake my head and get up off the couch. I need a drink, but settle for filling up a glass of water from the dispenser on the fridge. "Listen, I know you haven't known Sayeh very long, but most of what comes out of her mouth is carefully crafted BS," I say shakily, even though she sort of proved me wrong on that today.

"I don't know," Millie says. "She seems forthright to me."

I need to get Millie off this subject. It was hard enough talking myself out of acting on the night Sebastian and I shared a bed. I don't think I can handle an out loud conversation—especially not one that's confirming something I wanted to hear so badly five years ago. I point to the TV. "Is that one of the actors from the British *Office*?" I ask.

Millie keeps her back to the TV, not even pretending that she doesn't know what I'm trying to do. "Can you just tell me why you don't love him?"

I'm at a loss for words for a few seconds. Finally, I settle on, "Millie. It's just not like that between us."

"Maybe for you. But I know it is for him."

"But you don't know that," I say, my voice going up in pitch. "*That* is fiction." I point to her notebook. "I mean, yes, we make each other laugh and we love *CoRaB* together and we were best friends. Maybe we can be again. But . . . nine years? Please. He spent freshman year making out with someone new at every Cornell frat party, the next three years pining after some girl named Belle, and the last month of senior year with Heather."

"Belle?" Millie asks.

"Yes," I say, taking a sip of water, happy that I seem to have finally reined in this conversation. "I overheard him talking about her once freshman year. And then again junior year. Seemed like a long, unrequited crush."

"Nina," Millie says, talking slowly, her hands folded calmly on the back of the couch. "You are Belle."

CHAPTER 25

SEBASTIAN

"I was surprised you called while Millie's in town," Heather says when we meet inside the lobby of the Stinking Rose restaurant on La Cienega. The Italian eatery is an over-the-top LA institution and their motto is "We season our garlic with food."

"I got kicked out so they could have a girls' night. Nina and my sister. And maybe Nina's sister, too. It was unclear." I grin. "Either way I'm outnumbered, and it occurred to me one-on-one with *you* sounded perfect."

Heather takes in her surroundings, peering past the check-in stand. Kitschy artwork adorns the walls, and each room has a different theme. I chose the Garlic Room, where bulbs hang from the ceiling and frolic in paintings, visiting California landmarks.

"What *is* this place?" Heather asks. "Have you been here before, or . . . ?"

"No, but I've been curious about it for a while. When you call to make a reservation, the voice on the machine says, 'Velcome to the Stinking Rose, if you vant to speak to a dead person, start talking now, mwahahaha,' like a low-rent Dracula. You know, because of all the garlic?"

Heather stares at me.

"They even have garlic ice cream, which I think we *have* to try."

Heather presses two fingers to her forehead. "Everything on the menu is smothered in garlic?"

"Yeah, that's the theme. You said the other night you wished my garlic noodles had more . . . garlic . . . Oh."

Her smile looks sad.

I duck my head. "You were being sarcastic. I get that now."

That was sarcasm, by the way. Maybe Roberto wasn't being mean. Maybe I'm that dense. (Or maybe I was paying more attention to Nina than Heather the night of our double date, which I still feel guilty about.)

"I'm a dick. Sorry, Heather. I thought I'd been listening carefully, and clearly, I wasn't. Should we get out of here, find a different place?"

"Yeah, let's . . . do that. And actually, Sebastian, I'm not super hungry. Maybe drinks and hang for a while?"

The valet's cool about it and doesn't charge us, but I slip him a five for his time.

"The atmosphere in that place was fun, at least," I remark, my thoughts still on the Stinking Rose.

"It did look cute. Sorry to veto it."

"You do not have to apologize—that was all on me. I wonder how they came up with the theme and how they decided which recipes to use and everything. I'm trying to make a cookbook," I explain, once we're settled in at Sur Lounge, mojitos in tow. Sayeh mentioned it as a reality TV hotspot during our citywide trek the other day.

Heather and I are cozy beside each other on a low, leather sectional beneath lush, dripping chandeliers encased in what appear to be birdcages.

She taps her glass to mine. "That's really cool, Sebastian. Good for you. California cuisine or something?"

"*Castles of Rust and Bone*–related, actually."

Heather takes a long, slow pull of her drink. "The show's pretty much your life, huh?"

"Well, it *is* my job."

"Yeah . . ."

"Remember all those parties in the dorm? I'd love to help like-minded people throw their own celebrations. I want my recipes to be creative but accessible for other fans."

"I guess for me it seems sort of passive, you know? Being a fan."

Not the way Nina and I do it. I think about the infusion of joy fanfiction gives Nina, both reading it and writing it. No one's getting paid to produce it: It's all conceived of and perfected in people's free time and shared with grateful strangers. Likewise, brainstorming my cookbook gets me out of bed in the morning because, let's face it, the actual show doesn't. Not anymore. Not the way I've been experiencing it.

"Whatever blows your hair back, though," Heather quickly adds.

I don't mention the downsides of fandom, the risks. It's a lop-sided relationship. The object of affection holds all the power, while the viewer . . . views, and hopes. Being a fan often means getting your heart speared in a joust you didn't know you were in. The characters might act in ways they never used to act in. They'll change, get killed off, or kiss the wrong person, and there's fuck-all you can do about it.

Still, when it's good, it's everything. To me, anyway. Even the stupid, wobbly, plywood sets of the places the characters live and hang out become important, as familiar to me as my own four walls. Nina inherently understands that and always has.

Maybe I haven't given Heather a *chance* to understand, though. It's worth a shot.

"The thing about fandom is that it's a shared language, a shorthand where everyone gets the same references and touch-stones." I take a risk with the next admission: "A way to belong."

"That makes sense." Heather looks me dead in the eyes be-fore her gaze drops and her voice grows thick with emotion. "I'm really homesick. I miss Chicago more than I expected, and don't know if I'll ever belong in this city."

I set my drink down, and gently tilt her chin with my finger-tips so we're looking at each other again. "As long as I'm here, you belong."

We lean toward each other, inexorably drawn together in a kiss.

Chapter 26

NINA

"What do you mean, I'm Belle? I'm . . . Nina," I add stupidly.

"It was his codename for you," Millie replies. "Something to do with Belle and Sebastian . . . get it?"

I just stare at her. "That can't be."

"Why?" Millie asks.

I try to think of the exact conversation that I overheard between Matty and Sebastian so long ago.

"Just go for it. You're clearly crazy about her. What's the worst that can happen?"

"Uh. It ends poorly and she's out of my life forever?"

"Okay, fine. But that doesn't mean you and Belle can't have a spectacular time in the meantime."

"Not worth it . . . I think . . ."

I sit down on the couch, suddenly feeling lightheaded. "I almost told him."

"Almost told him what?" Millie asks breathlessly.

I tug on my ponytail. "That I maybe had feelings for him. Senior year . . ."

Millie lets out such an enormous squeal, I'm surprised one of the hanging wineglasses doesn't shatter. "I *knew* it!!" She starts clapping her hands and I instantly regret sharing this bit of information.

"Okay, but hold on. He got together with Heather. He's together with Heather now. . . ."

Millie rolls her eyes. "Heather is an incidental character, Nina. Don't you see? You're the love interest. You've always been the love interest."

"Millie. This isn't fanfic. There isn't a stock 'love interest' character in real life."

"Who said anything about stock?" Millie says. "I'm talking about true love. OTP."

"OTP? Millie . . ."

"Look, just because I'm talking in fictional shorthand doesn't mean real love doesn't exist. And you two have it. Real love."

I hear footsteps in the hallway and my heart drops. I'm so not ready to see Sebastian right now. But then, luckily, they fade away past our door.

"I need a minute to take this in," I say. "When Sebastian returns, please don't tell him you said anything. Can you do that for me?"

She crosses her arms in front of her body and, for the first time, I see the kind of antagonizing little sister I'm used to. "Why? So you guys can drag this out for another five years? Haven't you both already wasted enough time?"

"It just . . . if this is going to happen, I need to make sure it's right. Because if it's not . . ." I look at her.

She sighs. "'When you kiss a friend, the friendship dies,'" she replies tonelessly.

"Exactly." I say.

"Okay, but please don't keep stringing him along. Now that you know . . . please figure it out. And please, please, please figure it out the right way. You know, the kissy way." She grins at me and suddenly she's back to the bubbly, love-obsessed Millie I know.

"I'll do my best," I promise with a weak smile.

CHAPTER 27

SEBASTIAN

Heather breaks the kiss, but keeps her hand on my forearm for another moment of connection.

"Thanks, Sebastian. It's nice to know someone's got my back."

"It was brave of you to leave Chicago and everything that's safe and familiar to chase your dream."

"Brave or stupid, the jury's still out."

"If it were easy, everyone would do it, right?"

"Maybe." She bites her lip. "I want to be honest, though, and say I'm not sure I'm in the right headspace to date anyone. What I said the other night, about not knowing if I'm going to stay in LA, was true, and . . ."

"I get it," I assure her. "No worries."

A twinge of disappointment, born of nostalgia and the fear of loneliness rather than a specific pining for Heather, pulls at my heart.

I hadn't wanted to re-create the past—but I'm glad we reconnected too.

"We'll always have the slaughter-brothel," I say.

She laughs. "I'd rather have Paris."

"While we're being honest . . . you were my first girlfriend.

to drown it out but that might be awfully suspicious if I'm supposed to be sleeping. Eventually, I resort to taking a Unisom because I know it's the only way I'll get any rest tonight.

I still don't. My sleep is fitful, punctuated by dreams of bloody wedding dresses and Sebastian kissing other people: Heather, the real Queen Lucinda, even our RA, Stanley.

I'm out of bed by five a.m., but wait until six forty-five to leave the room, dressed and ready to go. Millie is leaving this morning to start her six-week tour of America and I need to say goodbye.

Sebastian is in the kitchen cooking up breakfast. "Good morning," he says. "Feeling better?"

"Hi, yes," I respond.

"Good enough for French toast?" he replies, tilting his pan to show me thick slices of challah bread.

I shake my head. "I wish, but I have to head into work early."

"No problem," Sebastian says. "If you give me five minutes, I'll get it ready to go."

"I'm so sorry. I can't. Really big conference call with Stu Stu's team in Australia again and it starts at seven thirty on the dot." I turn away from Sebastian to see Millie looking over at me skeptically. But I ignore that, too, instead walking over to give her a big hug. "I hope you have the best time."

"Thanks," she replies, and then breaks the embrace to give me a questioning look.

I smile back. It's easier to pretend to have an answer when you don't have to speak. She seems satisfied, giving me another hug. "See you in six weeks."

It sounds like a countdown, the ticking, ensuing explosion kind. "See you."

After work, I surprise myself and call Ennis, asking if he's free to give me a ride home.

"Righty-o, babe."

Up until twenty minutes ago, I was sure I was taking the bus, like most nights. But suddenly the thought of returning to Sebastian seems so much more daunting than anything, even being forced to flush Roberto Ricci's toilet.

As Ennis's car approaches, I look at him through the windshield, his handsome face bathed in moonlight. When I get in the passenger seat, he leans over to give me a kiss.

It's a perfectly good kiss. It's a kiss that goes where I want it to: a box in my brain labeled "sex and romance." It's a small box, hardly bigger than the box that says "chores" or "elementary school memories." There are other, more substantial boxes in there. Complicated ones like "family." Big, unwieldy ones that say "dreams" or "story ideas."

And then there's the one that is terrifying the hell out of me right now, the one that's threatening to spill over everything and ruin the neat, stacked version of my life that I know and cherish. That box is breathing—fuming, even—like an animal about to charge. And there's nowhere for me to run this time.

So I can let it overcome me, cowering and concealed. Or I can face it.

"Ennis," I say, a few minutes into our drive. "I want you to know that I think you're a great guy."

Ennis glances at me quickly before turning his eyes back to the road. "Uh-huh. Do I need to pull over for this?"

I hesitate. "I don't know. Do you?"

"That depends. Is this a breakup?"

I pause. "Yes."

He sighs but doesn't make a move to pull over. "I care about you, Nina. But I always got the sense . . . you didn't really want me to care about you. Not really."

"That's . . . true," I admit.

"But sometimes you care about someone whether they want you to or not. Whether you want to or not."

I bite my lip. "I'm sorry. You don't deserve to be hurt. Honestly. You've been great. You *are* great."

He shrugs. "I guess it's not like you weren't always obvious about how much you wanted to keep this casual."

"It's still not okay to hurt you," I say, realizing how true that is. And not just about Ennis. Because there's always been someone else involved in that romance box. Just because I never let myself get close enough to get hurt doesn't mean I haven't caused others pain in the process.

"Well, I'll get over it." He gives a small smile, not an entirely happy one.

"I know you will," I assure him.

I give Ennis a long hug before I get out of his car. After he's driven off, I stand for a few minutes in front of the gray, yellow, and white apartment building. I look at the tall palm trees that stand in front of it. There's something quintessentially LA about it. This place of big dreams and big heartbreaks, of sunshine and wildfires, it feels like everything shines or burns brighter here. Is it better though, to try to shine and burn, or to keep everything neatly stacked and forever dull?

I swallow as I unlock the front door, go to the elevator, and enter our apartment.

He's there. In the kitchen, of course, delicious scents wafting around him, enveloped in gossamer wisps of steam. *Shine or burn, Nina?*

"Hey," he says, looking, for some reason, a little sad and subdued. "I made dinner. I figured you'd be okay trying my Baby Backstab Ribs prototype."

If he's sad about something, I want to know what it is. If he's cooking me dinner, I want to savor every bite those hands touched. And in that moment, I know I love him so much that I can't say anything or it will all come spilling out. So I nod and slowly start walking over to him.

"I . . . um, need to talk to you about something," he says into his sauce.

"I need to talk to you about something too," I reply and by this time, I'm standing right beside him.

Except I don't need to talk. We've talked enough. We've discussed, and dissected, and discoursed. It's time to burn.

I place one hand on his cheek, cupping it, sweeping one thumb slowly across his jawline and over his lips in a way I won't be able to take back.

He stares at me, blinking, his lips falling slightly open.

And then I lean in and do it. I kiss Sebastian Worthington.

CHAPTER 29

SEBASTIAN

We call in sick the next day. *Lovesick.*

I don't remember the words we use to tell our respective bosses, just that we have to stifle our amused reactions while the other person affects a cough and raspy voice. We lie sideways across Nina's bed, covers tangled and half twisted off the mattress, last night's clothes decorating the floor. Dangling off Nina's lamp. Draped over her bedframe.

I curl around her like a hand around a mug of hot spiced rum, drunk off each other in the morning after. She nestles against me, all warm satiny skin, and shoots me a grin over her shoulder before she calls in to WatchGoNowPlus. When she's finished, I tell her that actually, her fake raspy voice is kinda sexy.

"Is it now?" she purrs.

"Oh, yes." I nibble on her ear and she leans into my touch.

"One of us is overdressed," she says, and tugs my boxer shorts off.

"I think I know why they call it *dope*-amine," I sigh between kisses, my body responding instantly to her nakedness and warmth. Her lips are soft and welcoming, and I'm soaring from the realization that this might be our new normal, that when I want to caress her hair or kiss her senseless or twine my fingers through hers or stretch her out on top of me, I *can*. I will never tire of her, never.

I lift her as I stand, and she wraps her legs around my hips. She's lighter than air and smells delicious, familiar yet thrillingly new, her usual scent tangled with sex, and me, and us.

We kiss for ages, passion building. Last night we made the bed shake and I can still hear the sounds she made, on a loop in my head. If my mission in life before was to make her laugh, my new mission is to hear those sounds from her as often as possible. Coming up for air, Nina drags her mouth along my cheek and gives me a gentle bite. I take the hint and set her feet on the floor. Then I turn her so we're both facing the full-length mirror.

It has handprints on it from the night before. I grin as sense memories wash over me, urging me on. Standing behind her, I cup her perfect breasts and whisper in her ear, "Want to watch?"

She nods. I caress her nipples with my thumbs until they stand at attention.

She bites her lip and rubs her ass against my aching cock. Nerve endings on fire, I coast my hands up her spine, pushing down lightly, and she bends forward so I can palm her hips and position her right.

Our eyes meet in the mirror, and we look at each other as I sink into her warm, wet heat. We both moan, and I move slowly at first, eager to make her writhe and beg for me again. We're so in tune with each other's rhythms and wants and needs, it's both extraordinary and utterly natural; the continuation of a dance, proof of our bond, an expansion of everything we've ever been to each other. I should've known we'd be good at this, that *of course* our bodies would parry and thrust in perfect harmony.

She lets her eyes fall shut, her face soaked in pleasure, and

I'm mad for her, for this—this fairy tale playing out in real time. We're the hero and heroine of each other's stories. Maybe we always were, regardless of whether we took this next step.

I quicken my pace and slip my hand between her thighs, teasing and circling until we reach the crest together, one after the other, in a brilliant crescendo.

We lie on our backs afterward, chests rising and falling in union. I reach for her hand and she brings our entwined fingers to her mouth, peppering each of my knuckles with kisses around a smile that's sweeter than any confection.

She dozes and I gently extract my arm from under her neck so I can get a glass of water. My entire body is sore as I wander into the kitchen. The apartment looks like a bunch of rock stars blew in last night for a competition over who could accrue the most lawsuits. We gained considerable knowledge about which surfaces were best at taking our weight and movements. The kitchen table, for example, has a wobbly leg, but the kitchen island is . . . Oh. The kitchen island is covered in last night's uneaten dinner. Whoops. I dub them the best ribs ever, in absentia, and set about collecting various items that got knocked over in sacrifice to our bodies' demands.

In the mirror next to the front door, I'm a cheerfully depraved sight: hair askew, fingernail streaks along my chest, hickeys on my neck. The smug, lucky bastard who stares back at me looks like he teleported in from an alternate universe. How is it possible that the smug lucky bastard is me?

After Nina kissed me, she told me Millie had opened her eyes to the possibility of us, but also that, back in college, Nina had almost come clean on the night of the costume party.

"Nina," I said, "I've loved you from the moment you walked into that TV lounge, and every moment since. Not in a 'I must have her' way—though I mean, you're gorgeous—but because I knew we'd be important to each other. I wasn't your friend in *hopes* of anything, it wasn't *leading* anywhere, but at the same time I knew that regardless of the form it took, we were—"

"Meant to be," she supplied, her eyes wet.

It's noon by the time we rise from our stupor. We take a bath together, though of course, a third of the bathwater ends up on the floor when we do what we do in it.

"I never want to go back to the other way. The non-kissing way," I say around a yawn. Our lips meet again.

"Me neither." She taps me on the nose.

I rest my head on her stomach and she caresses my hair, damp and matted to my forehead.

The sex is great of course, but I relish the other kinds of touching too. Stroking her back, massaging her scalp, pulling her legs onto my lap when we watch TV, draping my arm across her waist in bed, melting into each other like cheese on toast, timing our breaths so they match, a syncopated heartbeat.

The next night, after a rigorous, deeply scientific study, we deem her mattress superior to mine, which leaves the question of what to do with my bed.

"Let's turn it into a fort," Nina says.

Spoiler alert: The fort also becomes a place for sex.

Nina, propped on her elbow, finger trailing along my chest: "Do you wish we'd figured this out sooner?"

I press my lips to her forehead. "No, because then we might never have become such good friends, and that's what I needed the most back then." I'd told her about bits and bobs of my childhood throughout the years, and the fact that she'd never judged me for it was all the information I'd needed about her.

The night after that, a text from Millie arrives: **You will henceforth refer to me as The Architect.**

Attached is a photo Nina apparently sent her earlier, of Nina kissing my cheek. Millie has added animated hearts around our faces and a techno beat to the background. It's so over the top I laugh at the sight.

Nina pokes her head in from the bathroom, where she's brushing her teeth. "What's funny?"

"Millie's taking credit for us."

"Aw, let her have it."

Another text from my sister: **Content?**

Yes, I type back. *To put it mildly.*

Millie immediately video-calls me on WhatsApp. Her tour group is at a pitstop in New Mexico.

"Okay, send me some," she commands.

"Send you some what?"

"*Con*tent!" she shouts.

"I thought you asked if I was con*tent*?"

"No, I want *con*tent! Images! Multimedia! Fanvids! Etcetera."

"Of me and Nina? We haven't created any." *We've been a little busy consecrating the apartment, couch to floor to wall to door.* "Here's your content: Nina has the most kissable cheeks."

Millie frowns. "That's all I get?"

"I didn't say *which* cheeks."

She screams, covers her ears, and sways. "Nope, no."

"Hey, you asked for it."

"Content by midnight or I'll haunt you."

She clicks off and I wave Nina over. "Get in here." We take a picture of our faces in profile, noses touching, then draw a heart outline to frame the shape we've made. Beneath the image, I type *Worthington/Shams 4-Ever* in graffiti font.

My bastard autocorrect changes Worthington to *Worthy grin.*

I roll my eyes and show Nina. "How do you like that? All these years together and it still doesn't know my name. Though right now, I'm tempted to leave it that way."

"*My* stupid phone autocorrects to 'Scam.' Like, way to help with my imposter syndrome."

"That's downright offensive."

"I know, right?"

I fix my last name and send the photo to everyone in our social circle, because we might as well let everyone know at once that our relationship status has changed.

Then I put my phone on "do not disturb" for the rest of the evening.

This is how our days pass:
Sleep in late, race to work.
Leave work early, race home.
Kneel before my queen, tilt her chalice toward me, and drink my fill.

At Vasquez Studios, Roberto trips me as I pass by with the briefcase. I don't even feel the subsequent bruise that forms on my leg, I just add it to the collection of hurts that Nina will kiss better. Another day, Janine makes me drive to West Covina on an errand and then changes her mind when I'm five minutes from my destination, has me turn around, then changes her mind AGAIN, and I don't even care because Nina's on speakerphone with me the whole time keeping me company and pitching me ideas for spec scripts she might write. I'm so proud of her I bring home a vintage bottle of red with which to celebrate, only to discover Nina has beaten me there, leaving a trail of roses to the bedroom, where she waits, cheeks flushed, eyes mischievous.

We turn the now-spare bedroom into an office. Shove my superfluous bed flush against the far corner and add another desk so there's one for each of us, backs to each other, facing opposite walls. We build a bookshelf and fill it with our combined sets of novels, screenwriting books, and cookbooks.

I point to a spot over my desk. "I think right here I'm going to frame the check stub from when I was on the show. Assuming it ever shows up."

I test out new recipes: Goblin Cobbler, Centauraggon Chicken. We stay up way too late. Days turn into nights and nights turn into weeks. The Farmers Market, the Getty, the Hollywood sign, and my absolute favorite, the Antelope Valley Poppy Reserve in Lancaster, a four-hour round-trip drive worth every second in the car.

We take the 14 there, waving at Vasquez Studios as we pass by.

I'll remember that day forever: the wind whipping Nina's dark hair around her face, the delight in her eyes as we reached the peak of that first hill and she spotted the poppy fields in the distance, calling us toward them with a promise of bucolic, dreamy oblivion. The abundant crop this year was called a super bloom, the flowers so vibrant they seemed to hover and glow, spilling up and down the countryside in undulating waves, the color of blood oranges. It felt as though we'd discovered a world hidden beneath our own; a world that had always been there, waiting for us to pull back the curtain. The way she whispered "No way" and "I've never seen anything like this" echoed my own thoughts.

A stranger took our photo when we arrived, the awe still evident on our faces, Nina's hair and skin contrasting beautifully against the endless orange-and-green backdrop, me tilting my head toward hers. The photo turned out to be the missing piece—the artwork that pulled the apartment together as our shared home: the two of us in those poppy fields, printed on canvas, hung in our bedroom.

We buy surprise gifts for each other, as though we're making up for all the years when it might've been strange to do so, and in this way, we feather our nest.

She teases me endlessly for wearing boxers to bed instead of sleeping nude the way she does. (I have an irrational fear that if a fire alarm goes off, I won't be able to find my clothes and I'll somehow end up stark naked outside. I know, it makes no sense.)

One night she approaches me with a bow-tied box and a coy

look on her face. "Since you insist on wearing clothes to bed, how about these?"

Inside the box is a set of satin pajamas, and on the back of the button-down shirt are the words, "A Knight in the Streets and a Freak in the Sheets" embroidered in *CoRaB* font.

I press the satin to my face, savoring the cool fabric, enamored.

As soon as I can, I return the favor with a silk nightie for her. ("Although since you insist on sleeping naked, I should probably tear it off you.")

Not all our gifts are expensive. In fact, most of them aren't, and we like the cheap ones best. I find Nina a bobblehead Queen Lucinda, one of several editions, for her desk.

"I wish *you* came in a set of twelve so I could collect you all," Nina tells me, pushing me onto the floor.

Two days later, a bobblehead Jeff stares me down at my desk, wearing his eyeball necklace.

The day after that, Post-its appear on the walls and desks, in a rainbow assortment of colors, ever-changing speech bubbles written on them, originating from our bobbleheads. "Get back to work, Worthington," Jeff says in creepy script written in "blood."

A month into our relationship, I open the window in our home office for some fresh air, and a gust of wind scatters the flimsy Post-its off the wall and across the room like leaves. I slam the window shut but it's too late; the Post-its are everywhere. I apologize for the mess, but Nina doesn't say a word; pulls out a Sharpie, removes the cap, and holds it an inch from the wall. She looks at me and I nod back, a thrill swooping up my spine.

She writes "Hi, Sebastian" in big, round letters on the wall between our desks. From that point on we ditch the Post-its and write messages to each other directly on the building, around and above us, because we can paint over it anytime we want.

"Now we can say 'the writing's on the wall' and mean it," Nina declares.

Adulting's never felt better. (I ignore the dirty dishes in the sink, the clothes on the floor, the books stacked everywhere, the Post-its behind the desk and on the floor, and the steady stream of unanswered texts and voice mails piling up in my phone. None of it matters.)

If College Sebastian could see me now, he'd build a shrine to Adult Me and worship me like a god.

CHAPTER 30

NINA

If Sebastian and I were a fanfic, here's what our story heading would be:

> Category: RPF (real person fic), Fluff, HEA
> (happily ever after)
> Fandom(s): Each Other
> Relationship: Friends to lovers
> Additional Tags: Perky Persian / Hot Brit;
> Zelda Gamers Gone Wild
> SUMMARY: 20-something BFFs-turned-
> amours Sebastian and Nina hole up together in
> their mid-Wilshire love den, neglecting all basic
> duties toward friends, family, and the outside
> world.

Millie was right; HEAs and OTPs absolutely belong in real life. In fact, give me all the acronyms because I'm pretty sure that Sebastian and I could coin a few of our own. ILCARDCAK (If Lucinda's Crown's A-Rockin', Don't Come A-Knockin'). FGAI (our Fugue-GetAboutIt state, which Sebastian has informed me Matty used to always ride him about). TUTWAP (Turn Up the WAP, aka the Cardi B special for our foray into erotica).

For once, my life feels as satisfying as a really excellent piece of fiction. I float into work now, nothing bothering me: not the trolls or atrociously spelled memes on Twitter. Not the profoundly disturbing Reddit threads describing the minutiae of *CoRaB* beheadings (rated on a feasibility scale of one to ten), not even Sean yelling at me to get to the bottom of a panicked call from Sabrina, the show's publicist, about an unsavory blind gossip item clearly referencing Roberto.

To top it all off, not only did Lou Trewoski and his staff approve of the writers' room takeover but it's happening *today.*

All I want to do when it's over is to relive it by telling Sebastian every single detail. And I think I know just the place to do it. How would you feel about driving to Irvine for dinner? I text him. There's a Persian kabob place that's been on my list for ages.

I'd feel great about it.

At six p.m., as I see Sebastian's car approaching me on the curb in front of my office building, I'm forced to examine the overwhelming emotions coursing through me. Ennis had done this dozens of times and never, at the approach of his car, had I felt this. I'd felt relief at being done with work, a pleasant sort of geniality at seeing Ennis's handsome face, and a tiny bit of guilt for letting him be my personal chauffeur. Now, I feel like one of those Italian renaissance paintings of the Mother Mary that show sunbeams shooting out of her heart.

I don't even wait for Sebastian to fully brake, just throw open the passenger door, leap into the car, and scramble over the gearshift to give him a huge kiss.

"The writers' room went that well, huh?" he says with a laugh.

"You have *no* idea."

"Tell me," he says as he pulls the car back out onto the road.

"First of all, Lou Trewoski is . . . a dream."

Sebastian raises his eyebrows. "Like a dream . . . *boat?*"

I laugh. "No, like a dream mentor. He was so nice. I got up the nerve to tell him I'm an aspiring TV writer and he gave me all kinds of advice about what to work on. I thought I should be writing a spec script for an existing show, but he told me I should really try working on an original pilot. That it'd be a better calling card for me. He even offered to take a look at it when I'm done!"

Sebastian's jaw drops. "Nina!"

"But, wait, that's not even the best part," I squeal.

"There's more?" Sebastian exclaims, his hands turning white from how hard he's clutching the steering wheel.

I nod. "He let me pitch an idea in the room, Sebastian. And I pitched . . ." I give a pregnant pause, a little trick I learned from my few hours with Lou's team.

"What? What is it?" Sebastian looks like he's ready to explode.

"*Jeffcan!*"

"No . . ." Sebastian whispers.

"And they loved it!"

"Oh my God," Sebastian says, his eyes bugging out as he turns them over to me and then quickly back to the road. "This might be too dangerous a story to tell while I'm driving."

I laugh. "You're right. I'll save the rest for the restaurant."

"There's more?!" Sebastian's voice is almost as high as season four's choir of castrati.

The restaurant is in a strip mall, an unassuming beige building that doesn't prepare you for what happens when you step inside and are greeted with the gaudy but somehow welcoming sight of blue and green mosaic walls, a large painted mural of Persepolis, and white marble statues of griffins that are, for some reason, behind red velvet ropes and standing on burgundy rugs. (Because even imitation art gets the red carpet treatment in Hollywood, I suppose.) Dark green tablecloths cover rows and rows of large tables, and at the back is a stage bathed in blue and purple lights. A completely mismatched array of mirrorwork art, paintings of unibrowed women, large silver samovars, and colorful glass hookahs round out the rest of the décor. It looks a little like my mom's living room, if her living room also doubled as an impromptu nightclub, and I think that's precisely the point.

While we wait for the maitre d' to seat us, Sebastian turns to me. "Okay, I think it's safe for you to tell me the rest now. Do you think they're really going to do it? Jeffcan?"

"Maybe," I reply. "One of the other writers mentioned that it would be great if they had more LGBTQ rep in the show. And then Lou riffed off of it storywise and said if Jeff fell really hard, then maybe he'd give Duncan access to Mount Signon and that could be a great cliffhanger for the season. Oh and . . ." I giggle, thinking of this next part. "They all agreed that Roberto would hate the storyline. Which seemed to give them even more incentive to do it."

"He's a real popular guy, isn't he?"

"You reap what you sow, I guess," I reply. "Does *not* narrow down who leaked that blind item about him."

Sebastian looks down at me, his eyes shining. "I'm *so* proud of you, Nina. You have no idea."

I beam at him. "I wouldn't have even dreamed of asking to go into the writers' room without you. And, I have to admit, Sayeh."

He laughs. "We might owe Sayeh more than that. She kinda gave me hope before I dared hope this"—he lifts up our interlocked hands—"could ever really be a thing."

"She did?" My smile falters. "Oh God, what did she say to you?"

"Not to me. To Millie," he replies. "I believe something like: 'Those two should've boned ages ago since they obviously belong together. Or at least fuck and get it out of their systems.'"

"Jesus Christ," I mutter.

"I don't think I will, by the way. Get it out of my system." He lifts up my hand and kisses it this time, his eyes turning decidedly more wicked.

I smile slyly at him.

We're interrupted by the maitre d', who seats us and hands us the extensive-looking leather-bound menu. Sebastian had already told me that he's leaving the ordering up to me, and it's not a job I'm about to take lightly. "I need silence to study this," I proclaim.

After about ten minutes, I finally put the menu down. "We have a problem."

"What's that?"

"We have to get mast-o-khiar—cucumber and yogurt—as an app. But we also have to get mast-o-mousir, that's yogurt and shallots. And we absolutely need the feta cheese and sabzi. It's . . ." I look up at him seriously. "A lot of dairy."

He nods solemnly. "I think I can take it . . . oh! Speaking of which! Here's a blind item for you. Which gorgeous Shakespearean actress turned TV queen apparently has some sort of personality-changing relationship with cheese? As heard from multiple sources."

"Really? I wonder what happens."

The waiter comes over and asks if we're ready to order our appetizers. I give Sebastian a look and he nods. "Let's go nuts. After all, it is our one-month anniversary."

I laugh. "Yes, it's our very important one-month anniversary." I read the whole list of items to the waiter, deciding at the last minute to add an order of kashk-e-bademjoon to the mix.

With the waiter gone, Sebastian takes my hand, stares into my eyes and says, "Which drop-dead gorgeous social media coordinator, about to be Emmy-winning TV writer, is said to be stepping out with . . ."

"The next hottest cookbook author. And we do mean hottest, folks. Have you seen that Link-like physique? He can scale my Mount Hylia any day." I wink at him as his jaw drops. I can tell I just majorly turned him on—the nerd.

"I got you something," he says huskily.

"What for?" I ask.

"Duh. Our one-month anniversary."

"Oh," I say, flushing. "I didn't think we were really celebrating that."

"It's just a small thing," Sebastian reassures me as he reaches into his pocket and takes out a black box wrapped in a bow.

It does look small. It also looks an awful lot like a jewelry box. "Um, what is it?"

"Open and find out." He's looking at me like I'm being weird.

But I'm scared. I hesitate before reaching for the box, and, in order not to make it obvious my fingers are shaking, yank off the lid. I breathe a sigh of relief when I see what's inside.

It's an enamel pin of Caveman Tal with the phrase "You Can Club Me Anytime." I laugh, maybe a little too loudly.

"Are Neanderthals the official gift for one-month anniversaries?" I ask.

"Absolutely," he says.

"I love it." I lean over and kiss him.

"Nina?" a hesitant voice asks from behind me.

I turn around and see a face that I didn't think I'd still recognize after seventeen years.

But even though his hair is salt and pepper now, his stomach rounder, the circles under his eyes—always prominent— a deeper shade of purple, it is undoubtedly the man formerly known as Baba.

I just stare at him, unsure of what to say.

"I can't believe it's you. Sayeh told me you lived here now, but still . . ." he says.

I nod and then pick up my glass of water and drink from it, stalling. My father is looking over at Sebastian, clearly hoping to be introduced.

"Hello," he says.

And just as Sebastian opens his mouth to respond, I finally find my voice. "We're in the middle of dinner."

My father does an awkward little bow. "Of course, of course, I can see that. It was just too much of a coincidence for me not to come over and say hello."

"Right," I say. "Hello. And goodbye."

He reaches into his pocket and hands over a card. "I asked Sayeh to give this to you but just in case . . . If you ever want to talk, please just call."

He smiles at me and I nod. "Okay." I put the card in my purse, and his face brightens. Little does he know, it's just a formality. No need to cause a scene here in the middle of what had, up to this point, been a lovely date with my boyfriend.

"It was wonderful to see you, azizam," he says softly before he gives another little bow and walks, I'm relieved to see, out the door. Thank God he was at the end of his meal.

"Nina. You okay?" Sebastian asks.

I realize I've been staring into my water glass for who knows how long.

"Yes. Of course. Where were we?" I pick up the gift box again. "Oh right, we were talking about how exquisite this is. Where did you find it?"

He pauses. "Was that . . ."

"My father. Yes. And, no, I don't have any updates on him or our relationship since the last time we talked about him when I was nineteen. So you're totally debriefed on that situation." I smile tightly.

"Riiiight," Sebastian says slowly. "Okay. So do you want to talk about this now?"

"Absolutely not," I reply firmly.

"Got it," he says. "So you want to talk about it later."

"That's probably a negative too," I reply.

"Nina . . ." Sebastian says.

"Sebastian." I look him hard in the eyes, almost a dare to

ruin our night by pressing something I obviously don't want pressed.

"Okay," he finally says, looking away.

"Oh yes! Our apps are here." I look at the waiters bringing over warm pita bread along with our cheese, two types of yogurt, and eggplant spread. "Now, Sebastian . . ." I place my hand over his. I can forget about the mindfuck that just happened if I only focus on this food, this space, this man in front of me. The right now which is, after all, what I'm best at. "Let me school you on the myriad ways to pita."

CHAPTER 31

SEBASTIAN

Running late for work the next morning, I traverse the parking garage in long strides. I'm bushed from tossing and turning most of the night. Nina refused to acknowledge the unexpected cameo by her dad at dinner, let alone how she felt about it. During the long drive home from Orange County, she fiddled with the radio, darting from station to station, using music to fill the air where a conversation should have been.

When she lowered the volume during an ad break, I thought she'd changed her mind and decided to let me in on her thoughts, but it was only to run a new idea for her potential pilot script by me.

Succumbing to a yawn now, I unlock my car and wonder if I have time to hit the Starbucks drive-through. As I swing the driver's-side door open, Sam pulls up behind me in his metallic blue Genesis Coupe, aka his baby, and blocks my exit.

I wave, feeling weirdly caught out. We haven't crossed paths except to, well, cross paths in the hallway or elevator these past five weeks, but right now isn't a good time to rectify that.

"Hey, Sam," I call out. "Have a good day."

He leans his head out the window. "You got a second?"

"I'm afraid not. Could you text me?"

"I would if I thought you'd read it."

Ah. I place my laptop bag in the passenger seat, slowly straighten my spine, and walk the plank to Sam's car. Doesn't look like he'll be moving his vehicle until we talk.

"Have you spoken to Matty lately?"

I scratch behind my ear. "Define 'lately'?"

"Never mind. I *know* you haven't because he's been blowing up my phone asking where the hell you've been." He points at me, his face serious. "You need to call him."

Dread expands in my throat. "What's wrong? Did something happen?"

"I'm not going to say anything else. Find out for yourself. Now."

For dinner I make the fastest grilled cheese known to man, burning mine and undercooking Nina's. We're lucky I didn't trigger the fire alarm from all the smoke (though at least I'm dressed).

Nina homes in on the fact that I'm shoveling my sandwich in at a rate of knots. "I don't actually know the Heimlich, FYI."

"Okay if I have the guys over tonight?" My crumb-filled words tumble out so fast they bump into each other.

It takes her a moment to decipher what I've said. She swallows her last bite of barely melted cheese bread before answering. "You don't need my permission."

"I meant without you here."

The intense look she wore after last night's dinner returns, and the sight of it sends a warning flare through my brain.

"Matty's going through something, and I want to show him and Sam how we decorated the place, let them add some artwork to the writing wall—if that's cool with you—and shoot the shit for a couple hours."

She gnaws on her lip. "Where am I supposed to go?"

"You know what, forget I asked. You can stay."

Her expression is blank. "How magnanimous of you."

"I didn't mean it like that."

She moves to the sink and drops her empty dinner plate inside. It clatters against the utensils already there. "It's about time I got a library card. I could go there."

"Is it open this late?" It's gone half-six already.

She scrolls through her phone. "Yeah, until nine. Would that give you enough time?"

"How will you get there?"

"I'll take the bus. That'll add an unnecessary hour to my trip, all the more time for you to bro out."

"You really don't have to leave."

"They're my friends, too, you know," she says quietly.

"Not the last five years, they weren't," I retort.

Jesus. It's like some evil creature has taken over my brain and is making me say the worst possible things at every moment. "I'm sorry, I didn't sleep well last night, which isn't your fault, but . . . Could we start this conversation over?"

She takes a deep breath, either on the verge of agreeing with me or refuting me, so of course that's when Matty and Sam knock on the door.

"Your friends are here." Nina goes to grab her purse.

I follow her, supplicating. "They're *our* friends. But is it so awful I want to see them on my own?"

She stops. Cups my face with her free hand and runs her fingers through my hair. "Of course you guys can have the apartment. Just—give me more warning next time. Okay?"

"Definitely."

A quick peck on the lips and she throws the door open, says "Hello and goodbye" to the guys, and moves down the hall. Naturally, this prompts Matty to sing a Beatles verse as he and Sam walk inside.

Abruptly, Matty's off-key crooning stops.

"What the fuck did you do to my apartment?" he demands, scanning the walls and peering into his old bedroom.

* * *

"How far along is she?" I ask Matty. The three of us have gathered in the new office, drinking beer and "bro-ing out," as Nina put it. Though I'm pretty sure our topic this evening is decidedly un-bro-y.

"We had the twelve-week visit." Matty digs through his wallet and presses a wrinkled ultrasound photo to my chest. I glance at the black-and-white blob depicted in the film strip of squares and try to affect an expression of wonderment.

I imagine Matty as a dad, hoisting a kid up on his shoulders, taking it to a baseball game, or teaching it to dance with its feet resting on his shoes, and the feeling I was pretending to have genuinely manifests.

"You're going to be a great dad," I tell him.

"You know what the best part is?" Sam asks me.

"No, what's the best part?"

"One day the kid'll buy him ties for Father's Day that *aren't* Red Sox."

I crack up. "We'll never have to see those fucking ties again! Totally the best part!" Sam and I slap hands and proceed to torture Matty for ten minutes straight. A sampling:

"What's on your baby registry?" I ask, faux-sincerely.

"I don't know, maybe a—"

"Daddy diaper pail?"

"Car seat with vomit bag?"

"A blow-up doll since Maritza won't have time for you ever again?"

"Fuck you, guys," Matty groans.

"No, really, what can we get you to help out?"

His eyes dart between us, wary. "Are you being serious this time, or . . . ?"

"Yeah, of course, what do you guys need?"

"We could use—"

"Retroactive condoms?"

"A one-way ticket to Belize?"

"A gun?"

"Jesus, Sam!" I smack him but even Matty is laughing now.

"For him, not for her!" Sam explains.

"Doesn't matter!"

"She'll get the life insurance. Right? Raise that baby in style? You need life insurance now, by the way. If you didn't know."

"Oh God." Matty slumps on the floor against the wall, below a Red Sox logo he drew in marker.

"Okay, we had our fun, let's dial it back," I tell Sam.

"You started it," he retorts, and we crack up again.

"It'll be all right," I tell Matty.

"Will it? Every decision I make from now on, I need to take the baby into consideration. If I stay late at work, I'll be missing out on baby-time or whatever, but if I *don't* stay late, I'm missing out on extra money, and shouldn't that be more important, if I want to give the kid a good life? And what about the Lemurs? Will I still be allowed to play baseball, or is that dead to me? Speaking of, we've got a doubleheader next week, if you and Belle-y Belle want to stop by."

"I'll ask, but that sounds good to me." Maybe it'll repair the damage from my foot-in-mouth disease earlier, if the four of us do something as a group.

"You dropped off the grid," Matty tells me.

"I know. Sorry I wasn't there for you when you found out about the baby."

"It's not that. We want to know how *you're* doing too."

"I live down the hall and I didn't see you for weeks," Sam points out.

"Do you think you and Nina might be moving a little fast?" Matty asks.

"Nine years is fast?"

"Come on, more than half of those years don't count. I saw the huge photo of you guys in the poppy fields. Every inch of this place is like a weird shrine to your history."

"It looks intense," Sam adds.

"Maybe I'd agree with you if I hadn't known her for so long, but if I don't lock this down, I'll become another six-weeker. No offense, Sam."

"None taken. We didn't last half that long."

I puff out a breath. "Right. Anyway, who wants another lager?"

I collect their empties and wander into the kitchen.

I could tell them the truth, that she refuses to talk about her family, and that I rarely get enough sleep because I'm dancing as fast as I can to keep her interested, but it's been so long since Sam, Matty, and I have spent time together that I don't want to waste the diminishing hours we've got bitching and moaning. Besides, Matty's the one we need to support right now.

Drinks in hand, I move toward the office to rejoin my friends. Their voices tangle together on the other side of the door and against my better judgment I linger outside instead of going in.

"What'd you call it in college, when he and Nina would ignore everybody? A Luge State?" Sam asks.

Matty's withering retort: "Luge is an Olympic sport like sledding."

"I meant fugue," Sam growls. "You know what I meant."

"Yeah. This is Fugue-GetAboutIt on acid." Matty's voice drops, but I can still hear what he says next, and the frustration fueling his words: "I know he doesn't do it on purpose, but when Nina's around, he can't see anything or anyone else."

Chapter 32

NINA

I don't stay at the library. Turns out if there are no utility bills in my name, and my non-driver's ID is still from New York, they won't let me sign up for a card. I'm too transient for even the library to trust, and suddenly I don't feel like hanging out there anymore

I end up calling the only other person I know in Los Angeles, besides my ex-boyfriend, who's not having a party at my apartment right now. Sayeh's free after a meeting with one of her product designers. I find her sitting at an outdoor table at the café at the Beverly Hills Hotel, a pair of sunglasses on her head, poring over some thick pieces of paper.

"Hello," I say as I sit down.

"Yo," she says, not looking up at me, continuing to flip back and forth between some drawings that I can now see depict several versions of an eyeshadow palette. Her name is written on it in different fonts and styles, some on the cover of the palette, some on the mirror, some etched within the powder itself.

Why don't I have any other friends in Los Angeles? I wonder to myself. *I've been here for over four months. . . .*

"So," Sayeh finally says, as if reading my thoughts, "why did you call me?"

"What do you mean?" I ask.

She rolls her eyes. "You never call me. So there must be a reason now."

"Do you *want* me to call you?" I retort. "It's not like you seem to enjoy my company."

"I could say the same."

"Maybe I don't call you because this is already exhausting." I snatch the drink menu and try to find something to take off the edge. Good Lord, these prices are insane. Nineteen dollars for a Bee's Knees? Nineteen!

"You find my honesty exhausting—"

"Some people call it abject rudeness—" I cut in.

But Sayeh continues as if I haven't. "Meanwhile I'm done with surface relationships. So. We may be at an impasse."

I roll my eyes, but when I look at Sayeh over the drink menu, she's not smiling, she's not giving me an arch eyebrow or side eye. In fact, she looks genuinely straight-faced. "Wait," I say. "Are you serious?"

"Why wouldn't I be?" she says, taking the last sip of the cucumber mojito she was nursing when I got there.

"Because . . . you're my sister. And you're never serious."

She shakes her head and puts down her glass. "Why do you insist on still thinking I'm eight years old?"

"Uh, how about because you act like an eight-year-old?"

She gives a harsh laugh and closes the folder on her papers. "Right. I got lucky, stumbled upon fame on the interwebs as a child, and am now trying to milk it for all it's worth as a talentless faux Kardashian who's about two years behind on the contouring trend."

"What? Where is this coming from?"

"Hi, can I get you something to drink?" the posh, vested waiter asks me.

"Sure, the Bee's Knees," I say, throwing caution and my credit card bill to the wind because I don't have time to analyze the menu.

"I'll have another one of these." Sayeh points to her mojito.

"Are you ready to order food as well?" he asks.

"Give us a minute," I tell him with a smile. And then turn to Sayeh, who looks—for the first time in memory—profoundly miserable. "What happened, Sayeh? Who said that?"

"A lifestyle blogger. Like, *the* lifestyle blogger."

I raise my eyebrow at her. "Sayeh. You know better than anyone not to trust personal comments on the internet."

"And why not?" she asks, her voice rising. "The internet made me. The internet can just as easily destroy me." She looks down and I could swear there's a tear hanging off one of her perfectly curled eyelashes.

I reach out my hand and awkwardly touch her fingers. "Hey. Are you okay?"

She takes the hand away, quickly wipes at her eyes, and looks up at me. "Of course I'm okay. I'm always okay. You're always okay. Maman's always okay. The Shamses are always okay."

"Look, I . . ." I'm not sure what to say. We are firmly in uncharted territory here. "I'm here if you want to talk," I say unconvincingly.

"I do," she says, and I see some color return to her face along with her composure. When she speaks again, she's back to her regular bored, snarky voice. "I want to talk about your fuck buddy and why I had to find the news out from a group text instead of social media, like God intended. Geez, Nina. You really need to reactivate your profiles."

I stare at her. "Uh. Didn't some stranger on the internet just totally shatter your confidence?"

She ignores me. "So. How is he?"

"Who? Sebastian? He's fine."

She rolls his eyes. "No, I don't mean, how is he doing? I mean how is he? As a loverrrr. Spill."

"Ew, no," I say, though I'm pretty sure a faint blush is creeping up my cheeks as I'm imagining two days ago, when he surprised me in the shower. There's something very delicious, and very hot, about being in the beginning of a relationship and already having the convenience of living together.

"I knew this time it was finally going to happen," Sayeh says smugly. "Now that he's the convenient one."

My erotic flashback dissipates in a cloud of imaginary shower sex steam. "What do you mean?"

She shrugs. "He's your roommate, right? It's easier to just be together and get all the sexual tension out. I mean, I don't know what's going to happen after, once you reach your four-month time limit. But for now, it makes sense for you."

The waiter comes over and places our drinks on the table. Sayeh immediately lifts hers up and gives me a wry "Beh salamati." But I'm frozen.

"That's a really shitty thing to say," I reply.

She takes a sip as she nods slowly. "Maybe. But it's honest."

I shake my head, pick up my own drink, and take a swig. She *is* exhausting.

"Baba told me he ran into you," she says.

"Yeah. Now, you want to tell me how I'm in the wrong there? Considering I was ten when he left and he was the adult?" It boggles my mind that they talk so regularly, that she would know about our run-in just last night.

"Maman was never the same after he left," Sayeh says.

"No shit," I say bitterly.

"You guys thought I was too little and maybe too self-absorbed to see it, but I saw. How everything made her cry for years. How she kept those wedding pictures of them up."

"I hated those pictures," I say.

"I know."

"Why would you keep up a shrine to someone who shattered you?" I say.

"Because before he shattered her, he made her complete," Sayeh says simply.

"And that's precisely why it hurt so much," I agree. "But she prolonged it. She could have chosen to hate him instead of continuing to love him, to pine for him."

"Could she? Can you *choose* to stop loving someone?" Sayeh asks.

"Sure you can," I say, finishing off my inordinately expensive drink way sooner than I expected. "I've done it plenty of times."

Sayeh looks at me. "Someone you *loved*. Really, truly loved?"

This night is a mess. I want another drink but then again, more alcohol probably won't make it better. Sayeh and I are on thin ice as is. Sebastian and I are on . . . not thin ice exactly but something murky that's making me feel uncomfortable. I should probably just go and sleep it off.

I check my watch. It's eight p.m. It should take me an hour to get home, which is around the time I told Sebastian I'd be back.

"I should go," I say as I dig into my purse for my wallet.

"It's an expensed meal. Don't worry about it," Sayeh says. "Do you need a ride?"

Yes, but also, no. I just want to be independent for once and call an Uber . . . a regular, no-strings-attached Uber, who can silently drive me home and not judge me or my life.

"I'm okay," I say. "By the way, I like the script font. Etched into the powder. I know you didn't ask for my opinion. . . ."

But Sayeh is looking up at me in surprise. She opens up her folder again, flips through the pages, stops at the one I just described, and points to it. "This one?"

I nod.

"Yeah," she says, with a small smile. "That's my favorite too."

CHAPTER 33

SEBASTIAN

A few nights later, Nina and I are settling in with some take-away on the couch—I'm too tired to cook, and she's too tired to taste anything that hasn't been vetted—when her phone dings with a news alert. She glances at it and her body goes rigid.

"Holy shit." Nina scrolls rapidly. "A guy was arrested outside Vasquez Studios this afternoon."

"What are you talking about?"

"It says he was caught trying to break into one of the cars in the lot, looking for scripts or something. He had a crowbar and a knife."

A horrified laugh explodes from my mouth. "Whaaaaat?"

Her eyes get bigger. "Apparently, he's been camping out overnight, or I guess, *hiding out* to be more accurate, in one of the rock formations with a pair of binoculars and a notebook, spying on the cars that come and go, writing down their license plate numbers."

"That could've been *my* car he tried to break into! What if I'd had the briefcase attached? Would he have tried to chop off my hand?"

"Oh my God." Nina slides into my lap and curls herself around me.

I pat her back, feeling dizzy. "It's okay, because they caught him, right?" I keep the next thought to myself, that there's no way he's the only one.

Nina kisses my neck and hugs me even tighter. "Is it worth risking your *safety* for this show?"

If I hadn't gotten this job, Nina and I might never have crossed paths again. We'd be two ex-friends living in the same city without knowing it. But we did, and we're together, we're in love, and we're both working at the show that created us, really. It *has* to be worth it.

Although, if I could change one thing, I wouldn't have disappeared on Sam and Matty. I have to pay better attention to that stuff, yet without insulting Nina in the process. Our argument's been put to rest, as far as I can tell, but it could've just as easily erupted. It's a fine line I'm walking lately, and I've never been good at balance.

We doom-scrolled Twitter, TMZ, and various fan sites long past midnight, looking for updates on the would-be thief, but there was little trustworthy information out there.

My text to Janine received a low-key, **Don't worry, stuff like this happens all the time; the public doesn't usually hear about it.**

Shockingly, this knowledge didn't make me worry *less*.

I do my best not to wake Nina at five-thirty a.m., but as I'm slipping out of bed, she panic-flails in her sleep. "Huh? Bees? *Leeches?*"

"It's okay. Go back to bed. I'm getting an early start," I whisper.

I haven't been to the gym since Nina and I got together over a month ago.

At first, I was cocky about it, like, "Who needs exercise? We're burning calories every night, hardy-har," until it dawned on me that burning calories wasn't why I went to the gym.

Short-lived catalog modeling notwithstanding, my workouts were about my mental health, not my abs.

I feel sluggish and groggy all the time. Nina and I stay up later than we should most nights, "burning calories" or watching TV because we both have a list of shows from the past five years that we want to see the other person's reactions to. In theory, it's a wonderful way to spend our time, if we didn't have other obligations or responsibilities, but the reality is my sleepless nights are wreaking havoc on my ability to function; and that's *with* the three cups of coffee I down like medicine throughout the morning and the two cups I choke back in the afternoon, guaranteeing I'll be up late again each night.

The cycle of caffeine abuse.

I've reached the dessert portion of my cookbook brainstorming, so it's unhealthy sweets and treats 24/7 to boot.

Operating on four hours of sleep, I nearly drop a fifteen-pound free weight on my foot in the gym, which prompts visions of me in a hospital bed, leg in a cast, zonked out in a private room. How luxurious would that be, to enjoy a deep, fulfilling snooze all by myself?

Wait, WTF?

The implications of such a bizarre fantasy shake me from my stupor. If a smashed limb sounds preferable to my current situation, that's a blaring indication I need to make changes.

I can't shake the feeling that if Nina's awake, I should be, too, basking in our togetherness. I don't want to miss a single instant with her, not when I lost her for so long. Not when I could conceivably lose her again at any moment.

Maybe I can convince her to hit the sack early tonight, at least.

The possibility calms me down just long enough for the universe—as manifested through my iPhone—to get wind of my tranquility and beep with a calendar reminder: We've got tickets for a screening at the Arclight tonight.

* * *

"Fuck, it's burned." I dump the blackened monkey bread into the trash and slam the oven door shut. "I have to start over."

"We're going to miss the movie." Nina's dolled up, standing by the door.

"I know, but I promised Matty I'd have his good-luck monkey bread for him tonight. It's his traditional good luck snack before his baseball game tomorrow."

Nina vibrates with impatience. "The bread doesn't have magical powers. He'll understand. Come on, let's get going."

"I can't." I tug my oven mitts off and face her. "Can we catch it over the weekend instead?"

"This is the only time the screenwriter's doing a Q&A, so . . . I'll report back." She opens the door to leave.

I wipe the sweat off my brow with my wrist and follow her, propping the door open with my foot. "You're still going?"

"Yeah, I've been looking forward to it all week."

"Okay. Have a good time, I guess."

"We're allowed to do things on our own, you know," she says.

"Right, but then how come you were upset when I made plans with Matty and Sam?"

"I wasn't upset you made plans."

"You kind of were, Nina."

"Can we talk about this when I get back?"

I keep my voice soft and steady. "I'm really asking."

"Okay, CliffsNotes version, I'm not upset that you want to make your friend good-luck sugar bombs or whatever. I'm annoyed that you let it take precedence over plans we'd already *made.* If you had told me you'd be busy tonight, I'd have known not to get you a ticket."

"I thought I could juggle both things."

She squeezes my hand. "It's fine, I'll see you when I get back."

The next day after work, I purchase a fancy stationery set from the Beverly Hills store where Millie bought her pen, along with a wax seal kit for Nina.

Presenting her with it feels different, though. It's not a spontaneous gesture born of affection or the desire to see her smile. It's an apology, and a blatant one at that.

"Another gift?" Nina says. She sounds . . . weary. "That's nice of you, but you don't need to be blowing your paychecks on me like that."

"I saw it and thought of you. It was on sale. No big deal." Lie. Lie. Lie.

She places the stationery on the bookshelf and tucks her hand in mine to lead me to the spare bed. It's more of a storage unit at this point, so we shift books and other detritus aside to make room so we can sit.

"What's going on with you? Last night you were so worried about that—bread."

The gap in her cadence tells me a choice adjective was removed.

"You know Matty would've understood, don't you?" she presses, her brown eyes searching mine.

I look away, because I can't have this conversation *and* look at her. "I have to be careful, that's all."

"You do a lot of things for them, grocery shopping and cooking, and that's great of you, but what do you think would happen if you didn't try so hard?"

"I don't have so many gobs of friends that I can get rid of them and grow new ones, okay? The ones I've got mean the world to me. You of all people should know that."

"I do. I just feel like we make plans and you agree to them but then the day arrives and you're all discombobulated, like it's *so* perplexing that—what?"

I tuck a silky strand of her hair behind her ear. "I love that you used the word 'discombobulated.'"

"Yeah, well, I'm a full-on wunderkind."

"I've never doubted it for a second."

I drop to the floor and hug her around the waist, pressing my face into her belly. She strokes my hair and I lean into her touch.

"I'm sorry," I murmur.

It's my most frequent phrase around her lately, and I hate it; that I've done so many things that apparently require apologies, and also that I can't seem to stop.

We live together, spend pretty much every night and weekend together, yet I feel with each passing day we're drifting further apart, snapping at each other, or refusing to have certain conversations. The problem is there's nowhere to retreat, regroup, or lick our wounds.

Maybe the edict is true: When the highs are this high, the lows are going to be correspondingly low. But lurching from one extreme to another is exhausting.

Nina slowly unbuttons my shirt cuff and rolls up my sleeve to reveal the handcuff marks from the briefcase. She presses her lips to the raised, red bracelet, tracing the circle, her lips like aloe, and I close my eyes.

"You don't have to try so hard with me, either," she says quietly.

CHAPTER 34

NINA

The next few days feel normal again, almost. We're blowing through seasons of old shows on Netflix and Hulu every night. Sebastian refrains from buying me any new gifts, which is a good thing. The stationery set remains unopened on the bookshelf and I wonder if I can eventually press him to return it, but I also don't want to bring it up and ruin the little bubble we've created again.

Because things also feel as fragile as a bubble, as if one wrong move and our rainbow-colored orb will burst, leaving us with nothing. I feel uneasy, but I try to channel it into something more productive. Per Lou Trewoski's advice, I'm working on a spec pilot—a sitcom about the disastrous behind-the-scenes world of an epic sci-fi/fantasy show reboot. I mean, they say write what you know, don't they?

This leaves me with an excuse to retreat into the office for hours at a time and, when I do, I can feel myself relax, release tension until my body slumps down in the old orange desk chair. It's tension I don't want to closely examine. Sebastian is the best friend I've ever had. I'm crazy about him and insanely attracted to him. This should be perfect. This *is* perfect. Inevitably, I end my train of thoughts right there and save the rest of the drama for the page.

Tonight, we have a date to go see Matty play baseball. His

girlfriend and Sam are also going. I think it's a little bit of a make-good for Sebastian acting like they weren't my friends too. I'm looking forward to hanging out with all of them, and Matty's girlfriend, whom I haven't met yet.

Maritza ends up being really nice, her baby bump just barely showing, and her bronze skin offset by a casual black dress and white Converse. When the boys leave to get us snacks, I start up a conversation.

"So how are you feeling?" I ask.

"Pretty good," she says, lightly touching her belly. "Now that the first trimester is over. You know . . ."

I really don't know but I nod anyway, then try to change the subject to something I can contribute to. "Sebastian tells me you're a teacher?"

She nods. "Kindergarten."

"My mom taught second grade," I say. "So you must really like kids?"

"I do. Though . . . I have a feeling they might be easier to deal with when they're not yours."

I laugh. "That's what my mom always said."

"You guys thinking about having kids one day?"

"Who?" I ask, caught off-guard. "Oh, you mean me and Sebastian?"

She gives me a confused smile. "Um, yeah."

"Oh, I don't know," I say, waving my hand. "We've only been together a little over a month."

"Oh, I'm sorry!" she says, looking flustered. "I thought Matty said you'd been together almost ten years."

"Oh, no. We've *known* each other that long. But we were just friends. . . ." And then we were nothing. And now we are . . . everything?

I'm luckily diverted from having to explain too much by the arrival of Sam, who's gotten back before Sebastian.

"For my favorite ex," he says, handing me my container of crinkle fries.

I snort. "Thanks."

"Wait. Did you guys date too?" Maritza asks, looking between us. I can tell her perception of what she thought was Matty's normal group of friends has suddenly been thrown for a loop.

I laugh. "Only for a minute."

"Excuse me," Sam says. "But it was ten days."

"Ten days of sticking our tongues down each other's throats," I add.

I hear a throat clearing behind me and look to see Sebastian carrying an armful of hot dogs.

"Um . . . what are you guys talking about?" Sebastian asks.

"Freshman year," Sam says as he reaches out to help Sebastian distribute the rest of the food. "We were giving Maritza some context."

Sebastian eyes me with a look I can't quite recognize. Is he actually . . . mad? Jealous? I turn to Maritza to clarify further. "Anyway, once we had a couple of conversations . . ."

"Once we came up for air," Sam says, looking over at Sebastian and chuckling.

"We pretty much realized we should just be friends," I finish. "And then we all became friends."

"I see," Maritza says. "Until recently. When you and Sebastian became something more?"

"Exactly," I say, smiling over at Sebastian. He smiles back but it doesn't reach his eyes and I really don't know why until right before the sixth inning. I come back from the bathroom in time to hear Sebastian and Sam having a surprisingly heated conversation.

"I can't believe you brought up that you dated Nina," Sebastian says.

"It was only a joke," Sam says. "Nina was just explaining to Maritza how we all met. You really need to chill."

Sebastian pauses for a minute and then turns to Sam. "I feel like all I've been is *chill* for nine years. Every time you talked about her or called her 'my favorite ex' when you knew how much it bothered me."

"First of all, that was mostly a ploy to try to get you to admit how you felt about her, ideally *to* her. And secondly, how can you be jealous of me kissing her like ten years ago? You kiss her all the time *now!*"

"I'm not jealous," he mutters.

"You could've fooled me," Sam replies.

I decide now's a good time to clomp down the two metal stairs between me and our seats, letting them know I'm coming. They abruptly end the conversation and I decide it's for the best that we all pretend I didn't hear it.

But Sebastian is in a funk. He's quiet for most of the rest of the game. He's quiet during our ride back, with Sam in the back seat since we're driving to the same building. Sam spends most of the ride talking about a sponsor he's chasing for his podcast, some very LA-sounding naturopathic startup company.

When we say goodbye to Sam at our door and go into the apartment, I pour two glasses of wine and hand one to Sebastian. I see him futzing around with the remote, about to cue up the next episode of *Veep*, but I put my hand on his to stop him.

"Hey," I say. "I think we need to talk."

He looks over at me, alarmed. "Why?"

"Because you're upset. And I don't know why."

"Oh," he says, looking relieved. He runs a hand through his hair and then gives a short bark of a laugh. "I don't really know why either. I mean, I do, but it's a stupid reason."

I settle into the couch, indicating that he should go on.

"I just . . . I hate when Sam pulls that 'my favorite ex' shit. He's done it for forever and it drives me crazy."

"And you've told him not to do it before . . ." I extrapolate.

"Actually, no. I haven't," Sebastian says. "Tonight was the first time I ever told him how much it bothers me."

"Oh," I say. "So he never knew?"

Sebastian shakes his head. "I guess he does now." He looks at me, worried. "You think I should go and apologize?"

"Uh, no. I don't think he's particularly upset. He seemed fine in the car."

"You're right," he says as he puts his head back on the couch. "Maybe I can just bake him some of his favorite blondies. I can use the recipe as a starting-off point for the cookbook, too. 'Castration Bars?' You know, 'cause of the chopped nuts?"

He smiles at me and I smile back, but I don't focus on the TV even when he turns the episode on.

"Sebastian," I say after two minutes of President Selina Meyer saying hilariously horrible things that I'm not able to fully appreciate right now.

"Oh, I'm sorry. I didn't even get us a snack." He pauses the TV and starts to get up, but I put an arm on his hand to stop him.

"No, that's not what I want. Can I ask you . . . why didn't you tell me? All that time in college? That you had feelings for me? Was it because of Sam?"

He settles back down on the couch. "Yes. Well . . . not just Sam. There was always *some* guy around. Some guy you met because he sat next to you in class or sold you a sandwich. Some convenient guy."

It's not lost on me that Sayeh used the exact same word last week. But I try to let it slide. "But none of them were important. . . ."

"Exactly. I didn't want to be another unimportant guy to you either."

"You wouldn't have been . . ." I say, but then stop myself because it sounds empty. If he'd told me how he felt freshman year, he would have been another four-monther, another guy I had fun with for a while and then left behind when things got too serious. In fact, a couple more months and we'd finally pass that threshold. Wouldn't we?

But then I look over at him. He's gotten skinnier over the past few weeks, his eyes hollowed out. I don't know how because I feel like we've just been eating prototype sweets and lounging on the couch. I know my jeans aren't quite fitting the way they used to. Sebastian looks tired.

And the thing is, I bet I do too.

I put down my wine.

"Sebastian," I say again, and look him in the eyes. "I don't want you to be unimportant to me, either. I don't ever want that."

He looks over and smiles, reaching over to put his arm on my shoulder.

I swallow and try to smile. "So how about we give this one more week. And then we go back. To just being best friends."

He blinks at me. "Are you . . . joking?"

I shake my head. "Look, what Matty and Maritza have . . . what a lot of people have . . . it's just not for me, you know? I mean, you *do* know, because that's why you never told me how you felt before. So I think you'll understand why this is the way it has to be."

He gets up from the couch, running his hand through his hair again. He never got it cut after my chop job so it's gotten longer and shaggier again. He looks at me. "Nina. I love you," he says, managing to make the words sound both true and angry.

I nod. "I know. And you have to understand I love you too. As much as I can. But, just . . . I don't think I can give you what you need. Maritza asked me today whether we'd ever have kids. . . ." I let out a nervous gulp of laughter.

"And what? That was funny to you?"

"It was . . . terrifying," I answer honestly. "I've never thought about having my own kids. I've never thought about getting married. I've never even thought about being in a real relationship with anyone. This"—I point around at the apartment, at the giant picture of the two of us, at the literal writing on the wall—"is just too intense. Because it's with you. You mean too much to me to keep this up."

He stops and looks at me. "So you're saying you can't do this . . . because you care about me too much?" His tone is disbelieving.

I nod. "That's exactly it."

"And you want to keep being intimate for another week and then just . . . stop?"

I stand up and touch his cheek. "I think it would help give us some closure on all this. Besides, there were a couple of things I came up with over the past week that we haven't tried yet," I say, trying—and failing—to lighten the moment. I lean in and kiss him softly on the corner of his mouth. When he doesn't reciprocate, I lean back to look at him.

"Does breaking up with me turn you on?" he asks coldly.

"No. *You* turn me on," I respond, but step away from him.

"Has it ever occurred to you that sex and intimacy actually go together, Nina? Like, that's what a real relationship is."

I pick up the stationery set from the bookshelf. "Well, has it occurred to you that a relationship isn't about giving everything of yourself all the time to another person?"

"That's your problem with me?" he laughs bitterly. "I *give* you too many things?"

"You give everyone too many things!" I burst out. "And I don't just mean gifts. I mean your time. I mean monkey bread."

"Why is that goddamn monkey bread such a sore point with you?" he shouts.

"It's not about the monkey bread!" I get loud right back. "It's about you feeling like you have to become a doormat for anyone to like you. We want you to just be Sebastian."

"But you don't," he replies. "You don't want me to just be Sebastian, because you don't want to be with me, Nina."

I have to try to make him understand. "It's the total opposite. I do want to be with you. I want to be with you all the time."

"Then why the hell do you want to end things?"

"Because friends stay together. And lovers don't." I say it very calmly because I feel it's the mantra that's been stitched on my heart, even though I've never said it out loud before.

"How can you say that?" he says. "Just because your parents didn't . . . Lots of people have. What about Paul Newman and Joanne Woodward? Tom Hanks and Rita Wilson?"

"Do you really want to keep giving me examples from Hollywood?" I ask wryly.

"My parents," he says. "Our neighbors in Sherborne have been married almost fifty years. Matty and Maritza are going to make it work. I know they will."

I sigh. "I hope you're right. I really do. But I just don't see it for myself. I never have. It's not you. . . ."

"Don't," he says forcefully. "Don't you dare end us with a cliché."

"'Sometimes tropes are tropes for a reason,'" I mutter, and I don't even know why. Except that when things get their roughest, I tend to retreat into writing analogies. I like the worlds I can control, the drama that goes how I say it will.

"I have to go," he says as he takes his keys and wallet from the side table and opens the door.

He turns to me before he leaves. "I think you did this to spare your heart. But you did it with no regard to mine." He chokes up on the last few words, but then turns and leaves, slamming the door behind him.

CHAPTER 35

SEBASTIAN

When you kiss a friend, the friendship dies. That's what I always told myself. Turns out it's a lie; or at least, it's not the full story. I know, shocker, a fantasy series about time travel, centaurs, and queens didn't accurately portray someone's inner journey in twenty-first-century Los Angeles.

Don't get me wrong; the moment Nina kissed me, our friendship perished. But a phoenix emerged from the ashes, majestic and beautiful. I will never regret that kiss and everything it led to. We were fucking perfect together. We were endgame.

Either she values us, *this* version of us, or she doesn't. Telling me I'm "too important" to be with is utter tripe.

After storming out of the building, I walk past the Grove and all the way up Fairfax. I linger over a matzo ball soup at Canter's Deli, but it doesn't comfort me. I can't even taste it; all it does is scorch my tongue.

I walk home, dread accompanying each step, but when I pass my apartment door and continue down the hall, the dread lifts. If Sam's not around, I'll get in my car and drive to Matty's because I can't face Nina right now.

Luckily, Sam's there, headphones on, brandishing a message.

"Hey." He ushers me inside and takes off his headphones.

"Nina stopped by looking for you. She seemed worried and out of it but wouldn't tell me why. You guys okay?"

I shake my head. I can't elaborate or I'll lose it, so I text Nina the bare minimum (I'm fine, won't be home for a while). There's no reply, and I hate looking at those words on my screen.

It's not home anymore, if she doesn't want me.

Sam and I hash things out and I'm honest for the first time about how his history with Nina—or more accurately, his repeated *referencing* of his history with Nina—gets under my skin.

"It was over in a nanosecond. Yours is the real relationship. Everyone knows that."

"It's not about that. Not really. Every time you call her your favorite ex, it reminds me I was too shy to act back then. It reminds me how *easy* everything is for everybody else. Making friends, having girlfriends, fitting in. Nobody else has to try so hard for those things. All I do is try hard. My whole fucking life."

We navigate a path through his apartment and sit at the breakfast bar. Sam turns off his monitor and microphones. He must have been in the middle of recording when I showed up, which sends another bolt of guilt through me.

"Start at the beginning," he says, eyes meeting mine.

I clear my throat. "I never told you guys this, but when I moved to the States in second grade, I didn't fit in. I didn't have real friends until college. I had classmates and neighbors and people my family knew, and that was just how I thought life was for me. How it would always be—on the edge of the room, watching a party I wasn't part of. You, Nina, and Matty changed all that. We got along so great, so effortlessly, that I felt normal for once, you know? But now that I'm finally with Nina"—(or *was* with Nina, I think bitterly)—"I'm worried the price is I'll lose you and Matty. I can't keep up with everything anymore, like groceries and Sunday dinners, and good-luck meals, and podcasts—I'm literally twenty-four episodes behind now—it's so tiring, and I hate that I haven't been a good friend lately."

He folds his arms. "First of all, we're not friends, we're family, and you don't 'lose' family. Secondly, I wasn't exactly Mister Popular growing up, either. I think Ithaca brings together misfits and thank God for that. But my point is, no one wants you to do any of that stuff you just mentioned unless *you* want to. Do what makes you happy and forget the rest! If something's legitimately important to us, we'll let you know, but otherwise, don't assume we expect things to be how they were. We know you've been preoccupied with Nina, and sometimes we give you a hard time about it, but we're all rooting for you."

I'm touched by his words, but considering Nina ended things tonight, they're rather beside the point. I slump into my seat and rest my face in my hands.

"Don't bother. *She's* not even rooting for us. She wants out."

"What? Why?" he yells, shocked. His response is vindicating, and I wish Nina could see it. If only majority rules could compel her to return to me. I know it's immature, but it's all I've got.

"She said she likes me 'too much.' Whatever *that* means."

He exhales and tugs on a lock of his hair. "What are you going to do?"

"I think the thing we need most right now is time away from each other." I don't know fuck-all about what we need, though. If I did, I'd give it to her.

Although wasn't that part of the problem? Me giving her too much?

"Crash here all week if you need to," Sam says. "If you stay longer than that, though, you automatically become a guest on my podcast. A multiple-episode sidekick."

"Fair. Did you hear back from the, what'd you call it, nature-pathic sponsor yet?"

"You'll be the first to know."

I take him up on his offer and spend the next two nights there, stopping by my own apartment for a change of clothes in the late afternoon before Nina arrives home from work. I feel like a stranger in my own place, in and out in five minutes, simultaneously hoping she'll show up and praying she doesn't.

The numbness that overcame me at Canter's Deli spreads throughout my body.

I get up each morning and I drive to work and I handle things for Janine and I drive around LA running errands, and all the while there's a lead ball in my stomach. I choke back just enough food and drink just enough water to provide the bare minimum strength to finish my tasks so I'll be allowed to go home each night.

I'm not living. I'm a witness to time passing, slower than I thought possible.

I spend the darkened hours between midnight and six a.m. paralyzed, thoughts racing, making up for the torpor of my days, trying to convince myself that *maybe*, if I give Nina enough space, she'll change her mind and summon me back.

If she did, though, what would that make me? Her prince, her knight, her court jester, or her whipping boy?

Doesn't she know I'd be all those things—any of them, whatever she desires—if only she would ask? (But shouldn't I have an identity that's separate from her desires?)

It's moot, anyway. She doesn't ask.

Sam wants to help, do something concrete, so I perform a mild act of vengeance for all my past grocery runs and send him to Ralphs with a list a mile long. I commandeer his kitchen and cast him in the role of sous-chef.

I can't do anything about Nina. She's made her position clear. What I *can* do is focus on my goals.

At Vasquez the next morning, I flick on my hazard lights and park in a loading zone so I'm mere feet from the entrance when I step out with by far my finest Seraphim Cake. It's a tower of perfection, glistening in the sunlight. No galloping warhorses knock me on my ass, no slowpoke Ennises force me to slam on my brakes, no Ramblers (*CoRaB*'s version of zombies) in full makeup startle me, and no Robertos trip me. I finally, finally make it to craft services without a single dribble of blood icing or frosted feathers out of place.

I lower my arms and set my creation down. A swarm appears, Francis Jean among the crowd. I dart back to my car for utensils and paper plates, and when I return, Her Royal Highness Queen Lucinda has tucked in, feasting on an enormous slice she apparently cut for herself with the bagel knife. In my humble opinion, she's never looked more luminous in real life *or* onscreen.

"This is absolutely scrummy." She flicks her white hair over her shoulder and licks her fingers clean, then serves herself a second slice, right into the palm of her hand. She swivels around and calls out, "Whoever's birthday it is, God bless you!"

I mean. It's clearly not a birthday cake, but who cares, she loves it! I wish I could snap a photo of her literally licking her lips, but of course my camera phone has a sticker over it. Roberto barrels past and shovels in a slice as well. It makes me a bit ill to see him mashing and gnawing around it, but cheers, Rob Slob.

"Our scene got pushed up, so move your ever-expanding ass," he tells Francis Jean between mouthfuls. She shoots him a reverse peace sign ("fuck you" in the U.K.), and finishes her second slice before gliding toward the set.

I want to follow them and eavesdrop, but I hang back to observe other people's reactions, which are overwhelmingly positive. I can't wait to tell . . . Oh. Right.

Thirty seconds later, a voice over the loudspeaker thunders out like the voice of God: "Whoever brought the cake, report to soundstage B immediately."

I glance around but no one's looking at me; no one knows I

brought the cake, so it's my choice whether I answer the command. I cautiously navigate toward soundstage B, Lucinda's throne room, where a sight I did not anticipate greets me.

In front of cast, crew, film cameras, and today's director, Francis Jean holds forth, brimming with ideas and scattershot energy.

"Can we do a comedy take? Actually, can we do a *musical*-comedy take, really quick, love? It's always so grim and dour in the throne room." She squeezes the director's arm, pulls her dress up an inch or two so she doesn't trip on the hem, and then, the leader of the Kingdom of Six launches into a full-on song-and-dance number, spinning, leaping, two-stepping, and blaring out at full volume what I can only assume are her lines for the day in song form. No one moves. We just watch in stunned silence, shifting on our feet and looking to the director for guidance.

"Cameras rolling!" Francis Jean shouts, and twirls past me.

"Do not roll cameras," the director shouts back. She motions for her underlings to form a huddle, then sends one of them away with an impatient flick of her wrist.

"Can we do a pantomime take?" Francis Jean starts her scene from the top, this time silently, with wide-eyed, swooping movements to indicate her character's dialogue. No one knows what to do. Minutes tick by, but Francis Jean can't be stopped. She cycles through the same scene again and again, always with a fresh theme, which she announces beforehand. There's a "backward" version, a "children's" version, and one "as giraffes."

"What fun!" she bellows. "Just like RADA. Did we get all that?"

A woman holding a robe (today's AD?) tries to corral *CoRaB*'s lead actress, but Francis Jean sidesteps her, waggling a finger in admonishment as the assistant lunges inefficiently. Just when I think Francis Jean is losing steam, fresh inspiration strikes her. The Royal Academy of Dramatic Arts would be proud.

"Oh, oh, can we do a take where he and I swap lines?" She elbows Roberto, who looks genuinely freaked out. "What's the matter, scared I'll show you up, Robbie? Do a better job? Bet you can't memorize what *I* have to say today."

The director's underling has returned with a few guys in suits. The director throws her hands up and tells them, "Do you see this? We're going to lose an entire day of filming. *Who gave her dairy?*"

"Oh, shit," I whisper.

Sharp, furious eyes laser in on me. "You, what are you? Are you here for something?"

"Nope, my mistake, bye."

I slink off, heart pounding, and make haste back to craft services. Security now surrounds the cake table, their headsets crackling. Only then do I notice the sign taped to the table that reads, DAIRY-FREE.

Onlookers chime in, a rush of gossip.

"Who brought it? Where'd it come from?"

"Someone's getting fiiiiiired."

"Throw it in the trash! Just get rid of it!"

My fists clench. *No, please! I worked so hard on it—please don't throw it away! Please don't dump it out like it's nothing!*

The security guys pick up the cake, and I can't watch anymore, so I bolt for the elevator, ride to the second floor, and make a beeline to Daniela and Dominic's office for the briefcase. The siblings look up from the couch, where they're filling the briefcase with . . . hexagonal, marble tiles.

"You're early," Dominic remarks, shutting the briefcase and locking it. He approaches me with his usual agitation, but I hold up a hand to forestall him.

"Why is the briefcase filled with tiles?"

Daniela covers her hand with her mouth. Is she laughing? "He doesn't know," she tells her brother.

"It's always a briefcase filled with tiles," Dom says, like I'm an idiot.

Dizziness washes over me. I sway on my feet, light-headed, and leave my body for a moment. I look down on myself standing there, dumbfounded.

"We thought you knew. You're a decoy, to protect the real messenger. Gives those psycho-fans hiding in Vasquez Rocks someone to tail. Don't be mad—it's important work. . . ." she trails off. "The show relies on secrecy. We need people like you."

Rubes like me.

My body slams back into place. Brain on fire, energized, I pace to the opposite wall and back. Okay. It is what it is, right?

I call Janine and when she answers, I spit out, "I'm here at Vasquez and I've just learned what's in the briefcase. Every time I drove out here, killing my wrist, shoulders, and neck, tense on the freeway for hours at a time, thinking I was helping the show with something important, it was pointless."

Silence on the other end. I'm about to repeat myself when Janine's voice comes on the line. "Pointless? That's not a designation *you* get to make. This is a job. It's not a self-esteem generator or an identity. *Or a fan convention*," she adds in a tone that makes me think I wasn't as clever at hiding my love for the show as I thought. "Can you do the job you've been assigned, or not?"

I swallow, every muscle in my neck and back taut with anger. Pain. Exhaustion.

Right, right. It's a job. Nothing more, nothing less. That's how most people live, right? Get up, go to work, drudgery, drudgery, get paid (not nearly enough), go home, repeat, repeat, repeat, *die.*

Welcome to the Golden State, the Big Orange, Tinseltown, Lotusville, La La Land, the Big Fat Fucking Lie.

I should suck it up and say, *Yes, of course, Janine, you can count on me!* I should eat shit and apologize. But I don't have it in me for any more apologies. Not to her, not to anyone.

I was terrified five minutes ago that I'd be fired over my stupid cake. Now there's nothing I want more.

"Mm, let me think about that, gosh it's so tempting, you paint an absolutely enticing picture, a real fucking corker, but no. I quit."

I don't even keep my security lanyard as a souvenir. I slam it in the garbage on my way out of Vasquez Studios, right on top of the splattered cake.

Out in the car park, I pass an enormous ship surrounded by a water tank. The set dressers stand on scaffolding to remove a house banner and replace it with a different one. Vaguely I register what this means, that there's only one ship. All along it's been the same ship. During battle scenes, they swap out the banners and film from a different angle. Another illusion falls away, so quietly it doesn't make a sound.

Elsewhere, a stuntman's been lit on fire, his entire body in flames, staggering around. I watch for a second, bored.

I reach my car to discover the passenger-side window has been shattered. Someone broke in looking for show-related items and my car served its purpose well; it saved someone else's car. My sacrificial lamb routine played out precisely as it was intended.

Raging, I take the carpool lane all the way home because fuck it, who cares if I'm caught. I arrive unscathed, but when I unlock the door of my apartment, I can tell right away something's wrong.

Nina has moved out.

I sleep until two p.m. the next day. Get all the sleep you want now, Sebastian! No job, no girlfriend. Is it everything you dreamed? Do you feel gloriously reborn, refreshed, well rested? Good on you! And you didn't even have to drop a weight on your foot, or a briefcase filled with tiles, to achieve it!

I open the freezer to see what's still inside: a pint of half-eaten pistachio ice cream. I bought it for Nina our first night of being roommates. It lasted longer than we did.

I don't know why, but that pint of ice cream nearly wrecks me. A sob tries to climb up my throat, but I push it down and I push it down and I push it down.

How did all my dreams turn into nightmares? Were my expectations so high that nothing could live up to them? I loved the show *so much*, but it was never, ever going to love me back. Neither, apparently, was Nina. Wishing otherwise was childish.

The next day, Millie arrives post-TrekUSA, face and arms sunburned, hair mussed, and full of camping tales. I was so wrapped up in my problems I'd forgotten she was coming. She deposits her rucksack on the kitchen floor, takes one look at me, and says, "Where's Nina?"

I show her the note Nina left on the fridge: *S—I didn't want to make things any harder than they already are.—N*

I'm not even sure when she put it up. It could have been yesterday, or three days ago. I have no clue when she actually left. Somehow that makes it worse.

"Oh, Seb. Oh, no. I'm so sorry."

Millie opens her arms for a hug, but I shake my head. I don't trust myself to speak or move or accept a single ounce of comfort. The sob I've been holding at bay tries to climb up my throat again, and it gets higher this time, making my eyes slick, but I push it down and I push it down.

She lets her arms fall to her sides. "Do you want to tell me what happened?"

I shake my head. I push it down.

Millie doesn't rally. She doesn't tell me a love like mine and Nina's is worth fighting for.

I think I expected her to *fix* us somehow. But if Millie thinks it's impossible, we really are through.

So my sister and I get my car window replaced, and then we paint over the office wall. Angry, sloppy brushstrokes to cover up the past month of love notes and drawings. One by one I make them disappear.

Hi, Sebastian is the first to vanish, absorbed back into the beige landscape, as though it were never there at all.

We take down the large canvas print of Nina and me in the poppy fields, looking dewy and radiant and younger, somehow. I probably cursed us by hanging it up, by daring to announce to the world that we were forever. How stupid I was, thinking we were special, that Nina's rules for dating wouldn't apply to me.

Around ten p.m., thunder rumbles overhead and sheets of rain pummel the side of the building.

"Oh, come on," Millie groans, shaking her fist at the ceiling. "You had one job, LA."

Metaphors don't spontaneously appear to torment fools. They show up when we need to make connections, when we don't know how to bridge our feelings to the world. The rain is expressing all the things I haven't allowed myself to feel.

I'm up and moving before I can think too hard about it.

"What are you doing?" Millie calls out as I grip the handle of the balcony door.

"I just need to feel all of it, all at once, or I won't be able to . . ."

"To what?"

"Go on," I whisper.

Through the sliding glass, I see my pack of cigarettes lying crumpled on the rusted chair outside, melting in the onslaught of water. I didn't smoke the entire six weeks Nina and I were together.

Part of me wants to scour the apartment for my emergency backup pack, chain-smoke until my fingertips reek and my throat turns to ash and my eyes burn. But I'd rather go outside and drown.

I yank the door open, close it behind me, and step into the storm. It's raining buckets and within seconds I'm drenched. I shiver and tilt my head up, offering myself to the elements. The rain feels like thousands of tiny needles stabbing me, my face, my neck, my skin, dripping down my arms and legs and plastering my shirt and jeans to my body.

The sliding door opens again, and Millie joins me in her sweatshirt. She pulls me tightly into her arms. I return the hug, holding on for dear life, and I cry so hard I can't breathe.

You're not alone, a voice reminds me. Millie's right here, Sam's down the hall, and Matty's one text away.

"I've never seen you like this," Millie says before bed, once we've dried off and made ourselves hot toddies. "I'm changing my plane ticket to next week, okay?"

I don't argue. My face feels stretched out, pinned back. My eyes are raw, my lips cracked, and I've got a massive headache, but giving in to my emotions in all their ugly truth has helped, somehow; taken the lead ball in my stomach and shrunk it. Famished, I finish Nina's pint of ice cream as well as two sandwiches and several glasses of water.

When I crawl into bed I can't smell Nina anymore.

CHAPTER 36

NINA

"Neal, you can go see him now," I say with a smile to the tall, jittery twenty-four-year-old sitting outside Sean's office. His suit is about half an inch too short for his ankles, but he's the first candidate wearing a suit at all. Most of the people Sean has been interviewing have been dressed in jeans and T-shirts of varying degrees of distressed.

Sean's been seeing candidates for the social media coordinator position all day, and with every person who walks in, I feel more and more relieved. I can't wait to leave Twitter and Instagram and the rest of them behind again forever. It's taken every ounce of strength I have not to check up on Sebastian's socials over the past week, despite not having any of my own. I want to know he's okay. I mean, I know he's physically okay, but I want to know he's emotionally okay too. Even though I recognize that, even if he weren't, the chance of him putting anything on his social channels to indicate it are pretty slim.

I busy myself by doing QA on the new teaser microsite that the show's about to launch. We're four months away from the premiere, and everything—from the digital promotions to the Comic-Con bookings—is ramping up. Soon everyone will know what happened to Lucinda and Duncan and Jeff after that cliff-hanger of a final scene.

And I'll know too—in greater detail than that glimpse I got in the writers' room. But then there's the problem of who will I watch the show with?

Sebastian, a little voice says. Once Sebastian's had a little while to cool down, I can broach us being friends again.

But then that little voice goes on. *Are you going to be able to sit on a couch with him and not lean your head on his shoulder? Are you going to be able to listen to him make jokes and not immediately kiss him because he knows just how to make you laugh?*

Are you going to let him go ahead and kiss someone else?

A vision of Heather in that wedding dress floats in front of me and I physically put my hands over my eyes to blot it out.

Yes, I tell the voice angrily, *because I have to let him go. He deserves something I can't give him. Now shut up and let me work.*

Luckily, Neal emerges from the office before I can get too deep in the throes of bickering interior dialogue.

"How did it go?" I ask him with a smile.

He clears his throat. "Good. I hope." He takes a look at Sean's closed office door and then leans over to quietly tell me. "I didn't want to sound too desperate, but this is basically my dream job. I'm just such a fan."

"Of *CoRaB*?" I ask.

"No. Well, yes, I like it well enough. But I meant of Mr. Delaney. The ladders he's been able to climb. And he's only thirty-eight? He's amazing. I can only aspire. . . ."

I guess I could tell Neal about the endoscopy appointment I just had to make for Sean because he's likely flared up his ulcers yet again. Or the HR file on him that's three miles long. But I don't. I think coming to terms with the messy reality of our fandoms is something we all have to do on our own.

"Well, then, I hope you get it," I tell him.

"Thanks!" he says brightly.

Sean sticks out his head from his office. "Nina, can I have a word?"

"Sure," I say, grabbing my notebook, giving Neal a small wave and going into Sean's office.

I sit down across from his desk and click my pen, poised to write down whatever 450 things he needs from me next.

"I wanted to ask you why you didn't apply for the social co-ordinator position," Sean says.

I look up at him, surprised. "I . . . was I supposed to?" I ask.

"Let's be honest—you're the ideal candidate for it," he says. "You're already doing it. You have solid ideas because you know this show, and I have the feeling that you'd have solid ideas for other shows too. Plus . . . you put up with me." He says this last one with a pained face. "I mean . . . my moods don't seem to faze you. So let's just consider this your official interview. Make sure to fill out the application when you get back to your desk. You know. For *them*." *Them* means HR. Sean was advised a few weeks ago by his therapist to replace his usual term—Horrendous Rectum-monkeys—with something more neutral.

Sean returns to typing furiously away on his computer, which is usually the sign that I'm dismissed to go. But I can't move from my chair. He looks up at me after a minute and frowns. "That's it. Interview over, Shams."

Righty-o, boss—or something equally inane—is what I'd normally say, no matter what he's asked. Instead, I clear my throat. "Um, I say this with all due respect, Sean, but I really don't want to be a social media coordinator. In fact I kinda hate social media. I'm not even on it myself."

"What?" he asks. "Oh, you mean you deleted one of your apps cause some celeb you liked got canceled or something?"

I shake my head. "No. I mean, I don't have any social media profiles. I haven't had one in five years."

He stares at me. "Okay, well, whatever. We'll try to internally promote you into a different department within a year or two. Marketing, PR, whatever floats your boat. Just fill out the application tonight so I can get the ball rolling on this. I assume you'll want the raise that goes with it too."

A raise. I could use a raise. If nothing else, my living situation would improve, meaning my life would improve—cosmetically speaking, anyway. Like a face-lift that doesn't actually make you younger. Saying yes to more responsibility at this job I don't care about would take away my time to write. It would take away my time to . . . what else do I have going on? Without Sebastian, I have no friends. Without Sebastian . . . I have no Sebastian.

"Okay," I say numbly and then a belated, "Thank you."

He nods as I get up from the chair and leave his office.

Luckily, it's near the end of the workday because I can't concentrate on much. I open up the application that Sean was talking about, but besides filling out my name and date of birth, I can't get myself to punch in anything else. I AirDrop the bookmarked page to my phone. Maybe it's something I can do tonight from the very unpeaceful floor of my temporary digs.

I'm sitting on the air mattress on the floor of Sayeh's room, fka my room, staring at the application on my computer, when my sister walks in.

"Celeste and I are about to go out for some boba. Want to come?"

"And Botox?" I ask.

"Strictly boba," she responds before adding, "this time."

I don't know how but apparently Celeste and Sayeh are soulmate roomies. They *love* each other, constantly spending their time out of the apartment grabbing dinner or drinks. Sayeh has apparently been helping Celeste develop a far more robust business plan for her spa, and Celeste has in return been performing free Reiki cleanses for Sayeh. They must be working because I have never seen my sister so relaxed. Relatively speaking.

I shake my head. "Thanks, but I'll take a raincheck."

"No, you won't," Sayeh says, coming over and putting out her hand to help me up. "You haven't been outside except to go to work in three days. You're coming with us."

I could argue but, honestly, I'm tired of arguing. And she's right. So I take the proffered hand and let her pull me up from the floor.

True to her word, we go to a non-Botox boba place that's still within walking distance. The sun has just set, leaving the last vestiges of a pink and orange sky fading up into a velvet blue, silhouetting the palm trees like a postcard. *Wish you were here.* I don't have to think too hard about who the "you" is.

I place my order at the counter and then go sit down at a corner table. Celeste orders next and sits across from me while my sister is still waffling between a lychee or a honeydew bubble tea.

"I hope you don't mind me saying this, Nina," Celeste says. "But you seem down. Your aura is very murky."

"I'm okay," I respond.

"Yes," she says. "But okay is not the best way to go through life. We should aim for incandescent happiness at all times."

"Um . . . yeah, sure, I'll do that," I say, as Sayeh comes over, her phone under her armpit as she balances a tray holding all of our drinks. I grab my Thai tea.

"What are we talking about?" Sayeh asks as she plops down with her green drink.

"My lack of incandescence apparently," I respond.

Celeste nods vigorously. "Of course, the operative word there was aim. We have to *try* for our own happiness. Sometimes there are factors out of our control that make that impossible. But to the best of our ability, we have to find the small things we can do to lighten our loads."

"Oh, all of the factors here are within Nina's control," Sayeh says. "She just refuses to acknowledge that's true."

"What are you talking about?" I ask Sayeh.

"Here," she says, dramatically taking her phone out from under her arm and flipping it over to reveal a round smiling face with short, dark hair.

"Maman!" I say in surprise, then turn to Sayeh. "Did you just have her staring at your armpit for two minutes?"

Sayeh shrugs. "Sometimes you gotta make sacrifices in service of the element of surprise."

"Nina, azizam," my mom says, beaming. "How are you?"

"I'm fine," I say, smiling. "I'm sorry I haven't called you as much as I should have lately."

"Oh, I know you're busy . . ." Maman starts, but Sayeh cuts her off.

"She's not fine, Maman," Sayeh says, turning the phone so that we're both in frame now. "She's heartbroken."

"Oh," my mom says and I worry her face is going to crumple at the mention of heartbreak. But it doesn't. Instead, she looks thoughtful as she says, "Sebastian?"

I nod. If anyone would understand the need to stay away from someone you're too emotionally attached to, it's my mom. "It just didn't work out."

"It didn't work out because Nina was worried about it not working out," Sayeh butts in. "So she broke up with him."

"Um, no," I say. "That's not what happened."

"Then what did happen, Nina?" Sayeh asks. "Did *he* break it off?"

"Of course not," I mutter. I can't even follow that up with a *but he would have* because it's not true. Sebastian never would've broken up with me. I settle for, "But we would have hurt each other eventually. It's not worth it." I turn to my mom, knowing she'll understand.

Now I see the tears I was expecting earlier. "Oh, Nina," she says. "This is my fault."

I blink at her. "No, it's not."

"When your father left, I never should've let you see me fall apart," she says. "You were just kids."

"You're only human, Maman," I respond. "And you've never been very good at hiding your feelings. How could you have hidden that from us? Besides, if I blame anyone, it's Baba."

She sighs. "I know. And that's my fault too. Your father hurt me, that's true. But I was the one who let it take over my entire life. And what's worse, I let it take over yours. But I'm working on that now. Did Sayeh tell you I'm seeing a therapist?"

I gasp as I look over at my sister, who shrugs and mouths an *I know, right?* "No . . ."

"Well, I am," Maman says. "And she's helping me to, what do they call it? 'Unpack' a lot of stuff."

"That's great, Maman," I say, smiling. Now that I take a closer look, her face seems a little smoother, a little more relaxed than I'm used to seeing it.

"Yes," she says. "But I need to talk to you, too. Both of you. Because I don't ever want to be the reason either of you is unhappy."

"You're not," I say firmly. "This has nothing to do with you. I chose this. And I'm not unhappy."

"You are, azizam," Maman says. "I can see it in your face."

"And what's more, you've *never* been happy, Nina," Sayeh adds. "Incandescent or otherwise, except in college. And then again for the past few months. What do you think the common denominator is?" She's looking at me expectantly.

"That's not true," I sputter, looking at my mom for validation.

"It is, Nina," she says quietly. "You love Sebastian."

I sigh. "Well . . . obviously. I've never made a secret of that. Of course I love him. But that's exactly why I need him as my friend. I want him to be in my life forever."

"And are you friends now?" Sayeh asks. "Now that you've broken his heart?"

I gulp because hearing it put so bluntly hurts, even though I know that's exactly what I've done. "Not at the moment," I say weakly. "But I'm hoping he'll come around."

"The worst part is, you've broken your own heart too," Sayeh continues. "And for what? Because our parents had a crappy marriage twenty years ago? Because nothing lives up to the stories you publish on the internet? None of these are good reasons to deny yourself something that, yes, makes you incandescent. I mean, annoying AF . . . but incandescent."

"It's not worth it," I mutter again, staring into my drink, trying to will myself not to cry.

"Yes, it is," my mom says emphatically. "You deserve to be happy, Nina. And you need to do everything in your power to accomplish that."

I see Celeste, who has been quietly sipping her drink but watching us, enraptured, nodding emphatically. "That's what I was trying to say," she whispers.

"Sebastian makes you happy," Maman adds.

I open my mouth to respond, but I get another flash of an image. This time, it's not Sebastian kissing someone else, it's me kissing someone else. It's two lips touching. It's an exercise, like one of the stretches my physical therapist would lay out for me.

1) Place arms around other subject's neck.
2) Lean head closer to him.
3) Bring lips together.

What it's not is friendship and romance and laughter and intimacy all rolled into one. It doesn't burn through my heart and my brain and my thighs all at the same time. It's empty. Safe and empty.

I look up at the three expectant faces staring at me, tears in my eyes. "But what can I do? I can't undo what I did. I can't unbreak his heart."

"At the risk of contradicting the iconic Toni Braxton, I think you can," Sayeh says, causing me to give a very loud snort. She reaches out to touch my hand. I can't remember the last time she did that, maybe when she was five and she still needed me to hold her hand while she crossed the street. I look up at her. "We just have to figure out how."

Chapter 37

SEBASTIAN

"So. Do you want to tell me why you really quit? And with a scathing speech, no less. I had to look up the meaning of 'corker,' by the way."

Janine and I eat lunch across from each other at her desk, instead of separately, or as was often the case for me, in my car.

"The briefcase revelation wasn't a good enough reason?"

I roll up my slacks to reveal a goose egg along my shin from the briefcase's repeated, rhythmic slamming into my leg the past few months.

She winces. "I knew about the handcuff mark, but I didn't know about the bruising on your leg, or your neck and shoulder getting so tensed up while driving. Why didn't you tell me?"

"It has recently come to my attention that I tend to push that stuff down. Also, I figured it was the price of getting to work on my favorite show. I knew there were fifty people lined up behind me who would take the job in a heartbeat and never complain."

"That's Hollywood's most insidious claim," Janine acknowledges. "And unfortunately, it happens to be true. I could've made your position a non-paying internship, used your salary to redo my kitchen, and still had Harvard grads applying for it."

The look on my face must seem murderous because she quickly adds, "I'm joking. Somewhat. Should we take a look at these cover letters?"

Two days after my dramatic exit, I'd apologized to Janine and offered to train a replacement over the next few weeks, as well as tie up any loose ends. In return, she presented me with a severance check, reimbursement for gas and the shattered car window, and workers' comp for my ailments. Most Hollywood producers would've cut me dead and blacklisted me, so I'm trying to count my blessings. To her credit, she'd always been upfront about the fact that this job had no internal promotions and that its purpose was to give me an overview of the business. On that count, it more than exceeded expectations. My crash course in the worlds of script research, casting, acting, preproduction, production, and postproduction would have served me well if I planned to go into any of those fields. It turns out it's perfect for realizing I *don't* want to do any of those things either.

"I'd offer to make some calls and find you a new gig, but I get the feeling that's not what you want. Or am I wrong?"

"You're not wrong. I was treating everything the way a fan would, with a fan's wide-eyed gaze, because that's what I prefer: watching the story on a screen once it's been edited and presented as entertainment. I just want to *enjoy* the show again. Speaking of, I have an idea for a show-themed cookbook. . . ." Sadness creeps over me at the words. Without Nina's encouragement, I never would've pursued the book in earnest.

I present Janine with the binder, images, and recipes I've compiled. She impassively flicks through it. "I know someone who runs an event planning company, would that interest you?"

"I'm not sure, but I'm willing to give it a try. Thanks, Janine."

"By the way, you're not the first assistant to quit on me. You *are* the first to come back to make things right, which is the only reason I'm extending that offer."

* * *

On the last day of her prolonged visit, Millie and I visit the Broad museum. It was on Sayeh's checklist all those weeks ago, and Millie thought it sounded cool.

We're only allowed sixty seconds in the Infinity Mirrored Room, the crown jewel of LA-based social media. They time us, and I know I'm supposed to frantically take a selfie while pretending to be serene, but I deliberately left my phone in the car.

I use my allotted minute to stare at all the versions of me, these alternate-reality Sebastians, these shards of lives unlived, paths untaken.

Nina and I gave everything to each other.

But there are so many pieces and elements to a life, maybe we should've kept some in reserve, held back a little. Maybe if we had, we'd still be together.

The kicker is, I'll never know. The only closure I'll get on this heartbreak is going to have to come from me; she won't be providing any.

Her reasons for ending us were flimsy, absurd, even, but that's not on me. What is on me is my reaction to her, both in college and during our short-lived romance. I gave her too much power over my emotional state. She controlled me like a goddamn puppet, but *I let her*. The pedestal I built for her, and shined and glossed each day beneath her feet, needed to come crashing down.

Because the truth is, she's not a queen and she's not perfect. She never was.

Quite frankly, she's a mess.

I loved that mess with everything I had, though. I can be angry at her for her choices while also mourning the loss of what we had.

"I need to move out," I tell Millie while she packs up. "I don't want another roommate, but I can't justify a two-bedroom place anymore, either."

She nods. "I get that."

"Maybe Sam's parents will take me in." They've been saving his old room for him, and the thought makes me laugh, briefly, and that's something, I guess.

Millie will start uni soon and I'm excited for her. I have to keep myself from giving unsolicited advice, specifically, *Don't fall in love*. Of course, I know that's not the advice I'd give even if she asked. Besides, I'm too late. Her cellist in Yeovil adored the postcards and will be waiting for her at Heathrow.

Still, she's mourning the end of Nina and Sebastian in her own way, right alongside me. "You guys were the only het couple I shipped. Guess I'm back to viewing life through slash-colored glasses. If Nina doesn't see how special you are, she's not worth the pain. Not anymore. And I was rooting for you more than anyone."

"I know."

"I love you, Seb."

"Love you too. Don't get too blotto during freshers' week, okay?"

"Call me whenever you need to talk. You'll be in Sherborne for Christmas, right?" she confirms when I drop her at LAX.

"Yep." It's strange to think about what my life will be like by then. The Infinity Room reminded me there are a million ways my life could splinter. "Thanks for staying longer. I really appreciate it."

We hug and I think of fairy dust and carrying her in my arms when she was five and I was thirteen, after she fell asleep in the car. She kisses my cheek and that's that. My little sister is gone.

When I return from the airport, I check my woefully neglected mailbox and what do you know? The paycheck for my under-five role has arrived. My old agency took a cut because of course they did. They also took additional money for unspecified "promotional expenses." What remains: seven cents. A check for seven cents.

That makes me laugh too. (*Somewhat*, as Janine would say.)

My rueful smile falls off my face when I reach my apartment door. An envelope's been taped to it, my name written in elegant calligraphy. I swallow tightly and peel the envelope off the door. Terrified of what's inside, I don't open it right away. I sort through the rest of my mail, kick off my shoes, and make myself a simple dinner first, eating quickly while trying to pretend I'm eating slowly, as though I'm completely unbothered by the mystery envelope THAT CLEARLY CAME FROM NINA. I recognized the stationery set I gave her before we crashed and burned, as well as her calligraphy art.

The instant my last bite of food hits the back of my throat, I slide my finger under the flap and brace myself for more devastation. A more thorough explanation of why she can't be with me, probably.

But it's not a letter, it's an invitation, crafted in the same impeccable, inked calligraphy as the envelope:

> You are cordially requested to appear at the following event.
> Where: Sam's apartment
> What: You'll have to find out
> When: Sunday, 7:30 pm, until Sam kicks us out
> Why: See "What," above
> What to bring: Yourself and ONLY yourself, we mean it, no food, no drinks, JUST SEBASTIAN.

I wear a nice button-down shirt and a new pair of jeans on Sunday. I'm five minutes late, for which I have no defense considering I live down the hall.

I pull my shoulders back and knock on Sam's door. As specified, I haven't purchased or cooked anything, and it's distinctly odd to arrive empty-handed. Unnerving.

Freeing, too.

"He's here! Everyone, shh, get ready!"

"Shut up, he can hear us."

"Just open the door!"

Scattered footsteps, then Matty swings the door open.

"Wait, do you live here now?" I joke lamely.

"Enter," he says.

Sam's studio apartment has been cleaned and organized to accommodate a crowd. There's music playing, a table full of snacks and alcohol, and a banner on the wall: HAPPY SEBASTIAN APPRECIATION DAY. I think of how I felt when I was younger, as though I was perpetually on the outskirts of a party I hadn't been invited to. Today, I *am* the party. I laugh, embarrassed but touched, as various Ithaca alumni greet me.

There's one Ithaca alum I'm holding out hope for, though she's nowhere to be seen.

"In case it's not already clear, you don't need to *do* anything for us to be friends," Matty says quietly. "Just be you."

"I told you, he and I already hashed this out," Sam informs Matty.

Matty slings an arm around my shoulder. "Just making sure."

I salute him. "Yes, sir."

Matty steers me to the table and unveils a gargantuan, lop-sided, yet instantly recognizable creation. "We made your Seraphim Cake and it was a fucking ordeal."

I laugh again.

More guests greet me, asking how I've been. It occurs to me that if I hadn't been lonely when I was a kid, I might never have taught myself to cook, found so much joy in it and become so good at it. I might never have appreciated how *wonderful* it is to have true friends. The empty space inside me from back then is overflowing now, but if I'd never had that empty space, it couldn't be filled so deeply with gratitude as an adult.

"It's exhausting being you," Sam says, referring to the cake.

"It took us two days and three attempts! Didn't it, Nina?" Matty calls out.

My heart jumps into my throat when I see her. She wears a

pencil skirt and sequined top. She looks breathtakingly, terrifyingly beautiful.

"Hi, Sebastian." Her expression is hesitant as she meets my gaze.

I don't reply.

She cuts the first slice of the cake, her hands shaking, and holds the plate out to me. "Have you ever had the chance to try it, before giving it to everyone else?"

"Thanks." I take the plate from her. "It looks good."

Instinctually, we move to a quieter location in the room.

"I'm *so sorry* I broke your heart," Nina says, her eyes glistening.

We stand there looking at each other, and my heart is a bass drum reverberating through my entire body, my entire soul. I'd like to reach for her hands, stroke her hair, pull her to me. But I don't do any of those things.

"I'm a catch," I tell her simply.

I don't say it to hurt her, or prove anything to her. I hadn't planned on saying it all. It just fell out.

Janine was right. A job doesn't give you self-esteem. Other people don't give you self-esteem. Self-esteem comes from within, and I know what I bring to the table: myself. My loyalty. My caring nature. My love of cooking, my love of taking care of friends and family, of making them laugh. I'm a fucking catch, as a friend *and* a boyfriend, and it doesn't matter if Nina agrees, because I know it's true.

"Yes," she says quietly. "You are."

I nod, and pick up the slice of cake she gave me. "I'm going to say hi to everyone. See you later."

I turn and walk away.

"Wait! Please?"

I look back, to see Nina get down on her knees.

As though maybe, for today, in this one moment, I'm her king. The eyes of everyone in the room fall on us.

"What are you doing?" I ask.

"Sebastian Worthington, will you do me the honor of dating me? From a distance, in separate apartments?"

I gaze down at her. "You want me to date you?"

"Properly. Slowly."

I must seem confused because she quickly explains. "We've basically lived together since we met, either down the hall in the dorm, or in the next room, or shacked up."

I never thought about it that way before, but it's true.

"This thing between us is far too amazing and singular to burn through quickly," she says. "I want us to last forever and I think we forgot a few steps. I don't want to skip any of them. Let's carve out a deliberate space for us, not a convenient one. Let's build in time apart so the time we *do* share with each other is sacred. Something to plan for, and look forward to, and delight in."

A grin slides onto my face. "Does this mean we'll talk on the phone?"

"Yes."

"Phone sex?"

She grins back. "Why not?"

"La la la, youngster in the house." Matty covers Maritza's belly as though protecting the baby's ears.

Nina looks up at me from the floor, resolve written all over her face. "I promise to say good night and leave, but always, always come back."

I respond with a solemn vow of my own: "I promise to slow down, to give us space so I can value the time we *do* spend together. I promise to see you as you are, a person in the world who's allowed to have doubts and fears and make mistakes, just like me."

"I promise to be open and honest, to tell you the truth, and have uncomfortable conversations. To not spend the night and stay up late except on special occasions," Nina adds.

302 / TASH SKILTON

"That sounds awful," Sam jokes out of the side of his mouth.

"It sounds perfect," I breathe. And it does. Perfectly messy. Perfectly us.

"Is that a yes?" she whispers. "Will you date me?"

I pull Nina up so she's standing, so we're face-to-face, equals. So we can fall into the best kiss of our lives.

Epilogue
NINA

Five Months Later

I'm putting the final touches on the Bacon-Wrapped Water (Sprite) Chestnuts, a galley of Sebastian's cookbook propped up on my kitchen counter. It's paperback and flimsy so it keeps closing on me, but the hardcover—which releases in two months, just in time for the *CoRaB* season finale—is going to look beautiful. We went through several channels to ask Francis Jean to approve a blurb ("The cake's so good, it makes you want to sing and dance!"), but never heard back.

There's a knock on my door and when I open it, the real-life version of the author photo I was just staring at is grinning at me. He bends down to give me a kiss and I reciprocate so warmly that we are full-on making out within seconds.

"Uh," Sebastian says after a minute. "Are you sure we need to have other guests tonight?" He keeps kissing me, finally forcing me to playfully push him away.

"Yes! Come on, it's your big night!" I take the postcard that's sitting on my mail table and hold it in front of my lips to deter him from kissing them. It's a picture of Sebastian in his debut role as portly, balding Brothel Owner in episode 602 of *Castles of Rust and Bone,* airing tonight.

Sebastian grimaces. "Well, at least we now know what that

'unspecified publicity' on my pay stub means." He takes the postcard that his agent mailed out all over town and shakes his head. "This is the most unflattering photo anyone's taken of me, ever. And that includes the three months Millie tried to document our lives *Big Brother*–style and I didn't know she had set up a hidden camera aimed at our toilet."

"I think you look hot," I say as I kiss him on the cheek. "Now have a seat. Take a load off."

My new apartment is small and it's going to be a squeeze to fit ten people in here tonight, but the beauty of it is that it's all mine. Sayeh loaned me the money for the deposit and when my dad offered to help subsidize some of the rent, I let him. My new temp agency job doesn't quite help me make ends meet all on my own, but it did let me finish my spec script. *The Reboot* has currently been entered into two screenwriting competitions and—most excitingly—an HBO fellowship program that would provide me with a year of mentorship in a real writers' room. I should be hearing back any day now.

Sebastian has just settled on the couch when the door buzzes. Sam comes in with Trina, a girl he met at PodCon. She's brought a bottle of prosecco and is dressed as a punk centaur so I already like her. Dina and José come in next. They're my new friends from the office where I've been stationed these past six weeks. Dina immediately launches into a conversation with Sam while José compliments me on the hors d'oeuvres, for which I immediately offload credit on Sebastian.

"You made them!" Sebastian says.

"Yes, but I just followed the recipes you created. You're the real star here," I say.

"How about we just give you split credit and leave it at that?" José says. "You can be the hors d'oeuvres version of the Coen Brothers. Or the Wachowski Sisters."

"Um, can we not be related though?" Sebastian says as he puts a very unbrotherly arm around my waist, cupping my bottom.

I shrug. "I mean, in *CoRaB*-land, it's the only way to have a lasting relationship."

Sebastian laughs as he gives me a kiss.

José looks confused. "Just what is it I'm about to watch?"

"The greatest time travel/high fantasy/centaur-appreciation mindfuck of your life," Sebastian says. "Walk with me. I'll give you a down and dirty prologue."

The doorbell rings again and it's Matty and Maritza. I give a loud guffaw when I see them. Maritza, who's set to pop any day now, has taken advantage of her huge belly to cosplay as Sebastian's brothel owner character . . . and so has Matty. They're both sporting bald caps, warts, and two sets of terrible teeth.

"Are you kidding me?" Sebastian says when he sees them.

"We wouldn't celebrate your big debut with anything less," Matty says solemnly as he claps him on the shoulder.

Celeste and Sayeh arrive next, with two bottles of Goop-endorsed organic wine.

"Is Celeste back with her ex?" I quietly ask Sayeh, who rolls her eyes.

"This week. Like, I don't have time to constantly be a love doctor for all of you all the time, you know?"

I smirk at her. "It ain't easy being a mogul *and* wise beyond your years."

"Don't I know it," she huffs as she pops a bacon-wrapped date in her mouth.

Sam joins our conversation, looking delighted. "How do you know my podcast sponsor?"

"Your what-now?" I ask.

"Celeste is my first podcast sponsor. Killing it with the holistic therapy subscription boxes."

I have so many questions but they'll have to wait; the doorbell rings again and I catch a glance at Sebastian's perplexed face.

"Who's missing?" he asks as he counts everyone in the room.

I grin as I hold the doorknob. "I have a surprise for you," I say, and open the door with a flourish.

Standing there, about twenty pounds lighter than we last saw him, is Stanley, our old RA.

Sebastian's eyes widen. "Stanley!" he says, as he goes over to give him a hug. "How are you, buddy?"

Stanley remains standing stiffly, unsure what to do at the unusual show of affection. "Uh. I'm good. Here's the cover charge Nina said to bring." He holds out a bottle. Sebastian takes it, reads it, and gives a burst of laughter. Then he turns to me, his eyes shining with love and memory.

I hear Matty and Sam greet Stanley warmly and ask him if he's excited to see the show. "I mean," Stanley says, "it'd be pretty hard to fuck up worse than season five, but I have faith. No one minds if I live-tweet this, right?"

I walk over to Sebastian and lightly touch the bottle of farm-fresh goat's milk Stanley just handed him. "I've achieved power beyond my wildest dreams," I tell him with a wink.

We look at each other, barely able to hold in our giggles.

"I've achieved *everything* beyond my wildest dreams," he says, as he leans in and gives me a soft kiss on the cheek.

"Me too," I say as I clasp his hand. "This is my favorite show." But I'm not looking at the TV. I'm looking at our entwined hands, and then up at Sebastian's beautiful face, the face I can lean over and kiss anytime I want. Because when you kiss a friend, the friendship doesn't have to die. It can be transformed into something even more profound; rooted in camaraderie, but with wings.

I touch my lips to my best friend's and I can hear him say, right before we kiss, "And it was ever thus."

Acknowledgments

A huge thank-you to agent Victoria Marini, for her grace and guidance during the particularly tough challenge of pandemic writing (and living).

So many thanks to all the wonderful and hardworking people at Kensington: Alicia Condon, Jane Nutter, Jackie Dinas, Alexandra Nicolajsen, Kristine Noble, Lauren Jernigan, Carly Sommerstein, and Elizabeth Trout.

—Sarvenaz Tash

Hollywood Ending was written in 2020, during personal and global turmoil. The books I read that year provided a true escape, and I hope any readers going through a tough time right now were equally transported by these pages. I needed this book for many reasons, including as a reprieve from the outside world.

Sarvenaz, thank you for pouring your talent and humor into Nina and bringing her to life so beautifully. Celeste's antics made me laugh out loud, the details you created for *CoRaB* and the Kingdom of Six were brilliant, and your narrative voice is unmatched.

Super-agent Victoria Marini, thank you for your steady hand and calm assurances.

Alicia Condon, thank you for your spot-on editing wizardry! I had fun brainstorming titles with you.

Also at Kensington, thank you to associate publisher Jackie Dinas, creative director Kristine Noble, director of social media Alex Nicolajsen, production editor Carly Sommerstein, publicist Jane Nutter, social media manager Lauren Jernigan, assistant editor Elizabeth Trout, and proofreader Kate Brandt.

Thank you to all the folks at Droemer Knaur, our German publisher, for your enthusiasm.

Thank you to my rapid-fire beta readers, Rachel Murphy and Amy Spalding, for your encouragement and insight. Rachel, I'm so grateful we could be together that June. Amy, I owe you for keeping me sane (as much as possible). To my parents, Earl and Ros Hoover, thank you for all the FaceTimes and babysitting. Your sage advice and loving support mean the world.

The book *Fire Cannot Kill a Dragon: Game of Thrones and the Official Untold Story of the Epic Series* by James Hibberd provided fun research, as did a certain internship I took at a certain network TV show during college that certainly did not inspire any moments in this book. Myriad fabulous and/or bizarre jobs I had in Hollywood during subsequent years made a few fictionalized cameos as well.

My POV character Sebastian Worthington hails from Sherborne, Dorset, a place I hold dear. Thank you to my mom's side of the family for letting me borrow it! I also want to thank Ithaca College (where, yes, Vivarin actually came in our welcome packs—back in 1995 at least—and where I met my IRL "friend-to-lover" Joe), and Los Angeles, in all its wackiness, for being my home since 1999.

If *Ghosting* was a love letter to New York City, this book was LA's chance to shine; and if "work is love made visible" (Gibran), Elliot and Joe are my forever inspiration.

—Sarah Skilton

Ghosting: A Love Story

LEAVE IT TO THE EXPERTS—TO BREAK ALL THE RULES

Online Dating Ghostwriting Rules to Live by

MILES

Dumped by his fiancée, not only is Miles couch-surfing across New York City, but downsizing has forced him to set up shop at a café. Also, he no longer believes in love. Not a good look in his line of work . . .

Do not present a "perfect" image. No one will trust it. Nor should they.

ZOEY

Zoey's eccentric LA boss sent her packing to New York to "grow." But beneath her chill Cali demeanor, Zoey's terrified to venture beyond the café across the street. . . .

Think of your quirks—such as cosplaying B-movies from the 1980s—as a "Future Honesty." Save these as a reward only for those who prove worthy.

The only thing Miles and Zoey share is their daily battle for Café Crudité's last day-old biscotti. They don't know they're both ghostwriting "authentic" client profiles for rival online dating services. Nope, they have absolutely nothing in common. . . . Until they meet anonymously online, texting on the clock . . .

Never remind the client you're their Cyrano. Once you've attracted a good match, let the client take over ASAP.

Soon, with their clients headed for dating disaster, both Miles's and Zoey's jobs are at stake. And once they find out their lines have crossed, will their love connection be the real thing—or vanish into the ether?

CHAPTER 1

To: All Tell It to My Heart Employees
From: Leanne Tseng
Re: New "Office Space"

Team,

Although the last couple of months have been challenging, I want to take a moment to commend you for being so open and adaptable to our new direction. I also hope you are all enjoying the freedom and independence of working remotely. (I came across this article in *Wired* about the future of offices. We're trendsetters!)

Also, whoever programmed my phone to play "Tell It to My Heart" for all incoming messages . . . I appreciate the joke. It played very well at our "Farewell Office" office party. But no one—not even the so-called geniuses at the Genius Bar—can seem to disable it.

Would you please come clean and get over
here to change it back? For obvious reasons,
if I ever have to listen to that song again,
I will 100% murder someone. And no one gets
paid if your CEO is in jail.

Yours,
Leanne

MILES

It's fine. It's absolutely fine.

So what if my ex-fiancée just posted a photo of her ringless fingers cradling what is very obviously a baby bump. So what if we only broke up six weeks ago and, look, I cannot claim to be an expert in women's reproductive health or anything, but I'm pretty sure that is not what six weeks pregnant looks like. So what if I, in a split second of confusion and elation, texted her "Are we having a baby?" with an actual goddamn baby emoji next to it just in case she needed a visual representation of the word "baby" and got absolutely no response even though the read receipt confirms she saw it.

So either the baby is mine and Jordan has decided she's not going to let me be a part of his or her life. Or . . . Jordan was cheating on me before she dumped me, shattered my heart, and stole the apartment.

I'm not sure which is worse.

I get a ping on my laptop, a message next to a tiny picture of a smiling brunette girl.

Jules478: Hi, how are you?

Fucking great. And now I have to work. Now I have to work trying to get other people's love lives in order. What a cosmic joke. Not only that, but I no longer even have an office to go to, or colleagues to make small talk with, or a coffee machine that will dispense caffeine to me at will. Just a totally unfathomable espresso maker that could double as a 747 cockpit and a corner of this borrowed couch that I swear is made from burlap, because my friend Dylan lives in a Pottery Barn catalog. (You may say that couch surfers can't be couch choosers, but I—in the throes of my melancholy and with half my hair in a permanent state of static cling—say we can all be critics.)

I close my eyes and try the breathing exercise that, of course, Jordan once taught me—inhale for four, hold for seven, exhale for eight—before I respond.

PerseMan: Hey there. I'm great. How are you doing?

It's okay. I can do this sort of idle chitchat in my sleep. I haven't spent the past two years becoming the top ghostwriter at Tell It to My Heart for no reason. I've honed these skills enough that I can practically be on autopilot. Right?

Jules478: Good.

Right. Except I just broke the cardinal rule of online dating: Much like improv, never ask a question that can be responded to with a one-word answer.

I try to rectify.

PerseMan: Have you seen the summer concert schedule for Forest Hills Stadium, by the way? It's pretty amazing this year.

My guy . . . I scan my open files for his name . . . Farhad. That's it. He's a music buff, so I know this is important.

Jules478: Yes! Belle and Sebastian and Greta Van Fleet? Amazing!

PerseMan: I know, right?

I type the response automatically and then scroll over to the schedule myself, trying to figure out which one of these goddamn stupid bands Farhad might be into. Oh, right. He had mentioned LCD Soundsystem in his questionnaire.

PerseMan: Super excited for LCD myself.

Jules478: Yeah? They're cool too.

Okay, so she's less excited about that one. But, hey, they can each bring different musical tastes to the relationship. That's the beauty of romance, right? Everyone brings their own interests into it, and then they mix and mingle, and sometime later, there is a little embryo that has genetically combined those passions into something that can be cradled in an artsy, black-and-white Instagram post.

PerseMan: Do you like kids?

Whoa. WHOA! What the hell are you doing, Miles? As the *Tell It to My Heart Style Guide and Freelancer's Handbook* suggests on page twenty-two, there are certain things you never, ever bring up on a first chat: politics, religion, marriage, meeting the parents, and—of course—children. Not in any way, shape, or form. I know this because I *literally* wrote the handbook. As Leanne's first employee, I got to sculpt a lot of what my job—and the company culture—is.

There is a noticeable pause before Farhad's match writes again.

Jules478: Yeah. I like them.

PerseMan: Do you have any idea what a six-week pregnant belly looks like?

I have no idea what's happening. My fingers are 100 percent working independently from my brain.

Jules478: Uh . . .

PerseMan: It's not obviously pregnant, right? Like, usually, you wouldn't be able to see a bump?

At this point, what the hell does it matter? Jules might have more insight into this than me considering she, at least, has the requisite parts and has, I don't know, probably attended a baby shower or something.

Jules478: I don't think so?

PerseMan: That's what I thought.

The thing is, I know the baby isn't mine. I probably always

knew it, but the blank screen on my messages, gut-punched by that *Read 8:37 AM* confirms it. Jordan wouldn't raise a baby alone, not if its father wanted to be an active part of his or her life. How many times had I held her while she told me another example of why her absentee dad was such a shithead and how it had directly impacted some aspect of her life or personality?

Jules478: So . . . listen. I think I've got to go.

Shit. I've been spiraling into a deep, dark thought hole instead of doing my job and convincing this girl that Farhad is a great match for her and worthy of at least a meetup.

Time for some damage control.

PerseMan: Ha! Sorry, I didn't mean to freak you out.

I'm now racking my brain for some sort of valid excuse to ask this girl about pregnancy symptoms.

PerseMan: I'm writing a song. And this is research.

Look, if there can be songs about lady humps, why not about baby bumps, am I right?

Jules478: Oh . . . are you a musician?

PerseMan: It's a hobby.

I scan Farhad's questionnaire again.

PerseMan: I work in finance by day.

Good, good. Worked in the stable job bit smoothly. I might be back on track here.

Jules478: What kind of band are you in?

I scan the questionnaire one more time. Oh, fuck.

PerseMan: A string quartet.

There is another long pause.

Jules478: Right . . . I'm sorry, but my lunch break is over and I really do have to go.

It's 8:52 in the morning.

Jules478: Maybe talk later?

But then she logs off before I can respond.

Honestly?

I probably did both Farhad and this girl a favor.

There is no such thing as love anyway. Not to get all hair metal power ballad about it, but love is an illusion. It's just a smokescreen for future heartbreak. Why do it to yourself? Why? Either they'll leave you, or you'll leave them or—best-case scenario—you live together happily until one of you dies and leaves the other one completely destroyed and a shell of their former self.

Why the fuck bother?

A message pops up from Leanne.

Leanne T: Miles? I think you need to come into the office for a meeting.

Fuckity fuck fuck.

Miles I: I'll be there in twenty minutes. Is that okay?

Leanne T: Yes.

And then, before I can think better of it.

Miles I: Hey, Leanne. Question for you. Do you know what a six-week pregnant belly looks like?

Leanne's office is in a building that was clearly a warehouse until maybe three minutes ago, when some enterprising real estate mogul realized he could create about 450 closet-sized offices in there and charge people an exorbitant amount of rent for the privilege of working right next to the West Side Highway, which is at least a fifteen-minute, windswept walk from any subway line.

I wait for her to buzz me up, and then take one of the many freight elevators up to the ninth floor, until I end up in front of Leanne's cupboard.

Up until two and a half months ago, Tell It to My Heart was located in a small, but airy office space in the Meatpacking District. Full-length glass windows looked out over the cobblestone streets where high-end shoppers in designer sunglasses and Jimmy Choos and/or hungover clubbers in designer sunglasses and taller Jimmy Choos hobbled to and fro. I used to look out and think it was very possible one of those clubbers was a client of ours, coming back from a successful date night that ended at seven a.m., rushing to get home and change and look presentable for work, but unable to hide that secret smile only a hot date with someone new was able to conjure up. It wasn't a walk of shame, it was a walk of *pride*. Who wouldn't feel proud and exhilarated to have come off of a night of passion and connection? And, maybe, just maybe, I'd had a hand in that. It used to make *me* feel proud and exhilarated, by association.

Now I know better.

Now I know one hot night will probably turn into agony somewhere down the road—whether it's because of unreturned text messages, or fights over the other one's overbearing parents, or splitting up and trying to figure out who gets the houseplants. I'm facilitating nothing but ruin and damnation.

And as for the office? Well. We can chalk that one up to another brilliantly catastrophic idea from Leanne's ex-husband, Clifford.

To paraphrase Taylor Swift, once upon a time, many mistakes ago, Leanne and Clifford were two of those idiots who thought they were in a loving, long-lasting relationship. So not only did they exchange vows, and buy an apartment (a co-op no less, another nightmare), and adopt a cat together—they decided to take it to the next knuckleheaded step: co-owning a business.

Yup, they started Tell It to My Heart together, although it was Leanne's idea originally. As both a writer and a person enthralled by love, she'd been watching her single friends struggle through the tortures of online dating, of constructing the perfect profile, and of saying the right things over e-mails, IMs, and texts. And one day she realized: She was a copywriter. She could help them craft their message better.

It snowballed from there, the idea to create a ghostwriting agency that would help people get their foot in the door on their paths to true love. "We're not ghostwriting, we're cupid-writing," Clifford said.

That was Clifford's task: taking care of the marketing and operations.

Meaning it was Clifford's idea to name the company Tell It to My Heart (which was probably the last time Leanne and Clifford agreed on anything). And then his next logical step was to get the rights to that Taylor Dayne song to use in all the commercials.

It sounded fine in theory, of course. Except Taylor Dayne and the songwriters did not want to be associated with some weird, unknown, online dating ghostwriting agency thing, and had asked for an exorbitant fee to secure the rights.

Any normal person would have tried to either negotiate or realize the song wasn't worth it.

If Clifford is one thing, it's abnormal.

He agreed to their terms right away, without consulting Leanne or the lawyers or anybody.

Leanne got the company in the divorce, but she was also stuck with the consequences of Clifford's poor business decisions.

So, yes, do have the pleasure of getting "Tell It to My Heart" stuck in your head if you come across any of our radio or occasional TV ads. While I and the other three full-time TITMH (pronounced *tit-mee*) employees have the pleasure of no longer having an office.

And poor Leanne, CEO, is relegated to this musty, windowless closet that can barely fit her desk and two chairs let alone all of the cool, eclectic artwork and sculptures she used to have as her backdrop at our old digs.

Still, despite her surroundings, she looks as impeccable as always. Leanne is Chinese-American, with long, straight black hair, the posture of a prima ballerina, and a wardrobe that almost entirely consists of structural pieces that look like they ought to come with blueprints. She somehow makes them work, whereas I'm pretty sure anyone else wearing them would look like they were dressed as the Empire State Building in a questionable Miss New York pageant.

"Care to explain what happened today, Miles?" she asks in her calm, deep voice, the kind you know has the potential to unleash a tsunami of devastating barbs if necessary.

I clear my throat. "What do you mean?"

"Let's start with not knowing our client was in a string quartet. And move on to the whole pregnant belly debacle."

"You know about all that?" I ask weakly.

"Miles. After the fiasco of the last three clients, I told you I'd be logged on to your computer to see your chats. And then you accepted my remote access request this morning."

"Oh, right," I say. Shit. I definitely had. And I definitely planned on being on my game today, but that was before Jordan announced to the world (and, oh yeah, me) that she was with child.

Leanne sighs. "Look. I know you're going through a hard time right now." I haven't told her too much about what's been going on, just that Jordan and I broke up. And that I moved out of our apartment into Dylan's living room. And that Dylan's boyfriend, Charles, has been passive-aggressively leaving me notes about how disruptive I am to their lives. And that he made me return the single-ply toilet paper I bought as a thank-you gift because, as he claimed, nobody's ass deserves the degradation of single-ply, not even mine.

Okay, so maybe I have told Leanne a lot. The problem is that in the eighteen months we were together, I ended up co-opting most of Jordan's friends, and now I'm stuck trying to scrape together some semblance of a social circle.

"Here's the thing," Leanne says, "I can't afford this meltdown, Miles. I *literally* can't afford it. Clearly, we are in some serious trouble here." She waves her arms vaguely at the horror show of peeling paint and Formica office furniture she's somehow ended up captaining. "And losing *four* clients in the span of a month? That's just not acceptable."

I nod, suddenly realizing it's very possible that—on top of everything else—I am about to get fired. I'm like the pilot episode of a sitcom about a man whose life goes to shit before he changes careers and decides to become a cattle rancher in that quirky town his grandmother lives in. Except all of my grandparents are dead and, in the real world, losing your job doesn't actually lead to a hilarious but poignant epiphany about what you're supposed to be doing. Just a sudden need to add LinkedIn to the daily ritual of social media that makes you feel like crap about yourself.

Leanne must see the panic in my face, because she tries to soften the blow. "It's no secret that you've always been my best employee, Miles. You were great at what you did. Nobody has as many success stories as you. How many weddings have you been invited to? Three?"

"Four," I mumble. Always as an old friend of the groom because, of course, none of them could bear to tell their future wives that their relationship was built on what is—let's be honest here—something of a lie.

"That's incredible," Leanne says gently, before her voice takes on the firm but fair tone that made her a superstar creative director back in her agency days, when I was working as a copywriter under her. "But I can't rely on what you *did*; I have to rely on what you *do*. I have to know I'm sending someone out there who's going to listen to our clients' wants and needs and work his hardest to get them to meet up with their perfect match."

"Right," I say, not adding that what Leanne needs is someone who actually believes in such a thing as a perfect match. Once upon a time, that was me. But not anymore.

"So this is what's going to happen," she says, and I'm expecting her to produce—if I'm lucky—a severance package from within her desk to hand to me. Instead, she takes out her iPad. "You have one more chance to make good here. One more client who's going to need the old Miles to reappear and give him the real Tell It to My Heart Experience™." Obviously, she doesn't say the trademarked bit, but I can practically hear it in her voice. Another one of Clifford's brilliantly expensive ideas. "So, pick one. Go ahead. There are three to choose from."

I reluctantly take the tablet from her, and flip through the familiar file format of our clients: a smiling photo and the answers from the initial questionnaire. This one ideally wants to be married within two years. That one is new to the city and wants someone to "eat his way through New York with." (His words, not mine. And obviously we are going to have to do something about them if I take him on.)

And then there's Jude Campbell. There's nothing very special about Jude's profile. He's good-looking enough. His answers are normal enough. Or, I should say, there's *almost* nothing very special about Jude's profile.

Jude apparently moved here from Scotland a couple of years ago. Which means Jude has an accent. And if I am going to stake my whole career on one guy's love match?

I'm picking the dude with the Scottish accent.

Connect with U(s)

Visit us online at
KensingtonBooks.com
to read more from your favorite authors, see books
by series, view reading group guides, and more.

Join us on social media

for sneak peeks, chances to win books and prize packs,
and to share your thoughts with other readers.

facebook.com/kensingtonpublishing
twitter.com/kensingtonbooks

Tell us what you think!

To share your thoughts, submit a review,
or sign up for our eNewsletters, please visit:
KensingtonBooks.com/TellUs.